ALSO BY ERICH ANDERSON

Hallowed Be Thy Name

THY KINGDOM COME

a novel

ERICH ANDERSON

FRIDIUM PRESS

FRIDIUM PRESS
http://www.fridiumpress.com

Copyright © 2014 by Erich Anderson
Cover design by Katie Pyne
More information at http://www.erich-anderson.com
ISBN: 978-0-9882511-3-7

Thy Kingdom Come / Erich Anderson.

To Saxon

"He who has a why to live can bear almost any how."

— Friedrich Nietzsche

MOTOR CITY

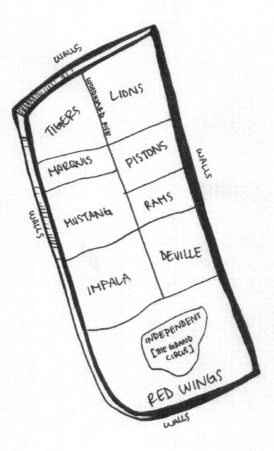

THERE WAS NO way that Houston—a city in the former state of Texas—was ever going to survive as a viable community in a world nearly devoid of petroleum. The devastation of the industry in the Middle East, the exponential expansion of need in China and India that effectively sucked anything available off the world market, and the eventual dissolution of the Union all contributed to Houston's sudden and complete diminishment.

Most experts would agree that the mishmash of urban planning projects undertaken at the end of the twentieth century contributed mightily to the situation that left the citizens exposed and vulnerable to every form of incursion by the various groups seeking to establish some type of "post-apocalyptic" hierarchy.

Where once there were countless residential communities occupying the flatlands twenty miles from the city center—the same communities that appeared to travel en masse along the serpentine mazes of a confusing freeway system—now there were nothing but ghost towns with fatuous names like Candle Creek and Piney Woods Village.

Not long after the city and its citizenry devolved into irrelevance, two factions of insurgents met for battle in an area in the Southwestern sector that was home to the defunct amusement park once called Six Flags AstroWorld.

Under the rusting metal sculptures that once supported rollercoaster rides with names like "The Texas Cyclone" and "Greezed Lightnin'," desperate people sought to kill each other over their wanton desire to push their own specific ideologies.

The skirmish between the Redeemers and the Barbers lasted nearly two weeks. As the hit-and-run battle extended north toward the junction of State Highway 59 and Interstate 610, the civilian collateral damage rose to over a thousand souls.

The two groups of warriors shared a similar nihilistic desire to destroy life, so it was a bit of an oddity that they should find themselves on opposite ends of a battle.

The Redeemers' agenda was well known and had catalyzed among the populace as an entity that engendered terror. Their faithful firmly believed that the only path to heaven was to kill all of the people who didn't accept their messiah as the true Son of God. They worshiped the legacy of Russell Reading, a serial killer from Kansas. The Redeemers believed that he was the only person raptured to heaven on a date that the world was supposed to end.

Russell had killed over thirty people on the spree that resulted in his death-row incarceration. He subsequently proclaimed at his trial that God, his Father, had asked him to cull the sinners from an amoral world. Ruthless and unrelenting, the Redeemers had cultivated new devotees rapidly over the last thirty years. A census had never been taken to confirm their true numbers, but they appeared to be ubiquitous, and the entire population of what was once the middle of the country feared them the most.

The Barbers had endeavored to become an equally frightening adversary of the public. Their desires were rooted in the belief that financial compensation was a much more satisfying goal than any kind of spiritual reward.

Delivered by the creation of the physical walls that separated the haves and the have-nots as the country's metropolises began the process of creating their protective enclaves, the Barbers were a motley collection of militiamen and militiawomen hell-bent on destroying the new infrastructure and pocketing anything they could in the process.

Initially a hodgepodge of disparate groups with ridiculous names, like W.I.D.O.W. (Wealth Is Death One Wishes) and R.B.M.D. (Rich Bastards Must Die), the now-unified Barbers did share a common devotion to the eponymous Gary Barber, a disgruntled former U.S. congressman who first noticed his country dissolving at the onset of the twenty-first century. (Special emphasis should be placed on the phrase "his country.")

Unlike the Redeemers' progenitor, Russell Reading, Gary Barber was a man in love with anything that would elevate his name to the top of the day's news. Portly and bald, severely myopic, Gary Barber had grasped the country's ear with his stentorious opinions that the role of the white man in society had been diminished by a culture that had seemed to transcend the notion of race.

His plaudits about the raw deal that he and his ilk had garnered provided another vessel for people to toss their anger into as the jobs dried up and the middle class frittered away into nothingness.

Barber blamed people of color, wealthy Wall Street folk, paper money, regulations and laws, and the government's seemingly neutral stance to all of the preceding. After nearly a century where the poor white people felt superior to the poor people of color, the lines had blurred and the penurious white people could no longer consider themselves marginally better than their ethnically diverse brethren.

To the wealthy, the Barber's treatise read, "I will never have what you have, so I will fucking take it from you."

The Barbers had been the first group to acquire weaponry and munitions as the shit came down, and because of that hardware, they had initially proven to be somewhat unstoppable.

The battle that was fought in the shadow of the roller coasters had not to do with a clash of ideology, as one might have assumed, but with the proximity of a National Guard Armory in the vicinity. Both the Barbers and the Redeemers had been in the process of raiding the degrading weapons caches of these poorly defended facilities. That they should meet on the outskirts of one such facility was merely coincidence. By the time the battle ended, Houston had been turned into a smoldering field of spectral emptiness. Nearly all of its previous residents had vacated. Both groups set up camps and recruiting centers at either end of the city center with the no-man's-land of the former University of Houston between them.

But the story does not begin there.

PART ONE

ONE

OUTSIDE AKRON

J IMMY HAZEN KNEW he had never felt terror like this. Just a month
into his twenty-first year of life, he had been of the mind that his
young virile body was capable of synthesizing enough testosterone to
overcome anything. But this shit looked bad. Notions corroded with
self-defeat were trying to elbow their way into his thoughts. It was an
all too familiar refrain—the voice in his mind that persistently proclaimed that his hereditary biochemistry might not be up to the task
at hand.

He put the brakes on the chaos in his head and tried to direct a serene
mind to the situation. Had he really seen that movement in the trees?

He hadn't had a lot of sleep recently. Maybe all the deprivation
had caused his brain to create some type of waking dream.

But there it was again.

When he saw the flashes of steel and carbon arcing off the moonlight, he felt his stomach flip over. It was an epitasis that was a response
to the sudden increase in the pace of his heartbeat. The ensuing spasm
caused him to vomit most of his half-digested breakfast on the ground
next to his right boot.

Staring at what his stomach acids had done to transform the contents of the canned ravioli, he became saddened. Even with all the
training, all the supposed mental transformation, he was now convinced that he would never be able to transcend his inherent DNA.

Jimmy had come onto the watch at 1 A.M. A hazy moon had just
finished teetering to the left of Venus. He had cleaned and reloaded the
mounted .50 caliber machine gun they had installed on the upper deck
of the armory while constantly keeping an enhanced night-vision eye
on the tree line.

Jimmy knew that Joe had done some scouting the day before and
had expressed a belief that the bad guys would be attempting an attack
on the facility within the next couple of days. The two of them were
into their second month at this particular site. By all accounts, by every
measure, they were as ready as they would ever be for the arrival of evil.

When Jimmy saw the dim headlights of the silent vehicle approaching from the east, he knew that he had to wake his partner.

Things were about to become a lot more complicated than they already were.

———————

Joe Smith was dreaming about a black sand beach in a land where everyone spoke Esperanto. Of course, he had no idea that they were speaking the international auxiliary language, but he did see subtitles in the images that offered him the translation. People kept saying "dankon," and, somehow, he knew that meant "thank you."

The walkie-talkie crackled by his ear.

"Joe?"

Joe extricated his subconscious from a swirl of umbrella-accented cocktails and bronzed beauties in skimpy bathing suits. As he oriented to the noise coming from the handset, he thought he could hear a fair amount of panic straining Jimmy's voice at the other end of the transmission. It was either that or the batteries were low. The nine-volt he had loaded into the unit four days ago might have been the last one in their inventory.

"Joe?" Jimmy asked again.

"Yeah."

"We got a situation here. I see movement in the trees and some car just came out of nowhere. They're passing the facility now."

"Any markings on the car?" Joe asked as he slipped on his dirt-encrusted fatigues.

"Uh, no. Wait, there's a white cloth hanging out of the passenger window."

Joe had to stifle a laugh. As if the symbol for peace would mean anything to those savages in the trees that were probably close to executing a plan to flank the building.

Joe cinched his belt another notch. He figured he'd lost close to twenty-five pounds off his six-foot-two frame in these two months. He hadn't been able to stomach the canned provisions except for the fruit, and the reduction in his protein intake had taken its toll on his musculature.

"Is the fifty loaded?" Joe asked into the handset.

"Yes, sir."

"I'll be right up."

Joe threw on a black shirt and augmented it with a black down vest. It was well into April, but the recent mornings had somehow missed the message that the vernal equinox had taken place some three weeks prior. An unrelenting chill remained in the misty air. Old Man

Winter still had his boot on Spring's neck—that was the way his father would have phrased it.

———————

The report from the single shot of the deer rifle created a diminishing sequence of six echoes.

On hearing the discharge, Jimmy ducked behind the wall of sandbags and swiveled his view over to the vehicle. Where before he had seen that the car carried a driver and three passengers, there now appeared to be only three registering fully on his thermal-imaging gear. Somebody's light was going out.

And then the muffled screams from inside the car began to circulate with the recession of the concussive echoes.

Jimmy could see someone trying to get the door open. As the interior light of the car blazed on, he was briefly blinded. He flipped the imaging rig up, and with his naked eyes he clocked the sight of the driver slumped over the steering wheel. An amoebic pattern of splattered blood now obscured the front windshield.

"Holy shit," he said into the mist.

He resumed his view through the night vision. He drew vectors in his mind, working back from the patterned diagram of the blood of the victim, and swiveled his head to locate the general area where the sniper might have unleashed his headshot. He saw nothing through his eyepiece that gave him any indication of the murderer's emplacement.

———————

Joe had heard the shot from inside the reinforced concrete superstructure of the armory's main hall. He was just about to scale the stairs to the roof when something convinced him that the simultaneous presence of the vehicle and the gunfire was more than coincidence. He slipped out the steel side door and saw the idled car parked fifty feet away.

Joe withdrew his nine-millimeter and crept slowly toward what resembled a theatrical display. Two hysterical mimes were acting out a scene of displeasure in the backseat. The passenger in the front seat was facing them, endeavoring to get them to calm down. He appeared to be gesturing that they should keep the doors closed.

Joe thought it might be best to appeal to the mediator in the forward cabin; the other two looked crazy. He knocked on the passenger window.

The one in the forward seat reacted to the aural stimulation like an animal that suddenly finds itself enclosed in a cage. Startled by the presence of someone just outside the car, separated only by a sheet of aluminum and window glass, he freaked out. The force with which he threw the door open knocked Joe to the ground. Joe looked up to see a large, hulking figure of a man with eyes full of menace hovering above him. The man's right hand held a KA-BAR knife with an eight-inch blade. Joe could tell by his light grip on the haft that he was no novice.

"Who are you?"

"Easy now," Joe replied.

He let the *e* sound linger as if he was trying to calm a young, un-broken horse.

"You're the bodyguard, right?" Joe asked.

The man flinched—yes.

"I'm Joe. We've got to get your people out of the car and into some cover."

The big man wasn't buying it. He looked off to where Joe had exited the armory and tried to discern whether the skinny man in the fatigues he currently held sway over was a good guy or not.

In that instant, Joe disarmed him. The man took a wild swing at Joe who parried the blow, knocked the wind out of him with a kick to the gut, and brought the bodyguard to his knees.

The back door opened and the two frail middle-aged men crawled out.

"Don't hurt us," one of them pleaded.

Joe just shook his head and pointed to the door of the armory.

"Make yourself small," he said to the older of the two.

The younger one had a prominent stain on the front of his pants and some of the driver's blood-streaked brain matter on his forehead. His spectacles magnified his already widened eyes and he resembled a character from an old, Italian art flick. The two men zigzagged, dipped to the ground, crawled for a bit, and eventually made their way to the threshold of the door.

Joe turned his attention back to the muscular security man. The big dude, still kneeling, was attempting to gather in something ap-proaching a half breath by this point.

"I didn't mean to hurt you. No hard feelings, huh?"

The bodyguard nodded in comprehension, though both men knew that this might have only been the culmination of round one. Though Joe appeared to be ahead on points, the hired hand of the two men would likely be seeking recompense for this act of humiliation in front of his employers.

"What do they call you?"

"Udo," the man grunted.

Back up on the parapet, Jimmy Hazen was perplexed. He had seen the scene go down with Joe and the tourists, and he was wondering why he (and they) hadn't heard a second shot. The sniper had shown a deft touch in effecting a headshot from what appeared to him to be at least a thousand yards, so why hadn't he taken out the large targets that appeared so vulnerable in the moonlight? Jimmy eventually concluded that the reasoning behind the absence of a follow-on attack was because the shooter did not desire to expose his position, or that he was on the move when the opportunity had presented itself.

He scoped the forest again. There was a rustling of foliage—a group appeared to be massing southwest of his position. Jimmy did not see anything that resembled a rifle being held by any of the crazies.

Joe hustled Udo through the side door, clanged the solid steel barrier shut, and installed all three of the civilians in the former commandant's office.

"You'll be safe in here. Don't get too comfortable. We may be forced to move quickly," Joe said as he handed each of them a can of tomato juice.

"Sorry, this is about all we have left," he added.

The older of the middle-aged men was intent on getting a briefing of some kind, but Joe was already headed for the door.

"Who's out there?"

"Redeemers," Joe said.

It was a word that no one in the room, save Joe, wanted to hear.

"Are you fucking kidding me?" the younger man said, looking at the bodyguard.

"Take it easy, Steve, we're inside now. We're safe," the older man said to his compatriot.

But Steve's eyes lased into the man they had hired to protect them.

"You said it was a short cut, did you not? 'Just make a left and we can save an hour.' Where the fuck are we anyway?" Steve asked.

"Ten or so clicks northwest of Rubber City. For your safety, I would again advise you not to leave this room," Joe said.

"Jesus fucking Christ, Harry," Steve said, addressing the older of the two. "Jesus fucking Christ," he said again to no one in particular.

TWO

Jimmy Hazen thought he had accessed the position of the sniper in a grouping of pine trees that he was certain must have provided the perch of advantage. He unlocked the rotation arm on the .50 caliber and swiveled the sight over to the area of his estimation. He switched the gun's mode off automatic, removed the night vision eyepiece he'd been sporting, and looked down into the laser sight. Why not squeeze off a round? What difference would make? All of those maniacs lurking in the woods knew that they were up here.

Jimmy's finger tensed at the trigger. He'd been a spotter and, at times, the shooter, but he had never done both at the same time.

When Joe tapped him on the shoulder, he nearly jumped out of his already thin skin.

"What's up?" Joe asked.

Jimmy released the first joint of his index finger from the trigger, returned the latch to the safe position, and turned to face his mentor and superior.

"I think I've located the sniper's position," Jimmy said.

"Guy's a pretty good shot. What do you think is his range?"

"A thousand yards?"

Joe looked through the sight. He didn't see anything that indicated the presence of the sniper.

"The grove you're looking at has to be at least fifteen hundred meters. Unless our shooter has a fifty cal of his own, he isn't even hitting the car from that distance. That was a clean headshot from what was likely a pretty good deer rifle, but it wasn't taken from fifteen hundred meters. Even I would be three out of ten from that far away."

"Maybe he got lucky."

"True, one cannot account for luck," Joe said.

There was movement in the trees to Joe's right.

"There."

Jimmy peeked over the wall. He could see the flashes of orange clothing and the glint of the machetes and sharpened gardening tools moving around the foliage.

"That's the first wave. The fodder. They'll try to distract us while their main force attacks from another flank."

"When?"

"Sometime before first light, I reckon. This group isn't blessed with a great deal of brains. I've seen them use this tactic before, and if they had their shit together, they would wait to attack when the fog arrives."

"Fog? There's mist, but I wouldn't call it fog."

"The barometric pressure's dropping. Whatever front is coming through will most likely produce rain and/or fog within the next forty-eight hours."

Jimmy hadn't even thought about the weather conditions and how they might affect the battle. God, he had so much left to learn.

Joe put on a pair of night vision viewers and looked at the rabble that he had designated to be the diversionary force.

"Newbies," he said, "not a single hole in their jumpsuits."

Joe took off the goggles and gave Jimmy a look of disappointment.

"What?" Jimmy asked.

"It's just such a waste."

Jimmy had never known Joe to ever have any feelings of remorse in regards to his doings with the Redeemers. He had seen the man kill their ilk without even a scintilla of emotion. Come to think of it, his behavior was, in many ways, the mirror image of these savages.

Jimmy knew there were deep-seated reasons for this; he'd heard the rumors and the myths of Joe's vendettas against these psychopaths. Jimmy knew that, for Joe, it was personal, not a job. Jimmy had overheard particles of conversations from previous colleagues who mentioned Joe's mother and, possibly, a wife as the explanation for Joe's need to avenge. God knows, he had never asked him to confirm or deny the scuttlebutt.

"So, how do you think we should handle this?" Joe asked of his student.

Jimmy took a moment to answer. He knew this question would be posed and he had desperately tried to come up with a strategy that Joe might endorse. He culled through all that he had learned and observed in an attempt to make his mentor proud.

"Forget the diversionary force, let them come toward us with their crude weapons and concentrate on the main assault?"

"Is that a question or a statement?"

Jimmy wavered.

"C'mon man, you can't just try to imagine what I would do. You have to assess the situation and make decisions on your own that will produce effective results," Joe said tersely.

Joe waited a beat or two—hoping that the gears in Jimmy's mind might engage. Finally, he let the kid off the hook.

"You got it right, Jim. I was just commenting about the way you presented it. Don't make it a question, okay?"

"Okay."

Jimmy noticed Joe looking at the puddle of vomit on the ground next to the big gun. Joe never gave him the impression that this was anything out of the ordinary.

"How does the arrival of those travelers affect us?" Jimmy asked.

"They're just going to have to go with the flow, I guess," Joe replied with a shrug.

Down in the commandant's office there wasn't much flow present. Steve had examined the expiration date on the can of tomato juice and, noticing that it was some ten years beyond this day, tossed it toward an empty trashcan.

Harry, on the other hand, was thinking about his family. His wife had warned him of the dangers of embarking on an excursion such as this, but he had assured her that they would have more than adequate security.

They had hired the chauffeured car and the security consultant, Udo Lewandowski, from a well-established C-town business that specialized in itinerant travel. The company lavishly insured their human cargo for a million-credit benefit and had advertised that they'd never paid out a single, solitary sou in damages. Hell, it was just a quick trip from Cleveland to Cincinnati to meet some surplus drywall suppliers. One day out, and one day back.

Udo drained the viscous red fluid from the crimson-lettered can, crossed to the trashcan, and exchanged his empty for Steve's discarded portion.

"May I?" he asked.

"Knock yourself out," Steve said.

Udo popped the top, and as he raised the four-ounce container to his lips, he saw Steve lean in close to Harry.

"What's with this stiff?" Steve whispered. "That skinny fucker dropped him before you could say his name. And I don't mean his last name."

Harry didn't respond, but his eye did wander over to the enormous man sucking down the can of salted tomato pulp. Steve had spoken the truth. This Udo fellow got his ass kicked, but good.

Udo could feel the sense of the scrutiny emanating from his charges, and instead of allowing himself to offer a response in his defense, he wandered over toward the door of the office.

"Where do you think you're going?" Steve asked.

"See if I can help," Udo said.

"Bullshit. You stay here with us. That's what we're paying you for."

"I'll be right back," Udo said, breezily disregarding Steve's admonition.

Fifteen seconds after Udo's exit, Steve and Harry heard two charges explode outside and the nerve-rattling noise of an unbaffled machine gun springing to life.

"Holy shit," Steve whimpered. "We are so fucked."

———————

Just as Joe had anticipated, the diversionary group of raw Redeemer recruits made a charge for the building from their position in the trees just to the right of the front entrance. And just like the two defenders of the facility had planned, they ignored these rookies and their animalistic battle screeches.

Instead, they blew the two charges of dynamite they had laid up in the trees to the east. The explosion startled the first group of attackers, as they had been left wondering why they were drawing absolutely no fire.

Jimmy opened up with the .50 caliber, raking the tree line from the northeast to the east. The tracer fire hit more than just wood as a couple of the orange-prison-jumpsuit-wearing murderers stumbled from their cover and died, twitching on the bare ground.

As if the deaths of their comrades were some type of signal flare, fifty Redeemers sprung from the trees and sprinted straight for the armory. Jimmy could make out an array of more sophisticated weapons within this group. There were wooden-handled axes, a variety of small arms, and gleaming swords of stainless steel.

It was at that point that Joe tapped Jimmy on the shoulder and bade him to hold his fire.

When Jimmy turned to Joe, the younger man's eyes were fixed and dilated as if he was in a trance. The rush of adrenalin coursing through Jimmy's body had rendered him with a condition akin to shock.

Joe made certain that they made direct eye contact and that there would be no improvisation; they would stick to the plan in place. Jimmy shook away the pounding in his head and nodded his assent. Joe strapped on his goggles and peered over the edge of the sandbags.

The last intelligence report they'd received, some four months prior, had mentioned that bands of Redeemers had gotten their hands on some rocket-propelled grenade launchers. Incursions at armories such as the one they were defending had become a consistent strategy employed by all of the so-called insurgent entities that roamed the countryside. Even though the pilfered munitions were usually old, way past their expiration dates of effectiveness, one could lay odds that some of them might still be operational.

This is what Joe was scanning for: the confirming presence of a cluster of Redeemers gathering within range, with the sole purpose of aiming such a weapon as a grenade launcher or mortar at their position.

Jimmy's job was to be ready if Joe should spot a group readying that type of weapon for deployment. He had switched the gun back to the single-shot mode and awaited the order.

"There," Joe said. "Shit, it looks like an old Russian RPG."

"Where?" Jimmy screamed.

"Four hundred meters north, northeast."

Jimmy swiveled the sight, but as the scope lacked night vision, all he could see were shadows.

"Fuck!"

"Take it easy. You got another ten seconds or so. Breathe, find your target, and fire."

"You'd better do it, Joe. I can't see shit."

"Breathe," Joe repeated.

But Jimmy was choking. He had no clue as to the whereabouts of the projectile that was soon to be headed their way.

Joe grabbed the spotter scope and located the enemy combatants.

"Follow me," he said.

Jimmy did as he was told and allowed the spotter scope to guide the sight on the rifle to their target.

"Take the shot," Joe said calmly.

Joe could see that the grenade had been loaded into the breech of the Redeemer's recoilless rifle, and he was bringing it up to aim it at their position.

"Take the shot, Jim," Joe repeated.

Jimmy squeezed the trigger and unleashed the chambered round.

Joe watched through the spotter scope as the bullet whizzed by the left ear of the attacker. Like swatting away a precocious gnat, the attacker meekly waved at the annoyance before leveling his weapon.

Jimmy had qualified with this particular gun and could easily hit a dime from this range, but as Joe had predicted, Jimmy's predilection toward a condition of nervousness had blocked his path to success.

Joe resisted the urge to push the young man out of the way and deter the attacker by lodging one of the full-metal-jacket bullets between his eyebrows.

"Try again, Jim," Joe said calmly.

Jimmy bore down through the scope and felt a bead of sweat work its way out of a pore by his temple. He feathered the trigger again, but Joe knew that it was going to be too late. The attacker was bearing down on the release mechanism of the RPG.

The two foes fired simultaneously.

Joe would never know whether Jimmy's shot made purchase or not because the grenade the attacker had tried to fire at them exploded while it was still clinging to the end of the rifle. The attacker and two members of his troop were reduced to mounds of viscera as the shrapnel tore them apart.

"You can't account for luck," Joe said with a hint of irony. "Okay, let's finish this up."

———

Udo wandered through the facility in amazement. It didn't matter which room or corridor he explored; the entire place had been wired with what appeared to be the armory's entire inventory of plastic explosive. A lot of the material was old—a mere caress caused it to crumble—but even if only a quarter of it was viable, he knew the whole place was sure to be leveled.

Udo traced the wiring to a back office, where an old amateur radio stood on top of the desk that had once been manned by a supply sergeant. Judging by the permanent dent in the chair that was tucked into the desk, Udo concluded that the previous occupant must have been quite portly.

Above him, he heard the constant barrage from the machine gun come to a climax before being silenced, and his first thought was that the ammo had run out. Thinking that he had only a finite amount of time, he quickly disconnected the detonator from the power source, threw the radio to the floor, stomped it into the ground using his sizable weight as leverage, left the room, and sauntered back toward his employers in the commandant's office.

———————

Jimmy watched as all of the predictions Joe had listed in his agenda came to being. The raw recruits were attempting to enter the facility through the steel door using their crude weapons. Their progress could be qualified as minimal, at best.

Freed from being pinned down by the machine gun fire, the flanking force was storming toward the front of the building and the cover that the overhang would provide. Most of this group hooked up with the initial attackers and began trying to open the door of the facility with a coordinated earnestness.

Joe signaled Jimmy to switch the .50 caliber back to automatic and shim the trigger with the makeshift block he had welded together from the legs of a steel table.

When the big gun went off again, the noise shook the forest. The tracers arced toward the tree line, providing an illuminating effect not unlike the pinpoints of light from a fireworks show.

As the two defenders escaped from their perch and hustled back into the facility, the gun continued to suck in what was left of their conserved ammo in a rapid fashion. There was no target, no hope of killing any of the raiders, just the noise and the strategy deployed by the principals that would make the assailants think they were still up there. Everything was pretty much on schedule, with the exception of what to do with their surprise guests in the commandant's office.

Back inside the armory, Joe immediately hustled over to the gun cabinet. He withdrew a nine-millimeter semi-automatic and six loaded clips of ammunition. He stuffed the ammo into the thigh pockets of his fatigues.

Jimmy gathered up their pre-packed belongings and headed for the debarkation point——a manhole in the middle of the main hall. The clanging of steel on steel coming from just outside the door competed with reports from the unmanned machine gun until the weapon was silenced by starvation. The end was near. This job was moments away from completion.

THREE

S TEVE AND HARRY had heard the steady stream of cacophony from outside and were understandably unnerved. Udo, on the other hand, appeared placid as he occupied his time by rolling himself a collection of cigarettes from a pouch of bootleg Canadian tobacco.

When Joe burst in, his weapon out and pointing to the ground, the three men weren't sure whether he was friend or foe.

Steve tried to jump up from his chair, but the vinyl seat covering had bonded with his urine-stained pants, and he ended up being embarrassingly pitched forward onto the ground at Joe's feet.

"We're moving," Joe said, with just the right amount of urgency.

He ripped the chair away from the groveling Steve before reaching into his own waistband and withdrawing the impotent Beretta.

He handed the weapon to Udo.

"Here," Joe said.

Udo pulled back the breech to see that the gun was unloaded.

"It's empty," Udo said.

"Yeah, sorry about that. Maybe if I knew you better. It will still scare the shit out of someone. Make them pause. Perhaps give you an extra second or two."

"Yeah, right."

Joe caught the inference that this act was likely to be added to Udo's growing list of slights. This wasn't Joe's intention, but he determined that maybe this was just one of those situations that carried the appellation "no-win."

"Make your way to the center of the main hall. My partner is waiting for you there."

"Where are you going?" Steve asked.

"I'll be there. Just go now."

The three men filed out of the room and turned left on Joe's indication of direction. They could hear the grinding sound of metal meeting metal coming from the side door that Joe had used to rescue them. This continued to discombobulate the two businessmen as they stumbled toward the main hall and the voice of Jimmy beckoning them to come forth.

Joe crossed through the corridor and checked the security of the door. At this rate, it would take many more blows from the cadre outside before they would be able to make entry. He rushed back to the staging area and arrived in time to find Steve protesting to Jimmy that exiting the facility through an air conduit would not be possible given his predisposition to a debilitating form of claustrophobia.

"Get the fuck in the hole," Jimmy screamed to him from down in the elbow of the drainage pipe.

"You want me to crawl into a goddamn sewer?" Steve asked, exasperated.

"It hasn't been a sewer for a hundred years, so all the shit in it is probably fossilized," Jimmy joked.

"Fuck, Harry. What the fuck?" Steve mumbled, as he turned to his partner.

"Just do it, man. It will be a hell of a lot safer than staying in here," Harry said.

As if on cue, one of the axes made a crease in the door down the hall, and the slim opening allowed the screams of the bloodthirsty legion to filter over to where the five men stood.

"Ah, shit. Fuck this!" Steve muttered.

He climbed down into the hole. Harry followed him. Udo dallied before finally joining the other men in the pipe. Joe followed, replacing the heavy metal cover.

Jimmy held an LED flare that provided all of the illumination the group needed.

Being roughly four feet in diameter, the pipe could be traversed by either crawling or squat-walking. For Udo and Joe, the former was the only possible gait. Up ahead, Steve and Harry were trying to do the squat dance, but years of inactivity had tightened their hamstrings to the point that they would never be able to make themselves less than forty-eight inches tall for more than twenty seconds at a time.

Jimmy had covered this distance many times in preparation, and because he had duties to perform on the other end, he handed the torch to the next in line—Harry.

"Take this, and keep up the pace," Jimmy said before hurriedly shuffling to the pipe's termination.

On Jimmy's exit, Steve reacted queasily to the departure of one of his protectors. He steadied himself by grabbing Harry's shoulder.

"Where do you think we're headed?" Steve asked.

"My guess is to safety, don't you think?"

"I just . . ."

"Shut up, and keep moving forward," Harry barked.

When Joe smelled the acrid air of the outside and the waterlogged garbage rotting in the Pigeon River, he knew that their two months of preparation were finally culminating in a conclusion. He thought about the ramifications of the assessment he would have to fill out on his underling, Jimmy Hazen. Their employer, Tynan International, Ltd., required a detailed analysis of each commission, and Joe knew that he would have to massage a few details to allow Jimmy to progress forward with the company.

It had not been easy, these preceding months. The kid should have been a lot farther along, and Joe blamed himself for not demanding that Jimmy accede to the dogma of Joe's timeworn wisdom. He knew now that he had been foolish to allow the kid so much latitude in the area of creative thinking.

Then, Joe could see the light spilling through the opening. The sun had just crept over the horizon and was trying to peer through the mist, but didn't have the leverage of a hard angle to pierce the fog.

It was an eight-foot drop from the end of the pipe to the natural arroyo that at one time had functioned as a flue that carried the facility's waste to the river.

Knowing that this day would come, Jimmy and Joe had installed a rope ladder to make the descent less than ankle crushing. Jimmy unfurled the conveyor and climbed down to the ground. Holding it taut, he helped Harry negotiate his way to terra firma, but Steve, sweating profusely, gulping for air, became entangled in the second step. As he pitched forward, the twisted coil choked his calf, causing a skirmish between gravity and the tether. Dangling headfirst, he screamed out something incomprehensible.

"You're wasting our time, goddammit! You're going to blow the whole deal," Jimmy said.

Harry pitched in to help his business partner, and, fighting through Steve's fright, they got him righted and safely to the ground.

Udo shunned the ladder, grabbed onto the lower arc of the concrete, and hung in the air briefly before dropping the couple of feet that represented the gap.

Joe followed Udo's lead, and the quorum gathered at the base of the yawning pipe.

"What now?" Harry asked.

"You three should find some cover," Joe said.

Before Steve could ask him to give them a reason why he might need to protect himself, Joe and Jimmy dashed off down the arroyo, scaled its earthen walls, and took a position on a knoll that offered an unobstructed view of the armory.

From his backpack, Jimmy produced the spotter scope and a handheld walkie-talkie. He handed off the scope to Joe.

"They must have made entry by now," Joe said.

"Does it matter?"

"Not really."

Joe gave the area one quick scan with the scope before turning to Jimmy. The clouds had lifted a bit, but their heavy, gray weight still pressed down on the old building at its rooftops.

"Light it up," he said.

"Fire in the hole!" Jimmy screamed.

Jimmy brought the walkie-talkie up and pushed the send button. He had calculated the lag to be somewhere in the neighborhood of three seconds. When five had passed, he knew something had gone wrong.

"Battery?" Joe asked.

"I replaced it yesterday."

"Maybe the signal's blocked."

"No way. I've tested it. This should not be happening," Jimmy said.

He opened the radio, adjusted the battery contacts, restored the cover, and tried again. Nothing.

"Fuck!"

Before they could discuss another option, Jimmy pushed up off the ground and sprinted back to the pipe opening.

"Jim, no!"

But Jimmy had already climbed up the ladder and was, once again, slithering through the pipe. Joe ran over to the three travelers.

"Give me the gun," he said to Udo.

Udo reached into his waistband and came up empty handed.

"I must have dropped it somewhere."

"What's going on?" Harry asked.

"Give me the fucking gun, now!" Joe repeated.

Udo stared him down. Joe got the message five-by-five: You want it? Take it from me.

Joe's reaction was entirely visceral. Had he paused to wonder why Udo was withholding, it would have laid on the table an entire litany of questions. Instead, triggering the deltoid muscles surrounding his scapula, he thrust his open palm at the larger man's nasal cavity, knocking him off his feet and thus giving him an ample window to rifle through his clothing and to claim back his property. He found the weapon clinging to the waistband of Udo's pants at the small of his back.

Without so much as a word, he loaded the gun with one of the clips and sped away for the ladder at the pipe opening.

———————

Back inside the armory, Jimmy slid the manhole off its inset and peeked out into the breadth of the main hall. No one was yet in the vicinity. From the sound of the continued banging on the door, he surmised that the attack force had yet to make a big enough hole to allow entry.

He climbed out of the sewer, cocked his weapon, and headed toward the supply sergeant's room and the malfunctioning detonation device.

As Jimmy moved through the corridor, he could see, at the end of the hall, that the hinges of the steel door had been partly compromised and that the invaders were trying to free it from its moorings. He hurried to the room containing the radio and discovered the destruction of the receiver that was designed to provide the spark needed to blow the building to kingdom come. What had happened here? He had checked it the day before, so he knew this happenstance was deliberate and not just an unfortunate occurrence. There was just one assumption that his frantic mind could muster. Only Joe could have done this. It was just the two of them, right? That supposition made absolutely no sense, but it was the only conclusion that he could draw from the fragments circulating through his addled brain.

He had a decision to make. This was the moment, he told himself. This was his opportunity to remove the doubt as to whether he could perform under pressure.

———————

Joe's height was hindering his progress on his return trip through the tunnel. He knew that if the raiders had gotten through the door, Jimmy was, mostly likely, already dead. Success in an environment of one against one hundred did not exist in reality.

Coming upon the opening, he could see some light spilling through the portal. The manhole had been reopened. This confirmed that Jimmy had returned, and it left Joe feeling sad as well as culpable. Jimmy had so wanted to impress his superior. And to gain that credibility, he had acted rashly.

As Joe emerged from the hole in the floor, both guns cocked and ready for bear, he could hear the screeching of steel as the door was finally breeched.

"Jimmy!" he yelled.

Getting no response, he angled into the hall just as the first of the Redeemers entered. A single shot to the torso felled the man in the orange jumpsuit with the tattooed arms. No one else dared to enter in the ensuing seconds. With both of the guns leveled at the horde now massing outside the door, Joe sidled toward the room that held the detonation device. From the mob outside, he could hear shouts of encouragement to the newbies that martyrdom lie ahead for them if they would lead the assault.

Joe popped off another round from each gun in an attempt to construct a virtual wall, but he was pretty sure that some overzealous fool would probably try to cross the threshold before he was able to make it to the radio room.

When he heard glass shattering behind him, he became aware that the invaders had not confined their intention for entry to just the steel side door. He spun around quickly to find four machete-wielding Redeemers moving toward him in the hall.

Bang! Bang! Bang! Bang! Four discharges. Four incapacitations.

He triple-timed it to the door of the office to discover Jimmy trying to find a power source to detonate the explosives. The smashed radio lay in a heap of non-degradable plastic on the floor.

"Forget it, Jim!"

Jimmy looked up to the voice. Joe was struck by the realization that the boy he had come to know this past year was no longer there. It wasn't that Jimmy had been transformed into a man; there wasn't anything resembling a human quality in his visage.

"Did you do this?" Jimmy asked, pointing a finger at the electronics on the floor.

"What?"

"Why would you do this?"

"What would make you think that?"

"Who did this, Joe?"

"Does it matter now?" Joe asked.

The kid had lost it, and Joe suspected it would not likely be returning during this particular interim. Jimmy's sense of logic and reasoning had been jettisoned in favor of some kind of primordial, instinctual response. There were many factors at play here, including elements of childhood, parenting, and genetics. Joe had been trying for these past twelve months to get him to reveal all of it in the hopes that it would enhance his maturation, but certainly not in the context that was currently on display. Jimmy now saw this as his duty, maybe even his life's goal.

"Get the fuck out, Joe."

"Jim."

"I'll give you twenty seconds."

Jimmy had dragged an old car battery out of a metal cabinet. It was one of many they had liberated from the stable of defunct vehicles that cluttered the main hall. Joe calculated the odds of whether or not it could have retained any charge in its corroded sodium cells. A couple of amps were all that Jimmy would need.

There would be no further warnings. Jimmy exposed the poles of the batteries and reached for the wires.

Joe's first thought was to shoot him in the leg. He figured that would give him about a 30 percent chance to get them both out alive. He'd have to assist the wounded man and drag him to safety, but they would have a shot at surviving. He leaned back out in the hall and saw another of the Redeemer rookies maneuvering through the steel door and around the body of the man he had gunned down. Another round from his Beretta took off half of the attacker's face.

The sound of the shot caused Jimmy to snap back into the present.

"I have to do this, Joe," he pleaded.

"No you don't."

"You'll never understand why."

"Try me."

"I'll give you fifteen seconds. That's it," Jimmy said. He grabbed his own nine-millimeter from the top of the desk and pointed it at Joe.

"You can't stop me. You can only save yourself. Don't think I won't fucking shoot you," Jimmy said.

"Jim . . ."

"Ten seconds."

Jimmy put some tension to the trigger of the handgun. In that moment, Joe could see the intention that now filled the being of his partner. This was going to happen. He could be a witness—albeit briefly—but nothing more.

Joe made his decision. He had done this before when confronted with an individual as adamant as Jimmy. Why was an image of his late wife coming up for him now?

Joe backed out of the room, his arms forming a cross with each gun pointed horizontally at both ends of the hall. He fired a round in each direction before calculating the amount of his remaining ammunition. He had twenty-five rounds between the two guns when he had reentered the building and, to this point, he had expended ten. Fifteen left without reloading.

He headed back toward the manhole. More Redeemers had come through the second entrance, and he discharged the contents of the gun in his right hand to keep them at bay.

The estimate of ten seconds was certainly just that, an estimate. Joe needed to get to the tunnel now. There could be no impediments. If more invaders popped up, he would not have the time to reload, so he tossed the empty gun away and switched the other to his dominant hand.

He ran over toward the hole and slid on the ground as if he were ballplayer trying to stretch a single into a double. With his free hand, he grasped the railing of the internal ladder to keep himself from plunging down the eight feet to the terminus of the elbow.

By the time he heard Jimmy's screams from the corridor, he had partially replaced the cover and had starting crawling back down the pipe.

When the knife flew through the open door, Jimmy had been bent over, checking the water levels in the battery, hoping to find that not every one of the cells was desiccated. The blade lodged itself in the back of his upper right thigh, severing the connection between his hamstring and his gluteus maximus.

The searing pain was intense, and he screamed out in response. He swung around, fired his weapon. One body fell to the ground as Jimmy collapsed to his knees.

He attached one of the wires to the battery and turned to see five of the maniacs standing in the doorway.

"Enjoy hell," he said.

He crossed the other wire against the grounding pole, and as he smiled at the assassins, he felt the rumble of the first charges going off somewhere in the building.

The chain reaction had begun, and the assembled could tick off the few seconds until they were no more.

"Fuck you, Dad," Jimmy whispered to himself right before his brain concussed.

———

Joe was only ten or fifteen feet into his crawl when he heard the first of the explosions—a thunderous harbinger of an oncoming crescendo. He felt the air being sucked into the building from far down the pipe, and he knew that he had only a few more moments before there would be a corresponding effect as a torrent of flaming exhaust sought a venting route to the outside atmosphere.

There was a bit of an alcove to his right, something that might have diverted the pipe to another opening in some previous time, and he hoped that the small space would allow him to clear himself from most of the destructiveness that would accompany the effluxion.

When the fireball hurtled down the pipe, he had his breath held and his arms crossed above his head. He heard nothing other than a roar and the pinging of metal as the long-buried manholes that existed along the line exploded from their housings. Their departure filled the tunnel with dust and the burgeoning morning light.

———

The three travelers felt the rumble of the ground underneath them before the sight of flames gave way to the sound of the explosion. The building completely imploded a couple of hundred yards away from their position. A mild shock wave blew across them like a mutant summer breeze.

Udo was nursing his broken nose, wondering if the bruising was already visible.

Steve and Harry were trying to figure out what the hell had happened and how they were going to get out of there.

When the pipe burped up the smoke and a bit of flame released by the explosion, the assumption by all three was that they were the only survivors.

"Well, that's that," Udo said as he spit a mouthful of blood onto a nearby river rock.

Steve and Harry could only concur. It was just supposed to be a little jaunt down to Cincy. Two measly days. This was crazy.

Steve suddenly became overwhelmed by a creeping paranoia that he began to project toward the bodyguard they had hired. He began to sift through the sum total of everything that had happened to this point. Udo had suggested the short cut that took them by the armory. He had disappeared during their time of refuge. He had refused to return the gun to that Joe guy. Who would stop him from robbing them, killing them, even leaving them out here in the wild? Steve looked over at the man who was now transforming into a monster in his suddenly dissociated mind. The fact remained: They didn't really know shit about this guy.

"Do you think the car will still work?" Harry asked no one in particular.

"Yeah, why don't you go and find out if it's operational," Steve said to Udo.

Udo nodded and climbed out of the arroyo.

"Let's get out of here," Steve said to Harry when Udo was out of earshot.

"Maybe the car will work," Harry said.

"I don't trust that guy. Something's not right."

"C'mon, Steve."

"Do you think all of those psychos died in that blast? If even one of them was still alive, would you go back there?"

Harry pondered the question.

"He didn't even blink," Steve added.

"You think he's in with them?"

"I'm not hanging around to find out. Look, if we stick to the river, we'll stumble upon something that resembles civilization," Steve said.

Harry stared at Steve for a long time. The same thoughts about their bodyguard began cycling through his mind. He was beginning to draw some of the same conclusions.

"All right."

They began to trek around the outside of the arroyo to head in the opposite direction from where Udo had made his exit. A coughing sound from the mouth of the pipe caused them to pause.

"Jesus," Harry said as he scrambled down the bank and ran over to the opening.

Joe Smith was sprawled at the ingress. There were haloes of smoke swirling around his arms. The material of his down vest was scorched black, and he reeked of burnt hair. To Harry he appeared to be half-dead.

"Help me, Steve," Harry said.

"Fuck," Steve said, as the resignation set in.

Harry scaled the ladder as Steve held it taut.

"Are you all right?" Harry asked Joe.

Joe stared back at him with hollow black pupils. Harry thought, for a moment, he could see into Joe's brain and read his thoughts. He had never seen a stare like this in his fifty-one years of existence, but he knew, from that look, that this smoldering man, sucking in half-breaths, twenty years his junior, had already been through more in his life than Harry would ever be able to recount on his own deathbed.

"Where's your bodyguard?" Joe croaked.

"He went to check on the car."

"Then he's gone."

"I told you," Steve said to Harry.

"There's a place I know up the river. They can help you get home," Joe said.

Harry reached out to offer his hand, but Joe propped himself up under his own power.

"Are you going to be all right?"

"I haven't been all right for long time," Joe said.

And then he rose into a squat before jumping the eight feet to the dirt below.

FOUR

MOTOR CITY

Lon Brassey had waited his entire life for this day to arrive. Until today, the only tangible highlight had occurred the previous January when he had been installed as the Impala captain. He hadn't even thought to bring milestones like his high school graduation, his wedding day, or the birth of his children into the criteria for comparison.

It had been years of lobbying and backstabbing that resulted in his being awarded the title, and today he was going to prove to the whole canton that they had chosen wisely by electing him as their leader.

He finished his cup of coffee before knotting his tie, ever conscious that his accessories must remain unblemished. There could be no gaffes forthcoming, and he planned to eliminate the possibility by fastidiously inspecting his family before they made their way out into the street.

"Karen?" he asked as he exited the dressing room and headed for the stairs.

"Yes, dear?" she replied.

"Let's gather the troops."

"We're waiting for *you*," she said.

On Lon's arrival at the ground floor, he could see that the fiat he had issued concerning the mode of fashion had been carried out.

His wife, Karen, two years younger than his forty-six, with a fountain of strawberry locks and a matte of faint freckles speckling her flawless skin, had chosen an outfit that accented the colors representative of their ward. Her kelly green skirt and black-and-white top incorporated all of the hues that flew on the flags that lined every street of their neighborhood.

Lon and Karen's seventeen-year-old daughter, Holiday, a willowy five-foot-nine-and-a-half-inch beauty completing her transition from tomboy to heartbreaker, had shown remarkable restraint by trading in her customary appliquéd denims for her Sunday best, a black skirt and jacket surrounding a white shirt. An Impala silk scarf with the requisite colors was knotted around her neck.

John, Lon's fifteen-year-old son, had opted for a green sport jacket to mirror his father's kelly green suit. His accoutrements included black slacks and a white shirt.

"Here we go," Lon said as he released a huge breath.

He opened the front door of the townhouse that led into their courtyard. Beyond the alley, he could see his constituency waiting to escort them to the Impala clubhouse on Temple Street. As the family strolled down the walk to join up with their neighbors, a round of applause broke out among the reception group.

Orchestrating the outburst were Lon's two lieutenants, Kevin Gatz and Billy Klock, two sycophants in their mid-thirties who had been instrumental in helping Lon attain the mantle of captain. Billy had been the muscle, Kevin the conniving manipulator, and with their aid, Lon had usurped the man who had ruled their ward for nearly thirteen years.

In succeeding his predecessor, Lon had offered but one promise to the horde: This would be the year that they would win the race. The previous captain, Ed Fisher, had scoffed at Lon Brassey's claim, but given his woeful record in delivering any victory in the most important event of the year, he was left without a leg to stand on in his attempt to wring out another term as their captain. The previous year's result of finishing second in the race was the final insult to the population of Impala. Ed Fisher had to go.

Through his functionaries, Lon had intimated that he had a radical strategy to employ should he be anointed as their leader. It has been said that the denizens of Impala were not all that enamored with Brassey or his tactics, but they voted for him anyway because their curiosity had been piqued by the rumors that he had somehow conjured a path to prosperity. At today's All-Impala fall soiree, Lon was going to open the curtain on the idea that he'd secreted offstage.

―――――――

The walling-in of the city of Detroit turned out to be a perilous task for the people that desired security in the days after the oil ran out and the insurgent groups proliferated. Unlike municipalities such as Dallas, the infrastructure of the Detroit city center had ceased to be a vibrant entity long before being tabbed as a place of sanctuary. To this day, there are some who are quick to say that this was all part of a master plan—concocted by the suburbanites who populated neighboring upscale burgs like Grosse Pointe and St. Clair Shores—when the automobile industry and home mortgage business began to show signs of finally tanking not long after the first third of the century had elapsed.

The exchange of nuclear weapons between adversaries in the Middle East could not have a come at worse time for the struggling transportation industry. Only ten years out from being able to fully switch their propulsion systems away from gasoline and other fossil fuels, the car companies were caught with their pants down when the experience of finding available petroleum to fill the need suddenly became akin to mining Burmese Painite, the rarest of gems.

Domestic oil production, neglected for decades because of the cheap prices and big profits attainable by buying foreign supplies, attempted to plug the gap, but when prices jumped to over twenty-five dollars a liter, only the wealthiest could afford to operate a motor vehicle.

Executives at Ford, General Motors, Chrysler, and their subsidiaries had foreseen the possibility of the scenario that became reality and had begun purchasing large swaths of the urban landscape at rock-bottom prices long before the "big bang in the desert." They were joined by a handful of other haves from the technology and tourism sectors of the business community.

Cobbling together large groups of like-minded individuals—family, friends, and colleagues—they began the urban planning phase to create the community in a series of meetings that were held in the banquet hall of the Country Club of Detroit.

The first rifts that would eventually become endemic amongst the founders were exposed in those early meetings. The enmity that had grown for more than a century during the era when these people competed for the nation's automobile business showed no sign of abatement, and eventually the tentative partnership was dissolved. The parties were left to create the patchwork of neighborhoods that would become the protected enclave with their own sense of jurisdiction, given their domain over a particular swath of real estate.

The only issue dealt with collectively was the actual walling-in of the city center. All of the nine disparate groups contributed to the pool that was used for the wall's construction.

As the walling process began, the poor residents who existed in the derelict parts of the city were forcibly moved to camps set up near River Rouge Park. Many of the newly displaced burned large sections of the city during the "Devil's Night" festivities on the eve of the Halloween that would be their last in the urban area. These wanton acts of destruction actually made the process of demolition easier for the wealthy émigrés.

Once the wall was complete, construction on the residential and commercial sectors began in earnest, and many of the refugees were brought back in from the River Rouge Park encampment to function as day laborers.

From the outset—as the new villagers began to populate their respective neighborhoods—there were turf wars as each respective ward felt a need to establish itself as the alpha region in the areas of commerce and physical prowess.

Again the heterogeneous collective was forced to convene to put in place the rules and laws that would govern the entire enclave.

The nine wards were called Impala, Mustang, Ram, DeVille, Marquis, Lions, Tigers, Red Wings, and Pistons. The first five were named after the car models that their progenitors were affiliated with during the days of their employment.

The other four wards, the Lions, the Tigers, the Pistons, and the Red Wings, had their own differences. Named after the former major league professional sports franchises that occupied the city, their followers were made up of the elements that were connected to the tourism and technology sectors. There was no commingling among this group that the central dwellers often referred to as "the rabble."

Because of their churlish behavior, everyone in the city roundly reviled the Red Wings, whose area of occupation consisted of the region around the old Joe Louis Arena down by the banks of the Detroit River.

As in the early days of other enclaves throughout the Midwest, Motor City's growing pains tended to include incidents of violence promulgated by both insurgents from the outside and warring factions of the various neighborhoods. Incentive to keep the peace and bind the community together to repel the outsiders was needed. Many different remedies were proposed, including the formation of a citywide militia, rewards for the least amount of incidents of aggression against the other wards, and once-a-month citywide parties (from February to October) hosted by each ward in their specific neighborhood. Every attempt at diversion inevitably devolved into some type of fracas, and when the entire Marquis neighborhood was trashed after their beer supply ran low during one August event, the communities' fear of being able to survive behind the walls became readily apparent.

Finally, Mitchell Stephens, a young scholar recently returned from studying the history of the Middle Ages at a university in Canada, presented a plan to the governing council that he felt might decrease the desire among the residents to resort to nastiness.

Combining Caesarian ideals with the present situation, Mitchell proposed setting aside one week out of the year for a festival of competition. Winners would be afforded prizes of prestige and bragging rights that could keep them warm through the tortuous winter months.

No one, save Mitchell, was really sure why the first week in July was chosen as the dates of the festivities. Deference to the former country's independence observance was assumed to be the case, but Dr. Stephens knew that the seventh month was also the common temporal period that gladiator competitions and Christian slayings had been featured in days of yore. Hell, Mitchell had mused, July was named after the most famous of Roman emperors.

Built into the planning was the directive that if any one of the wards acted foolishly throughout the months leading up to the saturnalia, they would be banned from competing and forced to sit out the proceedings until they had served a year's period of probation.

The first year's festival included cooking competitions, track and field events, matches between combatants, and over a hundred different games meant to determine who was the best in a variety of disciplines. It was only moderately successful. The overwhelming number of events caused dilution in the importance of being the victor. It was impossible for large numbers to attend most of the events, and despite a publication that listed the day's winners, no one, other than a household and their neighbors, knew who might have carried home a crown as champion.

The following year saw a return to the behavior that had plagued the environment from its inception.

Mitchell Stephens had claimed that he originally lobbied for the council to authorize only a singular event, not a chaotic schedule of hundreds. He claimed that he believed that this would be the only way to focus the community on a goal. The ruling junta initially saw things differently, but after the debacle of the first festival, many began to see the wisdom in Dr. Stephens's suggestion.

Thus the concept of the race was born.

The structure that had once been the Detroit Masonic Temple had been converted into the Impala clubhouse in the early day's of the ward's formation. The GM executives had chosen the particular plot of urban landscape because the temple existed within its boundaries. In a departure from the preponderance of Greek and Egyptian architecture that most of the Masonic temples built during the early part of the twentieth century brandished, the Masonic Temple of Detroit had been constructed in a neo-gothic style. It incorporated limestone, steel, and brick, and on its completion stood as the largest Masonic facility in the world. Features included a fourteen-story tower, a theatre, and a massive drill room.

To the members of the Impala congregation, the muscular nature of the edifice made it the most magnificent meeting facility in all of Motor City.

Yet there still existed a collective depression amongst the citizens, and the source of that despair was their performance in the race. Lon Brassey was determined to alter that reality, and when he and his entourage arrived to greet the Impala nation on the night of the soiree, there was a faint aura of optimism gripping the two thousand strong. At least it wasn't the same old song that Ed Fisher had been singing, they thought. Everyone in the room could feel that something was different, and it was this spontaneous deviation from the normal attitude of abject malaise that Lon Brassey was hoping to harness.

The bullet points of the speech he would give that afternoon had been crafted over the ten-year period that had elapsed since the moment he realized he wanted to lead this clan. It took a full decade for his goal to mature and required a large amount of relationship development to maneuver himself into the position he currently held. He planned to rouse the residents by citing the planks of his administration and spelling out the three specific precepts that he'd based his campaign on. These were:

1)   The ridicule that was foisted on the Impala community by the other wards would no longer stand as acceptable behavior.

2)   Impala's futility would cease to be included in the definition of their ethos.

3)   And finally, let the other wards return the quality of their loathing to the substantive realm of reverse snobbery, and let them hate the Impalas for what they were: wealthy and attractive.

The comments related to this creed were not really supposed to be part of the captain's duties, but Lon wanted to jostle his neighbors' expectations. By getting them riled up, he hoped to settle their emotions on the area that was actually related to his job description: preparation and success as it related to the coming festival.

It certainly wasn't a parroting of the generic Ed Fisher "state of Impala" speech. One had to go all the way back to Ted Schmidt, an early founder and former Delco CEO, to remember the kind of fire that Lon was prepared to breathe now that he was the grand dragon of this gathering.

Young John watched his father pumping hands as he made his way through the theatre before Lon clambered up the steps and jogged over to the lectern that was positioned on the stage's apron. John spied one of his classmates sitting with his family in the second row.

"Nin hao," John said in greeting.

"Nin hao," replied his friend, Mike.

Mike's parents frowned on hearing the youngsters conversing in Mandarin. Like many of the older folk, they had come to believe that the speaking of Chinese had become a subversive act displayed by the youth. They were of a mind that the youngsters had co-opted the language as some kind of crypto-kidspeak.

John and his peers would deny the link, but all of them secretly knew that their parents' misgivings were grounded in more than a smidgeon of truth. They had all become fluent in the language by watching the only television programming they could get on their satellites.

"What's the word?" Mike asked.

Anyone hearing that query would have thought that Mike had recycled a phrase from the mid-twentieth century, but the question, because it was directed at John, had a literal component to it.

"Teratogeny."

"What's it mean?"

"The formation of monsters," John said with a wink as his eyes followed his father to the dais.

Mike laughed at John's inference. This simple exchange further unnerved Mike's parents. They knew a lot about this strange kid with the rampant vocabulary who had taken to reading a dictionary daily because he was forbidden to participate in anything physical as a result of his medical condition. They did not like their son to associate with this freak, but now that his father was captain, they had little choice.

Lon asked the crowd to dispense with the applause and signaled the piano player in the orchestra pit to commence with plinking out the introduction to the Impala song. The entire throng rose as one and belted out the signature tune to the melody of "See the USA in Your Chevrolet":

See . . . the . . . way we play,
We're the kings today,
Impala is the reason you will fail.
That's why we all say,

She's the only way,
We are the Motor City's Holy Grail.
When you see us, you will want to holla',
Nothing is sweeter, nothing can beat her,
Life is completer in Impala."

There was a well-known tagline to the tune that was not normally permitted to be uttered in mixed company, but a couple of the men and some of the young adults could not suppress their desire to add that last verse which was shouted, not sung.

"Fuck Mustang!"

Immediately, the room was vocally split between gales of laughter and admonitions as mothers tried to clamp their hands over the ears of the young.

As the revelry abated, Lon Brassey strode to the microphone.

"I'd like to welcome all of you to the All-Impala Fall soiree. This will be a very special year for us. Be grateful that you are alive and well and can be present for the dawning of a new era for our beloved neighborhood."

At that point, a sprinkling of tentative applause interrupted Lon. Deep down he was hoping that there would be a greater display of enthusiasm, but he knew that once he revealed his secret plan the whole place would likely go totally bonkers.

He then proceeded to tick off the agenda items he had assembled, allowing for the tension to build.

As he wound up for the last paragraph of his speech, he was comforted by the fact that each one of his statements had been received with a much greater response than the one that preceded it. He made sure to allow each spontaneous outpouring of applause to wane before his oratory continued on to the next declaration.

Finally, after soaking in the adulation that was being directed at him by the totality of his constituents ensuing a particularly stirring portion of his speech, he paused for a very long time. The gap continued to extend and the patrons—as well as Lon's family—became unnerved by the protracted silence.

He continued to pause, letting the tension coalesce into a visceral entity before delivering the clincher.

"We will be victorious in the coming year, and I want you to commit to the concept that your maximum effort will be considered the minimum contribution. We have some plans, some internal competitions to select the drill teams and the punch-out squad, but we will also be making a radical departure from the normal protocol by bringing in a professional driver to pilot us to victory."

There it was. The crowd immediately hushed and contemplated the possibilities. Lon remained stoic. Nobody could have guessed that this was the protected concealment. It had never even been thought about, never discussed, and never attempted by any of the other wards. The collective thought was this: If Impala could pull this off, the shit was going fly. As the ramifications cycled through the crowd, a prevailing sentiment emerged from the faithful. They would be the first, and if one of the other wards didn't like it, they could go fuck themselves.

The effect that Lon had envisioned began to spread like a rapidly dividing virus as members began to stand and shower their new captain with thunderous applause and verbal accolades.

As the tumult grew, Lon felt like he owned the whole world.

FIVE

W HEN DR. MITCHELL STEPHENS convinced the board of elders that the correct course of action should be a competition around a singular event, he had no idea that the event would end up being a race.

Because of the romanticism he displayed for all things Roman, his first suggestion for the spectacle was a gladiator-style competition based on physical prowess, and he used the festival of the Puglia as a template. A "Puglia" was an Italian tradition last practiced about five hundred years ago. It involved a contest where the strongest men would try to force their enemies out of an enclosed area, such as a large piazza. Stephen's re-creation involved the gathering of members of each ward at a neutral, enclosed site and letting everyone have at each other until one or more members of a singular ward stood alone. He proposed that either of the two stadiums in the mid-eastern sector of the enclave could be used.

He also suggested that—beyond the swell of pride that the winning ward would carry for the year—they should receive some other benefit that would increase their wealth. His choice was a suspension of the local tax for the year's period that the champion reigned.

Many of the elders resisted Dr. Stephens's plan to return to the barbarous nature of some ancient rite and tabled his recommendation. As the year progressed with no discernible plan in place, the council kept returning to a discussion on the viability of the idea that was now being referred to as "the punch-out."

During a contentious proceeding where a vote on the proposal appeared imminent, the battle lines were drawn. Four wards, the Lions, Tigers, Pistons, and Red Wings, were down with the concept of the free-for-all. The other wards considered themselves to be more sophisticated and projected an air of disdain for the blood lust. They argued that the event would just exacerbate the problem of violence within the city.

After withstanding the fusillade of insults declaring the automotive sector to be fairies and pussies, the elders, representing the subjects of the ridicule, suggested that the matter should come up for a vote.

Since the automotive sector carried a majority of five wards to four, they felt they could silence the bullies by exacting a defeating closure to the matter being debated.

But the members of Mustang, always the provocateurs, had other ideas. A rumor swept through the meeting that the Ford boys would consider siding with the pro-punch-out folks for a price. Only negotiations never ended up being entered into because Harold Getty strode to the front of the council with an easel and a large black portfolio.

"I would like to ask the council for a few minutes of their time," Harold said.

The angry buzz in the room had yet to subside as Harold set up his presentation. Finally, one of the bickering principals noticed the first item Harold had placed on the easel. It was beautiful painting of a car—a lime-green 1971 Plymouth Barracuda.

Four bangs of a gavel were required to cede the floor to the aged man standing before the three-legged prop.

"I have a proposal that I think we should all consider," Harold began.

Most of the council members were still staring at the painting and permitting their minds to wax nostalgic to a different time in their lives. If one could have collated a consensus of their thoughts, they would have determined that this nonet had suddenly been transported back in time to a place that was simpler and more defined.

"So this is what I was thinking," Harold continued.

He removed the rendering of the vehicle and exposed a map of the city center.

"A race through the streets using the cars that I've archived at my museum."

The effect of his statement was akin to the condition that is achieved when air is forcibly sucked out of a room. To the right or to the left, one could hear gasps and view confounding looks of astonishment. Harold, the eremite collector, couldn't tell whether the council's response tilted toward the negative or the positive.

Poor Harold had been cursed with a fetish for V-8 powerhouses ever since the day his father first brought home a stunning '69 Chevrolet Chevelle Super Sport when Harold was still in diapers. His first memory may have been having his bare butt placed on that gray tuck-and-roll upholstery as his mother held him between her legs on the way to get some ice cream one sultry summer evening.

Being a child of means—his father was a prominent class-action personal injury attorney—Harold began acquiring, at the age of twelve, the machines that would eventually make up the contents of his museum. By the time he was legally able to drive, he had three vehicles:

his father's Chevy, a 1970 American Motors AMX, and the lime-green 1971 Plymouth Barracuda that had caused the attendees to swoon.

At the end of their time in Grosse Pointe, the Getty's family garage contained twelve vehicles, though three were in the midst of restoration. As his suburban cul-de-sac became uninhabitable, he purchased a space a couple of blocks off Woodward Avenue and began moving his treasures. The nine that made it to the facility included a 1968 Ford Mustang Shelby GT, a 1969 Chevrolet Impala SS, a 1971 Dodge Challenger, a 1972 Ford Gran Torino, a 1971 Plymouth Roadrunner, a 1968 Pontiac GTO, and the aforementioned three vehicles he had acquired pre- and post-puberty—the Chevelle, the AMX, and the Barracuda. All were in the condition that appraisers would only classify as mint.

Harold wasn't exactly sure when he came up with the idea for the race, but he had gotten sick of seeing these beasts just sitting indoors, submitting to the fronds of the feather duster, their crankcases as arid as a Saharan afternoon. The course he devised included a section through each of the southeastern wards, with the starting and finishing point being the grounds of Ford Field, the decrepit former home of Detroit's NFL franchise.

When he completed his presentation, there was nearly a full minute of silence as everyone ingested and sorted through the possibilities. In the end, Harold's question as to the worthiness of the concept was rendered moot. The assembled were universally enthusiastic about the idea, but logistics, format, and the council's stubborn attention to detail commenced immediately after the crowd allowed itself a conscious breath.

"So these are all electric now?" the elder of Marquis asked.

"No, sir," Harold said.

"Are we supposed to push the damn things, then?" the elder of the Lions asked.

"That would be funny, but no." Harold said.

"I can see that you have a plan, Mr. Getty," the elder of the Tigers said.

"I do."

"Would you care to indulge us?"

"Yes, sir."

He removed another chart from his portfolio and placed it on the easel.

"As some of you know, there exists a reserve of crude oil in a vault down by the river. This was placed there to serve Naval ships of our former country during what had been commonly referred to as the Second World War."

The murmurs emanating from the gathered confirmed to Harold that—even though he was privy to the existence of this cache—not many of the attendees had even heard of the reserve.

"Now, I have no way of knowing what is contained in the reserve, but I would have to believe that the total is more than just a couple of barrels. Turning to my chart here, you can see that each barrel of oil, once refined, could produce something along the lines of thirty-six gallons of 97 octane gasoline. As there are nine cars and nine wards, each could receive four gallons of fuel for such an event, and if one were to figure that the maximum efficiency of one of these vehicles is somewhere in the neighborhood of ten miles per gallon, the range works out to some forty miles. As I have shown you, one lap around the racecourse I have sketched out is six miles. If the race's duration were a total of three laps, that would leave plenty of fuel for practice, moving the car to and from the staging areas, and the race. There are still multiple refineries down by the river that could be returned to functionality without a lot of effort. As far as the products that would be needed for engine lubrication, I have those in my possession."

That silence came again. A couple of the elders were looking curiously at Harold and trying to figure out if he had an agenda that extended beyond his offer. Finally the representative of the Red Wings spoke up.

"And what are you going to get out of this, Mr. Getty?"

"I'm getting on in years. My health hasn't been that good. If I could get to see my cars run wild again, well, that would be my compensation."

One could see the level of emotion he was holding back as he made this disclosure. As he started to disassemble the elements of his presentation, he surreptitiously wiped a tear from his eye.

In the end there was no formal vote, just an agreement by acclamation. There would be a race, and for good measure they would have a punch-out during the festival week as well.

———

There was a significant change in the consciousness of the Impala faithful after Lon dropped his bomb on them. But, intentionally, he'd left a little on the table, and more than one glad-hander had a question or two for the new captain. Nearly all chose to focus their personal inquiries on the identity of the professional driver. Lon remained tight-lipped—smiled and deflected them all—as he and his coterie had yet to interview any candidates.

His initial plan involved offloading some of the recruitment process to a group larger than the three that made up the hierarchy. This was meant to function as protection in case the whole thing did not work out the way he'd envisioned. It was important—especially through his first term—that he had a patsy or two when it came to accountability, but after witnessing the outpouring of excitement engendered by his declaration, he formulated a strategy for a way to manipulate those emotions for his own gain.

Up until now, the duties of piloting the car through the racecourse fell upon one of the residents. An internal competition to determine the best candidate took place every May. Mental acuity and physical prowess were assessed. After a winnowing, the ward's representative would be anointed only after a final contest employing the race simulator housed at Harold Getty's museum.

The burden shouldered by the eventual winner of the contest often proved to be crushing in its weight. More than one of the drivers for the various wards had taken their own lives after a humiliating defeat. Finishing second was the worst possible result, as most people believed that you could have won, but didn't. It was far better to finish back in the pack than to narrowly miss victory.

Bringing in a driver with experience was definitely considered to be a radical idea because, to date, no one had attempted that strategy. Lon Brassey's ploy was sure to be met with resistance by the other wards, but the bylaws of the event had never contained a provision that stated that the pilot must come from the entrant's neighborhood.

In Brassey's mind, the need to seek approval from the rest of the wards or the organizing committee was a non-issue. He had little doubt that word would leak out of Impala's plans, but that could only serve to stir the pestiferous pot at blender speed. It could only amount to an ancillary advantage if their foes were drawn into an eddy of dismay as the festival dates approached.

John watched his father bask in the glow of the attention being beamed his way. The scene evoked another word for him, perihelion, defined as the closest point an orbiting celestial body achieves in relationship to its sun.

Conceptualizing the scene, John determined that his father was the orb and not the sun. *There it is*, he thought. *There it is in a nutshell.* This event was a distillation down to the essence of how he actually experienced his father, a man seemingly content that his effect on the world be limited to his bottomless desire to be lauded. Why didn't his father strive to be the source of light? Why was his esteem emboldened by the absorption of the warmth of others? *This is vampire-like, this sucking on the energy of others*, John thought. In that moment, he made a silent vow that his path in life would be in opposition to the one that needed to have this parasitic kind of relationship to the world. His brain processed words relating to the emotion he felt, but they did not leave his lips. They did bounce around inside his noggin, though—: *Fuck you, dad.*

SIX

GETTING HOME

AFTER THE COMPLETION of his duties outside of Akron, Joe Smith kept his promise and escorted Harry and Steve to safety. He led them to the Pigeon River, where they floated on a derelict boat northwest toward one of the many tributaries that lead back to Lake Erie. Once out in the openness of the river, it didn't take long for Joe to convince a kindred spirit among the passel of captains that helmed the heavily fortified wind-powered barges to let them tie onto her vessel. On their arrival at the banks of the Great Lake, Joe parted company with the two men who had been marooned by their flaky bodyguard.

Eternally grateful, both Harry and Steve profusely thanked their savior and offered him lodging should he ever make it up their way. Now atop the deck of the barge, Joe watched them melt into the mobs that swarmed the entrance to their C-town enclave before he turned his attention to the west.

With a stiff helping breeze, the deadhead trip to Toledo did not take long. Joe could see the outlying areas of the open city approaching on the horizon as he cataloged a loose itinerary for what was sure to be an arduous journey back home.

The first leg required him to book passage down the Maumee River, taking him from Toledo to Fort Wayne. From there he would have to travel by land to access the banks of the sycamore-lined Wabash River, the primary conduit in that region to the west and south.

He was not without issues—the most paramount being that he was nearly destitute. That meant that his very first stop when he hit the shore would have to be at the Tynan International, Ltd., branch office so he could get paid for his last six months of work.

The Toledo office had been the entity responsible for dispatching Joe and Jimmy to the armory in Rubber City. They retained the corporate responsibility for generating all of the reports related to Joe's mission, so he had to eventually check in there, but the timing had suddenly become critical. He needed to pay for the trip he had already taken before the ferry that delivered him here headed back across the lake.

Joe's hope was that he would only be saddled with having to go through a casual debriefing; they were many years down the road from having to detail anything that could be classified as formal. The gist would be: "We blew it up. We killed or maimed nearly all of those moronic maniacs that were intent on looting the place."

But the normally truncated debriefing would have to be expanded this time around. Jimmy's demise would have to be accounted for in the specific. That could keep him here for a couple of days at the very least. First, though, he needed to have his credit restored.

He disembarked, jogged up Jackson, turned left on Eleventh, and angled to the right side of the street. When he arrived at the outpost, he found the offices locked, the windows boarded up with Kevlar panels. The entire facility was vacant.

Initial inquiries as to the whereabouts of the employees who should have been manning the branch proved to be unanswerable. Joe asked the neighbors, the other business people in the area, even the loitering local militia, but their responses were never stronger than a noncommittal shrug of the shoulders.

Catching his reflection in the leaded glass of a restaurant window, Joe wondered whether the people's reticence to offer any information was related to his appearance. He looked as raggedy-assed as a god-damn Redeemer, for chrissake.

He checked into a daytel, a high-end public toilet for transients. He quickly showered, shaved, and sanitized his clothing. Thankfully, he had enough to cover the cost. His balance was announced after he paid for the transaction—one measly credit left. That was quite a ways short of what he needed to pay the purser on the ferry that had conveyed him across the lake. Shit. Joe hated to owe anyone anything, and he knew that the guilt associated with the unpaid debt would lodge itself into the recall portion of his long-term memory. It would be another broken promise that would reverberate when his mind went searching for sadness.

Determining that he had achieved something akin to the metric referred to as presentable, he ventured into the streets to again assess the tenor of the town folk. It seemed to him that everyone was on edge, and when he eventually got a local to relate the recent news covering the region, he understood why.

Barbers had been through the area within the last month, and a battle had been fought against the local militia on the grounds of the historic Woodlawn Cemetery near the town of Five Points. The attackers had been repelled, but the collective consciousness of the city had been infected by an intense anxiety.

Rumors abounded about a return of the Barbers along with gossip that bands of Redeemers would be making their way north as well. Joe confirmed that indeed, Redeemers had been seen around Rubber City recently, but he had heard that their progress had been halted. He never let on that he was the reason for their retardance.

Joe could find no one willing to offer a credible explanation for the sudden abdication of the Tynan International, Ltd., personnel. The ambivalence of the interviewees in response to that specific question led Joe to believe that there wasn't collective subterfuge afoot—these people just had no clue as to the disposition of his employers.

One of the respondents, a bartender named Brad, thought that they might have left because of a lack of funds. He had overheard a conversation between two employees—a few too many beers into one afternoon—that municipalities had stopped paying for the protection that Tynan provided. Short of taking or extorting the money, Tynan was left with only one alternative: leave. The company's theory had always been that once they disappeared and the assaults began, the company would have an easier time demanding higher fees for their return.

Brad asked for his order, and when Joe told him he could not afford any of the establishment's wares, the barkeep poured him two fingers of cheap Canadian Rye on the house.

Joe tossed it back in one quick gulp. As the alcohol blazed a corrosive trail down his throat, he thought about Jimmy Hazen. Poor sack of shit, he concluded. And then an overwhelming sense of remorse began to ravage every constructive thought his brain was endeavoring to form.

It wasn't the first time he had felt an onslaught such as this. It was an affirmation that, deep down, he knew he should have been able to prevent Jimmy's suicidal act. It led him to allow the memories of his mother, his wife, and his children to creep in—others he had been unable to save.

Jimmy was from some tiny shithole town just north of Memphis. Joe determined that the honorable thing to do was to make a stop and explain the circumstances associated with Jimmy's death to his kin.

He humbly thanked Brad and walked out of the bar and into the midday sun. The wind from the lake smacked him in the face like a bullwhip as he headed for the banks of the Maumee River. As he rounded the corner and put the lake and the bay behind him, he caught sight of the vessel that had brought him to this shore and noted the number spray-painted on the hull. Maybe one day he would be back through these parts and he could settle his outstanding debt.

He could not afford the transit to Fort Wayne. Hell, he basically couldn't afford to go down the block. There was a chance that he could recharge his money card at the end of the next leg of the trip, but he wasn't going to try to make that deal again. He felt a warehouse of remorse already, and he wasn't about to continue to lower the threshold levels of his psychic pain.

Boarding a wood-burning, steam-driven, screw-propelled riverboat, Joe asked the purser if he could perform some type of duty on the scow in lieu of a fare. Before he could answer, the inebriated captain nearly tripped over Joe on his way to the helm, and Joe made the same offer to him. The captain focused his rheumy eyes on the skinny man in the black shirt and camouflage pants.

"You got a weapon?" the captain asked.

"Yes, sir."

"What gives you the authority to carry a weapon on my boat?"

From the cargo pocket of his pants, Joe removed some coffee-stained paperwork and a badge that identified him as an employee of Tynan International, Ltd.

"Tynan?"

"Yes, sir."

"That outfit is all but kaput, ain't it?"

Joe didn't answer as he pocketed his identification.

"Look, there would be nothing for you to do until we sail through Napoleon. When the river narrows, I might need you to provide some extra security at night. We've been sailing pretty light since the river thawed, so I guess I don't see much harm in taking you down the line.

"That would be great."

"You get that I don't want you to have to exercise your talents and abilities?"

"Yes, sir."

"All right. I don't want to see that gun out at anytime unless I make a request, got it?"

"Yes, sir."

"Carry on, then," the captain said as he half-stumbled away.

The captain had been prescient in his assumption that there would be little or no trouble where the river ran in wide and deep water. As night fell and the wind subsided, Joe could hear the chugging of the steam engine as it fired up. He lay out on the deck and looked at the stars.

As it did every spring, the planet was passing through the trail of dust left by the Thatcher Comet. After locating the star Deneb in the Cygnus constellation, Joe worked his way up to the Hercules constellation. Halfway between the two, he focused on the Lyra constellation and its planetoid, Vega. It was from this specific area that he knew the meteor shower would appear. He had a few hours before the fireworks began. Joe closed his eyes and allowed himself some much-needed sleep before the rain of ore began in earnest.

When Joe awoke, there was a quality to the darkness on the water that allowed the starlights from above to shine with a vibrancy that he had not witnessed for a while. All those battery-lamp-lit misty nights in Akron had continually showcased a sky that featured only the brightest elements of the heavens. Finding constellations beyond Orion or the Big Dipper was a virtual impossibility in that environment.

He reoriented back to the celestial bodies that would frame the gush of meteorites. But as the first signs of the meteor shower lit up the sky, he heard the boat's engine sputter to a stop.

Feeling no wind, Joe knew that they were not in the midst of a changeover to a different power source. Maybe they were out of the wood that provided the fuel, or perhaps the captain had found a sweet spot in the current that might allow for some measurable speed without any assistance of the motor.

Joe took his attention off the sky and looked both port and starboard. From what he could sense, they were the only vessel on the river. But something didn't seem right. He stretched his frame to an erect position, grabbed his sidearm, and walked back to where the helmsman was ensconced.

"Everything all right?" he asked of the first mate.

"Why?"

"I heard the engine shut down and I was just wondering if there was a problem."

"We always shut down for an hour or so before the narrows. The captain likes to get some sleep, you know?"

Joe nodded. The first mate's response seemed credible. However, figuring the amount of booze that he had witnessed sloshing inside the captain, Joe couldn't help but think that the skipper would not need something akin to absolute silence to catch some z's.

"So what aren't you telling me?" Joe asked.

"I don't know what you mean."

"Someone got a camp on the banks before the narrows?"

The first mate flinched. Joe could see some perspiration leaking through his shirt. He pegged the ambient temperature to be around fifty-five degrees on the Fahrenheit scale.

"You can tell me," Joe said.

The first mate chose to stay mute. Joe pulled the nine-millimeter from the front of his pants and loaded one of the clips into the breech.

"Do they have boats?"

The first mate was staring at the gun.

"Yeah," he said.

Joe took a seat on the aft deck and tuned his ears to try to discern the possible sound of oars slapping at the surface of the inky water. After an hour, he figured the threat had passed. When the first tendrils of light warmed the eastern horizon, he searched the banks for any sign of possible raiders, but there were none to be found.

The wind began to freshen, the sails went up, and the boat coasted into the narrows without incident. When the watch changed and a replacement arrived for the first mate, Joe headed back to his former place on the deck. As he made his exit, the first mate gave him a simple nod of thanks.

After docking in Fort Wayne, Joe disembarked and slithered his way through the vendors and pimps with the intent of checking in with the Tynan officials at their local facility. He had gotten lucky once with a free ride. It was not likely to happen again.

It didn't take him long to find out that this Tynan outpost had been shuttered as well. He was in no mood to investigate the reasons, as he had thirty odd miles still to travel so that he could hook up with the Wabash. How he was going to head west on that river with empty pockets was a question he could not answer.

Running into the first mate at a food kiosk, he asked him what might be the best way to get his body south. The man of silence downed the last of the meat that had been floating in a mud-colored broth and motioned with his head that Joe should follow him.

Outside a storage facility, the first mate unveiled a beat-to-shit battery-driven moto. He checked the connections, the levels, the tire pressure, flicked the switch to on, and bade Joe to climb aboard.

Not a word passed between them, and when the first mate pulled up to the banks of the Wabash, Joe climbed off the machine. The first mate dismounted, strode up onto the deck of the boat that was moored at the dock, and exchanged words with a member of the crew. The first mate then drove off without so much as a "by your leave" as the boatswain waved Joe aboard. No one asked him for a fare.

SEVEN

PULLULATION

Young Joe could speak before he could walk. He could climb before he could run. All could see that he had an extraordinary ability to balance himself on almost any abnormal surface. There would be more difficult times to come as he matured, but the infant Joe and his antics became the source of entertainment to the Smith family and their friends.

Joe's father was a fire captain in the enclave of the former city of Dallas, Texas, and his mother, Eileen, made knock-off couture-worthy dresses for the gentry of the walled community. They lived near the botanical gardens, just off Garland Avenue, by the southeast corner of White Rock Lake.

By the time he turned two years old, Joe's parents were aware that their child had more energy than the other kids in the neighborhood. Captain and Mrs. Smith were a little advanced in terms of their age to be rearing such a rambunctious kid, and after Mrs. Smith sustained a black eye from an inadvertent punch from young Joe, they wondered whether there might be something wrong with their little guy.

They knew that if they started the process of trying to seek a medical diagnosis for whatever condition the youngster exhibited, the doctors would be sure to confirm that a malady existed. That was just what doctors do, they told each other. The prospect of subjecting the boy to continuous medication was not a road his parents desired to take.

The circular discussion inside the Smith household centered on the concepts of perception and gave deference to facts, such as they were not twenty-something parents with boundless energy, and the phenomenon that suggested that this is what little boys always did.

There was no doubt that access to the child's genetic profile might have answered a multitude of questions, but the Smiths were not the biological parents of Joe. Thoughts of sifting through their own behavior during their growing up would provide nothing tangible they could use to aid them in understanding the feral tendencies of their adopted son.

In the end, the Smiths chose to forgo placing a label on the attributes of their son's puckish behavior and opted to try to channel this odd energy into an activity that the child might be able to draw upon later in life.

Too young to join any of the team sports programs offered in Big D, the Smiths enrolled a three-year-old Joe in a combination pre-school/day care/tumbling class.

After the second day, Eileen entered the gym to retrieve her boy. The instructor separated himself from a gathering of the other parents and took her into the alcove.

"I've been trying to reach you. We've got a bit of problem here, Mrs. Smith," he began.

Eileen intrinsically knew that something bad had happened. Her first assumption was that Joe had been violent with one of the other children. She caught a glimpse of the other parents gathered by the refreshment table. They were furtively stealing glances to see if their desires were being communicated clearly by the instructor.

"What happened? Did he hurt someone?"

"Nearly."

Eileen felt a rush of relief. Captain Smith was working a seventy-two-hour shift at the firehouse, and he would be none too happy if he had to come down to calm the angry parents of the other children.

"What did he do?"

"We were waiting in line for forward somersaults and everything was moving in unison until it was supposed to be Joe's turn. I was across the room watching the kids finish their runs, but I had counted only seven. Your son was missing."

Now Eileen became suspicious. Why didn't this ponce come out with the facts associated with the incident that seemed to have left everyone so traumatized?

"Well, where was he?"

"He had climbed the bleachers and was hanging from one of the light standards, swinging back and forth," the instructor said.

It was obvious that the episode had completely horrified him. Eileen stifled a laugh.

"So the only one that might have gotten hurt was him?" she asked.

"Well, yes, but he scared the other children so badly we had to suspend the class. I had to get ahold of all of the parents, and they were not pleased that they had been forced to deal with this situation. Collectively, they are very unhappy with your son."

Eileen looked again at the other parents.

"Well, I guess all I can say is, tough shit for them," she said.

"Excuse me, ma'am?"

"Did you tell Joe that he did wrong? Did you say that kind of behavior was not appropriate for this class?"

The instructor hesitated. Eileen frowned.

"No. You just overreacted. My guess is that you screamed and scared the children half to death. So, really, all the trauma they experienced was caused by you," she said.

"I beg your pardon?" he sputtered out.

"Don't worry. We won't be coming back."

She strolled away from the instructor, smiled at the other parents, and called for Joe. He was sitting alone, sipping on a juice box with the instructor's assistant.

"Rest easy, folks. He won't be coming back," she said to the gathering of parents.

They immediately averted their eyes as if that action would somehow absolve them from having any responsibility in the kid's dismissal.

Eileen wanted to add something about jealousy or provincialism, but she thought that silence would be a more effective denouement.

Back at home, the Legos spread about the floor in organized piles, Eileen watched her son play with the building materials. She noticed— even at this premature age—that his mind was working logically. Joe had separated all of the pieces into commonalities, be it size or color. When he finally began to construct his project, the joining together was uniform and consistent.

Eileen stumbled as she tried to coalesce her observations into a personal diagnosis of her child's pathology. How could this child exhibit both a deliberate and reckless nature? And why was she so vigilant about parsing his every tendency? Couldn't she just relax and let the whole thing happen without having to make a definitive judgment on every little thing?

Eileen knew little about Joe's birth mother, as the woman spent only six months with them after delivering her baby. When probed, the woman only offered that her husband had been sweet, gentle, and extremely intelligent. But there was something that lingered in these conversations. It was the suggestion that the woman, Katherine, was not entirely sure that her husband had actually sired her child. Further investigation by Eileen never wrested away the identity of the actual person who might have been Joe's biological father.

If Eileen were to guess, she suspected that Katherine's offspring didn't exhibit the genetics associated with the man she described as her husband, and therefore, Joe must have been the issue of another.

God, how grateful would Eileen be if the secret of guiding this child could be revealed to her? Unfortunately, the one person who possessed that information had disappeared and was not likely to ever return.

Eileen turned again to watch her adopted son at play. Joe had nearly completed his plastic edifice, a slightly lopsided isosceles pyramid. She praised him for his effort.

"Wrong," he said.

"No it isn't, honey. It's beautiful. There is no such thing as wrong."

"Yes, there is. This is wrong."

Joe proceeded to tear the structure apart, making sure to the return the pieces to their respective piles.

By the time her husband had finished his shift a couple of days later, Eileen had worked herself into somewhat of a tizzy. By this point, she had done a pretty good job of convincing herself that she was a failure as a parent.

In the moments after Joe Sr. returned from work, Eileen related the details of the incident that had occurred at the tumbling class a few days prior. She also gave some of the highlights about her subsequent subjective reactions to the event.

Maybe Joe Sr. was tired, maybe he was frustrated by his wife's inability to just handle things, or maybe he felt some guilt for being absent for long stretches of time. The conversation shifted from simple relation to debate, and then something that could only be classified as a fight.

In his work, Captain Joe had some expertise in being able to delineate how a spark became a raging inferno, but he had no access to those tools when it came to dealing with interpersonal relationships. The root causes of the combustion, the ignition and the accelerant, were from the underlying uncertainty that had consumed them since they first took over the responsibility for this unique soul.

For the first year they were convinced that Joe's birth mother, Katherine Harris, would return in due time and reclaim her child. But as one year became two, the odds of her return seemed to diminish and they were forced to reassess their positions as simple caretakers.

When word filtered into Big D that Redeemers had laid waste to Mercyville, Kentucky, Katherine's former home, the prospects of her return seemed to dip to nil, and the Smith's realized that they had been promoted to the title of full-time parents.

After their altercation, Captain Smith slept for fourteen straight hours, and when he awoke it was like the event had never occurred. When he entered the kitchen he crossed to the stove and hugged his wife, poured himself a cup of coffee, and settled into his chair at the table.

His son was perched on a booster chair, smearing some oatmeal into the placemat.

"Hey sport," Captain Smith said.

"Good morning, Dad," Joe replied.

"Do you two have plans today?" Captain Smith asked his wife.

She looked up from the pot she was scrubbing.

"Why?"

"Because I've got an idea," he said.

When he told her that it involved going outside of the walls, she was immediately dubious.

"You are going to have to explain this thing you call an idea."

Joe stopped playing with his food long enough to watch the ping-pong nature of the conversation between his folks. He could tell that his father eventually won this particular point.

Captain Smith had heard about a church based just outside the walls of Big D that housed a collection of monks who were versed in a form of martial arts that had its origins in Shaolin Kung Fu. He didn't tell Eileen that he heard about it from a flyer that had been left on the windshield of one of the firehouse vehicles.

He didn't know much about the discipline except that it involved some combination of meditation and movement. It was strictly to be used only in self-defense, and it appeared to be about balance. Having watched his child's uncanny ability to remain upright on the most un-even of surfaces, Captain Smith had convinced himself that he would be putting his son in a situation that might enhance his natural gifts, and, by excelling, provide him with a foundation that he could use to promote greater self-esteem.

He satisfied Eileen's fears about his and little Joe's travel to the outside by telling her that they would be part of a Dallas Security Administration convoy that would ferry them down the Marvin D. Love freeway to the church's location on the east bank of Joe Pool Lake. The armored convoy ran daily along the route to protect the goods and services that were leaving or coming into the city.

When they arrived at St. Michael's Church and were ushered into the monastery, Captain Smith realized that he hadn't done his research in determining the requirements for admittance. The minimum age for trainees was five years old, and since little Joe had half a year to even reach four, Joe Sr. was either going to have to return home or lie. Seeing that documentation wasn't required, he opted for the latter.

A young Somali man named Mohammed offered applications to the six parents who had accompanied their children to their first lesson. Mohammed was shirtless and wore a silk skirt the color of burnt orange.

With the paperwork filed, the children were escorted to a small room in a group of buildings that existed between the cathedral and the monastery. The parents were invited into an observation room that allowed them to watch the proceedings without the children knowing they were present.

As Mohammed had explained to them, there was knowledge to be acquired by both the participant and the observer. No part of the experience could be discounted.

Captain Smith watched as little Joe and the other five children (who ranged in age from five to twelve) were marched into a dimly lit room. The only adornments were a grouping of circular cushions placed equidistant from each other on the floor. At one end of the room, another monk, smack in the middle of life's years, also shirtless, sat with his legs crossed atop one of the cushions. No words were spoken.

The monk on the cushion held out his hand to infer that the kids should assume a position on the cushions that was similar to his. Strangely, the youngest of the lot, Joe, was the first to react, and he took a seat at the cushion closest to the monk and crossed his legs. Slowly the others joined him.

The time passed without a word being uttered by the master. No physical instruction was offered. Eight minutes in, one of the kids began to cry. This unnerved two others, who abruptly stood up and began to walk aimlessly around the room. There was more fidgeting, a couple of whimpers, and a plaintive wail from the crying kid.

In the observation room, the parents were starting to take on the same anxiety that appeared to grip their children.

"What the fuck is this? They have to sit for an hour?" one of the parents asked of the others.

"I guess so," said another.

"Where's the lesson?" another parent asked.

"I think this is it," Captain Smith said.

Where the other kids had shown how uncomfortable the exercise was turning out to be, little Joe hadn't moved a muscle. His entire focus had been on emulating the Zen-like state of the sitting monk.

And that was it. After a full hour had passed, the lesson was over. As the parents reunited with their children, Captain Smith could overhear some of their comments.

"That was total bullshit," the parent of the crying kid said to the parent of the child who had fidgeted the most.

"I agree. Where do we get a refund?" the other parent said.

Captain Smith, on the other hand, was astounded by his son's performance. He was not alone.

"How old is your child, really?" Mohammed asked as the observation room emptied out.

"Uh . . ." Captain Smith hesitated.

"He's not five, is he?"

Captain Smith was pretty sure that Mohammed thought he might be older, given his ability to stay stock-still for the entire time period.

"No," Captain Smith allowed.

"He's more like three, am I right?" Mohammed asked.

Captain Smith had been caught in his prevarication. Before he could admit his transgression, the other monk entered the room.

"I was right," Mohammed said to the other monk.

"Your child is how old?" the other monk said.

"Three," Captain Smith said.

"Have him return for the class on Wednesday," the other monk said as he exited the room.

Mohammed was impressed.

"Wow, that's never happened before," he said.

"What?"

"Your boy has just been skipped ahead to the intermediate level. Some people spend four years getting to that point."

"Is he going to be safe?" Captain Smith asked.

"The real question is: Are we going to be safe?" Mohammed said with a smile.

EIGHT

H-TOWN

Joe's trip down the Wabash was uneventful. When the waters gave way to the Ohio and, eventually, the Mississippi, he knew that the time of his arrival in Baton Rouge could be counted in days, not weeks. He had no idea how he was going to get from Baton Rouge to his home in H-town once the aqueous tributaries were no longer available to him. He would be required to make his way overland from there on out.

As luck would have it, his reputation preceded him. Hanging around the rail yards in Baton Rouge, he ran into some former associates of another security company, American Eagle, Inc. They were traveling in a solar pod convoy for some point east, likely to their fortified compound in the Florida Keys.

They introduced him to an independent operator who was trying to eke out a living shuttling passengers along the old Union Pacific line between Beaumont and Houston. Once a week, the operator would extend her route to cover Lafayette and Baton Rouge. She had a solar pod convoy of her own and a need for security. With his former business rivals vouching for him, Joe was summarily hired for the journey. His compensation for providing security would cover the cost of his fare.

Joe never asked the American Eagle boys what they'd heard in regards to the doings at Tynan. He felt little need to show weakness or ignorance to the corporation that had competed with his company for the last forty years. But somewhere amidst the back slaps and plastered smiles, he sensed that they were holding something back about what he was likely to find when he arrived in H-town. Something told him that their subtle expressions of glee were intended to evoke a polar opposite sense of dread.

The independent solar pod operator, Sally Freeman, was a rugged woman of fifty, sun weathered and muscular, with a mat of gray hair that looked like the bristles on a hedgehog. After the death of a husband during a raid on this very run two years before, she had assumed the role as chief operator of the four-car convoy. Her teeth were stained a green-brown with occasional streaks of red. Joe knew that Sally was an uppers freak and that she probably chewed whatever pharmacopeias she could get her hands on, be it Khat, Betel Nut, or tobacco. Seeing the evidence of the strain of having to run the line deeply etched into the wrinkles around her eyes, Joe made sure that his presence would not cause her any complications.

"You want me in the first car?" he asked.

"Affirmative."

"How many passengers do you think you will have?"

"Probably twenty or so to Lafayette; ten more will join there for the ride to Beaumont. Beaumont to Houston will be pretty empty."

"How many headed to Houston?"

"At this point, it's just you and me. I only run to H-town for the outbound travel. Lately, that's where the money is. No one goes to Houston. Except you, I guess."

She spit some brown juice onto the Louisiana clay and looked at the angle of the sun. Clouds were gathering for the afternoon thunder-showers, and she wanted to get going before the discomforting rumbles began in earnest.

Joe wanted to ask her why no one wanted to travel to Houston, but she had already sauntered away. He moved to the front of the con-voy and climbed the small ladder onto the first car.

As he sat, in the only area that was not covered by the aluminum canopy, his feet dangling over the side of the platform, he thought about his visit with Jimmy Hazen's kinfolk after his boat had laid over for a night in Memphis, a couple of days prior.

Using information from the kid's personnel file, he located the given address just north of the docking point in the Tennessee hamlet of Cuba.

The Hazen family home had once been part of a planned commu-nity, but only two or three structures still stood on the street that used a one-time state forest as their backyard.

Joe never found the number of the house, but he knew which one it was because Jimmy had described it down to the flagstone walk, the bent basketball hoop above the garage, and the red enamel mailbox.

A man in his late fifties answered the door, and Joe knew imme-diately that this was Jimmy's father, Myron. Two hours later, his belly full of roasted wild pig leg, Joe headed back to the embarkation point.

Joe walked the ten miles back to the dock, stunned by the colossal difference between the concepts of description and experience. Jimmy's description of his father had been one laced with malice and venom for an unforgiving patriarch whom he could never please. Joe's experience after meeting Myron elucidated the whole idea that there are always at least two sides to every story.

When informed that his only son had died heroically, Myron broke down. Later, he asked Joe if Jimmy had ever told him why he had so much hate for him. In the moment, Joe lied. He told Myron that Jimmy had nothing but the highest regard for his father and credited him with everything that was good about this messy world.

Myron nodded that he understood why Joe had chosen to be untruthful. He now knew that he would go to his grave without ever understanding the relationship between himself and his only son. As he made up a pot of coffee, that realization caused another spate of tears.

On the walk back to the boat, Joe thought about his own sons and wondered what they would have thought of him had they lived. He decided that like life, and, he supposed, their deaths, the whole thing was a crapshoot.

An earsplitting whistle from the back of the solar pod convoy broke Joe's reverie. Sally Freeman was ready to get them moving on down the line. From the looks of it, Joe would be the only occupant of the first car.

The solar pod cars were powered by electricity stored in an array of batteries that were affixed to the underside of each of the cars. The whole contraption was nothing more than a moving cache of misappropriated goods. Reclaimed railroad wheels were attached to a base of one-inch plundered plywood. The plywood supported an aluminum shed that had been pilfered from someone's yard, the same type of prefab shed that probably once held a lawn tractor and a couple of bags of fertilizer. Glued onto the entire skin of the shed was an array of photovoltaic cells that charged the batteries during the sunlight hours. The batteries were scavenged from many sources but most commonly from auto junkyards and electronic dumps. The stored power turned the windings of a multitude of electric motors ganged together to provide the torque to engage a chain that would turn the wheels. The sources for the motors were multiple and included former hybrid vehicle assisters, prototype power units, and, on occasion, swimming pool pumps.

Depending on the weight of the passengers and cargo, a single pod car could travel nearly forty miles on battery power alone. During daylight hours, the motors could run continuously. Top speed was slightly less than twenty-five miles per hour.

As night fell, it was the decision of the operator to either continue to run the batteries out or to shut down and conserve the power to get a head start on the morning. Cloud cover always presented a problem. This is why Sally Freeman was so impatient to get the cars headed west before the gathering storm hit.

Two hundred seventy-five miles separated Baton Rouge and Houston. With stops and the inevitable breakdowns, the trip would take a minimum of two days.

Sally was right. It was just the two of them that ventured on the final leg as they departed Beaumont. When they arrived, three days out from Baton Rouge, the number of refugees occupying the line in the train yard totaled in the hundreds. Sally immediately doubled the cost of the fare for all points east.

Joe thanked her for her hospitality, and even though there were no hints of trouble, she reciprocated and idly mentioned something about his free fare being no strain on her pocketbook. Her focus moved to the crowd clamoring to board. Her microscopic pupils sought out those who rose above the rabble, and she decided to split the fare into two classes. The rich would be on cars that gave them room to stretch out a bit. The others would be crammed together, leaving no horizontal space available. As the crowd surged toward her, she whistled to a group of roughnecks who loitered nearby. They immediately jumped into the impending fray with the intention of creating order.

Joe stopped in the yard to scan the faces of the people who seemed desperate to exit their former home. When he asked one of the men what was happening in H-town, the man just offered a negative shake of his head. Another interviewee mentioned the Barbers, and yet another said something about Redeemers.

By all accounts, the town was dead. And with its demise, Joe's livelihood—at least the paid portion of it—was most likely defunct as well.

He wondered what had become of Claude Tynan, the founder and CEO of the company, and it didn't take him long to learn that Claude, along with some members of the "Black Geese"—the shady special operations unit of Tynan's security division—had been rounded up and executed by a commando faction of Redeemers. His bloody body had been hung from a tree near the steps of the George R. Brown Convention Center, a de facto DMZ between the factions of Redeemers and Barbers that remained encamped on either side of the ghost city.

In one last call of duty, Joe found his way into the Tynan International, Ltd., Worldwide Headquarters, entered his coded key into a secret stairwell, and walked down to the vault that took up thirty thousand square feet of basement solitude, four stories below the building's Crawford Street entrance.

In their zeal to kill the head of the company that employed their biggest adversaries, the insurgents failed to gather some much-needed intelligence. The arsenal contained in the vault dwarfed the quantities that these savages lusted over in the National Guard facilities they had sought to storm over and over again.

Here there was state-of-the-art weaponry, meticulously inventoried and cataloged. It took four days for Joe to wire it all together.

He was preparing to depart with a week's worth of "Meals Ready to Eat," two more nine-millimeters, a Howa 1500 sniper rifle for hunting, and multiple bandoliers of ammunition for each weapon. He had also liberated two extra pairs of boots that bore the manufacturing seal of Bulgaria. Joe's experience informed him that they lasted twice as long as the other stocked models that had been shoddily produced in China.

As night fell on his fourth day in H-town, he emerged from the underground labyrinth, making sure to leave all of the access areas open and available. At this point, he really didn't give a shit who hit the trip wires that would send the building into space.

There appeared to be no one left from his old firm, as he had monitored the encrypted radio frequencies during his entire stay in the building but had not recognized a single instance denoting incoming communications.

He had done all of this idly, knowing that it might ensure a lesser loss of life in the future. Nearing completion, and a final survey of the offices, an actual plan took shape. He made his way to the fourth floor and entered the communications room. As he expected, the entire area had been ransacked. All of the batteries had been liberated along with cases of handheld communication devices. Scouring the room for evidence of the identity of the perpetrators initially proved fruitless.

The way he figured it, he could return to the secret vault, send out a signal over the airwaves that he had discovered a huge weapons cache, and allow whomever showed up to claim the prize: the destiny of perishing with the inventory.

The results were likely to have a tinge of the bittersweet, however, as he'd only have a realistic shot of taking down just one side in the struggle—those who had pilfered the radio equipment. He comforted himself with the thought that the side that didn't get blown up might take some future advantage against the weakened other. There would be a palatable shrinkage of the population of barbarians, but there would still be one side left standing—perhaps fortified.

It was only when he made his way back to the stairwell that he saw the strip of orange fabric dangling from the door hinge. Some clumsy Redeemer's jumpsuit had become entangled in the brass fitting. Cheered by the thought that his most desired target was assured to suffer, he ran the eight flights down to the emergency radio to broadcast his message to any of the Redeemers who might have their hand-sets clicked to the on position. He scanned for a hot frequency and pushed talk.

"I found it," he said into the microphone.

He waited for a response. Thirty seconds passed before he heard a crackle of static.

"Who is you?"

"I'm down in the basement of the Tynan building. They got anti-tank weapons, C-4, PETN, everything."

"Who is you?"

"A fellow believer," Joe said.

There was a long silence on the other end of the line. For a moment, Joe was certain that he'd blown it—only an idiot would confer veracity to a disembodied voice coming over a random radio frequency. Then, a more authoritative voice came through the speaker.

"I'll need your name and affiliation."

Joe took a flier.

"My name is Udo. C-town."

He could hear the whispering among the group gathered around the handset. Though the bulk of the off-air conversation was unintelligible, Joe could sense that the mention of Udo's name had changed the nature of the discourse. The reply from the authoritative voice confirmed his supposition.

"Apostle Udo, I am sorry for doubting you."

"You better get here quick. I'm in the basement. Bring whatever carts you have and all the people you can gather."

"Yes, Apostle Udo."

Joe shut the radio down. *Well, that wasn't so hard*, he thought. The act gave further credence to Joe's belief that the bulk of people who made up the Redeemers wouldn't crack a score of 80 on an IQ test.

He gathered his things and rushed to get out of the building in case there were any scouts stationed nearby.

Out on the deserted street, he flipped a coin in his head, it came up tails, and he headed for the west side of town. Jamming clips into both of the nine-millimeters, he followed the smell of some wafting smoke and angled himself toward the former Pennzoil Plaza. He decided that at least one of the camps of insurgents was most likely hunkered down in Sabine Park, and if the randomness of the coin flip just happened to point him toward the Barbers' bivouac, he could expand the parameters of his ploy.

Near the crossroads of Brazos and Lamar, stationed on a street corner, he saw one of the Barber scouts loitering by a looted market. The coin flip had given him the preferred outcome. He walked up to the middle-aged marauder in the tattered baseball cap.

"Hey, asshole."

When the guy spun around to the voice and saw the two handguns aimed at his torso, he tried to skedaddle. Before he could get five feet, Joe shot him in the thigh, making sure to avoid the femoral artery. The felled Barber screamed out in pain.

"If you can get back to your camp, you'd better tell them that Redeemers have found a weapons cache in the basement of the Tynan building. There's not much time."

"What the fuck?" the guy screamed to Joe.

"Better yet, you could just lay there and scream your head off, hope someone comes to your aid, and then you can tell them what I've told you. Either way, if they get into that arsenal before you, you guys are as good as dead."

Joe turned on his heels and headed north. It was going to be a long walk up to Big D.

NINE

JOHN BRASSEY

JOHN FINISHED HIS physical regimen well before dinner. The last thing he wanted to do was show up at the table displaying any visible signs of perspiration. The cat was still in the bag and it was far too early to let it slither its way out. Today he'd concentrated on the muscles in his upper back. He'd found a fire escape in the building next to theirs with hardened steel bars that ran parallel to the ground. With the aid of a wooden box to boost him to the correct elevation, he was able to perform the classic strengthening exercise known as a pull-up. When he first started—some five months ago—he could barely do two repetitions before collapsing to the ground. Now, behind the locked bathroom door, a damp towel absorbing the shiny patina of sweat that coated his face and upper chest, he congratulated himself on completing three sets of thirty reps.

Looking into the mirror, he studied the area of his face that would, one day, hopefully sprout the hairs of a beard. Fuzzy blond wisps were coalescing at the base of his chin, but the coarse dark filaments of his future were still being held in abeyance.

John thought about the day's word, "perlustrate." It had been chosen randomly. He had carefully opened the *Webster's New International Dictionary of the English Language* to a purposeless page. After all, it was Potluck Tuesday.

As far as John knew, the dictionary, copyrighted in 1912, was the only family heirloom that had made its way into his possession. Twenty-two pounds of slowly decomposing paper and fraying fabric, it occupied its own pedestal that John had experienced the good fortune to liberate from an abandoned church over on Ledyard Street. There were numerous warnings that no one in the household should even breathe near it posted by the site of its placement, as well as on the outside panels of the door to John's room.

John knew every page that had sustained some type of damage and could catalog the occurrence. Many a night he would experience nightmares about being separated from his friend and instructor.

On Tuesdays, John would slowly flip open the book to a random page, scroll down to the section that depicted the underused or arcane words, and select his word for the day. He found the word "perlustrate" on page 1607, which covered the words from "pelour" to "peroneus." The definition of "perlustrate" read: *to wander through thoroughly, to survey.* As he continued to examine the stalled follicles on his face, trying to will for the era of his puberty to commence, he realized he was doing just that.

John Brassey was an innie. Being born within the walls of Motor City, he was of a generation that had never known any type of life outside of the enclave. His parents had entered the former Detroit with their respective parents. They had spent most of their years on the road to adulthood in a suburb without walls, in a country that still existed. Not John, or for that matter, his older sister, Holiday.

There were no illusions among the young denizens that a re-migration would occur at some point in their lifetime and they would be taken back to the life their parents had briefly led outside the walls. This created an entire class of people who used their pre-Motor City experience to consider themselves as somehow more superior than the uninitiated.

That air of elitism chapped John's ass. His father and many of his cronies wore it like a badge. The next time he heard somebody preface their contribution to a conversation with "Back when we lived in Grosse Point . . ." or "You know, before they built the walls . . ." John swore he was going to say something along the lines of, "Who gives a shit about the past, motherfucker?"

Like his father, John was all about loyalty to Impala, his affiliation by birth and place. This was why he surreptitiously put himself through the series of strenuous workouts. This was why—as much as he was coming to dislike his dad—he supported his father's desire to ascend to the level of captain of the ward. He knew that anyone was better than that flaccid Ed Fisher, the previous leader who had served a term for as long as John had been alive.

His father's big ploy to bring in a professional driver was bit of a disappointment to John, considering that he had hoped to pilot the entrant one day. He wasn't exactly in line with all of the reasons why his father wanted to change the status quo. Fairness and sportsmanship were part of the ethos that John embraced. He certainly had yet to see his father share any of these ideals.

All of the Pickwickian games, political maneuverings, and intentional subterfuge surrounding the event had become so prevalent that there was no way to turn back the clock to the time when the fastest and the strongest prevailed. Now, it was all about how you might fuck over someone else, not how you were going to achieve an honorable victory.

The conventional wisdom was that this was the fairest race because it was the most rigged.

These tenets tended to turn the stomach of Brassey the Younger. John dreamt of a day when the concept of competition in its purest form would reemerge. Even he knew that there was a distinction between dreams and reality. Even he knew that they would never be going back to that other time.

And then he laughed, his perfectly straight teeth using the mirror to project illumination to the face he had so carefully perlustrated. What the hell? Here he was waxing nostalgic in the same manner as his forbearers. Somebody ought to ask him, "Who gives a shit about the past, motherfucker?"

Later, at the dinner table, the conversation was concentrated, as always, on the mundane events of the day. Holiday announced that she would not be attending the school dance that was being held on the approaching Friday.

"Why not, dear?" her mother asked.

"Because all of the guys are creeps."

"Your brother is at that school, and he is not a creep."

Holiday tossed her one of those faces that was supposed to intimate something along the lines of "enough said."

"Well, I'm going to the dance," John said.

Both of his parents looked up from their plates of Great-Grandma's recipe for roasted hen and potato cakes and made eye contact with each other.

"Did you ask us whether you could go or not?" Lon asked his son.

"No, I just assumed that since I was in the ninth grade now, I could go."

The parents shared another look. They had undoubtedly reached some sort of crossroads here, and they would need to schedule some discussion time amongst themselves to sort through the various contingencies.

"We'll talk about it, honey," his mother said in that voice that suggested the topic would be tabled for now.

"Okay, let's talk about it now," John said.

Holiday's eyes immediately went to her plate as she waited for her father to call attention to her brother's insolence by ordering that silence would ensue for the remainder of the repast.

Instead of opening his mouth, Lon just allowed his fork and knife to clatter upon the plate. His desired result was achieved, as no one uttered a sound for the next couple of minutes. But the truth was, John had tired of this protocol.

"I don't understand why we have a problem here. I'm old enough to attend the dance. I'm a student at the school where it is being held."

Lon made his preference known with his feet. He got up and left the table. *What a fucking coward*, John thought.

"There is a time and place, dear," his mother said after her husband's abrupt exit.

"Now, you see, that makes absolutely zero sense, Mom. Dinner is really the only time the whole family is together."

"Oh my God, this is about a girl, isn't it?" Holiday asked, punctuating the question by opening her mouth in mock shock.

"Shut up, Holly," John seethed.

"John, do not tell your sister to shut up."

"It's because I'm right," Holiday proclaimed.

As much as he had no desire to emulate his father in that moment, John also rose and left the table. When he had removed himself from the possibility of being within earshot, Holiday leaned in close to her mother.

"What's the big deal?"

"Your father's afraid of the loud music or the, how should I put this, pressure."

"Pressure?"

"Yes, dear, it is not easy asking a girl to dance," Karen stated.

"He's not going to be dancing, Mom. Have you ever seen him try? He would never embarrass himself to that extent."

Karen couldn't say that she had ever seen John dance. Either way, the decision wasn't likely to change. There was no precedent for this kind of thing, and there were just too many variables given his condition. John hadn't experienced a seizure in nearly ten years now, and no one, save maybe him, was interested in opening the door to anything that might lead to one.

Most epileptics are not diagnosed as being afflicted with the condition until they experience a second seizure. Many infants, by virtue of the softness of their skull structure, may experience a seizure that is nothing more than an anomalous event brought on by a bump of the head.

It is only when the next episode of seizure occurs that the determination of an actual pathology is confirmed.

John's first seizure happened in the first year of his life. At the time, it was considered to be a fluke. His parents rushed him to the hospital, but by the time they arrived, the symptoms associated with his seizure had dissipated to the point that the resident doctor had less than stellar evidence to make a diagnosis.

John's parents were sent home with the assurance that the episode could have been a singular extraordinary event. After weeks of vigilance and precautionary behavior, and with John not suffering a reoccurrence, the significance of that day began to wane in the minds of Lon and Karen.

On John's fifth birthday it happened again. The existence of the second episode of seizure forever labeled him an epileptic.

Young John described the sequence of that episode's progression with the doctor. He told him that as he brought a bite of his birthday cake to his mouth, he smelled the presence of something other than the chocolate and the butter cream. To his newly five-year-old mind, the aroma reminded him of burnt hair. His first instinct was to scrunch up his nose and drop the forkful of cake onto the table. He then felt a buzzing in his head as if a swarm of bees had become trapped under his skullcap. When he returned to consciousness in the hospital, he said he felt fine, but really, really tired.

He didn't remember to tell anyone that before the onset of the strange smells, he had knocked noggins with one of the older kids as they bounced on the trampoline that had been brought in to serve as one of the party's diversions.

The doctor explained to Karen and Lon the rudimentary foundation about the epileptic illness. Using the terminology of the laymen, he demonstrated how the disease presents itself: "It's like your son's brain doesn't have the right current to run his light bulb. There is an inconsistency there, and the light flickers off and on. Sometimes it burns so brightly that it blows out. These are the spikes in brain activity that lead to the seizures."

Lon and Karen listened to the doctor as they watched their son through the glass window. The boy was perched on a table, licking a lollipop in the exam room adjacent to where the conference was taking place.

Any observer could see the disappointment etched into Lon's face. Everything about his life was about to get too complicated for his taste.

He only turned back to hear the doctor's continued explanation when he heard the GP say something about mental retardation.

"He's retarded?" Lon nearly screamed in a horror he had no time to mask.

"Well, no, Mr. Brassey. But if he has consistent episodes, it is a possibility because all of that abnormal brain activity can dull the formation of certain centers in the brain. I'll go back to the analogy involving the light bulb."

"Please don't," Lon said.

The doctor was briefly taken aback by Lon's blunt interjection, and it had the effect of increasing the size of the chip on his shoulder.

"Can we treat it?" Karen asked.

"Sure, we have a variety of different forms of treatment."

"What is the most effective?" Lon asked.

"Well, that is a difficult question, Mr. Brassey. Each patient is different. May I suggest we start by putting him on a ketogenic diet and see if we can do this without resorting to medication just yet. It's not like he's having seizures every day or even every month."

"A diet?" Lon asked with an air of dubiousness.

"Yeah, something high in fat, low in carbohydrates. Lots of meat, avocado, and dairy. No sugar, bread, or pasta. How much of the birthday cake had he eaten before the seizure started?"

"The birthday cake?" Karen asked.

"Yeah, I mean, I understand it's a birthday, but maybe he overdosed on sugar. That can sometimes trigger a seizure. It's rare, but it happens."

Karen began to punish herself as if she were solely responsible for ushering this crisis upon her son. Lon sensed her distress but chose to not modify it by offering her reassurance that it had nothing to do with the fucking birthday cake.

"Where are we going to get avocado?" he asked blankly.

It was this question that caused the doctor to again examine the nature of this particular parent. Immediately the doctor began to sense that the only concern of the father seem to be how the revelation of his son's illness had landed on him with the thudding notion that his convenience was being adversely affected.

The doctor took a moment to look over at the young boy whittling away at the circumference of the sucker with his red-dye-stained tongue. Except for the two known episodes of tonic-clonic seizure, the kid appeared to be as normal as rain in April.

"I would suggest we start small and see where we are after the next little while. Who knows, maybe he'll never have another problem," the doctor concluded.

"I'd like you to prescribe the medication," Lon said.

"But honey, why don't we wait and see if the diet has an effect?" Karen said.

"No," Lon said.

"Aren't there side effects with the drugs?" Karen asked the doctor.

"Yes, of course. Determining the correct medication will take some time. Getting the dosage right can be tricky, and then it will take a little while until it settles in to take effect. The main side effects are stomach problems, and he may have to deal with things like unsteadiness, memory loss, and grogginess. Being so young, still developing, I think the drugs create more problems than they are worth. If he was having seizures regularly, I wouldn't hesitate, but this is not the case with him."

"Just write the prescription," Lon said.

The surprised doctor was trying to process the brusque request from the father. Hadn't he just tried to dissuade him from taking that tack? What was going on here? Why was this guy being such an asshole?

"No," the doctor said.

"No?" Lon asked.

"I can refer you to another physician, but I will categorically refuse to administer medication until I have more data."

"Okay," Lon said.

Karen let out a short breath. Her husband must be coming to his senses.

"Give me the name of the other doc," Lon said.

"Mr. Brassey, I want to go on the record that I completely disagree with your choice of treatment."

"Noted. Just give me the other doctor's name."

The doctor reached into a drawer and pulled out a business card. Lon snatched it out of his hand and headed for the exam room to retrieve his son. A stunned Karen lingered for moment.

"I would suggest you buy a helmet," the doctor said.

"Excuse me?"

"If you put him on the medication, he'll probably fall down a lot. If he falls down, a blow to the head could trigger another seizure. The smart move would be to get him some headgear."

Karen just stared at the GP, feeling many miles away from the conference room. After a moment, she nodded, and followed her husband and son toward the exit.

Lon got his prescription—1000 mg of Carbitol—and John spent the first three years of his elementary education wearing a helmet with a face guard.

He struggled with his studies in any of the areas that required memorization. On a quest to mitigate this issue, Karen liberated her great-great grandfather's dictionary from a box in the basement and presented it to him on his seventh birthday. She is credited with developing the concept of the "word of the day" in the hopes that the gambit of looking up a word in the massive tome might help his degrading retention.

Gradually, his memory did show improvement from that particular exercise regimen. As John began to excel academically, his parents shared a sense of relief—they would no longer have to deal with the possibility that their child was mentally deficient.

But the whole helmet thing was becoming a problem. Early on, John did take quite a few tumbles as the drug caused him to lose his sense of equilibrium.

He withstood all of the abuse that was heaped upon him by his classmates and became inured to the bevy of nicknames like "soldierboy," "bullet," "condom," and "penishead" that they insensitively hurled his way.

Over time, he was able to use his athletic nature to find a semblance of balance in his growing frame, and the falls became less frequent. As he turned eight years old, he petitioned his parents to be allowed to go to school without having to don the headwear. After much family discussion and consultations with both the doctor that prescribed the medication and officials with the school, a trial period was instituted that would permit John to go without the protection device except during the exercise period.

The taunts did not cease, but John did gain a measure of self-esteem after being released from his cranial confinement. For many hours of the day, he was just another boy with buzz-cut hair, not a freak with a crown of single-impact plastic.

At nine, John asked if there were any further tests he could take to show that his condition was a misdiagnosis. He had only experienced the two seizures to this point in his life, and he felt confident that he would not have another. During an interview with the doctor who Lon had sought out to prescribe the medication, he remembered the blow to the head he sustained on the trampoline before the last event, four years before. The theory that John was trying to float was based on the foundation that his seizures were not the result of an ongoing illness but were the result of an instance of trauma.

To John, the doctor seemed preoccupied and subsequently failed to draw the thread of connection. The doctor reiterated the benefits of the precautionary medicine and announced to his parents that the course should be continued until the child reached adulthood. Karen and Lon concurred with the doctor.

John embarked upon a plan to change the protocol. With the aid of some primers he found at the local branch of the library, he was able to teach himself some fundamentals in the art of close-up magic. By the time he turned twelve, he felt confident that he could use his newly honed talent in prestidigitation to make his medication disappear prior to having to ingest it.

Now, fifteen, it had been three years since he had taken any medication related to his supposed affliction.

TEN

HOLIDAY HAD BEEN prescient with her comment that John's desire to attend the dance was about a girl. Her name was Rebecca Lee-ann Voss, and to John, she was the paradigm of perfection. She had encroached on his thoughts for nearly two years now, and, if asked, he could pinpoint the exact moment she had left her searing brand on his brain.

Even though he could have attended school with Rebecca for nearly eight years, he believed he had somehow always been separated from her by the vagaries of the school's curriculum. There were multiple groups at each grade, and he concluded that he and Rebecca had never been placed in the same cluster.

As he matriculated into eighth grade, knowing that he would be proclaiming his presence five names into the roll call, he allowed his mind to wander to the preceding summer and the experiences he had cataloged that included his turning fourteen years of age.

He didn't even break his train of thought as the teacher's words requesting his response leaked into his reverie.

"Here," he proclaimed.

The sheer level of vividness of the daydream blocked him from hearing one of his fellow classmates mutter the words "foreskin face" in reference to his former helmeted self. He only barely heard the resulting guffaws from the classmate's coterie and never gave context to the subject matter that invoked the gaiety.

John was focused on the day the previous July when the punch-out was contested during the week of the race. As was usually the case, the teams from Impala and Mustang had no interest in winning the free-for-all. Their singular desire was to use the opportunity to express their enmities with their hated rival in the most violent fashion they could conjure.

As the Red Wings were beating the tar out of anyone and everyone on their way to victory, Impala and Mustang ignored the proceedings and wailed on each other.

It turned out to be a lopsided victory for Mustang. The Impala fifteen were undersized, as usual, and the Ford boys made quick work of them. The Impala weaklings suffered enough missing teeth that the tooth fairy could charge the children's-myth society for overtime pay.

Watching the debacle, John had been blessed with an epiphany. He would devise a structured program to address the issue of the ward's woeful performance. It would be something that he would achieve behind the scenes, and he figured it might take five years to pull off any kind of reasonable result.

He had already made an assessment of the strength of the boys at his school, and he felt that with the right training, he could put together a squad worthy of the Impala name that could participate at some point in the future.

He would start by testing his theories of fitness by transforming his own physique.

"Rebecca Leeann Voss?" the teacher asked.

"Here," said the girl sitting next John.

The proximity and the unique timbre of the voice broke John's concentration, and he looked over to the respondent, annoyed.

"Oh my God," he nearly said aloud.

She was stunning. Why had he never noticed her before? They must have been sharing the same grounds all of these years, yet he could honestly say that he thought this was the first time he had laid anything resembling a discriminate eye on her.

There was one other student to be called, the requisite Z name, before the teacher handed out some paperwork.

John accepted the decreasing stack from the student in the row in front of him, and as he twisted his upper torso to hand the papers to the person behind him, he used the opportunity to check out the girl.

His gaze landed on the quadrants of her face that included her eyes, cheeks, and the bridge of her nose. Their respective qualities included an Alaskan glacial blue tint to the irises, a slight vermilion glow to the skin that was tautly drawn below the orbital bones, and a nasal bone that projected at forty-five degrees in a straight firm line, extending from a point absolutely equidistant between her brows.

Wow. Again he asked himself, *Why have I never seen her before? Could she be a new immigrant? Maybe she is someone's cousin or niece and has only recently arrived inside the walls.*

He decided to see if he could get her attention by performing a magic trick he had practiced over the summer. It was a classic gag where he makes it seem that he is tearing up a piece of paper only to then make it appear that the shards have reassembled themselves into the original form. He made a big show of the tearing part, but that only seemed to attract the attention of the teacher, Mr. Fedder.

"May I ask what you are doing, Mr. Brassey?"

Now he had everyone's eyes glued to him in the midst of what seemed like an act of extreme pertinence.

"Nothing," John said.

He finished the illusion by then smoothing the paper back to its original dimensions. Mr. Fedder, having gotten his desired result—that John quit messing around—turned his back and moved to the front of the classroom.

In the end, John was rewarded for his efforts, as Rebecca had noticed his feat. Their eyes connected and they both offered the other a smile.

The prominent question remained, though. How had he missed her through all the years of his education?

It would take him awhile to find out, but he eventually learned that this object of his desire had absorbed her entire academic curriculum at home until her matriculation into this final year of middle school.

That eighth-grade year was fraught with many challenges for the scion of the Brassey family. The most frustrating was his inability to gather the necessary strength to actually approach this now-over-idealized vision that sat next to him in Mr. Fedder's homeroom.

He tried to build on his attempt to perform for her, but something always seemed to get in the way. It could have been the constant rebukes from Mr. Fedder or the efforts of his classmates to keep him confined to the stereotype that perpetually defined him as the boy who used to have to wear head protection, but it seemed that every time he attempted to advance his agenda, he was soundly thwarted.

As the days became weeks, and the weeks became months, he found his already shaky sense of self-esteem being pared down from a status that could have once been described as burgeoning to that of hopelessly conceptual. As the school year came to a close, the now-muted demonstrations of his interests consisted of subliminal nods and the occasional smile.

On the final day of the school year, John decided that he would force himself to alter the trajectory of the graph that measured his sense of self worth. He would attempt to engage Rebecca in something beyond the stunted banality of his actions to this point. When he entered the class, he saw that she was in the process of engaging in a somewhat static conversation with one of his tormenters from the back of the room, Richard, a hulking boy/man who had the good fortune to mature physically faster than all of the other male members of the eighth grade.

It took a tremendous amount of force to overcome the effects of the inertia that had increased exponentially once he had set his sights on this pair. He crossed from the door, shunned the relentless gravitational pull yanking him toward the safe niche of his desk, and strode over to the two. When Richard reached out to replace a lock of Rebecca's hair that had fallen across her eye, John halted. He froze in place and felt all of his manufactured will pouring out of his body onto the scuffed linoleum floor.

Mr. Fedder entered at that exact moment with a dose of residual pipe smoke leaking out of his nostrils. He noisily closed the door behind him, and the spell was broken. All of the students dutifully returned to their prescribed places.

"Let's do the pledge. I'd ask someone to lead, but I know I'd get exactly zero volunteers. Since it's the last day, I'm going to go easy on you. I'll lead," Mr. Fedder announced.

And with that, the collective rose and stood next to their desks.

"Ready? Begin," Mr. Fedder half-heartedly beckoned.

"We pledge our fealty to the people and principles of Impala and pray that God should look favorably upon our families and friends. We stand for justice, intelligence, and forbearance. Impala is the only way."

There was always some smart aleck in the back who would tag the pledge with its now-accustomed ending, "Fuck Mustang." People had become so inured to hearing the obscenity uttered after either the pledge or the song that no one gave it much mind. The usual delivery would be whispered or spoken in a low tone so that only the people in close proximity to the blasphemer could hear it.

That was not the case on this day as a full-throated bellow of the profane phrase rattled the framing of the schoolroom.

All eyes turned to the yeller. To nearly everyone's surprise, it was John. The sheer mass of the stored energy he had intended to use to engage Rebecca Leeann Voss had become fissionable.

"Well, Mr. Brassey, I believe you have earned yourself a trip to the principal's office."

But John did not cease his ebullition until all of the other students were treated to further evidence of his complete meltdown.

"Ah, the expected response of a quisling," John said.

"Excuse me?"

"Let's be honest, Mr. Fedder. There is no one here who is not loyal to this ward. Why would you send me to the authorities for voicing what we all believe?"

"You used profanity, Mr. Brassey."

"Did I?"

"Yes."

"Well, let's examine that statement, Mr. Fedder. Have you any idea where the word 'fuck' originated?"

"It was stamped on the foreheads of people who committed adultery a long time ago in England."

"So it's an acronym?"

Mr. Fedder began weighing the prospects of just how far he was going to let this act of insolence progress.

"It means 'for unlawful carnal knowledge,' or something like that, right?" John asked in continuation.

"That's what I've been told, Mr. Brassey. Now if you will come up here and take the hall pass, your classmates can bid you goodbye for the rest of this homeroom period."

John offered no resistance as he rose, grabbed his things, and crossed over to Mr. Fedder's desk.

"Actually, Mr. Fedder, the word 'fuck' is most likely derived from the German word 'ficken,' or possibly the Middle Dutch word 'fokken,' which both mean to strike, or to penetrate. Isn't that what we want to do to Mustang?"

"Well then, you should have said, 'Strike Mustang.'"

"Yeah, but that sounds lame, don't you think?"

"Just leave, Mr. Brassey."

"No problem, Mr. Fedder."

John headed for the exit. As the door slowly closed behind him, John heard a rousing round of applause erupt from the other students in the classroom. There was a certain amount of notoriety being reserved for him on the horizon, and he was cheered by the possibility that from this day forward, he might be known as a man of defiance, not the wimp he had been perceived to be for all of the years that led up to the beginning of high school.

The principal chose not to suspend him but issued a warning that the next occurrence would be met with harsh punishment. The principal knew that John's father might win the upcoming election for captain, and he chose not to inform the delinquent's parents for fear that he might not be looked at favorably by what was sure to be a completely new administration.

From the Impala point of view, the summer that ensued after John's eighth grade year was something of a bust.

As the solstice came and went, the beginning of July crept upon the city. The pre-festival fervor was reaching its heart-pounding climax when John gathered with his family for the punch-out.

They cheered for their side, but the result was the same: Impala got their blessed asses kicked up one end of the field and down the other by their mortal enemy.

John tried to watch the bloodbath for data he might be able to use in the future, but his attention had fragmented after he found Rebecca sitting in the stands with her family and Richard.

He tried to concentrate on the action, but his neck continued to swivel so he could be a witness to something that he hoped he hadn't actually seen—Rebecca appeared to be holding the hand of this guy. John's heart began to beat a little faster, and his brain tried to connect to the new feelings he was experiencing as he viewed what his instincts perceived to be a betrayal.

When he first felt the buzzing in his head, he began to panic that his whole world might be coming apart. Was he about to have a seizure? He sniffed the air for that telltale sign that his olfactory system was being countermanded, but all he could smell were the contents of the picnic baskets and the cloud of body odor that emanated from the crowd amidst the mid-summer swelter.

John panicked. He knew that if he had a seizure, his medication sleight-of-hand ruse would be uncovered. He knew that if he had a seizure, he would be back to wearing the helmet full time. He knew that if he had a seizure, the dreams he harbored about forming and possibly competing with the future punch-out team would sink like a torpedoed battleship.

As the battle continued to rage on the field, John staggered to his feet and tried to put some distance between himself and the crowd. He needed to remove himself from any situation that might end up being classified as a spectacle.

"Where are you going?" his sister asked.

John didn't answer because all he could hear was the megahertz band of static rushing into his ears. He made it to the rotunda area and the clear space that resided there. He waited, but there was no progression in his symptoms. As the buzzing blare that circulated around his head began to dissipate, he was left with nothing but confusion and sadness.

She was with someone else. She was with someone who could qualify as belonging to the demographic known as young man, not teen boy. He realized that she had pierced him in a way unlike anything that had ever happened before in his life.

ELEVEN

Never having experienced the quality of this type of psychic pain, the level of confusion and lack of context left John stunned to the point where all he could do was stare at the defined horizon through the opening in the stadium's stair ramps.

Ironically, it was his former homeroom teacher, Mr. Fedder, who saw his student standing dazed atop the crumbling concrete.

"Mr. Brassey?"

Mr. Fedder's voice sounded like it was coming from very far away.

"Are you all right, Mr. Brassey?"

John answered in a rote fashion. There couldn't be another human being alive that had been asked that question as many times as he had.

"Yes, sir."

"What are you doing out here?"

"I just needed a little air, sir," John said, his voice emanating not from his diaphragm, but at the upper limits of his throat.

"We got our asses kicked again, didn't we, Mr. Brassey?"

"Yeah."

"You know, I was at dinner last night and there was a young man there that talked about how things needed to change. He seemed pretty committed to coming up with a plan to ensure that Impala had more success in future punch-outs," Mr. Fedder said.

"Who was saying that?" John asked, testily.

"You know him; he was in my homeroom class. Rebecca Voss's boyfriend, Richard."

There was the definitive confirmation that John was hoping he would never hear.

"You had dinner with them?"

"Well, they were there. Her father and I go way back. Before I had to become a teacher, we had a small electronics firm that supplied GM. We made the motor assemblies for the retractable antennas."

John wasn't listening to his bona fides as Mr. Fedder continued to give him context on the subject of his relationship with the Vosses. He was starting to feel wobbly again.

They heard a roar go up from the crowd. One of the wards must have been awarded victory in the punch-out.

"Who do you think won?" Mr. Fedder asked.

"Lions or the Red Wings," John blankly replied.

"That's hardly going out on a limb, son."

"Yeah, I know."

After another minute, John could feel his bearings reassert themselves. A new threshold of resolve began to lay the first bricks of the foundation that would eventually support him when he made the vow that he would show them all.

"By the way, I'm no quisling," Mr. Fedder said.

John spun around to his former teacher.

"You looked up the word?" John asked.

"I didn't realize it was someone's name. Vidkun Quisling, the Minister President of Norway, traitor to his country by appeasing the Nazis during their occupation in the Second World War."

"Yeah, sorry about calling you that."

"Apology accepted. You know, John . . ."

Mr. Fedder let the preamble hang in the air as he wavered on whether he should continue with this train of thought.

"What?"

"Nothing."

Mr. Fedder had stalled as he looked at John's inquisitive face. He wanted to tell him to be careful. He wanted to tell him that not everyone was likely to find his precocious weirdness charming, that they wouldn't until he was a much older man. He wanted to warn him that the use of all of those hundred-dollar words—the words that he consistently slipped into a paper or conversation—might result in him getting his ass kicked by someone who failed to appreciate the breadth of his vocabulary. Mr. Fedder wanted to say all of that stuff, but he didn't.

They headed back into the tunnel and weaved their way through the throngs that were exiting. It would soon be dinnertime, and no one cared to be late to their respective ward's big party that evening. John kept his eye out for the Voss family, but they must have either passed him or taken another exit.

Enmeshed within Impala's embarrassing defeat in the race a day later and his father's jockeying to usurp the current captain were the desiderative feelings that arrived on John's doorstep the moment that he felt his heart shatter.

He tried to redirect the loop of sadness and despair that was cycling through his brain by experimenting with acts of sublimation and by the acknowledgement that he possessed free will. He worked out ferociously in the mid-summer heat, changed his protocol from the "word of the day" to the "daily double," and tried to keep the questions about the sudden depth of his emotional reactions far away from the moment he was experiencing.

In an attempt to transform the visceral to the mechanical, John wrapped an old rubber band around his wrist, and every time his thoughts veered towards Rebecca, he snapped it against his hamate bone. As Pavlovian as this act appeared to be, it freaked him out when he realized that he began to enjoy the slight pain that came with the mild violence he was perpetrating on himself from time to time.

Though the first day of high school was months away, anxiousness hovered around him like the swarm of white flies that hatched on his mother's rose bushes every June. As August gave way to September, he had multiple occurrences of heightened awareness that always led him to believe that a seizure was imminent. After a few deep breaths followed by no discernable signs of progression, he would chalk the incident up to the hysterical feelings of terror that he had conjured when realizing he might cross paths with the girl who opted for another. He was still in awe at how the gradients of the limits of his feelings had expanded to a level that seemed exponentially larger than what he had dealt with as a child. At first, he wasn't sure that he wanted to leave the innocence of his youth behind, but once the box had been opened—unlatched by his overwhelming response to the sight of seeing his crush otherwise engaged—he immediately knew that to keep the cover on his nativity would be an act of utter futility.

All of his pondering never answered his most important questions: Why had he reacted with such seismic force when he saw this girl with the other guy? Why did he feel entitled to her when he had barely interacted with her over the final year of middle school? Was this really love, or was it some cruel reorganization of his cellular activity brought on by a rush of concentrating hormones?

All of the attempts to apply logic to the situation proved unsustainable. He tried to reason his way out of his abyss, but the parameters of the hole seemed to expand. The whole process was fraught with more confounding dilemmas than he had ever been forced to confront. *Is this the process of maturation?* he continually asked of himself.

At a total loss, just three days before the fall term was to commence, he compelled himself to choose one of two paths.

He knew that the first one was the coward's road. It involved the process that would shut down his entire emotional response system, gird his heart with sheets of steel, and allow him to carry on with his life. The result of all of the technical work he had performed over the summer had brought him to the place where he was certain that this was a viable option, and that he possessed the requisite level of will power to accomplish it.

The second path was frightening and potentially more dangerous. In this scenario, he would wear his heart on his sleeve, exposed for all to witness, and try to see if all of these feelings he was experiencing were part of the process of acquiring adulthood.

In the end, he had no chance to predetermine his course because as the first day of school dawned, Rebecca Voss was not present. At every turn down a corridor, every peek through a classroom window, he was left wondering what became of her.

After the first week passed without her being in attendance, he ventured to the school office to see if he could find out where she had gone.

On the way, he spied the young man who he knew had already captured her heart.

"Excuse me, Richard?"

"What?"

The venom in Richard's response felt toxic, so John decided to edge his way around the question he wanted answered.

"Pretty pathetic showing at the punch-out, huh?" John asked.

"Why are talking to me?" Richard asked.

"Just making conversation," John said.

"Well fucking stop it," Richard said.

John's superior intellect was barking at him to continue on his initial quest to the administration office and push them for the answers he was seeking, yet he continued to speak to the lummox.

"Oh, by the way, you haven't seen Rebecca Voss around, have you?" John asked nonchalantly.

Richard's face instantly turned two shades darker.

"Why are you asking?"

"We use to sit next to each other in homeroom, but I haven't seen her since school started. Someone told me you two were friends."

"Were," Richard said.

"Oh, sorry."

"She got sick. I haven't seen her since she got sick."

"Oh."

Richard uttered some note of disgust and walked away. As he began to move away from the scene of their awkward conversation, John's gait became unsteady. She got sick? He hotfooted it over to Mr. Fedder's room, where the teacher's second period class was haphazardly gathering for his symposium on the nineteenth-century history of Europe.

John knew he would be tardy for his own second period class, and he tried to make a mental note to have Mr. Fedder write up some type of excuse so that his perfect attendance record would remain unblemished.

As he arrived at the door, he could see Mr. Fedder appear from down the corridor. A belated attempt to get his pipe lit on the patio of the teacher's lounge between the end of homeroom and the start of the education day had been curtailed by the ticking clock.

"What are you doing here, Mr. Brassey? Aren't you supposed to be on the other side of campus?"

"What's wrong with Rebecca Voss?" John blurted out.

Mr. Fedder wasn't expecting a question to be posed on this subject, and it took him a moment to process not only the query, but also the intensity lurking behind the eyes of its seeker.

"She's doing better," Mr. Fedder said.

"Better than what?"

"She's been through two cycles of chemo, and they removed the tumor and radiated the area. They're pretty sure they got it pretty early and it didn't make its way into the bloodstream or the bone marrow."

John felt himself falling. He needed to backtrack and figure out how all of this happened, but Mr. Fedder could sense a potential for unruliness about to take place inside his classroom. The period had started, and the supervision was standing outside the door talking to a student who was not longer a part of the middle school.

"She's doing better. You should go visit her," Mr. Fedder said again as he opened the door and allowed the build up of pressure to be released from the room.

John was left stunned. He wandered to his next class—intermediate math analysis—having forgotten to validate his lateness. In the coming days he would get the full story.

The object of his affection, the person he had deified without ever taking the trouble to get to know, had suffered a recurrence of cancer. It was the reason why he had not seen her for the first eight years of his education. She had endured the epic battles with the disease with her family being the only witnesses.

When the school day ended, he marched directly over to her house and offered his friendship. She readily accepted.

The dance that John said he would attending—the one that provoked the disapprobation from his father—would be the first time that

Rebecca would be amongst her classmates since the end of the last school year.

She and John had spent the entire fall and winter spending time together as the most platonic of friends. Mr. Fedder had been correct in his assessment of her condition; she was seeing significant improvement. As the time between them passed, John was able to replace his fantasy about this young woman with a new reality that was informed with firsthand knowledge. His initial instinct that she was worthy of his attention had turned out to be accurate. The more time they spent together, the more those feelings were confirmed. There was a commonality in their experiences in relation to the progress of their lives to this point, and they were both able to summon extraordinary strength—the foundation being their mutual sufferings from their unique pathologies. They were a damaged duo—two freaks against the world.

John's father's trepidation about his son attending the dance was not only rooted in his fear that something unfortunate would happen to John, but also in the guilt he felt. Lon Brassey had repressed many feelings in his life, but the one that needed to be kept at bay with the greatest of restraints was the sense that he was responsible for his son's ongoing physical problems. It was a secret he would attempt to take to his grave, though the fear that it would out itself haunted him on more than one occasion.

Not long after the abortive dinner, two of Lon's lieutenants arrived for their nightly confabulation. A couple of cocktails into their strategy session, John heard his father laugh behind the closed door of his study. He would use the shift in mood to reopen the discussion of his attendance at the dance.

When he heard bursts of laughs again as the front door shut and the lieutenants walked away from the Brassey residence, John caught his father expressing the remnants of a giggle in the foyer.

"What's so funny?" John asked.

"Nothing," Lon replied.

But Lon's smirk remained intact.

"Dad, I really want to go to the dance on Friday. I swear I'll be careful."

"Two conditions: You be back home before eleven, and you must wear ear plugs. If you can agree to those terms, you can go."

"Thanks," John said.

"You promise that you'll do both of those things?"

"Yes."

John would make sure to return at the assigned hour, but there was no way in hell he was wearing earplugs.

Lon spontaneously whistled as he headed off toward the kitchen.

"I think we've got a lead on a driver," he said on his departure.

"Who?"

"A suggestion from your Uncle Harry. We'll see."

John watched him leave, for once grateful that the man had consented to his wish. It was a rarity, and he knew it.

TWELVE

THE ROAD NORTH

JOE SMITH DIDN'T immediately leave the environs of H-town after the Tynan building was leveled. The forces that compelled him to hover on the outskirts of the city were not inertial. They may have encompassed a familiarity with the surroundings that led him to feel connected to the ground he was standing upon. There was a destination in his future that wasn't this, but he wasn't quite ready to embark.

He was conscious that he reacted with zero emotion upon hearing the blast echo through the corridors of the once-bustling city center. He recalled that, at the time, he had shrugged off all the factors that involved loss of life and property. It had been a long time since he gave a shit about anything. To anyone observing him from afar, this void in his personal reality was evidence of the success of his training.

His existence and the dispositional flatline that accompanied it was the way he had lived for some four years now, and it had become very much a part of him. It was akin to a sheep growing a burly winter coat to protect it from the external elements.

As he hiked toward the perimeter of the city and the once-lush suburbs that dotted the landscape, he found himself musing on some of the tenets of his nearly life-long indoctrination: How he had learned to be beyond attachments. How he had been instructed to produce action and not reaction. How he had been taught to understand the difference between being and recognizing. How well he understood the mantra that said that the target presents itself and the ends dictate the means, which dictate the tools, and that the enemy, when attacked, will offer up its weakness. And finally, how self-defense and self-protection are the catalysts for every action.

This thick fleece of protection that encased him had grown so floridly during this period that nothing short of a 88mm depleted uranium shell could penetrate it.

He thought about the consequences of shearing it, but wouldn't the mountain of repressed thoughts and feelings that would be displaced rival a cataclysmic tectonic shift? That he was actually even developing this line of questioning was an anomaly in itself. When had he last given purchase to the existential over the apparent?

It was vestiges of this force that caused him to veer away from his next destination, the monastery just outside the walls of Big D, and strike out for an area that was once known as the town of Aldine.

Slightly west and south of what had been the George Bush Intercontinental Airport, Aldine was a medium-sized bedroom community that existed between two spurs of the toll road that once hugged the metropolitan section of Houston like an obese grandparent.

The last incarnation of this unincorporated burg had a population that was Hispanic in majority. Now, many of the former inhabitants and their extended families had gathered in one of the housing tracts in an attempt to create a livable and protected enclave. It was within this enclave that Joe Smith had once owned and occupied a residence.

As he approached the wan fortification, laden with his instruments of war, the local gendarmes demanded that he halt his progress.

"¿Quién es?" a guard inquired.

"Me llamo Joe Smith."

"¿Qué quieres?"

"Yo soy . . . I'd like to see my house."

The two guards on watch shared a look of confusion. An older gentleman appeared from the shadows of the guardhouse.

"Where did you live?" the older man asked in non-accented English. "Did?"

"Look, man, don't be an asshole. If you owned property here, we can prove it. I can't guarantee that it's unoccupied."

The other guards were whispering in Spanish in the background, amazed by the amount of weaponry that this single man was sporting. Beyond the obvious sniper rifle strapped to his back, the guards could see both of the Berettas hanging limply in their shoulder holsters. There was no escaping the sight of the multiple bandoliers of .308 caliber rounds and clips of 9mm ammunition.

"You are going to have to surrender the firepower."

"Will I get it back?"

"Of course. We just don't allow guns in the haven."

Joe nodded and decided in that moment he could trust this fellow. He began to relieve himself of the guns and the ammunition. The older man beckoned him inside the guard shack.

"Where's your house, Joe?"

"645 Baxter Street."

The older gentleman pulled a book from the drawer of an old steel desk. Embossed on its cover was the title *Harris County Public Records*. He scanned through a street plat and found the location of the parcel.

"You're Josiah Smith?"

"Yeah."

"Got any proof?"

Joe pulled his Tynan credentials from his duffel bag and offered them to the lead guard.

"Tynan?"

"Yeah."

"I heard their building just blew up in H-town. Killed a whole bunch of Redeemers and Barbers."

"Good."

The older gentleman scrutinized the skinny man, his coffee-colored irises scanning Joe from his feet to his face. He held Joe's gaze for a long moment. He was looking for context that he could relate to Joe's flat response that appeared to suggest an allegiance for the side that did not include the bad guys. He turned his focus back to the ledger.

"You co-owned the property with a Cynthia Smith?"

"My wife."

"Where is she?"

"Dead."

"I'm sorry."

"Thanks."

The older gentleman decided the interrogation was over. He snapped his fingers at one of the younger guards.

"Tome esta hombre a su casa."

The younger guard put his own gun in one of the lockers before opening the log book and signing out.

"He doesn't speak English but most of our residents don't. You'll be safer if he escorts you."

Joe nodded and allowed the young man to usher him away from the guard shack.

When they turned onto the cul-de-sac that was his street, Joe felt himself break out in a cold sweat. If he had taken a moment to check his pulse or look at his extremities, he would have noticed that his heartbeat was elevated and his hands were shaking.

There it was, just off to the left.

When they bought the house, the neighborhood had been in existence for nearly thirty years. His house represented the plan B design for the tract and was sandwiched between a plan D and a plan A. All of the houses sported a hue from the earth-tone quadrant of the color wheel. 645 Baxter had the hue Tierra Fuego blended into its stucco. One might say it was a light pink. Joe always thought it looked like a salmon that had beached itself and allowed the sun to bake its flesh for a couple of days.

The young guard led him up to the doorway and knocked on the fake mahogany door. It was opened by a woman in her twenties who was holding a sleeping infant to her chest. The young guard spoke rapidly in the local dialect, and the woman immediately backed away from the door and offered Joe entrance.

There was a party going on, and the house sported the sort of decorations that had once graced the home's interior to evoke joyousness regarding a birthday, anniversary, or holiday. There was a crowd of about twenty and they were looking at Joe with a mixture of fear and pity. He made it a point to show that he was no threat.

"Please, don't stop your revelry. I'm just going to grab a few things," he said.

Joe misinterpreted the confused looks on their faces that suggested to him there was an undercurrent of panic that the abode's owner had returned to claim what was rightly his. The fact was, they hadn't understood a single word he'd said. He looked around the space and was amazed to discover that not a single thing had been moved or removed from its original placement. His family pictures still graced the mantle above the hearth. The crayon drawings of his deceased children still covered the refrigerator door.

Joe moved to the fireplace and removed the pictures of his parents and his sons from the frames. He left the photo of his wife in its silver and glass enclosure and started for the hallway.

Just before the door that would give one access to the garage was an empty bookcase. He dragged the particleboard-shelved monstrosity to one side, reached into his back pocket, and withdrew a large ring of keys. A recessed door was secured with a padlock of tempered steel.

As he began to sort through the items on the key ring, a crowd began to gather in the hallway. It was likely that no one knew that this extra room even existed.

There was a succession of die-cut gleaming metal templates on the key ring, an indication of all of the access he had once had. Pretty much every one was useless now. Pretty much every one only worked on a lock for a building, vehicle, or storage facility that had been destroyed.

If he could resurrect the images of all of the barriers he had crossed, all the entrances these pieces of steel, brass, and synchronized chips had afforded him, he could reconstruct his existence and whereabouts for the four-year span that had just been completed. But as he spun through the items on the ring, that thought never crossed his mind.

Fairly sure that he'd located the correct size and configuration, he fit the jagged teeth of the corroded metal probe into the mouth of the lock and released the bell-shaped bar.

How that much dust could accumulate in a place that had been virtually sealed was a conundrum that no one could explain. The group standing at the door peered into a haze that hovered in the room like a cinnamon mist.

Joe reached for the light switch, but the fluorescent elements had long since been rendered dormant by virtue of their prolonged disuse.

Instead, Joe flicked on the emergency battery-powered lamp. The room lit up and revealed its contents. Every available wall space was covered with cabinetry that displayed at least one iteration of nearly every version of handheld weaponry known to man. There were a wide variety of guns, knives, bows, iron bars, and tools used for hand-to-hand combat. Someone screamed. There were a couple of melodramatic gasps.

Joe nonchalantly crossed to a red enamel toolbox, used the same door key to unlock a similar restraint that would have prevented entry, and removed a wooden box that was intricately carved with an inlay of bluish-green nacre.

He placed the ornate box on a workbench, found the secret latch, and opened it. From its interior he withdrew two items that he stuffed into the front pocket of his pants. He closed the box, returned it to its internment, left the lock on the workbench, opened one of the wall cases, withdrew a couple of sheathed knives, and turned to exit the room. When he saw the crowd massing at the entrance, their collective mouths agape, he realized that what was normal for him was not customary for this warm, welcoming clan.

The group backed away to give him berth as he locked the door again.

"I'm going to give the key to the old guy at the gate. Maybe some of this stuff will come in handy should you ever be attacked," he said to no one in particular. There was no indication from the witnesses that they had comprehended a word of his suggestion. The gathered could do little but try to manipulate their dropped jaws back in place.

"Have a nice party," Joe said as he walked down the hall and out the front door.

The items he withdrew from the jewelry box would carry no significance to anyone but himself. They were the only things that had true value in his former residence. It wasn't just that the items were small and would not add to the burden he was already laden with; it was that they were the only things he possessed that connected him to the woman who had given him life.

As he left the community and headed north, he found himself continually caressing the two small items in his front pocket as if they might disappear if he allowed his attention to wander.

With the tips of his calloused fingers he was able to trace the physical properties of each item. He could feel the difference between the precious metal and the plastic band. These relics represented the sum total of his inheritance.

He was headed up to Big D, and Texas in the early spring wasn't Ohio. The heat during the daylight hours simmered his blood. It was constant and unrelenting, and he likened its daily duration to the time it would take to cook a pot of shoe-leather stew. Even after sunset, the area of the Texas hill country radiated a temperature only slightly less than when it was seared by sunlight.

Joe started to wish he had the assets to trade for a horse or mule, and after four days on the road, just outside of Crabbs Prairie, he made camp and decided that he would make some inquiries the next morning. He ate an MRE that was labeled "beans and franks"—his first meal in over forty-eight hours—and washed himself in a random creek that had somehow wandered away from the Trinity River.

As the day's brightness gave way to the gloaming, he pulled the two small items from the front pocket of his camos. In his hand he held both a small cameo of sterling silver with a cross of Murata pearl inlaid on its face and a polypropylene hospital identification tag loaded with small silicon chips. The ink-scratched name, Katherine Harris, had faded in the years since he last had his hands on it.

———

The tracker had his orders. He was to find a guy who probably couldn't be found. It was two days ago that he was summoned to the office of that sleazy lawyer in the center of Motor City and handed the task. He had acted cool, and he did his best to hide his gratitude. He hadn't had a gig in over two months.

The tracker had the quarry's name, an approximation of the subject's physical characteristics, and a couple of contacts in C-town who might possess some elements of specificity. The last known sighting of the individual was on the banks of Lake Erie two or three odd weeks ago. The intelligence said that he was probably headed for Toledo. The tracker had no picture of the subject but knew that he was never without a weapon. That would be the place to start.

Motor City to C-town was an easy commute, and he had no trouble booking the excursion. It was just a lazy wind-driven jaunt across the Great Lake.

On arrival, he was met by one of the men who had last seen the subject. His name was Harry Brassey, a building contractor and the brother of his third-party client, Lon. It was Lon Brassey who had retained the shitheel attorney to provide someone for this job.

Via a session of direct questioning and the help of an artist he knew in C-town, the tracker was able to construct a photo-realistic depiction of his subject.

A file was opened and the entries included all of the historical and personal information that Harry Brassey could recall from his encounter with the man.

There wasn't much. The elder Brassey brother centered most of his recollections on the harrowing adventure that he and his business partner had borne witness to. The tracker tried his best to cut through the bullshit and get to the facts. The subject's age was pegged at around thirty years old; he was projected as medium-tall (somewhere over six feet) and was subjectively considered to be unnaturally skinny. He had dark hair, green eyes, and a normal complexion that appeared to be weathered by the sun.

Harry Brassey's assessment of his physical abilities and leadership qualities were unabashedly enthusiastic. This was the first bit of information that piqued the tracker's interest. He listened as Harry described his dismantling of their bodyguard and the survival of the explosion at the armory. The tracker realized that his interviews in C-town must include at least one other subject—the man who had received the aforementioned beat down, Udo Lewandowski.

THIRTEEN

THERE WAS AN underground livery in Crabb's Prairie that Joe had patronized before. The old codger who ran the concession had passed away in the five or so years since Joe had last been there, but the entrepreneur who had taken his place had not let the quality slip. On hand was a stable full of stately animals that were available for long- or short-term rental.

Joe gazed at the steeds that had been put out in the pasture for their morning exercise session knowing he had a little problem: he was completely broke.

The new owner, Marsha Owens, a niece of the former proprietor, spied him longing after the palomino that frolicked at the far end of the property.

"He's a handful," she said as she approached with a jingle of her spurred boots.

"I gathered as much," Joe replied.

"He ain't cheap," she said.

"Well, that doesn't really matter. I'm flat busted."

She allowed herself a brief scan of his physicality; there weren't many men his age that stopped into her facility. He was a little old for her taste—she liked them young and eager—but loneliness had begun to creep upon her since her uncle, husband, and child had been claimed by the flu epidemic so many years before. There was only so much intimacy she could achieve while perched on the top of an equine. She had figured out a way to get it to work, but it certainly wasn't the same as something that could qualify as the real thing.

"Maybe we can work something out," she said with an air of definite flirtation.

When he didn't respond in kind, she grew dark. She didn't put herself out there like that very often. Getting blown off was rare, and her immediate reaction was to get pissed.

"Well, I guess you're shit out of luck, tinhorn."

She turned and walked back toward the barn.

"You got anything that needs to be returned up north?"

"I do, but I don't know shit about you and I ain't going to send you up there with the idea that you'll be paying later."

"I get it."

She continued on her way.

"How about a trade?" Joe asked.

"What are you offering?"

"I've got a gun. Nine millimeter, plenty of ammo."

"Good for you."

"So, that's a no?"

"I have guns."

"Okay, what else?"

"You got any meat?" she asked.

"No."

"Get me some meat and we'll barter," she said as she headed away from him for good.

Joe returned to his camp to find that nothing had been disturbed. Only the most savvy would be able to find his camouflaged cache up in the branches of the tree above his bedroll and the fire pit. He brought the Howa down from its perch and set out to find an animal to kill. He hoped that the lady at the stables liked venison because that was the only being he was likely to encounter. He briefly calculated the weight of the available meat in a normal-sized deer and realized that anything larger would not be transportable.

Joe knew that if he kept to the flatlands he might find himself a stray steer or cow, but even after it was dressed and butchered, he felt the amount of waste would be too great. It might make the vultures and others that feed on carrion happy, but he wouldn't be able to stomach the guilt over the unused excess.

As he stalked the rocky hillsides searching for deer spoor and any signs of hoof tracks, he began to once again notice things like the angle of the wind, the arable quality of the earth, and the density and age of the stone. Was there a return to a different level of consciousness in his future? He tried to process the feelings to see if he could elevate himself from his current state of a life of muffled emotion. As elusive as gossamer, the harder he tried, the farther his target began to recede in the distance. It was an experience that was not foreign to him.

———

After the initial class, Joe's father had done what the master said and brought his child back to the monastery for the Wednesday intermediate seminar. The toddler, Joe, was ten years younger than anyone else in attendance. The child didn't acknowledge the stares or titters from the other students and riveted his eyes and ears to the words and actions emanating from the master.

Joe Sr. watched from the observation room and worried that his son would get confused during the segment of the class when the master verbally discussed his teachings in philosophical terms. He kept watching for the presence of a frown, or the screwed-up face his son made when he was frustrated about not being able to achieve some sort of perceived perfection, but those expressions never once appeared—even on the periphery.

"First and foremost, you must not seek to harm others. You must only protect yourself from those seeking to harm you," the master explained as he instructed his charges to balance on one foot, the other leg bent at the knee and protruding forward.

What little Joe heard was that he was not to make another individual feel anything that could be construed as pain. The lesson that he absorbed was that the infliction wasn't just in the physical sense, but would also encompass behavior. After that first intermediate class, his youthful personality went through an alteration where the desires of others became paramount, and he began to persistently endeavor to grant their wishes.

The Smiths were amazed by the sudden transformation. To them, it appeared that their adopted son had become a responsible human being. He offered to help with the family chores, was constantly there to provide love when it was needed, and exhibited the manners and decorum society would attribute to much older children.

As the years passed and his developing brain was exposed to more of the master's wisdom, little Joe began to become the go-to guy among his friends and classmates. In school, teachers often used him as a third party to solve problems resulting from differences between members of the student body. Joe could always be called on to put a bully in his place or to raise the meek above their lowly standing.

He was promoted through the system at the monastery in a rapid fashion. By the time his eleventh birthday rolled around—having already completed the necessary training to reach what was considered to be the highest level—he began working on the "forbidden" degrees of the discipline.

The master had only achieved the status of the third degree of the highest level, an extremely rare feat among all practitioners, but he was now certain that his prized pupil would transcend that stratum before the youngster reached puberty.

As Joe's rapid maturation progressed, the master started to become somewhat intimidated by his esteemed student. The kid was moving toward the limits of the master's knowledge. How could the young man realize his vast potential without the correct instruction? Communicating with a Chinese high priest via a satellite link, the master explained his confusion. The priest's response was logical; it would now be the student's responsibility to teach the master. The goal was to creatively discover together where the discipline could go by pushing beyond the boundaries defined by the established curriculum. The high priest suggested that the next level would not be focused on the combat arts but on esoteric areas such as mind control and the mythical ability to disappear from plain sight.

The master—having lived many years in this world—knew that these were unattainable goals. His student did not.

———

Joe scrambled over another set of berms that had naturally been built up in the dry wash he was fording. He was experimenting with trying to clear his mind of all of the mundane thoughts that had seemed to preoccupy him during the last ten years or so. Ah, the simplicity of youth. He didn't recall having these many emotive fractures to sort through in the days before he was ordained as an adult.

When one fills the available brain space with a marriage, mortgage, career, and children, the ability to access one's Theta state of consciousness becomes a near impossibility. He used to be able to do it. Now that all of those elements had disappeared in the ensuing years, maybe he could again.

His immediate goal was to reverse the natural order of things. Instead of hunting his prey, he was attempting to use his mind to invite his quarry to find him.

As he climbed another bump in the rocky terrain, he tried to concentrate his thoughts on asking this animal to willingly make the sacrifice for him. He perched atop the outcropping and took a sip of the boiled river water from his canteen. In the distance was a clearing, a country meadow surrounded by a battalion of oak trees.

He unhooked the spotter scope from his belt and scanned the area. He was still roughly 1500 meters away from the open space of prairie grass. He was paying special attention to the densest foliage that outlined the area. Were those leaves rustling? They were.

Nose to the air, a mature doe nudged its way out of the green shield. Taking in all of the factors that could threaten her, she probed the environment searching for every reason why she shouldn't cross the clearing. For her, it was about sorting through a mass of negatives. That was natural for her. That's just the way she operated.

Joe slid the rifle off his back. He was at the limit of his range, but if he could make the kill from here, he wouldn't have to risk losing the doe and being forced to track her for hours in the anhydrating heat of the day.

He drew down and adjusted the scope for the wind. He would wait until she was fully exposed and he was presented with the bulk of her being. He was a long way from her, and he wanted the largest mass available to him to ensure he disposed of her with a single shot.

Then, she was out in the clearing, instinctually calmed, nibbling on the new shoots of grass that had been nurtured by the recent monsoonal flow.

He removed the safety and laid his finger on the trigger. He took a deep breath, let half of the volume leave his lungs, and settled himself. His technique was solid, impeccable to the point that there was nary a waver of the target in the sight.

His mind began to swarm with thoughts that told him that this was wrong. This lone animal had not tried to harm him. This wasn't about self-defense. In truth, this was about convenience. Nothing more. This was about making his trip up to Big D a bit cushier. He wouldn't be partaking in the bounty. He didn't need it for his own survival, as he had enough MRE's to sustain him through his journey.

Joe lowered the weapon, gathered his things, and decided to advance toward the target. He resolved not to abandon the effort; he just felt that if he moved closer, his reasoning for ending this animal's life might become clearer. Maybe he was queered by the thought that killing this beast with a high-velocity shell from such a distance would require him to make an entry in the ledger that would brand him as a "perpetrator of an unfair fight."

The wind freshened, and he used the increased decibel level of the environment to slither across the rocks undetected by his prey.

When he had advanced to a range of 800 meters, he paused again and brought the scope to his dominant eye. The doe had only moved far enough to graze on the next large patch of grass.

Once again, he unshouldered and aimed the rifle, and once again, he froze.

"Damn," he muttered before sitting down and laying the rifle across his lap.

It was as if his wits had suffered the same type of demolition that deuterium does at the culmination of its journey in a linear accelerator. He tried to gather them and glue them back together, but they were like metal filings in the sand, and the magnet he was holding was of the opposite polarity. The more he tried to gather them into cohesiveness, the more they were repelled.

He decided to move even closer and hope that the forward movement might help him to dissolve this stubborn resistance. He set an arbitrary distance of 200 meters as the span that would be acceptable. To catalyze his determination, he vowed that he could only kill the doe with an extinguishing headshot.

Again he was successful in traversing the terrain without disturbing the doe. He used a scrub oak as camouflage and brought the spotter scope to bear on her. The doe swiveled away from its former profile pose.

From this new angle, he noticed that something was odd about her physiognomy. There was a strange bulge to the frame on either side of her torso. When she wandered over to the next patch of grass and presented her dorsal side again, he could see that her teats were prominent and appeared to be engorged.

"Jesus," Joe said with just the breath of his exhalation and little enunciation.

He never left the spot, and as the sun began to set, the doe laid down in the meadow and fawned.

As he watched her fight through the pain, silently cheering her on towards completion, something inside of him broke. Whatever had been bound together inside of him to keep him moving forward, to keep his intentions clear, dissolved like sugar in rapidly boiling water. The formerly impenetrable crystal matrix degraded in just a few of those moments as the doe began to lick the placental rime from her newly minted issue.

By the time he returned to his camp, he had been crying nonstop for three hours.

———

The interview with the subject, Udo Lewandowski, was not going well for the tracker. They were meeting in one of the offices of the company that employed Lewandowski, Amalgamated Sentry, Inc.

"I don't really remember much. It was kind of a dangerous situation," Udo explained.

"That's what I've been told."

"I'm also not legally permitted to discuss incidents surrounding that event. There is a matter of litigation on the table being pursued by those clients you mentioned."

The tracker was looking for the lie. He knew that the two C-town contractors had been abandoned by their bodyguard and had been forced to rely on the subject of his search to provide them with safe passage back home. He also knew that the two were suing Amalgamated Sentry for non-performance of their duties.

What he didn't know was that Amalgamated Sentry was a Redeemer front company and that the man he was talking to was very high up in the organization of the movement. Within the Redeemer community, the name Udo Lewandoski commanded a large amount of deference.

What the tracker also didn't know was that there were entities out there creating revenue for the Redeemer movement, and that Udo Lewandowski was very interested in the whereabouts of Joe Smith as well. Udo had heard the reports of the Tynan building being razed in H-town and the use of his name to lure some of the unsuspecting victims. When he put the variables together—including the facts that Joe worked for Tynan and that Joe had heard his name and probably suspected him of collusion in that mess at the armory—the outline of a sketch began to emerge that a thorn in the side of the movement could be removed if they could put this Joe Smith down.

So, Udo subtly became the interviewer.

"So, does this Joe Smith guy owe someone money?" Udo asked.

"No, not that I'm aware of," the tracker said.

"And someone's paying you to find him? For what?"

The tracker had the invitation letter from the client in his front pocket, but he had no idea of the text that was contained inside the sealed envelope. Until that moment, when the question had been posed, he had never even thought of why he had been dispatched to find this wraith. In truth, having to know the reasons was not part of his concern, nor included in his job description. But this big guy sitting across the table from him had introduced curiosities that were sure to erode his ethics over time.

"Where are you from?" Udo asked, as if the original subject of the conversation had been closed.

"Motor City."

"You like it there?"

"It's all right. It's kind of tough to live there if you don't have a lot of resources, but it feels safe. The food's good. They have power for the daylight hours. It's all right."

Udo nodded in unison with his interrogator.

"C-town could learn a lot from them is what I'm hearing."

"Yeah, this place ain't no Motor City, that's for sure," the tracker said.

"You got a card or something? I'm sometimes in need of a tracker, and maybe you can recommend someone here. Or do you sometimes take jobs outside of Motor City?"

"I'm freelance. I'll work wherever the job is. If you want to get a hold of me, get a message to this guy."

The tracker pulled a card out of his pouch and handed it to Udo. It read: "Leo Rascone, Attorney".

Joe never returned to the livery. He decided to abort the attempt to seek the capital he would need to haggle for a horse. He would walk the rest of the way to Big D.

This was not the first time he had put hundreds of miles on his dogs, and he knew all of the techniques to preserve his footwear and the skin it protected. He was able to make the entire trek on just the boots he started out on and one other pair.

It took him a total of nine days and nights. He took a day off to rest in the middle somewhere, but other than that he had little problem with the monotonous task of putting one foot in front of another. As the trip progressed, he unloosed himself of the empty MRE's and the pair of degraded boots, but he could hardly say that the end of the journey was easier, as fatigue filled in the spaces of convenience provided by the decreased weight.

When he arrived on the doorstep of St. Michael's Church, he weighed in at somewhere south of 140 pounds. An acolyte answered the doorbell. Upon seeing this disheveled man standing on the steps of the rectory, his arsenal having been lowered to the ground, the assistant rushed inside to gather clothing and water. This was the custom of St. Michael's, an institution dedicated to tolerance. The acolyte had no idea that the man who stood at the entrance was the myth that every one of his teachers had invoked as the paradigm student. As renown as Joe Smith was in this particular world, only his parents, the master, and the master's assistant, Mohammed, would have had the ability to recognize him.

The acolyte attended to the waif on the doorstep. He offered Joe water and washcloths perfumed with the juice of fresh lemons.

It was Mohammed who noticed Joe first. Returning from his morning run, he leapt up the steps, two at a time, passing the acolyte attending to what he assumed was just another transient. Something, perhaps an aural emanation, made him stop and study the recipient of the acolyte's attention.

"Oh, my God," Mohammed said.

"What?" replied the acolyte.

"Lord Smith?" Mohammed inquired as he moved closer to study the wasted figure of Joe.

The acolyte—having heard the name that had only been uttered in reverence—gasped and stared at the rumpled man.

"Hey, Master M.," Joe said.

The acolyte started to wobble before he sought stability by falling to his knees. This is the man he had heard about, the legend of all legends.

"Get up, kid," Joe said.

If one could see beyond the sunken cheekbones and the grime, they would have noticed a look of embarrassment portrayed on Joe's face.

"Let's get you inside," Mohammed said.

Mohammed signaled to the acolyte to pick up Joe's effects as he reached out his hand to lead the wayfarer into the facility.

"I just walked up from H-town; I'm not a cripple."

Mohammed laughed.

"You haven't changed at all, have you?"

"Yes, Master M., I have."

Mohammed let that statement land. He knew something of Joe's recent history; the poor man had experienced a litany of gruesome tragedies with deaths of some of the members of his immediate family. Many of his daily prayers had included the plea that the horror Joe had been forced to deal with would be divinely mitigated somehow.

"Let's get you to a bed. Have you eaten recently?" Mohammed asked.

"I'm not hungry."

"Take him to the visitor's cell," Mohammed barked at the acolyte.

"Yes, Master M."

Mohammed rushed to the storage area to gather the necessary implements to make Lord Joe Smith comfortable. He couldn't wait to tell his boss, Casey—the master who had brought Joe along in the early years until the tables had turned between the teacher and the student.

FOURTEEN

ST. MICHAEL'S

THE TRACKER CAUGHT a break outside of Fort Wayne when the first mate that had ferried Joe Smith down to the Wabash recognized the man in the artist's depiction and told him of their contact. It was a fluke that he had run into the guy, but the incident was further evidence to the tracker that some forces related to destiny and collective consciousness blessed his searches.

The power of the universe being in play here or not, the tracker was grateful for this particular episode of kismet. During his discussion with the first mate, he caught another unforeseen break: information that his subject's ultimate destination was H-town. The tracker deemed this nugget as the first major break in his quest.

The tracker had briefly toured the site of the destroyed Rubber City armory, used his contacts with the recently unemployed Tynan people who he had once had business relationships with, and begun to compile a portrait on the subject replete with a growing mass of substantive data.

One of the former Tynan executives, Ned Maker, a VP of the regional office in Fort Wayne, had the subject's employment history. It revealed details of the subject's non-stop four-year crusade to complete Tynan's contract to close the orphaned armories.

"Who was paying off on these contracts?" the tracker asked Ned.

Ned shrugged the shrug of a former spook who was wary of passing any information to a civilian.

"So this guy continued to do all of this work for no pay?"

"He was getting paid. The company wasn't. They were having trouble collecting on the contract since the entity that offered the original contract no longer existed."

The tracker knew that this was a government contract at one time, and the government hadn't related to the center of the country for a good long while now.

"They were just covering their asses until they could cover their asses, you know what I mean?" said Ned.

The tracker did not, but he chose to change the topic of the inquiry.

"Those pricks to the east wanted to keep all of the psychos busy until they could build their own wall," Ned continued.

The tracker nodded but didn't record Ned's statement. He wasn't interested in Ned's personal tastes, distastes, or political philosophy.

"All of these partners that he had. Do you know their whereabouts now?" the tracker asked.

Ned smiled and held one finger up to the sky. For a moment, the tracker thought that some of the subject's partners were in the apartment building that was hosting their meeting, occupying the upper floors. Maybe this was where the Tynan organization abdicated after their CEO was killed. Only after Ned chose a different response—the clichéd mime of a blade slashing across the throat—did the tracker understand the initial inference.

"All of them?"

"Pretty much."

"Why?"

"If you ever do run into him, you'll understand. Ain't no one got the training, the ability, and the balls to keep up, you know? I only met him once and I certainly wouldn't want to be in the field with him. But nobody got the job done like he did. You asked about pay? He didn't give a shit about that. His job was his religion, his reason for being. He performed it with a fervor that could only be described as fanatical."

The tracker inscribed Ned's response verbatim into his notebook. He scanned the list of all of the men who had worked with the subject. They couldn't all be dead, could they?

It had been roughly a month since Joe had slept with an actual roof over his head, much longer than that when it came to having anything that resembled bedding. In the past, the presence of these luxuries was never required when it came to his getting the needed rest and recovery; he could grab a couple of z's at any time and in any position.

Joe certainly was not ready to simply dispense with the vigilance that had kept him alive in the face of certain death for so many years. Even though logic would dictate that there could be no safer environment than the one he currently occupied, he could not embrace those obvious concepts and relax. There was the condition of the four confining walls of the visitor's cell to be pondered, and that initially unnerved him as he stretched his gaunt frame onto the four-poster queen-sized bed.

His first thoughts concentrated on the possible exits should he need to escape an attack. Having just the oaken door as the only exit put him in a defensive state of mind. He decided that, if required, he would have to blast his way out of the room. So, he loaded both of the nine millimeters and placed one on the nightstand and gripped the other with his right hand.

Subsequently, he conjured what lay outside the claustrophobic cell. There was the hall and its acrophobia-inducing ceilings, the doors that buttoned either end, and the three other rooms that existed on this wing. One of the doors at the end of the hall led to the sacristy and the gym beyond; the opposite one led to an open courtyard.

Joe played out the various scenarios like action scenes in an old movie. Before his eyelids would close and he would offer himself up to Morpheus, he played out the simulations of a multitude of harrowing situations, adding another armed attacker for every distinct iteration. Like the shepherd might lull himself to slumber by counting the members of his flock, Joe, the warrior, counted the enemies and punctuated each sighting with a precise placement of a hollow-point bullet in the center of their torso.

He did not dream.

The knock on the door introduced an otherworldly sound into the nothingness that accompanied the deep delta state that suspended him. His eyes fluttered open and the first thing he saw was the butt of the gun being gripped by his right hand.

"Joe?" someone whispered from the other side of the door.

The voice was familiar, and he relaxed the reins on the firearm and slid it under the extra pillow.

"Yeah," he croaked.

He got out of the bed. He had to pee something fierce.

Joe unlocked the door to reveal the smiling master, still in his sweat gear from his morning PT and sparring sessions.

"I gotta pee," Joe said.

"Please, go," the master replied.

Joe made a beeline for the bathroom down the hall. The master entered the room. One full intake of breath told him much of what he needed to know. It wasn't just the rank smell of the unbathed that entered his nostrils; it was smell of someone who had been in the proximity of death. The master knew that Joe possessed the tools to clear the stench of his aura because Joe had taught him the technique. The Master assumed that he would come to that when he was ready.

When Joe returned, the two men embraced, as was their custom. For the master it was an unbridled envelopment of his former pupil. For Joe, it was an attempt to accept a transfer of some of the master's power into his being to compensate for the utter weakness that he felt in the moment. Both men were able to understand and consider the motivation for the osmosis-like exchange of energy and information.

After they separated, the master shuffled to the door and called out for an acolyte.

"I might like to stay here for a little while, master." Joe said.

"You can't call me that anymore. The title must live up to the billing, and next to you, that mantle sounds ludicrous."

"Whatever."

The master laughed. Joe had never been able to call him by his actual name.

"You can stay as long as you'd like. You can work out with us. You can mentor. It's up to you," the master said.

"For right now, I think I'll just be wearing out a path between this room and the garden, master."

"Stop it. Say my name."

"I'd rather not."

"Say it."

Joe's mouth moved to form the opening consonant, but somewhere before he could put his breath to it, he lost his nerve.

"Can we just drop this, master?" Joe asked.

"No. You want me to be the teacher again? Fine. First lesson: Say my name, Joe."

The master knew there was a method in his desire to elicit a response. By badgering Joe, he was attempting to start the process of bringing him back to a world that wasn't assessed by a body count. Joe was getting pissed. The master saw this as a good sign.

There was a tentative knock on the door. Two acolytes were revealed at the threshold. One of them held a porcelain bowl; the other held a stack of towels and a murky liquid in a mason jar. Both averted their eyes, staring at the cracks in the tile floor.

"Who knocked?" the master asked.

"I did," one of the acolytes stuttered.

"What is this?" the master asked.

The master proceeded to mock the acolyte by brushing his knuckles weakly against the vertically grained wood of the barrier.

"I asked you here. Please, in the future, make your presence known. Knock with purpose."

"Yes, master."

The master welcomed them inside.

"What is this?" Joe asked.

"Your feet stink."

The acolytes knelt before the legend and waited for him to offer his feet for cleaning and annealing.

"Thanks, guys, but I can do it," Joe said.

"But . . ."

"You aren't going to wash my feet."

"It would be our honor," one of the acolytes said.

Joe looked up at the man he still considered to be his superior.

"You're kidding, right?"

"They had a contest last night. There were a series of bouts designed to produce a winner. The winner was allowed to select one of his fellow combatants to join him. Danny here chose the boy he beat in the final, Larry. These boys fought for the right to do this. The depth of their disappointment will be on you."

"Fine. Your name is Casey," Joe said to the master. "Casey, I can wash my own feet."

"And so it will be, Joe," Casey said with a smile.

He ushered the two acolytes out of the room. Before he exited, he stopped, with his back to Joe.

"You can stay as long as you like, Joe, you know that. Do you want me to contact your parents?"

"Not now. Maybe later, but not now."

As Casey slowly closed the door, he could hear the splashing sounds of Joe's ripe feet meeting liquid.

The tracker rode the solar pod convoy from Baton Rogue to H-town on the same forward car that his subject had taken more than a fortnight before.

Sally Freeman and he weren't the only passengers headed west this time. News of the culling of many members of the cults that had threatened the former Space City had been passed along the line to its former residents, and some were returning to reclaim their homesteads or collect items left behind amidst their hasty retreat.

It was in H-town that the tracker hit a cul-de-sac. County records got him to Aldine and Joe Smith's former residence, but that is where the trail went cold. There was not a great deal of cooperation from the residents of the housing tract that included the address 645 Baxter, so any clues the tracker hoped to glean by poking through the house were left secreted.

The tracker knew that time was running out on his contract. He had come so far with nary a detour, and yet the wall that he now faced appeared to be beyond his ability to scale. He was going to need some of that odd intervention, that good old mojo, to get the thing done.

———

Joe did indeed wear a path in the floor between his cell and the garden courtyard. As his joints began to stiffen from under use and his belly became less flat, he eventually began to loiter around the dojo, watching the acolytes receive their verbal training before they tentatively attempted to transform the words into action.

One afternoon, the master, Casey, asked Joe to address the intermediate class. It was the same level at which Joe had begun his journey in the discipline over twenty-six years before. There was hunger in the eyes of the students, a ravenous disposition to acquire the knowledge quickly. After the lesson, Joe moved over to one of the mats to spar with Casey.

"Was that all right, Casey?" Joe asked.

"What do you mean?" Casey asked.

"I didn't know where they were in the curriculum. I fear that I might have jumped a little ahead for their level. I could see a little desperation and frustration in their looks when we passed from the theoretical to the practical."

They moved about each other in near slow motion. They were performing the mirror exercise, and to the few observers that were allowed to be in the dojo during this interval, it looked like violent ballet. Every aggressive movement was not met with a parry, but the reverse of the particular ploy.

"You did fine. Hell, half the kids didn't hear a word you said. They were a little in awe of your celebrity."

Joe's facial hue morphed from ashen to rouge, and he briefly lost his concentration and with it, the rhythm of the Terpsichore.

"I suppose I looked like that when you spoke way back when," Joe said.

"No, you did not, Joe. The truth is, you never showed any emotion, any evidence that you comprehended anything we said. From our standpoint, it was very disconcerting. Our first reaction was to think we had failed you, and it had a negative effect on our self-esteem for a time. But when you put it into action, we all knew that you had absorbed every word, every nuance. I haven't seen that type of behavior exhibited by any other student in all of the years since. I keep looking for it, praying for it, but I know now it will never happen again in my lifetime."

Joe took over the lead and picked up the pace. He was feeling stronger physically, but his mind was still as mushy as the pre-packaged gruel he had been forced to eat during some of his more lengthy missions. He watched in amazement as his former teacher immediately got up to speed.

Joe wasn't a good judge of subjective metrics like someone's age, but he figured that Casey must have been alive for over sixty-five years. He knew that Casey was in his mid-thirties when he'd arrived here at St. Michael's with Mohammed and the two of them first gathered the initiative to open the monastery and the training facility. As to Casey's past—the era before his arrival at the outskirts of Big D—Joe knew virtually nothing. He was aware that Casey was homosexual, but it had never been anything other than an observation. Joe had no feelings of negativity about Casey's or anyone's sexual orientation. Joe knew that Mohammed had arrived with Casey and decided to stay. As far as Joe knew, the two men were strictly friends and colleagues.

Looking at his mentor now, trying to find his breaking point by increasing the intensity of the exercise with each pass, Joe thought about the comment that Casey had uttered when he referred to his lack of emotion. If that was a quality, Joe ventured that he might be the epitome.

He saw Casey begin to wobble. Joe became acutely aware that their session was not entirely private. He had no desire to embarrass his mentor in front of his devotees. He began to wind down the effort.

"Don't do that," Casey barked.

"What?"

"Don't slow down."

Joe could see that his mentor was having the slightest difficulty in drawing a full breath. Casey's sweat-flecked face glistened with the moisture that was probably in need of being restored to his aging body. The heat in the dojo was stifling as it always was from early spring to late fall.

Joe knew that Casey would never quit. He would die first. So, Joe pulled up, stopped the exercise, and rested his hands on his knees as if exhaustion had made it impossible to assume any type of stance that involved erectness.

"I've had it," Joe said.

"You are such a liar," Casey said.

"I'm cooked," Joe reiterated.

Casey walked over to Mohammed, accepted a towel that had been soaked in ice water, and laid it over the back of his neck.

As Joe crossed over to them, he saw them giggling at some private joke.

"What's so funny?" he asked.

"Nothing," Mohammed said.

The exchange put Joe on the defensive, and he wondered if he should give Casey what he seemed to be asking for—a session that might ultimately be injurious to his mentor.

"You know the master has legs of titanium," Mohammed said.

"Yeah, I know," Joe said.

There was no quantifying the level of respect that Mohammed had shown Casey over the decades. He was always there to elevate his stature in any situation.

"I'm not being metaphorical. The master's legs were crushed when he was young. Most of his bones disintegrated. Both of his femurs are metal."

"Really?" Joe asked as he looked over to Casey for confirmation.

"Yeah. I'm a robot," Casey smiled.

Joe was left wondering if all of this was true. It reconfirmed for him that he knew little about the man who had guided him for so many of his waking days.

He would have to ponder the reasons why there was this obvious hole in his education. He would have to ponder the direction of his future. And he would have to ponder why he felt the presence of something in his periphery ever since he had that emotional break, now weeks before, down in the Texas hill country.

FIFTEEN

FUCK TRADITION

EVERYONE KNEW THAT there would eventually be a leak and that the other wards would become aware that Impala was in the process of flouting the accepted norms. It could be assumed that through intermingling with third parties, one couldn't keep the secret inside if it meant that divulging the juicy tidbit might provide an advantage in a social situation. Those that might have let the scheme out of the vault could have been using it to appear smart or cool, to project omnipotence, or to release some pent-up energy that had required them to keep the confidence for longer than they were capable.

It wouldn't be strange if one of Impala's allies like DeVille became privy to the ploy. Whether or not they would support Impala's choice would be up for debate. Their sole goal, like every other ward, would be to win, no matter what the cost, no matter whom they had to best.

The issue came to a head not long after the all-Impala dinner, where Lon Brassey announced that they would be seeking a pilot for the race from outside the neighborhood. Mustang had their spies afoot, but they were under the belief that all of this was just fluff. Their instincts informed them that Impala was just trying to be provocative by intentionally putting out misinformation.

When Lon contracted with the lawyer Leo Rascone to aid in his search for a possible candidate, the veracity in the intent of the captain of Impala could no longer be denied.

Leo Rascone operated out of the area of town that had no affiliation to any of the wards. Encompassing the region around the stadiums and what was once known as the Grand Circus, the independent archipelago housed neutral businesses and residents that provided services to all of the different wards. The people of this insular community were called "Indies," "Un-coms" (as in uncommitted), or "Mugwumps" (a somewhat inapt appellation derived from those who bolted the Republican party in the mid-1800s because they thought they had more character and intelligence than the other members of the party). The area was considered the Switzerland to the rest of the enclave's Europe.

Housed within the aging office spaces and the high-rises were the janitors, maids, security personnel, legal professionals, some doctors, and city management.

These residents were usually imported for their expertise in a certain area and took the opportunity to live within the enclave as a privilege that could be taken away should they not live up to the ideals espoused by the naturalized occupants of Motor City. The cynics among them would refer to themselves as indentured servants. The more optimistic hoped for a miracle—that they would marry into a ward and legitimize their residency.

Leo Rascone had built a thriving practice by accepting cases and tasks that were not settled by simple mediation and accepted logic. Reviled by many for his ethical high-wire act, Leo was often the butt of jokes delivered by the Motor City snobbery. But, when push came to shove, when the rubber needed to hit the road, or when one needed access to things deemed undesirable, Leo was the guy.

Leo emigrated to Motor City with the first wave of outsiders. Immigrants were only allowed in on a perceived-need basis, and early on, the founders felt that a man like Leo—unaffiliated and unaffected by some of the arcane rules—would prove indispensable in situations where the courts and the ward officials would be in need of a certain type of antagonism. There was always the thought that the exclusionary tactics employed by the "powers that be" might eventually lead to a city-controlled quasi-fascism, and an interlocutor such as Leo would always provide a stumbling block to any of the fellow travelers that might try to bring about such a condition of the state.

Even though Leo was thoroughly vetted in terms of his references, family history, and education, there were a myriad of skeletons that hung in his closet like the never-ending supply of natty suits he was in the habit of donning.

Before he became Motor City's go-to guy, he had been an advisor, litigator, and bagman for organized crime figures, fetishistic billionaires, dubious celebrities, corrupt aldermen, mayors, and state representatives of the crumbling former political establishments. He also had a multitude of indictments hanging over his head when the infrastructure of the government that had set about enthusiastically prosecuting him collapsed.

All of the information pertaining to those elements of his previous work experience was conveniently wiped away with an exchange of sop between the parties that were responsible for allowing his entry and some intermediaries that Leo employed. Once he was ensconced, the memories of his past appeared to have been wiped clean from the consciousness of the residents of Motor City.

When Lon Brassey sought him out to perform the benign task of finding a specific person out in the wilderness, he thought only about the remuneration that was to be extended from what was easily considered to be the wealthiest of the wards. He had employed the tracker and sent him on his journey, but not before surreptitiously scanning the letter of invitation that the tracker was engaged to deliver to the subject of the search.

To say he was mildly shocked by the content of the text contained in the letter would have been a gross misstatement, and it did not take Leo long to create an angle of maneuver. He knew that the knowledge would be worth a pot load of compensation, as well as a deposit of gratefulness from the entities who would be hungry to know the facts that he now possessed.

Leo decided to make his primary entreaty with a certain lieutenant of Mustang, a gentleman who Leo had done business with in the past.

John Brassey observed the breadth of his father's newly minted boost in self-esteem and pronounced it to be inorganic. Maybe it was the tribal continuum that determines that, at some point, the son rejects the teachings and guidance provided by the sire. Maybe it was the altered-consciousness-inducing influence of the love he felt for his woman. Or maybe it was because his dad was a fucking glory-hogging narcissistic prick.

John watched his father preen in front of his two lieutenants as they shared a cocktail on the day the letter was sent on its way. Lon's brother's recommendation that there could be no better candidate than the intended recipient of the letter had buoyed him to the point that he seemed to be floating a couple of inches above the leather club chair he was occupying. As John loitered in the terrace doorway, waiting to refresh their drinks, the masters of Impala bantered about the prospects of the man that Lon had designated as the invitee.

"It's not a skill that everyone has," said Kevin Gatz.

Kevin was the bespectacled mouse of a lieutenant with the heart of a sadist who had spent most of his life collating information that was meted out to produce an advantage for himself in all of the relationships he maintained. John was never without the urge to kick this pipsqueak in the soft area behind his knees whenever he offered some pithy phrase like "Hey, kid, you grown any hair on your balls yet?"

"You can learn a lot on the simulator," Billy Klock said, adding little to the conversation.

John thought Billy was a lunkhead. Billy was well over six feet high and nearly as wide. He had actually been the backup driver in his mid-twenties, some ten years back, but John speculated that he never graduated to the pilot's seat because he was so fucking stupid.

"Why are you guys worried? In the end, everyone will get what they want," Lon said.

"You are too smart for me, Cap," Billy said.

"I know, Bill," Lon said as he patted the behemoth on the thigh.

Everyone will get what they want? What was that supposed to mean? John thought the only goal was to win the race. What kind of crap was this three-headed hydra trying to pull?

John registered that Kevin's drink was down to just a sip or two. He strolled over to the table and picked up the finely etched crystal old-fashion glass. The etching depicted a hunting scene and displayed a water-loving retriever gripping a limp duck in his maw.

John nearly laughed. Not one of these men, especially his father, had ever gone hunting in his life.

"You ready for another?" John asked Kevin.

"Just a short one."

"Anyone else?"

Billy waited to see if Lon was going to have another pop, and seeing that the captain made no move to give his son the glass, he demurred.

"Hey, kid, you gotten laid yet?" Kevin asked.

"Kevin, please, my son is not yet sixteen," Lon said.

"Hell, Cap, how old were you when you lost it?"

John waited for his father to answer, but Lon was not interested in confirming the date of the loss of his virginity in any kind of a public setting. He had a look plastered on his face that fell between the cracks of embarrassed and pissed off.

"How old were you, Dad?" John asked.

John knew that there would be no way that his dad would ever answer him. He also knew that he assured himself of a tongue lashing once the underlings took their leave. He had been warned about speaking up in certain qualifying social situations, this definitely being one of those, but he was really enjoying watching his old man squirm. Kevin sensed the tension and chose to put the focus back on the younger Brassey.

"So, kid, when you do end up doing it, make sure you wear a helmet," Kevin said.

That one busted up Billy, who was actually smart enough to understand the double entendre in the statement, since everyone knew that John had been required to wear headgear for such a long time. It pissed John off that his father chuckled along with the others at the crack.

Dutifully, John exited the terrace and went into the kitchen to fix Kevin's drink. His mind wandered to the type of poisons that might be under the sink. Out on the patio, the conversation continued.

"So you think this guy is going to be able to drive, huh?" Billy said to no one in particular.

For all intents, the question had been asked and answered, but Billy sensed that something had gone off the rails here between the father and the son, and he thought that this might swivel the spotlight away from that relationship.

"Didn't you hear the captain, Billy? It doesn't matter," Kevin said.

Billy was still trying to get his mind around the concept that winning the race was not the first priority. It didn't matter? Then why were they bringing the guy in?

"I guess I don't understand why it doesn't matter," Billy said, looking into the bottom of his glass.

John returned with the Kevin's freshened drink. Kevin never gave a thought that its contents could possibly be tainted and immediately took a gulp.

"This is good, kid," Kevin said to John.

"Thanks," John replied.

He hadn't done anything but measure the correct amounts of rye and sweet vermouth. Poisoning him was a fantasy, a kind of alternative reality that John often used as personal entertainment.

John wandered over to the railing and tried to appear invisible. He really wanted to hear the rest of the conversation.

"Okay, Billy, hang with me here," Lon began. "One of the reasons it doesn't matter is because the intention of trying to pull this off has more to do with provocation and less to do with result."

Using a word like "provocation" to Billy was just cruel, John thought. Was his father not sensitive to that consistently quizzical look on Billy's face? John decided to help the big guy out.

"By 'provocation,' he means stirring shit up, Mr. Klock," John said.

"Oh, okay," Billy said.

"Watch your language, son," Lon said.

"Yes, sir. Sorry, sir," John said without even a hint of sarcasm.

Just the fact that his father hadn't banished him for opening his mouth was a huge step forward. If he could restrain himself from this point onward, he could stay for the rest of the confabulation.

"But what does that get us? I thought we were trying to win the race," Billy asked.

Finally there were no instances of opaque reference in regards to strategy—Billy had asked the question that had been poised on the tip of John's tongue for some months now.

"We're still going to try to win, Bill," Lon said, "but you know as well as anyone that there are a lot of factors that go into whether that aim is realistic or not. I mean, we could get a dog of a car, or the mechanics could screw something up, or Mustang spends a lot trying to undermine us."

"You can bet on that," Kevin interjected.

Lon gave him a look that said that he was not interested in being interrupted again. To center himself before continuing, he drained the rest of his drink.

"The people don't really think of these things; like you, like all of us, they just want to win. But we know that much of it is out of our hands. Sure, we'll work hard. We'll make our deals, hope we get a good ride in the lottery, pray like hell and do everything possible, but what if we don't win? Who's to blame for that? This last election told us that the people have a target for their anger and disappointment. That target is the captain. And by association, that means the two of you as well."

John checked in with Billy. It appeared to him that the meathead had comprehended Lon's monologue. At the very least, he was listening intently.

Lon also took a moment to check in with his doltish assistant. He was fully aware that he still hadn't completely answered the question about why the outcome didn't matter.

"So, you see where we're going here, Bill?" Lon asked.

"I think so," Bill said unconvincingly.

"It doesn't matter what happens because the one they'll blame is the driver, not us. Heck, they'll blame the car, bad luck, God, the other wards, but in the end they'll have this guy that they don't know, this guy who isn't connected to us. And we will get to run things for another year at least."

Kevin felt the explanation had been delivered to the satisfaction of all, even his moronic equal, but Billy still displayed a certain hesitation.

"What are we missing here for you, Bill?" Kevin asked.

"Well, if we're looking for a patsy or something, why go to all the trouble to track down this guy that your brother hardly knows? Why not get some loser over in Toledo?" Bill asked.

Wow, John thought. Maybe this Billy Klock wasn't a cretin after all. That was a really good question. Even John had not formulated it yet himself. His father echoed the same thought that was reverberating in his mind.

"That's why I love you, Billy," Lon said.

Lon and Kevin shared a look. It was an acknowledgement of the legitimacy and amazing foresight present in Billy's query.

"We are trying to bring this guy in because he seems to possess the qualities that the people of Impala expected when we said we were going to do this. Harry said that he'd never seen a braver son of a bitch in his life, and I believe him. Bringing this guy in will prove to the people of Impala and the rest of Motor City that we're serious and we're not trying to pull any funny stuff. We aren't trying to throw the thing, Bill. We are still going to try to win, but if this guy turns out to be a dud, he'll become the vessel that holds the people's disappointment, not us."

Billy absorbed it all. John could almost hear the clank of each idea trying to find its rightful spot in his short-term memory.

"To expand on what the captain had to say and in reference to the kid's 'stirring the shit' comment, we're also doing this because we know it's going to drive some of the other wards crazy. I mean, think about it. If you heard that Mustang was bringing in some hotshot pro to drive for them, wouldn't that freak you out?" Kevin asked.

Billy nodded.

"We'll be the talk of the town, and while all of those idiots are focusing their attention on us, they'll be neglecting the things that they should be paying attention to in their own worlds."

"Okay, I get it now," Billy said.

"Good," Lon said.

"When are you going to drop the bomb on the rest of the wards?" John asked.

Both Kevin and Billy were interested in the timing as well, and their expectant glances at Lon allowed John's father to consider the question, even though John ought not to have asked it.

"Well, my guess is that there are already rumors out there, but I wanted to meet this fellow, see where we stand, before we make it public. Hopefully that can happen sooner than later. I originally thought that we'd show up to the lottery with him, but there's no way the lid can stay on until then. There's a rules meeting of all the wards in a couple of weeks where we'll get the particulars of the festival, and if things seem right, I expect to announce it at that time."

The two ass-kissers gave Lon a look that bordered on adoration. John watched his father soak in their adulation and began to fantasize that the day would come when that self-confident grin would be wiped away by a wave of humiliation. *It just has to happen. It has to,* he thought.

John carried the glassware back into the kitchen and set about washing the fine crystal. He knew the rules: tepid water, mild soap, and thorough drying with a soft, lint-free cloth.

His father was seeing the men to the door, and John wondered if he would return to discuss the over- and undertones of everything that he'd heard this evening. He heard the parting salutations and the closing of the door, but he didn't hear his father make a return to the kitchen. He did hear the click of the door to his father's study as his old man once again closed himself off from his family, his scion, and the world.

SIXTEEN

MACHINATIONS

LEO RASCONE USED an intermediary, Ricky Lomes, to contact the Mustang lieutenant Tom Cobble. Ricky, a Mustang civilian, was a sometime employee of Leo's and specialized in fomenting enmity between the wards that had taken the identities of the sports teams: the Pistons, the Tigers, the Lions, and the Red Wings. By keeping these groups at odds with one another, Mustang was able to use them freely as allies to help their own cause whenever the advantage presented itself.

The need to maintain entropy within the groups that were not affiliated with the former automobile industry wards like Impala and Mustang was an example of some the long-term strategies that Mustang Captain Titus O'Keefe, had put into play during his twenty-year tenure as the Mustang leader. His theory was that any bloc that was greater than two would severely sway an edge toward the members of that cabal and could not be tolerated by the other wards that desired to remain competitive in the race.

Titus was the only one who had the foresight to understand the danger of such a hypothetical alliance, and he spent a lot of time and assets making sure that all nine of the wards, with the exception of the pre-existing long-standing relationships, operated in their own self-interest. Titus had used Leo Rascone to accomplish some of these goals, and the emissary that dealt with the lawyer was Ricky Lomes.

Ricky and Leo used the timeworn tactics of innuendo and rumor to bring about the desired effect that the Mustang captain aspired to achieve. By seeding the various entities with half-truths and out-right scandalous lies and then producing the minimal amount of physical evidence or third-party confirmation, the two could ride a wave of venomous intention smack into a nascent pact between two wards. As the tide of their subterfuge receded, the formerly friendly wards dealt with each other tentatively for the next year or so. Thanks to all the ratfucking, Leo and Ricky's antics had created a new basis for these suddenly warring ward's relationships, and sometimes, many years would pass before the trust was rebuilt.

Leo explained to Ricky that he had some worthwhile information that Titus and his staff might want to be kept abreast of. When Ricky saw that the lawyer was keeping the disclosure of said material close to his gabardine vest, he knew that he would have to bring in someone more senior than himself to begin the process of negotiation.

Enter Tom Cobble, an embittered former engineer, who had served as Mustang's senior (and virtually only) lieutenant for nearly ten years. Like his work history—he'd been chief of design of Ford's foray into the folly of fuel cell technology—Tom Cobble had been chosen for his position because the Mustang hierarchy believed that he would do his job and not covet the opportunity to eventually be the top dog. Titus O'Keefe had no desire to create a succession plan as he hoped to serve in the captain's position until his demise. Previous lieutenants had grown impatient that their path to leadership had been blocked by Titus's autocratic style and had resigned in disgust.

Tom, however, was a get-along guy. How else could someone glee-fully head up the effort surrounding an alternative fuel source technology that had never really worked? A savvy engineer, Tom knew deep down that the thing was a boondoggle, but it had allowed Ford to continually announce that they took the issue of alternative fuels seriously. Tom never gave an opinion to the contrary.

Tom's meeting with Leo did not start out well. There was a price to be negotiated for the information that Leo retained, but Tom thought that certain disincentives should be built into the deal in the event that the information was already in the Mustang pipeline. Tom touted Mustang's large intelligence gathering apparatus, and he felt that Leo might be selling them something that they already had a good deal of data about.

"You might know about some of the basics of this intel, but I have the specifics. I have a name and a job description," Leo said.

He sure makes shit like this seem enticing, Tom thought.

"All right, let me talk to Titus," Tom said.

"Tom, this information is time sensitive. It involves your arch-rival, but it also involves the entire community."

Damn, Tom thought, this guy is good. *He could probably sell bacon to Muslims and Jews.*

"I'll get back to you, Leo."

"After five today, you lose your exclusivity," Leo stated.

"Yeah, yeah, counselor, I'll get back to you," Tom said as he head-ed for the door.

Tom knew that they would pay for whatever pearl Leo was con-cealing in his oyster brain. This was a dance they had performed together before, and they both knew he'd be waltzing back to Leo's office before the deadline.

———————

Though they had been inseparable for the last seven months, John had yet to kiss Rebecca Leeann Voss. He had thought about it for nearly a year and a half now, but it still hadn't come to pass.

After being informed by Richard about the reason for her absence from school, he had arrived at her door with his heart stoked with compassion and his fear of rejection miraculously stored somewhere deep in the freezer of his consciousness. Something told him that he was needed here, and every month that followed confirmed his hypothesis.

Ewing's sarcoma is a form of bone cancer that mostly strikes the young and preteen. Often there is a correlation between the onset of growth spurts and the presentation of the disease.

In Rebecca's case, the discovery of her affliction came on a breezy pre-winter weekend during her second grade year. The revelation emanated from a seemingly innocuous act—her brother pushing her on a swing in their yard. As he reached for her approaching body to thrust her forward, his hands slipped and made contact with the rib area on her right side. The dissonant tone produced by her wails of pain and her brother's screams of defense that he had done nothing to hurt her created the siren call that brought her parents rushing outside. After everyone calmed down and the story unfolded, there appeared to be no rational explanation as to why Maxine and Frank's daughter was in such tremendous distress.

The tumor was discovered between the fourth and fifth rib on the right side of her torso. A biopsy was performed and the excised tissue qualified as malignant. Before they could surgically remove it, the doctor suggested an initial round of chemotherapy to see how much of the mass could be killed. The doctor didn't tell the parents at the time that he thought her prognosis was devastating and that one of the reasons he was delaying the tumor's removal was that he wanted to find out if a machine shop could mill a titanium insert to replace the bone he was sure he'd have to cut away. This would be the best-case scenario, the doctor determined. Because of the location of the tumor and its proximity to the soft tissue of the lungs and the linings of the heart, he was pretty sure that this pretty young girl was doomed.

Rebecca's beautiful flaxen hair began to fall out within two days of receiving that initial round of chemotherapy through a portal that had been bored into the side of her body.

The journey through surgery and follow-up treatment was a rollercoaster that the Voss family rode together for nearly four years. Every sniffle, every cough was met with fear and the ominous feeling that a recurrence was at hand. Data for red and white blood cell counts became as ubiquitous as the prurient items in the daily news.

It got to the point that Rebecca could no longer handle being the center of attention. She took responsibility for the dour nature that had invaded her household and pleaded with her parents and sibling that they should return to the happy-go-lucky mood the family displayed before she got ill. Their life was no longer a complete circuit, and the connection that provided light was often left open.

This was why John did not see her for the years that he took to complete his elementary education, as well as his first year of middle school.

When she arrived for her eighth-grade year, she had been pronounced cancer-free for the previous two years. She hadn't been left behind in her studies; Maxine made sure of that.

Throughout the entire school year, everything seemed normal. Even through the beginning of the summer, in the days and weeks leading up to the festival, she never announced to anyone that she was feeling anything but a notch above tip-top.

During a routine check-up, not long after the festival where John saw her with Richard, some swelling was discovered in the area around her lower neck. Lymph nodes removed in the area showed no sign of cancer, but as a precaution, three more rounds of chemotherapy were recommended. Though Mr. Fedder had implied that a tumor had been removed, in this instance, it was only the suspect lymph nodes that had been cut from her body.

John's sudden appearance in her world, only days after an especially grueling round of chemo, was a godsend to her. She expressed not a wit of reticence about his presence from the outset, and she often remarked that, though they didn't really know each other that well at first, she felt a kinship based upon their full year of experience sitting next to each other in Mr. Fedder's home room. Later, she would draw further bonding connections amidst his revelations that he had also been classified as a student with an ongoing medical condition.

She was grateful to this new friend in her life, as he provided the needed attention that her mentally exhausted family had been solely responsible for previously. This time around, the guilt for her was less severe because she had a friend to help shoulder much of her pain and nausea. John's presence seemed to blow away the clouds of depression that had hung over the household when she was younger. He was a beaming sun and a forceful wind that kept the dark storms of yesteryear out at sea.

However, there was more than just John's agenda being attended to here. Rebecca did not see her friend as anything other than the amazing companion he had become for her. She sensed that he might try to advance his standing at some point, but she was careful with any statements or actions that could be construed as encouragement.

Of course she consented when he asked if he could escort her to the dance, but she made it clear that they were going as friends; there would be nothing to suggest that there would be anything bordering on exclusivity as far as either of them functioning as the other's only dance partner.

She had no idea that his father had nearly forbid him from attending. She knew little about his life outside of their communion, other than the fact that his father was the ward's captain. The arrows of attention were always only pointed at her, and there was no space, given her circumstances, for anything resembling return fire.

Amidst the crepe paper decorations and the muted lighting, they entered the gym on the night of the dance. No one noticed them. Most of the other students were so self-centered that they weren't aware that she had been AWOL for the first seven months of the school year. Besides, she looked healthy and hearty at her debut—a far cry from her condition during the previous fall and winter when the poisons introduced into her body to promote a cure had rendered her feeble and wan.

But there was a moment of tension. A slow dance had permitted John and her to bring their bodies into a closer proximity than they had been at any time during their seven-month relationship. During a check to see if it was clear on the right, their faces met in perfect synchronicity. Just millimeters needed to be traversed between their lips, but, alas, John blinked and turned away. The moment had become too special—much too momentous, John would later rationalize. It needed to be spontaneous. It needed to be flabbergasting.

That moment at the dance had taken on the quality of watershed for John—it was the confirmation that a promise would be met—but for her the event carried with it a complexity that she wanted to avoid.

Her romantic feelings about John had already been sorted out. She wasn't interested in anything beyond their current state of amity.

Why was she so unwilling to accept John in his guise? It wasn't that he was unattractive. On the contrary, she could see the rugged lines and definition he had developed with his regimen, his impossibly straight teeth, and his goofy mop of dark brown hair. But something was missing. Some indefinable unifying principle that bade her to show restraint when he appeared to wordlessly suggest now that they become amorous.

The concept that she couldn't put her finger on, the concept that so bedeviled her, was that John was very much still a boy.

To John, this girl he had fallen so hard for, had become smitten with, still seemed fragile and incomplete. This was the most potent reason for his tentativeness in delving into the romantic situation he wanted so badly to commence. He had watched her progress from a condition that resembled a hospice resident back into the maturing beauty who had first caught his eye. He'd had a front-row seat as the toxins coursed through her body, bringing about the loss of so many things: hair, skin color, energy, mood, vitality, and stability.

In his fantasies, he would inject himself into her body and wield a bloody saber, slashing away the ugly cells as they made their mutations visible to him.

Now that she was seemingly well, he was having trouble reconciling the past that he had borne witness to and the present that contained more information than a fifteen-year-old should probably know about his crush.

She had presented him with her worst, so many things that she would have kept secret from her family let alone the non-related boy who had become a friend. And yet, John was still there, still feeling his heart beat at a more authoritative rhythm every time he was in her vicinity.

He had no idea that he didn't measure up in her account of ideals. He was simply blissful and assured that all of the things that hadn't happened yet in their relationship were chapters of a book that was still mired in conception. He was fairly certain that, like he, she was a virgin. He assumed that she had at least kissed the viripotent Richard, but he kept images of her touching him or vice versa out of his mind.

He was overjoyed that she was getting better and that the day of their lips finally coupling could be seen bobbing like an incoming skiff on the horizon.

No one in his family knew the whole story. This was why his sister Holiday's intuition in regards to the reasons John wanted to attend the dance was such a shock in the moment. All his family knew was that John had a friend who was sick.

———

Tom Cobble returned before the deadline with an offer that Leo would find difficult to let pass. With his function reduced to delivery boy, Tom held a handwritten note scripted in Captain Titus O'Keefe's hand inviting the lawyer to a private dinner at the Mustang clubhouse. Plenty of security would be provided, and only Tom, Titus, Ricky Lomes, and the chef would know that the communion between the two had ever taken place. Acceptance of the invitation would invalidate the deadline.

Leo had only run across Titus O'Keefe during the most innocuous of social situations, and the sum total of their interaction had resulted in nothing more than a nod of mutual acknowledgement. At the very least, Leo would be able to satisfy a curiosity about the fare and exclusivity of the private dining facility at the Mustang clubhouse. He made Tom sweat a little but eventually consented to meet Titus at the suggested time of 7 P.M.

Leo's meal with Titus did not disappoint. Not only was the menu sumptuous and the filtered candlelight in the room spectacularly focused, but the offer that Tom inferred would be tendered appeared to be as robust as the flavors of the two bottles of twenty-eight-year-old Bordeaux they consumed.

The short of it was that Titus was interested in putting Leo on a yearly retainer. For a yet-to-be-negotiated fee, Leo would use his "Independent" relationships with all of the various wards to acquire whatever intelligence Titus needed. The two principals who had feasted on a meal of lamb, farro, and Caesar salad would be the only two individuals with full knowledge of the contract's existence.

Titus was adamant that Leo's ability to remain in his position as an impartial civilian among the other wards should continue undisturbed. Leo accepted the terms, and after the plates had been cleared away, his quid pro quo finally aired.

"Impala is bringing in a driver from outside their community," Leo said.

"So the rumor has foundation."

"Yes."

"When you say outside, do you mean outside, outside? Or is it someone from Motor City? A Mugwump, perhaps?"

"From out in the wilds. I'm pretty sure that the Impala captain has never met this individual. The recommendation came from his brother out in C-town."

"A professional?" Titus asked as he leaned back in his chair and lit a cigar with the candle from the centerpiece.

"One would think. Otherwise why go to all the trouble of hiring a tracker?"

"I'll need a complete dossier."

"I can do that."

"And you have a name?"

"Joe Smith."

"Really?"

"Could be an alias, I suppose," Leo said.

"Sounds fake."

"Well, that's who the tracker's out there looking for."

Titus had the chessboard laid out in his head and was thinking five moves down the line.

"The whole thing sounds like bullshit. What are the odds that the new Impala captain is fucking with us?"

"He paid for the service up front."

"Well, of course, they have the resources. If it's a ruse, it's only natural that he would act like he was serious and pay the full rate."

Titus spied the rook nestled in the back of his brain and wondered how that piece might be used when the game got hot. He thought about the representation of the castle as a blocking tool, a way to hide something that was valuable to him. This shyster sitting across from him might serve him as more than just an information conduit, he thought. There would be loyalty tests to be performed in the future, but for now, Leo Rascone would not be given a position at the back of the board. He would have to graduate from being anything more than a pawn in the short term.

If Impala was actually going to try to pull this off amidst what was sure to be rabid opposition, what should he do? What was the most effective countermeasure?

Titus's first thought was to act as if he didn't care what Impala did. He knew that one of the primary reasons that Captain Brassey was pulling this stunt was to get under his skin. Step one was to act like the whole endeavor was okay with him and his kind.

Step two might be encouraging the other wards to go along with Brassey's desires and accept this deviation from tradition. Now, that would shock the shit out of those Impala assholes.

Titus would have time to formulate his plan well before the meeting of the rules committee. He wanted to have options though, and to accomplish this he would need the lawyer.

"So I need you to do me favor," Titus said.

"What?"

"Strictly on the QT. Find out where Mustang might find a driver of their own."

Leo had to hand it to the guy. He didn't fuck around when it came to taking advantage. He was not going to get caught with his pants down, this one.

"Sort of a back pocket deal, you know? Maybe I'll use him, maybe I won't," Titus added.

Leo could only nod at that point. Yeah, this guy definitely had his shit together.

For Titus's part, he was just beginning to draft his plan. He didn't even have the pencil out or the piece of paper on the table, but he wanted as many variables in play as possible before he started to sketch. As for the lawyer, this was a good test. Would the information that he was also seeking a driver from the outside come back to him through a leak? How thoroughly would the lawyer scour his sources to come up with a good candidate? Would it be better than the guy Impala was seeking?

"Oh yeah, and lay the groundwork for the immigration proceedings in case we find somebody who fits the bill."

"Okay," Leo said.

"It's going to be an interesting next couple of months," Titus said.

The day was at hand. John awoke on a Potluck Tuesday, stumbled over to his dictionary, and flipped open to a random page. He closed his eyes and aimed the point of his finger at the lower part of the page where the unused words lingered. He thrust his pointer down to the page but missed the lower section. Instead he lassoed a word from the more common usage part of the page: "veridical." The definition read, "Truth-telling or truthful," but it was an example that caught his eye and infused him with purpose as he went about preparing for the school day.

"Veridical" was used in the example denoting a veridical hallucination. A "veridical hallucination" was explained as "a hallucination corresponding with or indicating some real event, as when the apparition of an image of an absent person is coincident with his death."

During his sets of push-ups and sit-ups, he tried to conjure something akin to an apparition of his love, but he realized that it was nothing more than a fantasy. That was the problem, he thought. Everything that ruled his world lacked the sheen of reality. The dream of a romance with Rebecca, the dream of leading a team of bruisers in a future punch-out, and the dream that his manhood would arrive soon were nothing more than amorphous ideas that he seemed to have little control over.

Now was the time to enter an era of decisiveness. Living in a fantasy world had its benefits; there was no chance of being hurt either physically or emotionally, but he had tired of that alternate universe and the fact that he could not qualify it as real or actualized.

Today would be the day that he would announce to his love and the world his intentions. Today would be the day that augured the angle of his future.

With all of the affirmations urging him on, with all of the circulating hormonal activity affecting his judgment, he became hell-bent on staking his claim the moment he saw Rebecca sitting quietly in her first class, studying the material that was sure to be on the morning's quiz. She had returned to the classroom the Monday after the dance, and thanks again to Maxine, her mother, she hadn't missed a beat in the composition of her education.

The clock was ticking. The bell would be ringing the class hour into session in fifty seconds. She looked up from her notes, mentally tried to lock the precepts into her memory, and found John standing in front of her desk.

"Hey, there," she said.

He smiled, leaned down, and kissed her with an open mouth.

The shock of the moment was lost only on the one who had premeditated the event. Rebecca's eyes widened, and she stared straight into the face of a boy who had obviously become detached from the planet. His eyes were shut tightly, as if the preservation of the moment and not the actual act was paramount. Her first thought was, *Is this going to end soon?*

When the girl in the back of the class screamed that the math teacher's arrival was imminent, Rebecca tried to pull away. There would be no time for any words to pass between them, as the teacher, Mr. Yoder, grabbed John by his shirt collar and yanked him away from Rebecca.

"Just what the hell do you think you are doing, Brassey?"

John was prepared to announce to Mr. Yoder, the class, and the entire community of Impala that he was in love with this girl, but Mr. Yoder was pushing him toward the door in an effort to give him the bum's rush.

"I want to state for the record . . ." John began.

Rebecca cringed, but gratefully he never got his announcement out. Mr. Yoder clamped his hand over his mouth and began the forced escort to the vice principal's office.

Rebecca's visceral response to the kiss and the aborted attempt at his profession of love told her all she needed to know about the way she actually felt. She did not want this, and the sooner John knew that, the better.

With his butt glued to the creaky wooden chair, the security guard keeping watch as they waited for Vice Principal Flynn to finish making his between-class rounds, John was exultant. For the first time, he felt truly alive. He felt in touch with all of the things that had been written, filmed, and recorded extolling the wonders of love.

Another student, an acquaintance, crossed toward him from down the hall.

"Zhe shi zenme nui shi?" (What's going on?)

"Wow en le yige nuhai." (I kissed a girl.)

"Liang, John." (Cool, John.)

The VP was in no mood to allow this particular affront to pass with impunity. Yelling "Fuck Mustang" was one thing, but this could put the school in jeopardy from a legal standpoint. John was informed that if the young lady who was the recipient of his behavior disclosed that his advance was uninvited, he would likely be expelled. In any event, his parents would be notified of the indiscretion.

John didn't give a damn if his parents knew. And the "recipient" wouldn't be complaining. He knew that for a fact.

———

After that dinner with Titus, Leo had returned to his office with his blood chemistry altered by not only the wine, but also the excitement and anticipation that he was finally going to be part of something tangible in this claustrophobic protectorate. Maybe the deal he had struck was layered with Faustian overtones, but he knew that if he were going to be a whore, he would have no better john than Titus O'Keefe. All of the other wards lacked the stability that Mustang had, and Titus wasn't going anywhere for a good long while.

It was truly serendipitous that on his return, he found two notes on his desk that had been left by his secretary.

One was a message from the tracker stating that he believed that he had found the subject of the Impala captain's interest.

The other was from a man by the name of Udo Lewandowski, a security consultant from C-town. Mr. Lewandowski was requesting a return call from Leo at his earliest convenience.

SEVENTEEN

FOUND

Another week of Joe's life passed. He had given up on all of the routines that had functioned as distractions during his stay at the monastery. He had given up his walks down the hall to sit in solitude in the walled garden. He had given up viewing and assessing the daily bouts from behind the two-way glass in the observation room. And he had given up trying to figure out why he felt so fucking dead inside.

He sat alone in his cell and thought about where he might be headed next. His mental compass was pointing him in the direction of heading back out into the wilderness. What he would do once he left the monastery was still to be determined, but he knew it would involve the skills he had spent the bulk of his life honing. Deep down, he was afraid of losing the razor's edge that his mind and body had developed from its constant brushing against the strop that represented his need to exterminate Redeemers.

These thoughts of heading back out to continue his work without pay, to essentially be a zealot, began to buoy him above his mire.

He was keenly aware that his fanaticism was based in his all-encompassing desire to avenge. It comforted him to know he wasn't just a mindless killer; there was a basis for his desires, and it was rooted in this need to correct more than one wrong.

He spied the two items sitting atop his bedside table, the two items he had liberated from his lair back in Aldine: the hospital band and the cameo. It was Redeemers who had killed the previous owner of those items. It was Redeemers who had killed nearly all of his partners. And it was Redeemers who were responsible for the end of his marriage. The foundation was there. He wasn't just some savage butcher.

He rose from the bed and exited his cell. In the warm-up area—just outside the room where the daily bouts were contested—Joe found Mohammed readying a group of twelve-year-olds for a sparring session.

"I need my guns," Joe said.

"Of course, Lord Smith."

The mention of his name with the reverent modifier caused every one of the students to snap their heads in Joe's direction. It was probably the last thing that Joe wanted to see. He honestly felt that he was no more worthy of deification than the janitor who cleaned the bathroom in his cell, or the monastery's dog that often knelt at his feet hoping to get a bite of his dinner.

"I'll be in the garden," Joe said as he shuffled away at a pace repellently commensurate with the energy of the attention that the youngsters had placed on him.

The guns were delivered, and Joe went about stripping and cleaning each one. As he begin to break down the Howa, a cherry blossom, severed from its mooring by a sudden zephyr, floated down into the breech.

"Ohka," Joe said to himself, invoking the Japanese word for the petals that found their way into area between the barrel and the firing pin.

He searched his memory to try to remember how he knew that word. What tumbled back at him was the story of Japanese aviator Lt. Commander Goro Watamura that Master Casey had used to illustrate the concept of commitment to duty when Joe was probably no more than ten years old.

As he picked the blossom out of the breech, he tried to give the story context now that it could be filtered by his experiences as an adult. Would the morals and ethics contained within the text hold up to the heightened scrutiny that naturally came with living these last twenty years? Would he come to the same conclusions? Twenty years. Fuck.

———

It was one of those days in the summer in Big D where venturing outside had its perils. The death toll from the protracted heat wave that had begun in early August was approaching the thousand-person mark. This had been the pattern the last couple of years, as the average temperature had bumped up a full four degrees in a twenty-year span. Couple that statistic with the power restrictions, the ambling pace of the retrofitting, and the lack of good old common sense, and an environment was created that often led to the morgue at Baylor University Hospital having to withstand critical mass.

There had been an argument inside the Smith household that morning as Joe and his father prepared for the trip down to St. Michael's for Joe's Saturday examination. Eileen was worried that if their transportation convoy should become stalled out in the heat of the day, they might not be able to survive. She also made mention of the facility at St. Michael's and commented that they did not have any form of air conditioning.

Joe Sr. did not want to deviate from the routine, as he knew the precautions that one must take on a professional basis. He had spent a significant portion of his work life fighting fires, and before that, he had served many a military tour in the south Asian desert where the average summer temperatures were much hotter than the readings that pegged the thermometer on a Big D afternoon.

As his wife harangued him, he continued to silently gather the things that his son needed for his test. Finally, when he felt that she had exhausted all of the negatives, he spoke.

"I appreciate your concern, dear, but we will be fine. Look, you trust me to go to work every day and return alive. Trust that this will happen for us today," Joe Sr. said.

"I don't trust that you will return alive when you go to work, I pray that you will," she said.

"Okay, pray then."

That put the brakes on the discussion but didn't entirely throw the momentum of her anger into park.

"I need to have some say here," she pleaded.

"Sweetie, we're going. This is his graduation day. He has a commitment to duty. That's the only thing that has to be understood. Besides, are you really going to want to deal with the repercussions if you tell him that he can't go take his final examination?"

She did not.

Obviously, similar antagonistic conversations between husband and wife had been replicated throughout the enclave, and in most instances, the spouse who was advocating that their child shouldn't travel in the searing heat won the debate. Of the five youths scheduled to participate in the graduation examination, only Joe and an eighteen-year-old girl, Melody, showed up at the assigned time.

This created a conundrum for Master Casey. To have a ten-year-old boy spar with a teenage girl was not the problem; it was that he knew that the young boy would balk when it came to showing his full potential for fear that he might hurt the girl.

There was no question that the boy would graduate. He could actually be moved up more than just the single belt that was on the line here. As the fathers moved into the observation room, the master took his two students aside.

"You will not need to spar today," he said.

Both of the kids were shocked. So much work had gone into preparing for the final. The master led them out into the garden and had them sit amidst the cooling humidity that the fountain provided.

"Your graduation will not be based on your physical abilities. You have already shown me through your practice that you have reached the competency level required to move on to the next level. Instead, I am going to tell you a story, and after, I will ask you a series of questions. This, and this alone, will determine whether or not you advance."

The parents in the fan-cooled observation room were confused. The two middle-aged men wondered where their children had gone.

"Well, this is weird," Melody's father said.

"All we can do is trust him, I guess," Joe Sr. said. "We've come this far."

The men drank their tea and waited for the examination to commence, but no one would be entering the dojo this time.

Out in the garden, the master noticed that the boy had slid to the end of the fountain and was staring intently at him, waiting to absorb the story. *Good God, this kid is intense*, the master thought. He had never had a student like him and doubted that he ever would again.

"Twenty years ago, before the two of you were born, I came here to St. Michael's. I was confused and unsure of what would happen in the future. Someone told me that I should come here. But when I arrived, I wasn't comfortable that this was where I should be. Thankfully, my friend, Master Mohammed, told me that if I wanted answers, this place was as good as any to start."

The master retrieved a cushion from one of the chairs and sat cross-legged on the ground.

"The head priest at the time was an older Japanese man by the name of Ichiro Nakamura, and he immediately took me under his wing. With his guidance we built the dojo and started the monastery. Father Ichiro once told me a story about his father and the man who saved his life, and it is the story that I want to tell you now."

The master checked in with his students. He noticed that the boy was rapt and the girl seemed bored.

"Before Father Ichiro's father got married and had a family, he was a pilot in the Japanese Navy during the war with America many, many years ago. It wasn't going well for the Japanese. After years of battle, the Americans were on the verge of attacking their homeland. In desperation, the Japanese put together a group of pilots who would fly their planes as if they were bombs. They called these pilots kamikaze, which in Japanese means 'divine wind.' Father Ichiro's father was assigned to be a member of a group of pilots who would fly a new plane, the Ohka. 'Ohka' means cherry blossom in Japanese. This plane was the first rocket-powered plane to be built by the Japanese, and the pilot had but one purpose: to fly the plane into a ship."

"That's stupid. He would die," the girl said.

"Yes, of course. All of these pilots were willing to die for their country," the master said.

"Well, that seems stupid," said Melody.

"Shhh . . ." the boy said to his classmate.

"I don't have to shush," she said indignantly.

Before they could get much further with their sniping, the master clapped his hands. The clapping of the hands was the most serious of rebukes and caused the two students to freeze in place.

"We will have a discussion later. I will now finish the story. Where was I?"

"The cherry blossom?" the boy asked.

"Right. The thing about the Ohka was that it had to be carried by a bigger plane—it couldn't take off on its own—and as I said, it didn't need to make a conventional landing. Father Ichiro's father's leader was man named Goro Watamura, and it was his job to fly the plane that would deliver the Ohka. Lt. Commander Watamura felt bad that his job was to take men to die. He was supposed to fly out toward the enemy, drop the 'cherry blossom,' and then fly back and get another pilot and another Ohka. That he was not flying the Ohka himself, something he was prepared to do, was very upsetting to him. To carry these brave men to their deaths made him feel like a coward. So, he vowed to his wife and family that when he dropped off the first Ohka, he would follow his fellow pilot down to his death and crash into the ship as well. He told no one else of his plans."

The master could see that the boy was thinking about the significance of this choice. The girl was as impatient as she had been before, and the master knew it was because she hadn't come here to hear some cockamamie story about Japanese suicide pilots—she wanted to fight. Her enthusiasm for combat was partly why the examination had morphed from a bout to this exercise. Fighting for pleasure was not a part of the discipline.

"So what happened?" the boy asked.

"Well, nothing works out the way you think it will. Lt. Commander Watamura took off with the first Ohka and the pilot. We'll never know what would have happened because American fighter planes shot down Lt. Commander Watamura's plane before the Ohka was ever released."

"So he died anyway," Melody harrumphed.

"Yes."

"Okay, what are the questions?" she asked.

"Why did you say that this man saved Father Ichiro's life?" Joe asked.

Joe wanted the mystery solved. He'd been waiting for the solution since the master presented it as the basis of the story.

"It was Father Ichiro's father who was waiting to go second. He stood on the runway of the airbase for four hours preparing to die until he found out that his leader would never return to take him to his duty. By dying, the leader had saved his life."

What followed were a series of questions to test their comprehension. The boy retained every bit of the minutia presented in the retelling. The girl's responses were weak, but passable. When the discussion turned to the parables and morals to be gleaned from the tale, the boy spoke first.

"I think you told us this story because the Japanese were America's enemy, but you spoke of them as heroes. To be good in our work, we must understand how our enemy might see things so that we can gain an advantage," the boy said.

The master hadn't thought about that one. That wasn't the reason he told the story, but in future retellings, he would be sure to include that under the heading of themes.

"What else?" the master asked.

Melody didn't have a response. She started picking at a scab on her arm.

"Is the story about feeling bad that you might be the reason that someone gets hurt?" Joe asked.

"Yes, that's part of it," the master said.

"So instead of letting anyone else get hurt, he promised that he would hurt himself first?" Joe offered.

"That's it," the master said.

"Are we done?" Melody asked.

The master momentarily thought that maybe he wouldn't pass the teenager onto the next level. She was a fierce competitor, someone who excelled in technique and power, but her mind was muddled and distracted.

"I need you to respond to the story," the master said to the girl.

"I told you that I thought it was stupid. Why would this man kill himself—for his country? That seems dumb. He had a family and a wife."

"Okay, good. That's good. Let's discuss this in terms of duty. His job was to take men to their deaths."

This explanation made young Joe uncomfortable. To him, it was as if Master Casey had changed the story.

"His job was to take men to do their jobs. Their job was to fly their planes into a ship," Joe said.

"And die," Melody said.

"But their job . . ."

"Was to die!" Melody screamed.

"Okay, they died. But it wasn't their job," Joe said.

Again the master wondered where all of this wisdom came from. He had met the parents and he was sure that the talent this kid displayed on a regular basis must be innate. Nothing about the parents seemed remarkable to him. Joe looked up to Melody.

"I'm just saying that they had a job to do," Joe said.

The two students looked at each other for moment. Master Casey couldn't quite see if anything passed between the two that resembled respect. Joe seemed intent on her understanding the point he was trying to make, and she just wanted the whole thing to be over. Casey felt that the conversation had completed its cycle. Whatever morals were attached to the story would either be digested over time, or not.

"We're done. Congratulations, you have both moved to the next level," the master said.

———————

Joe rubbed the diaphanous panes of the cherry blossom between his fingers. Maybe his memory had distorted the actual text in his recollection of the story, but he now felt humiliated in the face of the heroics that the Lt. Commander had displayed. In his recent work life, he had been the opposite—the leader who had seen his subordinates vanquished and who had simply moved on to the next task. He had chalked it up to their inexperience or the rigors of the employment, and he had never entertained the idea that he had any responsibility in their demise.

But that supposition was wrong. Any objective observer would have seen that his assistants commonly took unnecessary risks in an attempt to emulate the abilities of their boss. In almost every case, those risks resulted in their maiming or their death.

He took the disassembled guns back to his room and went in search of Master Casey. He found him in his office, napping at his desk.

Watching the elderly man sleep, his eyes twitching with dreams of pleasure or horror, Joe decided that his needs could wait. He perused the bookshelf, figuring that he might sit and read something until the old guy came to.

There were books from a wide array of subjects, including religion, martial arts, and strangely, the theater arts. As he reached to pluck a copy of the play *Long Day's Journey into Night* by Eugene O'Neill off the shelf, he was struck by the presence of a large glossy trade paperback that occupied a place in the line just above the booklet he was removing.

To say he was shocked to think that the master possessed such a volume would have been an understatement of mammoth proportions. The only explanation could be related to the story of Lt. Commander Watamura and the need to understand the motives and nature of the enemy. He pulled the worn text out of its place among the other religious writings and thumbed through the pages. There were many instances of underlining and notes in the margins. *Holy shit*, Joe thought. *What the hell is going on here?*

"What do you have there?" asked a gravelly voice from the area of the desk.

Joe turned and faced his recently woken mentor and held up the book he had pulled from the shelf. It was copy of *The New Testament for Now* by St. Horace. It was the tome known to be the bible of the Redeemers.

"Huh, forgot I had that," Casey said with a smile.

Joe couldn't speak. He walked over to the desk and tossed the book on the surface. Casey picked it up and opened it.

"This was a long time ago," Casey began, "in a another galaxy, in another world."

He continued to muse over some of the notes he had scribbled throughout the text, reacting by shaking his head in wonder or smiling about the extremes of his youthful brio.

"Goes to show that life is a process, you know? I do have to give myself credit in that the quest for self-authenticity has been a successful one."

His index finger pointed at the tattered text.

"Now, this period of my life was an example of the absolute opposite. This was a person who was still craving ego gratification and financial wealth. I'd been going downhill for a long while. But this was the absolute bottom. It got so bad during this time, and I was so out of touch with the reality of what I was doing—who I intrinsically embodied—that I fear I might have become mentally ill. I began to hear voices. Well, one voice. The same voice that ironically brought me to this place."

He stopped and had one of those moments of clarity that designated the entire journey as a worthwhile enterprise. If this was the process that was required to bring about the synthesis of his current being, so be it, Casey concluded.

The questions formulating in Joe's mind began to pulse so strongly that he imagined that his brain had become an anvil and each new question was accompanied by the foundry-like bang of a maul.

"Sit down, Joe," Casey said.

Joe half-staggered to the wooden chair that was aligned perpendicular to the desk and plopped down. He suddenly felt weird making eye contact with the man who had been his teacher, his role model, and, by all accounts, a surrogate parent. How could his master be connected to the Redeemers?

"You have questions?" Casey asked.

"I do," Joe said.

"I know that what you might be imagining appears extremely grave on the surface. I know that you have a righteous axe to grind against these people. I dare say that your motivation to hinder these nuts might be shared by more than a few, but your desire to pursue them relentlessly is unmatched."

"What is your connection?"

"I just want to you know that my involvement predates anything that you've had to deal with. Take what I say in as detached a manner as possible. I am but a character in this tale, a character that no one would remotely relate to what I am now."

Joe saw that he was speaking somewhat in platitudes with special attention paid to this self-absolving preamble. *This must be mind-blowing*, he thought.

It was. Casey told him the entire tale of his return to Kansas after an abortive attempt at an acting career out on the West Coast. He told him about the strange man from the prison who hired him to play the pastor of the church that was being erected to pay homage to the serial killer, Russell Reading, aka the Redeemer. And he told him about the spoken directives from the archangel St. Michael that initially committed him to the cause, and later bade him to come to this very church outside the walls of Big D to establish the monastery. He told him of his years of rigorous study before the Shaolin School was opened, the ebbing of St. Michael's voice in his head, and the revelation of his true calling in this world.

He also told him of the irony associated with his star pupil taking on a life mission that involved wiping these lunatics from the earth. This wasn't the intent of the enterprise here at St. Michael's, but Casey couldn't help but admit that knowing that Joe was out there, disposing of this mess, gave him a certain comfort.

"But you created this," Joe said, pointing to St. Horace's text.

"Not really. I facilitated it. I exacerbated it. I didn't create it. There was a Zeitgeist out there at the time that left a whole portion of the country open and vulnerable to ideas that were deranged. Many screwed up people were trying to tap into it for monetary gain, including the people who hired me. Some of those sheep became Redeemers. Some became Barbers. Others became what they became. At the time, many believed the world was going to come to an abrupt end on the day you were born."

"I'm reminded of that fact every time I have to give out information related to my birth date," Joe said wryly.

"In the end, the people who employed me turned out to be some really bad guys. I feared for my life and ran away as fast as I could."

Joe knew there were parts of the story that were missing. Like the retelling of the tale about Lt. Commander Goro Watamura and his relationship to Father Ichiro, maybe Casey's terse recollections were meant to convey a larger meaning than just the listing of a couple of highlights from the master's biography. And yet, Joe was still blown away by the few facts that Casey had related. There wasn't enough empty space in Joe's brain to cram in all of this new data, let alone recalibrate his opinions about the master that were already stored there.

"There's something bothering you?" Casey asked.

"Yeah. I can't understand why you would do something like that."

"I've already told you. My priorities at the time were petty and vile. I had been through a period of disappointment, and I took an opportunity that would satisfy those base instincts. It's not something that can be judged by the likes of you—you gratefully lack that type of life experience. Thankfully, you have lived almost all of your life with the discipline. I had to come to it."

That much was as true as a diamond blade. Joe had lived nearly his whole life with the precepts of a discipline that included the basic fundamental of "be not there." Isn't that what had gotten him into so much trouble? This discipline, this way of being, was meant to alight amidst the vagaries of life, not take the form of a fucking indoctrination. How does one unwind it all and start over? *I'm nothing more than a robot*, Joe thought. *I'm a machine, crafted by that dude across the desk from me.*

"Why did you want to see me?" Casey asked.

Joe finally locked eyes with him. In that blinking second, Casey saw how truly damaged and confused his protégé was. There was so much loss to behold in Joe's eyes. Casey tried to see some light at the end of Joe's being. It was like staring down a mineshaft, dropping a pebble, and waiting for it to hit the bottom. In that moment, Casey would have to admit that—looking into all the darkness that represented Joe's current essence—he was not likely to ever hear the sound of that stone making contact with a floor.

"I wanted to ask you about the Ohka," Joe said.

Casey took a moment to put the request into context.

"The story about the Kamikazes that you told me when I was a child," Joe offered as a refresher.

"Oh, of course. God, that was a long time ago. I can't believe that you even remember that," Casey said.

Casey could see that Joe had not only remembered it, but was parsing it anew.

"What did you want to know?"

"The guy that got shot down, the guy that was supposed to come back and get Father Ichiro's father and take him to his death, do you really think he would have done what he said and crashed his plane instead of bringing any more young men to die?" Joe asked.

It was a question with no correct answer, one that asked only for speculation. Casey began to see that a lot would hinge on how he responded to Joe. He began to formulate the most laic response, completely devoid of any greater message. When he failed to come up with anything that would qualify in all the parameters he had set to limit any controversy, he said, "I don't know, Joe. What do you think?"

Joe had always believed in the myth that Lt. Commander Watamura was a man of his word. If he told people, especially his family, that he was going to disobey orders and honorably kill himself, then that was what he was going to do.

But the effort of living one's life had a way of distorting one's principles. If one includes the path-altering experiences like the end of a marriage, the death of children, the death of friends and compatriots, and the fact that the bastard principal in this case, Joe, had basically been abandoned by his mother, then one must reassess any conclusions one makes in regards to another's commitment to duty.

One can only affirm what they would do. At this point, Joe hadn't a clue.

"Do you think Lt. Commander Watamura had been brainwashed?" Joe asked.

"That is an interesting question, Joe. Do you think that he might have been? Do you think that is the only way he could have seen this task as a duty?"

Knowing what he knew now, Joe wondered if this guy, Casey, really got what he was asking here. Was he so clueless as to not see the provocation in regards to the use of a form of the term "brainwash?"

Joe did know one thing. He had to get out of here. It was going to take awhile to rethink this relationship that he had put so much faith in—this incontrovertible link with his master—and he knew that doing that without the perspective of distance would be impossible. At this point, the ledger was tilted to the negative. The master's tally of demerits had suddenly filled the entire page.

It was not the sort of thing Joe needed to experience presently—his teacher slipping off his vaunted perch and becoming human. It might have been a process of inevitability as it is in most of these types of relationships, but he didn't need for it to happen now. Maybe this was a form of graduation. Maybe once he shed the shackles of this hierarchy, he would be free to devolve into the person he was supposed to become before the training waylaid him.

As he walked back to his cell to gather his things—making sure to avoid any eye contact with the students and staff—he became exceedingly dubious that his sense of humanness could be restored. There was a flood raging under the bridge, and he was certain that a cresting wave would break over the span and toss him into the roiling river. No dam was going to stem the tide; one could only make the river deeper and wider. He was, by all accounts, fucked.

EIGHTEEN

BIG D

GETTING INTO BIG D had become slightly less difficult than the last time Joe had sought entry. The full-body scans were not required if one had the modicum of identification to prove that one belonged.

Joe was stationed in the long queue that had been designated as "tourists only." There was a subcategory for those who had pre-applied for a visa, but Joe shuffled along with those hoping to get in on the spur of the moment. Having decided to make the trip within the last two hours did not allow him access into the shorter of the lines, even if he had been a resident for the first twenty-one years of his life.

Joe watched the sloppiness in the procedure being meted out by the Dallas Security Authority and knew that they were only one intra-anal explosive detonation away from their having to wipe up a lot of blood and viscera while placing tags on the body parts of the deceased. Only then would the authority's decreasing vigilance that had resulted in this lax treatment return to the correct protocol of zero-tolerance and hyper-scrutiny.

It was a DSA officer, Teddy McMahon, trolling the line profiling possible infidels, who noticed his former classmate holding his paperwork along with a red receipt signifying that the man applying for entrance had weapons impounded.

"J-dog?" Teddy asked.

"Hey, Teddy bear."

"What the fuck, man?"

The two former teammates sized each other up. Joe looked nothing like the buff, golden boy wide receiver he once resembled, and Teddy had grown nearly double the girth he had once sported as the starting left tackle.

"Where did you go?" Teddy asked.

Joe tried to think of an answer that would make sense. The truth would be a saga worthy of a hardcover. The answer he wanted to give could be written on a piece of scrap paper.

"You know, working," Joe said quickly.

"No, I mean, you must weigh like 150, am I right? What happened?"

"You know how it is," Joe said with a chuckle. "I need some of my mom's cooking."

"And quick, my brother."

Teddy looked around to see where his partners were stationed.

"Come on, you're in the wrong line," he said.

He grabbed Joe by the arm and marched him over to the "merchants only" line. There was only one other person going through the entrance procedure. As the farmer gathered his paperwork and headed to the next level of screening, Teddy shoved Joe in front of the pretty female officer.

"Rachel, sweetheart, this here is Josiah Smith, Fire Marshal Smith's son. He's in town to visit his folks, he's a former resident, and he ran back the kickoff with no time on the clock that beat Knollwood when we won the city championship. I, of course, threw the key block."

"When are you guys going to live in the present?" Rachel asked with a grin. "That was a long time ago."

"Seems like yesterday to me, right Joe?"

"That's because you quit growing mentally after you graduated from high school. Obviously not physically, but mentally," Rachel said with a twist of a sarcastic knife.

"Rachel went to Knollwood," Teddy said to Joe in an aside.

"But not in the 'good old days.' I just graduated two years ago, and, for some reason, all of your heroics never trickled down through the years."

"Figures. You kids have no sense of history," Teddy purred at her.

Joe hadn't heard banter between the sexes like this for an awfully long time. The disorientation that he exhibited by his reaction to the flirtations lobbed at him by the stable owner down in Crabb's Prairie remained. His immediate reaction to this exchange was to think that this was going to end badly for one of them. Out in the wilderness, conversations with the hint of contentiousness like this usually led to bloodshed. One was careful with the words and tones that were chosen.

"So, sweetheart, could you just stamp his visa and let him be on his way?" Teddy asked in that way that suggested the act was a *fait accompli*.

Rachel scanned the vicinity for her superiors. Every one of the senior officers must have been having lunch or using the facilities.

"You're not going to do anything stupid, like blow something up, are you?" she asked Joe.

"Hmmm . . . I kind of had my eye on placing a few explosives in the trophy room at Knollwood," Joe said in an effort to blend into the repartee.

Teddy laughed. Rachel was looking at Joe, slightly unsure that there was a joke there. Teddy picked up on her low level of consternation.

"He's joking, honey. He scored the winning touchdown, but the Knollwood QB had a big day and was awarded the MVP. It hangs in the trophy case by the gym at your alma mater."

The spell had been broken. Now it was time for business. Rachel took the paperwork from Joe and briefly scanned through the two pages. She stamped the form with a device that placed a green hologram on the front page.

"You carrying anything that you need to declare?"

Joe only had two things in his pocket, the hospital bracelet and the cameo. He shook his head before hoisting his duffel bag up on the counter.

Rachel didn't really look inside before adding the same green hologram to the label tag.

"Don't throw this away. You won't be able to get back out without it."

"Thanks," Joe said.

"No problem."

"Yeah, thanks, honey," Teddy said.

"You're welcome, Officer McMahon," she said with a girlish grin.

"Where else do I need to go?" Joe asked her.

"You are free, Mr. Smith. I could send you to "body cavity search," but only if you're into that sort of thing."

"No, I'm good."

"Thanks again, darling," Teddy said.

She waved them away. Joe and Teddy parted at the gate. As Joe walked into the city, he could here Rachel yell across the quad, "Knollwood rules!"

It was a pretty good distance from the south gate up to his parent's residence on the shores of White Rock Lake, but Joe did not begin that journey. He headed northwest instead of northeast. Joe could have gotten through immigration effortlessly by just contacting his parents beforehand and requesting that they call in a pass, but he was tentative and it left open the possibility that this particular trip might not include a visit with the folks.

Whenever he envisioned that reunion, his feelings listed toward avoiding it altogether. He just wasn't in the mood for anything that reeked of the possibility of emotion. Four plus solid years of no contact had created a gulf for him that he was not sure he was willing to cross. It might just be better for the current state of his psyche if he slipped into town, took care of the business that beckoned him here, and exited as stealthily as he arrived.

He carried no animosity for his parents. They had done the very best they could with the tools they possessed. His mother could have been less over-protective and smothering, and his father could have been more understanding of the uniqueness that he displayed as a child instead of leading him into the discipline that muted many of those qualities. It wasn't like they knew better. It was what it was.

The last two times he had seen them was approximately five years before, six weeks apart, on the dates that marked the burials of his two sons. Since that was their last frame of reference about him, he knew any type of communion would start with that remembrance, and he really had no desire to go there.

It took him almost two hours to make his way up to Baylor University Hospital on foot. There were plenty of pedi-cabs and decrepit buses, but his pockets were empty of the currency required to purchase a fare.

During the trek, he passed many of the haunts that he had patronized during his youth. There were the virtual simulator arcades that he was sure still carried his initials as the high scorer. There was the park where he played youth soccer and the music store where he had taken trumpet lessons.

At the hospital, the elderly woman at the information desk proved to be of little help. Joe showed her the artifact hospital bracelet and asked if there was any way to find out the information stored in the different chips attached to the plastic. To the lady, it was an odd request—one that she had no experience in ever having to grant before.

When she said, "What exactly do you want?" for the fifth time, Joe knew that he would have to come up with an alternate strategy. He asked the lady for a hospital directory, hoping that the one doctor that he knew who used to practice there had not retired.

Dr. Dennis Harrington was the orthopedist who had set Joe's dislocated wrist after he fell off a horse at his first riding lesson not long after he turned six. Up until that time and since then, he had never had the occasion to stay even a minute in a hospital. It was a long shot, for sure.

He found that the good doctor was still affiliated with the hospital and that his clinic occupied half a floor in one of the low-slung buildings adjacent to the main towers. These bungalows had been built as temporary structures thirty years ago when a terrorist bomb destroyed most of the central buildings. Those structures were rebuilt, but as Big D continued to densify, the hospital decided to transform the temporary spaces into permanent facilities.

Doctor Harrington's receptionist had a better grasp of the present and went about verifying that the orthopod had, in fact, treated the patient who was standing in front of her window nearly twenty-five years before.

Joe held out the bracelet that had been marinating in his pocket since he left St. Michael's.

"I believe this is the bracelet that my mother had on when she gave birth to me in this hospital. She left not long after I was born and was killed when Redeemers stormed the community that she lived in. I'm trying to put together some type of history here, and if it wouldn't be too much trouble, would it be possible to download the information into your system? I'm hoping that something specific might be on this thing."

"Like what?" the receptionist asked.

"The name of my father. Uh . . . my mother's age when she had me. Any genetic abnormalities that I should be made aware of. Things like that."

These seemed to be legitimate requests, and the receptionist appeared to agree. She rose from her station and exited to the hallway. Not a minute later, Dr. Harrington came through the swinging doors.

"How's the wrist?" the doctor asked.

"Good. I guess you did your job. No complaints."

"No arthritis?"

"No."

"All right. You want to come on back? I'd love to have a look."

Joe acceded to his request, but he had no interest in knowing whether there was any abnormality in the way the joint had healed.

The wrist was scanned with a goggle device that produced an image of both the bone and the soft tissue in front of the doctor's eyes.

"Hmmm . . ." the doctor mused.

"What?"

"You don't feel any pain or stiffness?"

"No."

"Okay."

"Do you see something that indicates that I should?"

"A minor misalignment and fair amount of scar tissue. But if you've got no trouble, so be it."

Joe wasn't sure how to ingest that. He wondered—now that his consciousness had been altered by this new information—would he start to feel discomfort after all of these years?

It was a metaphor for his current state of mind. He realized that he had lived his whole life without any specific knowledge of his mother. Would things change if some of his questions were answered?

The receptionist entered the examination room and handed Doctor Harrington a series of printouts. The two health professionals shared a conspiratorial look before assessing how much of the information inked on the sheets of paper could be ethically divulged.

"So, what is it you wanted to know?"

"All of it."

The receptionist pointed at one of the lines of print.

"Jesus," Dr. Harrington said. "You were born on that fifteenth of March at 12:07 A.M.?"

"So I've been told."

"Did you know that a bomb had struck the tower that housed the obstetrics wing about seven minutes before?"

"Yeah, not in the moment. I'm not sure I had those cognitive abilities yet," Joe said with a smile.

"Well, of course . . ."

"I've been reminded of that occurrence through the years, though. The person who adopted me was one of the first responders."

"Jesus," Dr. Harrington repeated. "It's weird because I didn't make that connection until just now."

He held the pages for another moment. The information was from thirty years ago, the doctor thought. Whatever ethical limitations might have required censorship or the swipe of some black indelible ink had been diluted by the sheer amount of time that had transpired. He held out the pieces of paper and the bracelet to his former patient.

"Hope that's what you're looking for," he said.

Joe looked down at the first page of the printout. He wasn't sure if it was what he wanted, but he wasn't going to stand here, in this overly bright room, in front of these near-strangers, and go through it all.

"I'm sure that whatever is on here will be of great value to me and only me. I really appreciate the effort."

"You know, if you ever want to do some revisions on your wrist, I'd be more than happy to do them at no charge. I feel sort of responsible that it's not perfect."

"Yeah, I may take you up on that," Joe said.

He didn't mean it. Per his training, the word "perfect" wasn't part of Joe's vocabulary.

There was a small bar where Joe and his buddies had celebrated his bachelor party just down the street from the hospital. Since it was still early afternoon, Joe suspected that the place would be virtually empty and that the proprietor wouldn't mind if all he cared to imbibe was a glass of water. His assumptions on both accounts were accurate.

He sat at a table over by the front window and unfurled the pages of data that had been extracted from the bracelet. All of the information on the first page had been printed onto a pre-prepared form. The preset boxes were organized into the categories such as patient's name, sex, age, insurer, etc.

In the name box the listing read, "Katherine Pepper Harris." Her age was listed as twenty-three years old. Her blood type was listed as A+. There was no indication of any pre-existing conditions. There was a box that detailed all of the dosages and time of administration of all pharmacological preparations that she had received during the time leading up to the delivery of her child. At the bottom of the form the delivery time was noted and the sex of the child was indicated using an x under the heading for male. The box listing the baby's name was left blank.

The second page was taken from another source, another chip, and was presented as a scan of her previous medical history. It showed digital and handwritten results of a physical examination from before her pregnancy. Another paragraph showed no anomalies or annotations during the prenatal phase of her pregnancy. There were no results for any prenatal diagnostic testing due to the patient's declinations to submit to either CVS testing or amniocentesis.

The third page was from yet another source and was titled to reflect details related to the patient's husband and child's father.

Joe looked around the room. There were a couple of sots putting the brakes on the onset of their DTs by greeting the day with a pitcher of tap beer.

All of the information that he had perused to this point, other than the medical jargon, had been passed down in some way by his parents over the term of his life. He knew his birth date, his gender, and his mother's name. He knew absolutely nothing about his father except that he died of pneumonia a day before he was born.

How the data about his father had been uploaded to one of the drives of the bracelet would always remain a mystery, but this piece of paper he was holding held the only information about the man who, Joe believed, provided some percentage of his DNA. There wasn't much that had been put into the system.

His name was Donald Cameron Harris. He was twenty-three years old when he passed. And he was a quadriplegic. His blood type was O-. Other than some test results related to the viral pneumonia he was carrying, some machine data outputs, and a notation signifying the gravity of his condition, there was no other information contained on the page he held in his barely trembling hand.

He drained the glass of water and took the empty up to the bartender. He thanked him for letting him hang around for a few minutes and exited onto Hampton Road into the heat of the mid-afternoon.

As he traveled north, he began to ponder the possibilities of anomaly associated with the blood types of his parents and tried to recall his knowledge of Mendelian genetics to determine if these two parents could produce a child that carried the blood type that he had tattooed onto his ankle when he was first hired by Tynan. Along with his employee number and department, the sub-dermal black ink also denoted his blood type as O+. Fuck. What was the relationship in regards to the possibilities given known alleles of both parents? He eventually became resolute that these two parents could produce a child with his blood type. But why was he even thinking about it? He had no knowledge pointing him toward the contrary, but something was lingering in the back of his mind. Maybe it was the fact that he had never known either of them. To him, they were only myths—ghost-like figures with no form other than perhaps a wisp of imagined smoke. Conjuring any physical specifics other than the statistics he had been given would have been impossible.

He was wandering now, maintaining a heading that was due north. He was approaching University Park, which was roughly the same latitude as his parent's house, now about seven kilometers to the east.

He happened on a youth baseball game that was being played on one of the smaller fields within a complex of meticulously manicured ball diamonds. The teams were made up of youngsters who couldn't have been more than nine or ten years old. Joe noticed that they had graduated to the protocol that allowed the kids to pitch to each other, the next step beyond either the coaches pitching or the kids hitting off a batting tee.

The pitcher in the blue uniform had just finished issuing a free pass to the third batter in a row. With the bases full, the player's coach had come out to the mound to adjust something in the pitcher's motion.

"Timmy's holding up his mitt as a target. Just hit the mitt," the coach was saying. "It's not that hard, son."

Joe knew different. He knew what to tell the kid because he had to learn the lesson himself. Joe visibly shook his head in the negative. You didn't tell the kid to "just hit the mitt," you told the kid to focus on a point somewhere beyond the mitt, ten feet beyond the mitt, and that he should follow through to that point. It was the same in the combat arts. You didn't just hit someone in the face; you went through the face and out the back of the skull. If you aimed at the face, your momentum would be slowing instead of accelerating. During that deceleration, the small muscles would have an opportunity to get involved and knock your aim off its intended target.

The kid walked in a run before hitting a batter with the very next pitch. When the coach returned to the mound to remove the kid from the game, the kid was sobbing. Joe followed his walk of shame to the dugout where the kid buried his tears into a towel.

Joe had a desire to go over to the cyclone fence enclosure and tell the kid to hang in there. He wanted to tell him that the next time things would be different. He wanted to tell him that no progress comes without a little pain, and that learning takes effort.

He began to advance to the area of the dugout. As he arrived, he saw the kid's father walking briskly toward the same spot he was headed to.

"Why are you embarrassing me?" the father said to his son.

The kid removed the towel from his face and looked plaintively at his old man.

"I'm sorry, Dad, I tried," the kid blubbered.

"I'm not embarrassed by your effort, son, I'm embarrassed that you're frigging crying about it," the father said.

And so it begins, Joe thought. This was one of the many tiny lacerations—one of those mild suppressions—that often led to a man's inability to exhibit emotion later in life. It was a fine line, but nothing was going to be learned here if that was the tack.

Joe thought about the moment that he had broken down after seeing the doe fawning in the meadow. He had bottled it all back up not long after that and had experienced not a single recurrence since. It was about avoidance. It was about resisting the pressure and pushing those things out of his mind, out of his reality. It was about maintaining an affiliation to the discipline.

He continued to watch the exchange between father and son and did his best to try not to imagine himself in a similar situation. Part of him wanted to tell the dad that at least he had a son, and that he should tread softly on his psyche, and part of him wished that he could have been that father, worrying about the mental state of his child, making it a goal to forge a man from the molten steel that all boys have buried inside of them.

NINETEEN

THE HOUSE ON WHITE ROCK LAKE

JOE WALKED THE seven clicks to his parent's home. He was neither dreading nor welcoming the event. He had lapsed back into that state that had carried him through all of the shit that he had witnessed and endured. The state that proclaimed, "Be not there."

He did harbor some curiosities as to the fortunes of the people who had raised him. He knew that up until the day that he'd left the house, the triangle that represented the three principals of the household was constantly shifting from isosceles to obtuse. If there was ever a time that the angles were equilateral, he could not recall it.

There were the dynamics between father and son, mother and son, and father and mother that consistently shifted in form, power, and intensity.

Initially, with Joe's birth mother in residence, this union took on the form of a rhombus. After her departure, the three-sided trilateral geometry began its oscillations between the three occupants in the residence.

The initial rent that occurred when Joe had married Cynthia allowed for the entrance of their daughter-in-law, and eventually their children, into a new model with two configurations, with Joe occupying two points, one in each. But when the younger family exiled themselves to Aldine, everything went a little screwy.

Left without the binding of their hypotenuse, Eileen and Joe Sr. were suddenly just straight lines. Intersection required effort, and neither seemed up for providing it.

Joe was aware that this state might have been only temporary—complicated by the situations revolving around the deaths of their grandchildren and the disappearance of their son's marriage—but instincts told him that divergence was their graphic trajectory, now and for the future.

The residence had been attended to during the years of his absence. Joe Sr. took pride in having the nicest yard and facade on the block. It was an abode befitting of the city's Fire Marshal, and the exterior represented methodical order and an invitation to enter.

But God forbid that anyone answered that amorphous request, for inside existed chaos.

Poor Eileen, so conscious in the past to medicate and care for the erratic nature of her mental health, had finally had her apple cart upset for good. Her doctors never attributed her decline to any specific event, but the loss of the boy she had raised to the violence of the wilderness was most certainly a huge factor.

As far as Eileen and Joe Sr. knew, their son had been dead for many years. When he first vanished from his home in Aldine—a few months after both his sons had perished—and commenced his reign of terror on the Redeemers, the parents tried to track him down. They questioned everyone who Joe had been connected to at all the points of his life. Casey and Mohammed provided nothing in the way of tangible information; they were as much in the dark as the inquisitors. The bureaucracy at Tynan and the clearances required to access any information about Joe's duties were denied to all who didn't need to know. Before long, the wife, Cynthia, had been declared dead by the Harris County authorities.

So, the Smiths retreated to their domicile on the shores of White Rock Lake and began the process of mourning the disappearance and likely demise of their adopted child. The divergence that had been held in abeyance during Joe's presence in their life began to accelerate in earnest. The separating lines were headed to infinity at light speed.

Joe Sr. spent most of his time at the firehouse, and Eileen spent her waking hours—which were few and far between—building little temples to honor her dead child and grandchildren.

All of that changed six days ago when a knock at the red oaken door reverberated through the halls of the house. When she answered, Eileen found a delivery agent, wearing a yellow merchant's hologram pass around his neck, holding out a sealed letter.

She took the piece of mail and laid it on the kitchen counter. She took a seat across the room in a chair where the fabric had frayed on the arms because she had spent many hours picking at it while she stared into the void and waited for her husband to return from his shift. Joe Sr. returned two days later.

When Joe Sr. found his wife frozen in a vegetative state, sopping with urine, he thought little of it. His intention was to grab a change of clothes, maybe have a shower, and return to work. He didn't even feel a need to acknowledge that he'd arrived.

Passing by her, he saw the letter on the counter and picked it up.

"Don't open it," she said in a breathless whisper.

"What is it?"

"It's him. It's about him. It's a death notice."

"How do you know?"

"I know."

Joe Sr. looked at his wife with all the pity he could muster and opened the letter. He scanned the first paragraph.

"He's alive," he proclaimed.

Eileen jumped up from the chair and grabbed the letter out of his hands. She read the contents in a quick yet deliberate manner.

"This is nothing more than an invitation. What makes you think he's alive?" she asked.

"Jesus Christ, it's in the first paragraph—the part about the writer's brother having met him just a month or two ago somewhere around Rubber City."

She slowly reread that part of the missive, capping the period of the sentence with a widening of her eyes and gulps of air.

"Is he coming here?" she asked.

"I don't know."

"If he's coming here, we need to prepare."

"Calm down, dear. All we have is a letter sent by someone in Motor City who thought that he might live here or happen by. My guess is that this person has left a lot of letters in every place that he could possibly be."

"This means he's alive, though?"

"Well, he was a couple of months ago."

"That's a start," she said.

"Jesus, Eileen, you smell. Go take a shower, for chrissakes."

"Of course, dear," she said as she headed down the hall.

Joe Sr. looked around the room. *What a fucking disaster*, he thought. He didn't think his son would be happening by any time soon, but if the notion became the spark to start the engine that could propel his wife to an emotional life that wasn't this, he was willing to play along. He grabbed some clothes and shaving lotion. Before he left, he carried the stained and worn chair outside and tossed it in his truck with the intention of disposing of it in the compacting incinerator at the firehouse.

The effects of each day after the letter's arrival could have been plotted on a graph that when connected would have resembled a camel's hump. The first few days were taken up with getting the house, and Eileen's mental state, into some semblance of order. After three days, she peaked, and the trend became a drudgingly swift descent back to a bottom that probably allowed for more depth than she had experienced before.

It was at this point that an overmedicated Eileen, through the fog, heard a key slip into the deadbolt of the front door. In her state, it was hard to comprehend the occurrence of this act—her husband was not due back for at least a day or two. When the open door revealed her son at the threshold, she collapsed to the ground.

Joe rushed to her side, saw that she had only fainted, removed her arm from under her side so that it wouldn't fall asleep, and went to the kitchen to get her a drink of water. He saw the opened letter on the counter.

"What happened?" she asked from her place on the floor.

"You passed out," Joe said.

"Oh Lord, I'm so embarrassed."

"About what?"

There was no answer to that question. Joe felt responsible and wanted her to know that he didn't see her swooning as some form of manipulation, though he was aware that this was the first in a litany of acts that she was sure to use in an effort to emphatically state that his absence had been hurtful to her. He decided to get the ball rolling on his mea culpa before she opted for an encore performance.

"I'm sorry, Mom, for not getting in touch. I have a lot of excuses, but none of them are worthy. I'm ashamed for having not contacted you through these years. I love you," he said as he helped her from the floor and into, what he noticed, was a brand-new chair, still swathed in its protective plastic.

All of the slights that had built up inside of her—an edifice of pain—began to crumble as if the structure had been erected with poorly mixed concrete and no rebar. She had her son back. Was it a dream? The drugs were supposed to take away the aberrations and chimeras, were they not?

She ran her hand across the skin and bones of his face. There was no dermal slack, and he looked nearly skeletal. When he smiled back at her, she began to sob. She was still crying when Joe Sr.'s voice squawked over the two-way.

"Eileen?"

He did this periodically to make sure that she was still among the living. He never divulged to anyone the narrative of some of his fantasies that spun a yarn where she didn't answer him back because she was no longer a part of the earth.

When Joe picked up the handset and answered the call, Joe Sr. thought there was something wrong with the connection.

"Hello? Who is this? What channel are you on?"

Joe could hear his father ask a subordinate if he'd been messing around with the radio.

"It's me, Dad," he said.

"Joe?"

"Yeah."

"I'll be right there," the fire marshal said.

Both Joe and Eileen could hear the handset on the other line clatter to the floor.

The reunion was officially on. For four days and nights they were a family again. It took a little time to catch up, a little time to sort through the feelings, but when Joe headed out to collect his weapons, catch a pre-paid transport to the north, and begin his next adventure, all parties shared the feeling that reconciliation had been achieved.

The tracker had caught another break. Stifled by the guards at the tract in Aldine, unable to collate any information from the subject's last known residence, he was at a crossroads. The chilly trail had finally been reduced to block ice. His first reaction was to throw in the towel, call his contractor, and confess that he had failed to complete the assignment.

The next morning he approached the guards at the Aldine enclave and asked to confirm that a Josiah Smith had once occupied a house within their community. Luckily, one of the day guards complied with his request by showing him the bound copy of the Harris County Records. Listed on the deed were the cosigners of the mortgage loan: Mr. and Mrs. Josiah Smith, Senior. Next to their names was an address in Big D.

The tracker decided to give it a final attempt and had the letter delivered to the parents via an inner-city courier service. He started his trek back to Motor City, prepared to tell his employer that he had been unsuccessful. He was prepared to return the fee, less expenses. He got the congratulatory message at the communication center of a transient camp on the outskirts of Decatur. The message read: "Stellar job. Subject en route." A notation at the bottom indicated that one Leo Rascone, Esq. had transmitted the missive.

The receptionist for Doctor Dennis Harrington was finishing her work for the day, sorting through her data requests, and passing the patient records back to the hospital's central data bank. Before she could leave for the weekend, she needed to download all of the histories for the upcoming week's appointments.

Her tasks complete, she closed out of all the windows on her monitor. In the upper left-hand corner, a single document remained. A click of curiosity revealed it to be the data she had pulled off the bracelet for the mysterious skinny man who had showed up anxious and without an appointment.

She was about to dump it in the garbage when something struck her as odd. "Katherine Pepper Harris," she read aloud.

She picked up the phone and punched in a number. A male voice answered with the word "gynecology" mumbled in rote.

"Hey, its Jackie King in Ortho. Is Katy on shift today?"

"I think she comes in around 8 P.M.," the voice said.

"Can I leave her a message?"

TWENTY

KATY

KATY RETURNED THE call from her friend Jackie King, Doctor Harrington's receptionist, the following day. It had been an exceptionally grueling evening in the obstetrics unit, with two breech pre-
sentations and five inducements. Someone had obviously screwed up
the scheduling, and the chaos engendered by the mistake made for an
evening of non-stop intensity.

The note, handed to her by the colleague who took the call, did
not specify the reason that Jackie wanted to talk to her, so Katy stuffed
it into the top pocket of her nursing greens and went about preparing
the delivery room for the evening's first arrival. The shit hit the fan
soon after.

Katy waited until the afternoon—until she had a full complement
of sleep after punching out at 8 A.M.—and called Jackie at home.

"Hey, it's Katy, what's up?"

"Hey, sweetie, it's probably nothing. It struck me as odd because
we've known each other for so long," Jackie said.

"Uh-huh."

"There was this strange . . . well, not strange . . . let's say, interesting man that came by the office yesterday, and he had this bracelet of a
patient from thirty years ago. He claimed the patient was his mother,
and I didn't think too much of it, though it was somewhat bizarre,
until I saw the name of the patient, and . . ."

"What was the name?" Katy asked, her voice trying to stay on a
calm pitch.

"Katherine Pepper Harris."

"And who is that?"

"Well, didn't you say your married name was Harris at one time
before you changed it?"

"Yeah," Katy said.

There was silence then. There would be no admission coming
from Katy. Not now. Not ever.

"You'd never said that you had a child."

"Because I didn't," Katy said.

"Yeah, I know. I mean, I would have known, I guess. I just thought
it was weird."

"Harris is a fairly common name."

"Yeah, I know that, but the address that was listed for this Mrs. Harris was from someplace in Kentucky. Didn't you come from there?"

Katy tried to keep the quaver rising up from her diaphragm free of the timbre of her voice. There were a couple of dots that could be connected: Jackie only had to look at the readout. The name of the city this Mrs. Harris claimed to hail from was the one Katy had used as the basis of her own last name.

"I don't know what tell you, Jackie. It is kind of weird, though, like you said."

"Yeah, it is."

Silence shrouded them again, but Katy was determined to shatter it, lest the quietude be construed as an acknowledgement that she might have something to actually confess to her friend. The kibosh had to be maintained; there was no other way.

"That's pretty strange, huh?" Katy asked in a folksy tone.

"Do you want a copy of the records?" Jackie asked.

"No, why? It's not me, Jackie."

"I know. Well, have a nice day off, Katy."

"You have a great weekend yourself."

"Ta-ta.

Katy laid the phone back in its cradle and took a seat in the chair at the tiny kitchen table. She determined that Jackie would now believe that she was the person that the bracelet denoted and had delivered a child at midnight on the day the world was supposed to end. Jackie was being diplomatic, no doubt. She had to have made the connection between Katy's new last name, Fairplay, and the town where she lived before she had come to Big D with her son at full gestation, toting her ill, soon to be dead, husband.

Thirty years. Her child would've had his thirtieth birthday just a couple of months ago.

She rose and proceeded to make herself a cup of coffee. She would be having a birthday herself soon, she thought, her fifty-fourth.

Jackie's instincts had been right, of course. Katy, had given birth to a boy on the aforementioned night that had been designated as the end of time. And, yes, her real name was Katherine Pepper Harris before she changed it to Katy Fairplay once her residency had been established on her return.

After the birth, she had spent six months with the Smiths before departing. A note and the two items that Joe now had in his pocket were the only things she left behind, other than her child, of course.

There were a lot of complications in regards to remaining in Big D at the time of her departure. She had suffered three too many tragedies in a relatively short period of time, including the death of her beloved husband, the revelation that she had been sexually abused by her father during her teenage years, and the fear that the child she had delivered was not fathered by her husband, but by a beast of a man during an act that could easily have been categorized as rape.

Confused, depressed, insecure, and untethered, she disappeared in the middle of the night, exiting Big D through the main gate and hitching a ride to Springfield with a long-haul trucker returning to his hometown after carting provisions of Missouri smokehouse pork products to the exclusive enclave. A church in Springfield provided shelter for a night or two before she was able to continue her journey back to Kentucky as part of convoy of vans headed to a regional prayer retreat in Knoxville. One of the parishioners deviated from her course to drop Katy back in her hometown.

She arrived in Fairplay, unbathed and barely fed, on the fifth day of her travels. The bungalow that she had rented with her husband felt like the county lockup, what with its feelings of utter emptiness. The memories of her husband still lingered and were expressed by the presence of all the equipment that had helped him sustain life for the five years after his catastrophic accident.

She was able to unload most of the medical appliances at a fraction of their purchase price to a medical supply wholesaler, and the rest she donated to the local hospital.

The clearing did not work. Once emptied, the house no longer felt like a home. The four walls of each room created a condition of claustrophobia in her that did not seem to dissipate over time. Eventually, she took a job as a live-in domestic with one of the families in Mercyville that had once employed the cleaning service she had run back in the day.

Mercyville was a housing project in the city of Fairplay that had been swiftly constructed in the lead-up to the predicted date for the end of the world. Katy had been the chief procurement officer for the endeavor when she was under the employ of its developer—the Jack Clark Worldwide Ministries. Reverend Jack Clark was part of the cadre of religious leaders who had predicted that the world would end and their souls would be commended to their savior on that Ides of March.

When that day came and went, and the only soul that seemed to have been raptured to heaven was a serial killer in Kansas, the confused and bereft community set about trying to figure out what to do. The future that had been promised had evaporated like ether on warm stone. Most of the residents had sold and divested themselves of any non-essential belongings in anticipation of the judgment day, and many were forced to start anew in search of careers and avenues to earn a wage. The community was relentlessly close-knit, though, and gathered every resource to make a go of it as the banks continued to falter and countrywide anarchy appeared imminent.

When the retail grocery markets began moving out, they grew their own food. When the shoddily constructed infrastructure showed signs of decay, they pooled their talents to repair it. When a wayward soul like Katy appeared, they took her in and provided for her needs.

As the country's foundations became more rickety, the Mercyville community endeavored to be completely self-sustaining. Eventually, the Jack Clark Worldwide Ministries closed up their compound, and the hierarchy scattered to parts unknown. Any subsidies that the organization had provided to their sponsored community disappeared with their departure. Yet, the people of Mercyville soldiered on.

Years before anyone would know her as Katy Fairplay, Katherine Pepper Harris continued to be astonished by the community's collective resiliency. She prayed nightly that some of it might rub off on her. With the help of a friend of the family that she worked for, she was able to spend many sessions with a therapist who started her down the road of sorting through the stagnant morass that had cluttered her mind for so long.

As to the disposition of her child, she became more and more convinced that the process that she had embarked upon would preclude her from returning anytime soon to reclaim him. She was terrified of the effect that she might have on a burgeoning soul when she was so desperately out of sorts.

At some point in her past, she had been diagnosed with Munchausen's syndrome by proxy, a malady where the afflicted attempts to weaken his or her charges so that he or she becomes indispensable to their survival. She'd already seen the disease in action when someone on her watch—her husband—had ceased to exist. She was not going to inflict her dementia on her child.

As the therapy took hold and she became more emboldened, she began to ponder her own future. The catalog of possible career choices was slim, but deep down in her heart, she knew that whatever discipline she chose would involve being of service to people.

Throughout her brief existence, she had come in contact with a group of people who always amazed her with their professionalism and aptitude. Additionally, Katy observed that the nursing profession was always perceived as rewarding and informative, and except for one or two bad apples, its legions were filled with exceptional, compassionate individuals.

Even though she had been warned that people who had the same diagnosis as her often drifted toward this career with catastrophic results, she could see no greater use for her talents than to care for those who might be sick or were in need of medical assistance.

She took an opportunity to fill a position as an unpaid nurse's aide at the local hospital where she had donated her husband's medical apparatuses. Over a very short tenure, she was given greater and greater responsibility.

The hospital was not a training facility, however. Katherine knew that if she wanted to continue her education and eventually acquire accreditation, she would have to find a different venue to pursue those lofty goals.

Only a year had transpired since she'd left Big D, and during the early days of her exile she became convinced that the road to success in this arena may have to go through an educational institution that she had some familiarity with, namely Baylor University Hospital.

She was able to reenter Big D on the pretense of a follow-up examination with the ob-gyn who had delivered her child. Once ensconced, she applied for a student visa and began the formal training program. During the application process, she asked for a waiver to have her named changed to its current iteration, Katy Fairplay.

At the time, the plan was to complete her education, apply for permanent residency under the auspices of a special skills retention program, and return her child to her side.

Three years later, the first two tasks were completed, but the reality surrounding the accomplishment of her third goal—that of getting her son back in the fold—appeared to be problematic. From her voyeuristic observations, the child seemed to be thriving with his surrogate parents.

She never told his new parents that she had returned. She cut her hair short and dyed it a dirty blond. She wore glasses when she was out in public. Because of her workload, she was forced to cease most of her physical conditioning regimen, and as she approached thirty, she had morphed from her once slender figure to matronly zaftig.

From afar, she watched all of her son's exploits as he cycled through the youth sports programs. She never missed one of his high school football games and even witnessed his graduation. By every measure it appeared she had made the right choice to leave this child with these caring people.

Of course she fantasized that one day they would reconcile, but so much time had come and gone. As the years progressed, any reality that might include their mutual reintroduction slipped farther and farther down the list of possibilities.

Even if she could have found a way to validate her need to see him, there were the issues of her disappearance that would need to be dealt with, as well as reversing the belief of Joe's adoptive parents that she had died.

Two years after her return to Big D, Mercyville was destroyed by a band of demons that were later identified as Redeemers. It was their first organized foray on a community, and they chose the disciples of the late Reverend Jack Clark as their primary victims. The body count totaled nearly 600. The inhabitants who survived the attack scattered like beads from a broken necklace. The previously abandoned compound of the Jack Clark Worldwide Ministries and the Tabernacle were burned to the ground. Though never positively identified, Katherine Pepper Harris was assumed to be among the mortal casualties.

Deeply saddened by the deaths of most of the people she had come to love, Katherine retreated further into her studies and allowed her old self to be put to rest in the metaphorical and legal sense. Katy Fairplay took her place, and the only assumption that the Smiths could make was that she had perished along with the other members of the Mercyville community.

———

As Katherine sipped her coffee, she began to add up the content of the years of her life. She determined that she was nothing less than a failure. She had transformed from the girl with the energetic magnetism that personified her youth to the childless matron who occupied the four-hundred-square-feet where she sat, surrounded by cheap Swedish furniture and plastic utensils.

The questions came at her in waves. Why had she not reclaimed the fruit of her womb? Why had she stayed silent as the premonitions of the future that her husband had specifically told her would transpire did just that? Why was she letting the days and nights just come and go?

She had no idea what had happened to her son after his graduation from high school. She did not know that he had married, fathered children, and embarked on a career. She never knew that he had become a master in the art of Shaolin Kung Fu. She never knew that her grandchildren had been struck down by disease. She never knew the daughter-in-law who no longer existed. At this point, all she knew was that he was alive because of his recent visit to the orthopedic clinic.

She finished her cup of coffee and got dressed. She thought she would take a walk and loiter around the Smith's neighborhood. After all of this time, maybe she could catch of glimpse of him if he decided to hang around the city.

There was a park near the Smith residence on its eastern edge that afforded a fairly clear view of the front of the house. Katy settled onto one of the benches, a reader in her lap, her personage eclipsed by a large straw hat, and kept an owl's eye on the front walk of the smartly kept home.

Being a spring Saturday morning, the park was beginning to fill up with groups of revelers. The added congestion would be a welcome benefit to her desire to appear inconspicuous.

Just across the path from her bench, a family laid down a blanket and set out a sumptuous spread. A little beyond them, a father and son played catch, and still further in the concentric area directly in front of her, a group of teenage girls were tumbling and practicing with some kind of hoop device.

This was life, she knew. This was something that she had kept at arm's length for the bulk of her last thirty years here on earth. She mused, *What am I waiting for? Where did the time go? Why am I living like this?*

As clichéd as that sounded to her at the time, it did have the effect of bringing to her emotional surface many of the feelings that had provided the stumbling blocks to achieving these simple goals. The most prominent was the realization that she had spent nearly her entire life experiencing a steady state of mourning.

There had been so many deaths.

And those growing piles of ashes had provided no enriched loam to allow for the growth of something akin to a new life. *This is the root of my troubles*, she thought. *This is a symptom of my disease—a steady string of deaths without the promise of resurrection.*

As the afternoon waned, the scenes in her vicinity ebbed and flowed with the arrivals and departures of the park visitors. Her focus on the front door of the Smith residence had deteriorated along with the light of the day.

There had been no movement in the five or so hours she had sat on the bench, and her stomach was telling her that the need for sustenance would soon be moving its way up the priority chart.

Her assumption that he was even in the city was founded on the slimmest of hypotheses. For all she knew, his visit with the orthopedist was just before he exited the enclave, not the opposite.

On her walk home, munching on an egg sandwich cooked to order by a street vendor, the anxiety ebbed. Was it the comfort provided by the food, or was it that she had avoided the possibility of confrontation? *God*, she thought, *all of this crap wasn't part of the girl I used to be, but it is definitely present in the woman I became.*

TWENTY-ONE

THE FIRST

JOE HAD SEEN old movies and TV shows in which a perpetrator was brought to a room like the one he was sitting in, interrogated by a brush-cut hard-boiled cop with nicotine-stained teeth, and reduced to tears as he confessed the horrors of his crime to the audience.

Those same clichéd design specifications must have been in the minds of the builders of this room, right down to the padding on the walls for the crazed suspects and the mirrored window that allowed others in positions of authority to spy on the subject of the inquisition.

This might have been all well and good if these rooms—there were eight identical lined up and down the hall—were to be used to break the hard cases clogging up the justice system, but this was the immigration wing of the administration building, and Joe was only waiting to be interviewed by one of the officers of that department.

When the portly man in the short-sleeved shirt entered through the single door with his tablet aglow, he could not have been more apologetic in regards to his tardiness.

"My goodness, Mr. Smith, I am so sorry. There appeared to be a schedule mix-up, and I was still at home when they called me and told me that you had arrived."

"No, it's fine," Joe said.

The man laid his tablet on the desk and pulled out the chair.

"You comfortable in that seat?" he asked as he hesitated briefly before he made a move to put his butt on the padded gray vinyl of the chair opposite Joe.

"Do you need me to move so that whomever is behind that mirror can see my face?"

The question startled the interviewer, and he nearly missed the center of the chair as his hinging legs allowed for his descent. He quickly transferred his weight, landed square, and took a shallow gulp of breath.

"Goodness, no. I don't believe there is anyone viewing this interview. What made you think that?"

"I don't know, this room, I guess. Kind of makes me feel that I've done something wrong."

"No, no, Mr. Smith, you shouldn't think that. You have very powerful sponsors who have gone through the proper channels to secure
your visa. We just need a little preliminary information—boilerplate
stuff really—to open up the file."

"Let's go, then," Joe said as he straightened his posture.

"Okay. Some of this may sound repetitive, but I have a form, and
all of the boxes need to be filled. Your full name, please."

"Josiah Flavius Smith."

The tablet was having a little trouble transcribing Joe's first and
middle name. It was likely that at least one of them had never made its
way into the recognition database.

"Hmmm . . . Could you say it one more time?"

"Josiah Flavius Smith."

The tablet blinked that it could not acknowledge the response,
so the interviewer called up the keyboard function on the tablet and
handed it over to Joe.

Joe typed in the information and clicked the cursor down to item
number two—date of birth. He filled in that blank as well.

Here it comes, thought Joe. Should he have lied and made up a different date? The interviewer was switching the tablet back to the VOX
functionality when he noticed Joe's entry.

"Are you serious? That's your birth date?"

"I get that all the time."

"That is a first for me, I must say."

Joe waited for the moment to pass, but the interviewer kept staring at the number.

"Sorry. Address?" he finally asked.

Joe knew that he couldn't say that he didn't have one, but in reality, he didn't have one.

"645 Baxter Street, Aldine, Texas territory."

"Spouse's name?"

"Cynthia Cecilia Smith."

"Age?"

"She would have been thirty next month."

His response demanded a follow-up.

"She's deceased," Joe said.

"Date that she passed?"

"Don't know that one."

The interviewer sat back in his chair and offered a grunt that was
laden with the feeling of mild frustration. There weren't boxes for these

types of answers. The box requested: "if deceased, what date?" He called up the keyboard and typed the acronym "N/A" in the box.

"Children? Names and ages, please?"

Joe stretched his neck before holding out his hand and asking for the tablet. He wrote in the pertinent information and handed it back to the interviewer.

"I'm sorry," the interviewer said as he read the entry.

He switched the sound feature back on and laid the tablet back down on the table as if the blasted thing had become toxic. So far, the machine had logged mostly sadness, and, though its physical properties weighed practically nothing, it had acquired a definite avoirdupois by virtue of all of these inputs of darkness.

"Most recent employment?"

"Tynan International, Ltd."

"Position?"

"Special Operations."

Joe heard some commotion behind him. Even through the heavy insulation, he knew that at least two people had entered the observation room. He thought about turning around and tossing the voyeurs a cynical smile, but then he remembered that he had been invited here to be of service. This wasn't a situation that called for confrontation. On the contrary, he was grateful for the person or persons who had extended the opportunity to him.

Kevin Gatz jostled for position in front of the window. He didn't want to have to stand behind the big body of Billy Klock. Both men needed to give their boss, Captain Lon Brassey, the center, but both men were desirous of claiming an unobstructed view.

"Are you sure that's him?" Billy asked.

"Why would it be anyone else, Bill?" Kevin asked with a lilt of sarcasm.

"I know. It's just, he don't look like some kind of killer," Billy said.

Kevin understood where Billy was coming from. The subject, though he could only see the back of his head and upper body, looked slight, even possibly malnourished.

"We're not hiring a killer, Bill," Lon said.

"I know, Cap."

Lon listened to the timbre of the man's voice; he seemed to have a quality of command over his words and conviction in the way he answered the interviewer's questions. Once he saw his face, Lon believed his opinion was not likely to change. Besides, his brother Harry would only offer a recommendation if the person of interest transcended a mighty threshold.

The three men could see that the interviewer was wrapping up.

"Let's head out to the street and wait for him to come out," Lon said.

The interviewer hit a button, forwarded the form to his superiors, rose from the chair, and stuck out his meaty paw.

"Good luck to you, Mr. Smith."

"Thanks."

"As an Indie, I don't have a stake in the race, you know, but I'll be rooting for you."

Joe couldn't place the appellation of "Indie" into any sort of context. He reckoned there would be a lot of vernacular that was going to be new to him.

"Where do I go now?"

"My superiors are reviewing the file. It shouldn't be more than fifteen minutes or so, and then someone will come and get you."

"Okay."

"You're going to make history, Mr. Smith."

"You might be jumping the gun there."

"Regardless of the outcome, you will be the first, Mr. Smith. It's a goddamn precedent."

He exited and left Joe with the feeling that whatever task these people had summoned him to perform, their expectations were extremely high.

The interviewer had been accurate in his estimation. In the fourteenth minute after his departure, another functionary arrived to escort Joe to the embarkation gate. There was some paperwork to sign, an oath to be taken that proclaimed that every one of his statements were true and he intended to cause no harm to any of the citizens of Motor City, and the acceptance of his temporary identification. He was also given a money chip that had a small quantity of legal tender programmed into it, a gift that all new immigrants received.

Joe did not see his original interviewer pass by in the background—a new tablet in his hands—headed for another interview room to depose a recently arrived immigrant. He did not see that the subject who had been waiting in a room down the hall was a man by the name of Clarence Rigney.

The pressure in the hydraulics of the glass doors adjusted for the presence of someone standing before the sensor. The admonition from a disembodied voice proclaimed, "Stand clear!" Joe's atmosphere was transformed from one of non-odorous climate control to the unleashed environment of a city just beginning to enter the spring swelter.

There was also the striking contrast between the industrial gray decorum of the immigration building and the vibrant rainbow of colors that greeted him as he cast his gaze northwest up Woodward Avenue.

Joe heard a piercing whistle come hurtling from somewhere across the street. He located a quorum of three men standing on the steps of the Mariner's Cathedral. All three were waving him over to their side of the road.

As he approached, he could see the smile on the face of the middle-aged man in the center of the grouping and recognized him as the sibling of the man he had spirited to safety back in Akron a couple of months before.

The two men flanking the brother represented the contrary in body style and demeanor. The bespectacled one portrayed a look of acute intensity laced with a bit of intelligence behind his eyes. The other was ursine huge and sported a visage of confused congeniality. If it came to a fight, Joe would have preferred the latter, larger human, as an opponent. The former would, no doubt, fight dirty.

"Welcome, Mr. Smith, I'm Lon Brassey," the sibling said with an extended hand.

Joe offered a firm, incalescent clasp, but the reciprocation was decidedly wanting. Joe looked into Lon Brassey's eyes. There was something being concealed behind the brown irises, something that Joe could break down into two components: one long-term and one that appeared to him to be shorter in duration. It was the second sample that put him on the defensive.

"Let me introduce you to my two lieutenants, Billy Klock and Kevin Gatz."

Joe shook these men's hands as well. He noticed that both were better at keeping any commentary hidden—no doubt there was some type of premeditated shield in place. Joe speculated that the hierarchy must be rigid in its structure, and these two fellows had only recently attained the status of lackeys in the order. This Lon fellow was obviously the man.

Some small talk followed, but Joe's attention was drawn to his surroundings. There was not the drab, persistent, underlying malaise of Big D in this quarter of town. It was awash in vivacious color and populated by carefree, happy denizens.

As they started up Woodward Avenue, dodging the pedi-cabs and garishly painted electric carts, Joe noticed none of the enmity that he'd been told to expect from the system of segregation that compelled the various segments of the enclave to remain locked in constant competition.

He did not know at the time that this part of the city had only one filial responsibility, and that was to commerce. He would learn that, technically, this was the dominion of the Red Wings, but the shops and eateries paid the ward a separate tariff due to the desirable location near the front gates. For the Red Wings, this was a needed assessment given that their ilk were notoriously poor in comparison to some of the more wealthy wards.

This first impression confused Joe slightly. He had heard many stories that detailed life inside Motor City, and the prevailing sentiment tended toward an environment fraught with contentiousness. All of this iconography portended a fear that was present on his entrance, and it would take him a moment to adjust his thoughts now that he was having a first-hand experience. He was under the assumption that the threat of violence would be ever present, but this did not appear to be foreboding in any way.

He could smell the aromas emanating from the various kitchens that lined the route, and for the first time in a long time, he felt something akin to hunger. He knew that his face had maintained the status of placidity, as he had no interest in provoking any conversation that reeked of small talk. Yeah, he had questions, but to this crowd it might be perceived as showing some kind of weakness. He would not be offering that as a first impression. No sense allowing these men to think anything other than he was the man for the job. Whatever that job turned out to be. Yet, the big one kept checking him out, looking for an opening of some type. Joe decided to turn it back on him.

"I surmise that you might have a question, Mr. Klock?" he asked.

Billy was shocked. His utter lack of self-awareness had created a feeling of incomprehension that he was somehow being provocative by focusing his attention totally on Joe. He began to sputter something that sounded like a denial.

"So, have you ever driven a race car?" Kevin said to the relief of his fellow lieutenant.

This was the question that everyone wanted to ask from the get-go. They all turned to Joe in anticipation of his response.

"I've driven a car," he offered.

The cadre allowed that answer to appear to be satisfactory, but Joe could see that his response was being deemed incomplete.

"Is that why you've brought me in, to drive a race car?" Joe asked.

"Didn't the deliverer of the letter explain that?" Lon asked.

"No, I never met him. He just left the letter at my parent's house. It was coincidence that I happened to stop by. I hadn't seen them in four years."

Lon gritted his teeth. This was not the information he had been given by that scumbag lawyer. Being caught off guard was never a situation that he appreciated.

"This right here has a bit of an awkward tinge," Kevin said under his breath.

"Shut the fuck up, Kevin," Lon seethed.

Joe watched the dynamic between the boss and his underling and decided on a course of genial diffusion.

"So, you need me to drive a race car?"

"Yes. We have a big race on the streets every July. There will plenty of time to prepare. You shouldn't be worried," Lon reassured him.

"I'm not," Joe stated.

"Good. It's an important event for everyone in the city. You don't have to be here very long to grasp the significance. It is the only yearly obsession."

Lon noticed a couple walking toward them, an older man and a woman in her late thirties or early forties.

"There they are," Lon said with a nod of the head, "finally," he added to, once again, express the fact that he was mildly displeased by something.

Joe's gaze went up the road to identify the two that Lon had put in his sights. Closer now, he could see that the two were related, father and daughter perhaps.

"Joe Smith, I would like you to meet Frank and Claudia Concepcion."

Joe offered his hand. The woman shook it harder than the old man.

"I'll be leaving you in their hands for the time being. We have a meeting to attend. We'll rendezvous later for dinner at my house," Lon said as he signaled his two lieutenants to come to heel.

Joe watched the three men depart. Once again, the aromas of food tantalized his olfactory sensors. There was a small restaurant tucked behind the next door from where they were standing.

"What happens next?" Joe asked.

Claudia laughed. Joe could see the sinew bulging from her forearms and noticed the dirt and grease caked under her fingernails. She was nearly double the size of her parent, but they shared the same hue of straight jet-black hair.

"You know, I haven't eaten in awhile. Perhaps we could grab a bite to eat at this place right here," Joe offered.

Claudia threw a quick, concerned look at Frank. Taking in the response to his suggestion, Joe suddenly began to question his choice of restaurant. He wondered about the source of Claudia's sudden reaction, and her need to connect with her father. Was this an issue of delectability or hygiene?

"No good?" Joe asked.

"We wouldn't know," Claudia said.

"We wouldn't ever eat there," Frank added.

"Tell him why, Francisco," Claudia said.

Frank smoothed over an errant hair on his pencil-thin mustache and used the other hand to point to a small decal in the corner of the front window. It was a picture of a white horse in profile on a light blue backdrop. The horse was shying, its front hooves kicking impatiently at the sky.

"And that means what?" Joe asked.

"You got a lot to learn, buddy," Claudia said.

"The owners are Mustang. Impala does not patronize Mustang establishments."

"Oh."

"Come on, we're heading up Woodward," Frank said. "I know where we can get a great ham sandwich."

"Mimsy's?" Claudia asked.

"Yeah."

"Yum," pronounced Claudia.

"Lead the way," Joe said.

TWENTY-TWO

A FORGOTTEN PRIMAL DESIRE

THERE WAS A rumble in the room, a low-frequency hum that seemed to grow as the hour to commence crept upon the participants. Like bees returning to a burgeoning hive, the addition of each new person to the room increased the decibel level of the buzzing sound.

Lon took his seat on the dais. Kevin and Billy slid into chairs behind him, just out of the light that spilled from the overhead spots. Four places to his left sat a very smug-faced Titus O'Keefe, the Mustang captain, flanked by his only lieutenant, Tom Cobble.

The city commissioner, a Mugwump by the name of Carter Pleasant, banged his gavel upon the block of maple that he had constructed from a stray splintered baseball bat that he gleefully recovered from somewhere deep in the bowels of Tiger Stadium.

"Okay, let's get going here," Carter shouted above the din.

There was little change in the hubbub. Carter banged the gavel on the block again. Slowly the sonic squall abated as the gallery took their seats in the pre-assigned sections. As always, representatives of three other wards buffered Impala and Mustang in the general seating area.

"So we have the schedule for the festival week set. Nothing is really different here. Cracking ceremony will be on Monday the fourth. The Lottery is on Tuesday. Wednesday and Thursday morning will be reserved for practice. The punch-out will be Thursday afternoon. This is the same as every year. Nothing new. The race will be on Saturday at noon."

The buzzing began again. Carter beat it back with three swift hammers of the gavel.

"Look, if you all can't keep quiet, we're going to be here for hours. And I, for one, do not want to miss my supper," Carter shouted to the unruly crowd.

Carter knew that the cork—ever so slowly working its way out of the bottle for the better part of a year—was getting ready to blow. These last two months were always tense. Some would say that when spring fever was exacerbated by the anticipation of the July festivities, bad things were likely to happen. It had become so hard for people to keep their shit together after suppressing all of their base desires since the previous July. Nobody wanted to screw it up in May and risk being ejected from participation in the event, though. But the mood was always tense in the late spring. Always.

Carter threw a glance in the direction of the section that contained the Red Wings. They still led the city with four suspensions. Even though it had been five years since the last time they were excluded, he would have laid eight to five that another five years would not go by before they pulled some stunt worthy of a year's disqualification. One of the Red Wings' plebes started yelling at their captain, Gordon Brewer, to bring up a subject that had been bandied about within their ward.

"I do have a piece of business I'd like to talk about," Gordon Brewer shouted over to Carter Pleasant.

"The chair recognizes Captain Brewer," Carter shouted.

A couple of pounds of the gavel took the sound level down to a reasonable roar.

"We think that there is something fundamentally unfair here in regards to the fact that someone is always going to get stuck with a dog car. We all know that eight of the cars are fairly evenly matched and one is an outright piece of crap," Captain Brewer stated.

Everyone in the room knew that Gordon was detailing a well-known fact. The AMX, the only muscle car built by the company once known as American Motors Corporation, was just not up to the standard of the other cars. There was more than one reason for this— the company had shuttered its doors long before the other companies ceased to exist, so all replacement parts had to be cobbled from junkers that were built by other manufacturers or fabricated from scratch, not to mention the fact that the car itself had been branded a lemon immediately after its market debut. A staggering amount of recalls and bad reviews swiftly sunk the best efforts of the engineers of the AMX. There would be no revisions or extension of the line in the years after its initial appearance.

Any ward that was handed this vehicle via the lottery had no chance in attaining victory. The simple truth was the car had never won during the span of the race's history. The AMX had only been able to actually finish the race on just three occasions.

"We've got nine wards and nine cars," Carter explained. "If we only have eight cars, then someone isn't going to be in the race."

"You ain't in the race if you're saddled with that piece of shit anyway," someone shouted from the crowd.

The ensuing laughter compelled Carter Pleasant to punish the maple block again with his wooden hammer.

"We can talk about this in the future, but it's too late to change it this year. The executive committee has floated some ideas in the past that—should some of the cars become non-operational—one and possibly two wards would take a year off every year. You would be guaranteed to race seven years out of every nine."

Now, boos and catcalls became the noise emanating from the choir. Regardless of the conditions, no one wanted to take a year off. To this crowd, that was a non-starter.

"Nothing's going to change for this year, anyway," Carter assured them.

Kevin Gatz leaned over and whispered in Lon Brassey's ear. Lon nodded and raised his hand.

"Captain Brassey? You have something that you want to say?" Carter asked.

The recognition of Captain Brassey by the race's chairman caused the noise level to decrease exponentially in a matter of just a couple of seconds. Everyone had heard rumors about the ploy that Impala was trying to pull off. Was this to be the confirmation?

"Well, first off, I want to wish nearly all of the participants good luck in this year's festival. This is my first time at the helm, and I want to extend my gratitude to the other captains in attendance for helping to guide me through the process."

Kevin was having difficulty suppressing a smile. His boss could really pile on the horseshit.

"I just want to inform everyone that Impala has contracted with an individual from outside the ward to function as our pilot for this year's race. Actually, this is an individual brought in from outside the city. We've checked the rules on this, and there appears to be no statute that has been violated."

There were a few cries of "foul" from people in the crowd, but most everyone was curious about how the experiment would shake out in the long run.

Lon never used the word "professional" or gave away any details about the driver's qualifications, so the reaction of the crowd and their respective captains was one that could have qualified the attendees as intrigued, not necessarily defiant.

Carter Pleasant quickly pored through the race rules book, though he knew there was nothing in there that decreed that a ward's driver had to come from the insular community of that specific ward. Even so, he wasn't going to let an ounce of his authority be usurped.

"I am going to have to allow this on a provisional basis," Carter said.

"There is nothing that says we can't do this," Lon offered.

"We'll get back to you, Captain Brassey," Carter said.

Lon took a quick glance over to the Mustang folk and observed Titus O'Keefe wearing a tight smile. Lon was convinced that Titus and the Mustang faithful were a little stunned and envious of his coup.

"Anything else?" Carter asked.

It appeared to be over. No one raised a hand or proclaimed a need to say anything. People began to rise from their seats with the intention of making their way to the exits.

"We'd like to reserve the right to do that, as well," Titus O'Keefe suddenly said.

Everyone froze.

"We might be bringing in a driver from the outside too," Titus said in clarification.

Like the sudden release of a mute button, the buzz shot back up to deafening levels. When Titus looked over at the Impala crew, he would only see scowls and venomous stares coming from Lon, Billy, and Kevin.

Titus mouthed the words "Go fuck yourself" and polished off the exchange with an ambiguous shrug of his shoulders.

———

Joe couldn't remember an item of food tasting so delicious. His short-term memory certainly couldn't recall anything of memorable quality to rival the delights of this sandwich. The concept of food as anything other than a fuel source had become foreign to him. Anything that smacked of definitive sapor had been deemed as insignificant when stacked next to the needs of his body to ingest something to burn.

But this ham sandwich, so simple in its construction, had awakened some feelings deep inside him. The sandwich consisted of a crusty French-style baguette, a generous smear of butter, and two slices of salty, lean, smoked pig meat carved from the area just below the aitchbone.

Joe had allowed Frank to do the ordering—Mimsy's had a protocol that required that the requester speak clearly and without a hint of hesitation. When Claudia initially handed him the waxed-paper-wrapped sandwich, Joe knew he would have a hard time concealing the vestiges of a frown in his response. It seemed too crude, as if no thought had gone into its conception. He wondered if this was the level of quality that the citizenry had become inured to. Weren't these people rich? Did the tastes that once defined their culture not have to be catered to?

He took a bite, fully expecting the mass to land on his tongue and taste buds like a ration of oily cardboard that had been steeped inside a dank warehouse. Instead, he let out a verbal tone that sounded like a generic orgasm.

"You like?" Claudia asked.

But Joe was already into his second bite. It was such a visceral experience, and it shocked him that he had gone so long in his life with this basic of all fancies relegated to a state of utter dormancy.

After their meal, they continued north. They passed through the section of Woodward Avenue devoted to the residential area of the Mugwump, or Independent, population. Francisco did his tour guide's best to put words to the images that appeared before Joe as if he were visiting an amusement park for the very first time.

They progressed on past the stadiums and the old Fox Theatre and then up through the fringes of the Impala neighborhood, where a few people came up to greet him and wish him well. Joe did his best to accept their kindness, but the whole ordeal made him uncomfortable; he hadn't done a thing to warrant this attention.

As they exited the confines of the Impala portion of the immurement, Joe could see Frank and Claudia straighten their postures and become less relaxed about the circumstances of their surroundings. Claudia thrust her hand into her pocket and fingered something that Joe thought might be a weapon of some sort.

"Where are we now?" Joe asked in an attempt to put the level of tension in perspective. The neighborhood they were crossing through didn't look different or more threatening than anything they had traversed to this point.

"We're on the outskirts of Mustang. The Museum is technically considered neutral territory, but the Mustang ward exists around all four of its corners," Frank said.

"You know, I have a certain expertise if anything should come to a head. If it's all the same to you, if things get rough, I would appreciate that you steer clear of helping me out. It is the easiest way to avoid getting hurt," Joe stated.

A brief silence ensued after Joe's innocent declaration. Claudia smashed the veil of quiet as she suddenly exploded into gales of laughter.

"You're joking, right?" she cackled.

"I don't think he is," Frank said.

Joe immediately realized his mistake. These were complete strangers who were likely to see his suggestion as nothing more than a hollow boast. All he could do was offer a shrug and a sheepish grin.

"Some people don't get my sense of humor," he offered in apology.

"Are you kidding? That was fucking funny, man," Claudia said.

A group of young men in blue jackets strolled toward them. The duo of Impala folk and their new conscript scrunched up to the side to allow them to pass. One of the Mustang boys spat onto the sidewalk not five millimeters from Joe's worn boot.

"Fuck you, asshole," Claudia growled.

"What did you say, bitch?"

"We have a right to be in this part of town," she said.

"A right? Oh, you have a right. They have a right," the young Mustang explained to his friends with an emotive bit of sarcasm.

"Take it easy, boys, we don't need to settle this now. We all want to be able to race, don't we?" Frank subtly warned.

The boys took the statement as the threat it was meant to be: if this situation were to disintegrate into an altercation, they were aware of the consequences should a report be filed, and an investigation undertaken. The trick for them was to find a way to withdraw from this confrontation without losing face. The tallest of the boys decided to give Frank a half-hearted shove.

"I'd kick your ass, old man, but it wouldn't be fair," the youth said as he and his friends began to saunter away.

The boy who shoved Frank got only a few feet away before he felt a hand on his belt loop. Before he could react, Joe hooked his legs and flipped him onto the ground. His face met concrete so fast he had no time to break the fall with his hands. Joe rendered the ingrate impotent by applying his boot to the area of the downed boy's sacrum. The other two Mustangs took defensive postures, but they would not advance to come to the aid of their buddy. The bone-thin guy pinning him to the ground looked beatable, but crazy.

"We'll be on our way now," Frank said.

"Come on, Joe," Claudia added.

Joe lifted his boot off the back of the kid. The kid kept his face down on the sidewalk. He wouldn't be making any twitchy moves until the three members of Impala had surely departed. Joe locked eyes with the other two, and his gaze had the effect of temporarily paralyzing their voice boxes.

As the three aliens walked the last hundred yards to the door of Harold Getty's Museum, Claudia walked backward, keeping her eyes glued on their tormentors. If they had moved from their previous spots, she couldn't tell.

Francisco entered his personal code into the console to the left of the door. A monitor came alive, and a security guard appeared on the screen.

"What time is your appointment?"

"In fifteen minutes," Francisco said.

"You'll have to wait in the lobby."

"All right."

The door buzzed, and the three were admitted into a separate holding area and scanned with a weak x-ray. The discovery of Claudia's concealed switchblade knife had triggered a red blinking light on the screen on the wall.

"You'll have to put that in a locker, Miss."

"Okay."

She removed the weapon from her pocket and loaded it into one of the bus lockers that lined the wall to their right. She created her own combination before shutting the door. The completion of this act caused the inner door to release, and the three crossed the threshold and entered the climate-controlled museum. A different security guard—a ladder's worth of stripes on the sleeve of his buttoned-up tunic—greeted them.

"Welcome. I'm Teller. There is a team that is finishing up on the simulator. Shouldn't be but a couple of minutes."

"Thanks," Claudia said.

"You must be the one I've heard about," Teller said, addressing Joe.

"Yeah, I guess. Joe Smith."

"Hey, Teller, any chance we can get into the vault so we can show Mr. Smith what's what?" Claudia asked.

"That might be hard. Let me ask the curator."

"Thanks."

Teller moseyed away down the hall. Joe became entranced by a series of photo plates arrayed on the wood-paneled walls. They depicted action scenes taken from various races of the past. The one he was currently studying showed a car passing between the thresholds of a steel gate. It could have been the angle that the photographer shot from, but it appeared to Joe that the space between the steel of the gate and the steel of the car couldn't have been more than a few inches.

"The gates, yeah, you are going to love that," Frank said.

"So are you my coach?" Joe asked.

"Kind of. Claudia and I are the ward's mechanics. We've had the gig for the last eighteen years. I was one of the engine designers at GM a long, long time ago. She's had grease under her fingernails since she was a toddler. There were the guys who knew how to sculpt car bodies from clay, but they had no clue as to the practical aspects of putting a vehicle in motion. That was my area of expertise."

The door opened down the hall, and a woman with a radiating tablet emerged with Teller in tow. Dark haired, just under six feet of willowy grace, she marched toward the group.

"Look, I can give you only five minutes in the vault. Normally, we like to keep it off-limits during the run-up except under special circumstances. I figure that the presence of this gentleman here constitutes one of those extraordinary instances," the woman said.

"I'm Joe Smith."

"Welcome to Motor City, Mr. Smith. And welcome to the Harold Getty Museum. My name is Cassandra Montgomery."

There was something producing an arc between this woman and Joe. Francisco and Claudia noticed that the connection was not the result of simple static electricity. Part of the system that controlled things like electrostatic buildup within the building's environment would have excluded that hypothesis. It's not as if their handshake lingered or took on the quality of flirtation, but there was something that both the Impala mechanic and his daughter simultaneously allowed to be part of their consciousness. Soon, they would both feel compelled to issue a warning to their driver.

The five of them moved to the door of the vault. Cassandra keyed in her code, and Teller broke the seal on a biscuit that contained the concurring numbers. Teller read the numbers from the sheet of plastic into an imperceptible microphone hidden in the lock mechanism.

"Nine, four, five, four, nine."

Tumblers began to move, and all could hear the sound of the compression change between the inner and the outer. They entered a room enveloped in cavern-like darkness. When the fluorescents were flicked on, what lay before Joe was something that he had only seen in books.

The room was a small hangar that housed all of the vehicles that made up the entrants of the race. Red velvet ropes had been placed around every one of the gems of American motor science. Joe was stunned, and he approached the nearest car—a 1969 Impala SS.

"These are all electric?" he asked in awe.

The giggles from the other four answered his query. Frank put his hand over his heart.

"Internal combustion, friend. Eight cylinders of smooth steel bore. Each and every one encapsulating a piston that sequentially sparks and ignites that sweet flammable nectar. As the four-barrel carburetion feeds the beastly power plant, the energy is created, and the resulting torque rattles down the transaxle to a heavy-duty differential. So much torque that one can pull two g's accelerating out of a turn."

It was a reverent speech. No doubt, for Francisco, this was that part of his life that substituted for religious faith.

"Okay," Joe said, but he was distracted now, mesmerized by the clean lines of steel swathed in multiple layers of polished lacquer.

"I think this boy's in love," Cassandra the curator said with a girly lilt.

"Well, he wouldn't be the first," Claudia said.

Both she and Frank cast a wary eye on the comely curator. Teller's information module began to hum. It was the indicating signal that the simulator was free.

"Right on time," Teller said.

TWENTY-THREE

ROBBY THE MAGNIFICENT

TELLER USHERED THE three Impala representatives toward the hallway. Cassandra pulled the door closed, waited for the locks to re-
set, and headed back toward her office. Joe could not help himself from
allowing his gaze to follow her for fifteen steps or so. Again, Claudia
and Frank shared a look of dubiousness. Teller, concerned that schedules be adhered to, took no notice of the subtle exchanges between Joe,
Cassandra, Frank, and Claudia.

"You have thirty minutes," Teller said as he handed off the trio to
the simulator technician, Robert (Robby) Darnell.

"Hey, Robby," Francisco said, shaking hands with the sim-tech.

"So, this is the guinea pig?" Robby said with his dull green eyes
fixed on Joe.

"I'm Joe," Joe said with his right hand extended.

Joe knew from the outset that Robby was one of those guys who
lorded over his domain with the demeanor of a mid-twentieth-century
dictator. Anyone coming into contact with Robby's world was likely to
be diminished by both his glaring stare and his denigrating remarks.
No one could know as much as he did about the job that he did, and
God forbid they intimated any inkling that they might. Joe prepared
himself for the process of being led through the protocol as if he were
a first-grader on day one of the school year.

As Robby spoke, Joe did his best to block out anything that didn't
register to him as hard information. He had no reaction, no acknowledgement of intended or unintended humor, and he kept his mind focused on the machine that was known as the race simulator. Joe caught
and tried to hold on to phrases like "real-time telemetry," "actual struc-
tural integrity of the vehicle," and "delineated course realism."

They entered the simulator room, and Joe came face-to-face with
the most sophisticated automobile emulator that had ever existed.
Comparisons could only be drawn to military-sourced flight simulation apparatuses and other devices that provided a strictly virtual, not
tactile, experience.

Centered in the enormous room was a large plasticized dome that
resembled the cap of a button mushroom. The dome was centered on a

hydraulic tripod, and the whole system was perched on layers of double-railed track that covered the floor of the hanger like a steel checkerboard.

Robby used his remote to call the simulator to the loading dock—a jungle gym of scaffolding that ended ten steps above from where they stood. Robby led them up the stairway, popped open the door of the cockpit, and allowed Joe to have a look at the inside environment of the module. It resembled the driver's seat of one of the cars that rested on the museum floor, down to the tuck and roll leather upholstery and the shiny, not quite spherical, knob that was attached to the top of the gearshift.

Robby was rambling on about how one needed to keep an eye on the tachometer to gauge the optimal shifting window once the engine crested the minimum four-thousand-revolutions-per-minute barrier. Without registering whether Joe understood the protocol, he moved on to caution that far too many neophytes tended to ride the clutch on occasion, and that was the single most intolerable offense to the mechanical performance of the vehicle. That type of insult was responsible for more retirements from the race than any other, including crashes and flat tires.

Frank and Claudia were getting impatient with Robby's constant drone of admonitions. They knew that the thirty minutes that had been allotted to them started when Teller led them to the door of the simulator room. Joe sensed their fretfulness and threw caution to the wind by opening his mouth.

"I think I'm ready to go," Joe said.

"Really?" Robby asked sarcastically, both his eyebrows arched toward the heavens.

"I mean, I can't break this thing, can I? You can stop it before anything bad happens from your control room, can't you?"

He tossed that last bit in to let Robby know that he was still in control of his operation. It turned out to be the right amount of flattery as Robby stepped back slightly and dramatically waved his arm, inviting Joe to situate himself in the pilot's seat.

What Joe never divulged was that he had spent many an hour in simulators that were less sophisticated, but similar. He understood the concepts related to shifting and acceleration from his experiences in the arcades of his youth. As he moved into his teenage years, he had become notorious for his prowess in the machines that featured oval track racing and something that was once called Formula One.

With Frank's help, he strapped himself into the seat and took a quick scan at the cockpit gauges.

"We're going to start with a generic straight, flat country road. You won't have time to get to the race course program on today's visit," Robby said.

"You sure?" Joe asked.

"I'm sure."

"Yeah, because we've wasted so much time listening to your bullshit," Frank whispered into the air.

"What was that, Frank?" Robby asked.

"I was telling Joe that he should just listen to you and let you guide him."

"Roger that," Robby said.

From the first moments, Joe realized that he had overestimated the similarity between this unit and the shoddy impersonation of the devices that resided in the pleasure temples back home. This was real. Not a single detail of the experience of driving a car had been left out of the equation. Joe could sense the speed, the torque, the feeling of the tire rubber's coefficient of friction as it ran down the road, and the sensitivity of all of the elements that the activity required: the limits of the steering mechanism, the pressures needed to depress the accelerator and the clutch, and the visual interpretation of both the road ahead and behind.

He had many reasons for taking it slow at the outset. He had learned from his study of the Shaolin discipline that hubris in any form usually extended the time period required when traversing the length of a learning curve. Also, he didn't want to raise the expectations of the witnesses by taking this bull by the horns and steering it down the country lane at lightning speed, though it was something he was convinced he could accomplish from the get-go. Instead, he took a measured tack and allowed himself to make it through the first three gears in a uniform and sequential manner. He shifted when the tachometer read exactly 5000 rpms at each gear level. He was able to achieve a top speed of fifty-five miles an hour as he was winding out in third gear.

Robby took control after that—abruptly aborting the session because he felt that a shift to fourth could have taken place earlier.

"It's one of the quirks of this type of transmission," Robby began. "Gear spacing between third and fourth is minimal. You don't want to wind it out in third. You need to jump to fourth so you don't lose speed when you're looking to find the top end."

Most of what Robby was talking about was Greek to Joe. He really had no idea about the nuance of the mechanics of a car; he only knew what he had to do in a simulator to score the most points. Phrases like "top end," "gear spacing," and "winding it out," flew over his head like so many geese traveling north for the summer.

"I don't think we have time to drive the course, but I'm going to run the program that will give you the rudimentary routing through your visual. You seem like you know what you're doing regarding the basics," Robby said.

Joe intuited Robby's statement as a compliment of monumental significance given the persnickety nature of Robby. Joe took his foot off the pedals, his hands off the padded steering wheel, and sat back in the seat.

The next ten minutes were like a ride on a rollercoaster. Any details that Joe hoped to pick up from the display were reduced to a blur. Even as disciplined as his mind had become, there was no way to take in much more than the slightest of specifics. Each particular image was being shoved out of his short-term memory because room was needed for the next. The overall big picture would classify the course as one with long, wide straightaways followed by sharp turns—some of them less than ninety degrees.

Something truly funky happened when toward the end of the loop, the track took a route that required a right turn where the road actually banked left. The program took the viewer on a double move—an S-pattern—within the turn to accomplish the feat. Joe also remembered something that happened earlier where the road was intentionally narrowed by the presence of two steel walls.

As the screen went black, Joe closed his eyes to effect a moment of pure focus. He tried to replay what he had just seen in an attempt to create some level of formatting for his memory. The best he could do was place the images associated with the odd turn into some random place of his consciousness.

"Next time, we'll try it for real," Robby said.

The grating voice of this tormentor broke his reverie and destroyed his efforts to gather any of the other bits of information that could have provided him a starting point on creating a metric to measure future experiences. It was the beginning, though. It was only May. They had almost two full months to get up to speed. Frank later explained that they had a two-hour block scheduled for two days hence.

On the catwalk of the scaffolding, it took Joe a couple of minutes to reacquire his bearings before he felt grounded enough to climb down the stairway to the floor. That last thing, the racecourse route, had been a real rush. Robby came out of his booth and greeted them at the door.

"We'll see what you got next time out," he said.

"I guess we will," Joe replied in as humble a fashion as he could manufacture.

In the event that Robby heard the slightest sting in his comment, Joe added, "Thanks for all your help. Looks like you're going to be my Sherpa for the next little while."

A smile from the normally taciturn Robby indicated to Joe that he had pushed the correct button.

As they traversed the lobby on their way to the exit, Joe once again saw the photo plate of the car squeezing through the gap in the steel wall. It transported him back to that moment in the simulator when he had tried to recreate the race route. This was another jagged piece of the jigsaw puzzle, but in the moment, he wasn't in any way sure where it fit.

"Tell me about the gates," he asked the two mechanics.

"It has only been in the race for maybe eight, nine years now. Someone on the competition panel felt that there was this section—the last straightaway before you hit the turn at First and Adams—where the fastest car could make up ground and eventually win the race. The lore was that the race was always decided in that straightaway and not where it should have been decided—the wicked turn I just mentioned and the short tight run back into the stadium," Frank said.

"So they came up with the concept of the gates," Claudia said.

"When we get back to Captain Brassey's house, we can show you a map of the whole course. That might help to explain it," Frank said.

"Okay. But tell me about the gates first," Joe said.

Before Frank could continue on with his dissertation, Cassandra exited her office and appeared in the hall. Joe sensed the palatable tension she brought to his handlers with each step of her advance. This would have to be another question for his mechanics: What was it about her that so bugged them?

"What did you think?" Cassandra asked.

"Amazingly lifelike," Joe responded.

"Many a hotshot has been perfect on Robby's baby, but the real thing is the real thing, you know?"

"Nothing can substitute for the real thing," Joe said.

Again Frank and Claudia flinched. What had he said that made them do that? Cassandra looked down at her tablet and noted the time that this group would be returning.

"Well, I guess we'll see you in a couple of days," she said.

"Looking forward to it," Joe said.

The amount of force with which Frank tugged on his arm to seemingly drag him toward the exit surprised Joe, and when he got into the street, he turned to the father and daughter.

"What's up with all the eye-rolling and wincing when we're around that woman?"

"You like her, don't you?" Claudia asked with an air of accusation.

"What? No. I don't even know her."

"Stay away from her," Frank cautioned.

"Okay, but why? What's the story here? Is she a witch? Has she killed someone?"

"She's Mustang," Claudia said.

She leveled a stare at Joe that stood just outside the door of penetrating his soul. These folks were not joking around.

"Don't speak to her. Don't give her any insights into who you are, what you're capable of, or anything that she could use as intelligence to give her side an edge."

"Come on, I've only been here half a day. But if she can rig the thing from the inside, what's the point? Would they really let her have the job if anything funny was going on?" Joe asked.

"As curator of the museum, she is supposed to maintain an ethic of impartiality. There is a lengthy selection process for anyone who works there, but we will always maintain that you can never trust a fucking Mustang," Claudia said.

"Okay. Fine. So, back to my question about the gates."

Claudia, having retrieved her stiletto from the locker, decided to walk in front of them for the period that would get them through their immediate surroundings.

"As I was saying, the purpose of the gates are to create an impediment to anyone from bombing straight up Cass Avenue with the throttle wide open. The race is three laps, so the first time around the track the gates are open enough to allow three cars to pass side by side. For the second lap, only two can pass at the same time, and for lap three, only one," Frank said.

"Whoever thought of the thing is a genius because it also helps the drivers to count down the laps," Claudia added from behind them. "Too many times during the early races, some dumbshit who had the lead would drive right past the stadium because he couldn't count how many laps he had driven. I mean, the number is three, how hard is that? But it happened quite a few times."

Frank laughed at the memory of those incidents, though it had happened to an Impala driver twice in consecutive years. Both times the ward had the lead coming off the last turn, and their pilot drove right past the jog to the finish line in the stadium thinking he had one lap to go. That driver, Clem Mason, still had to apologize whenever he ventured out of his house and ran into members of his community. Now approaching his seventieth year of life, his brothers and sisters of Impala would never let him forget what he had done. Clem would, no doubt, have to live out the rest of his years being shunned, and one could expect his headstone would be defaced once they had placed his shamed carcass in the ground.

They passed out of the Mustang area, crossed the dividing line of Martin Luther King Jr. Boulevard, and reentered the safety of the Impala neighborhood. As the dusk came upon them, they took a shortcut through Cass Park, where recreating Impalans stopped their workouts to watch Joe and his mechanics pass. A sheepish Joe offered a few waves, and the tone of the tittering of the masses continued to reinforce a theme that this wasn't the guy they were expecting at all.

Frank and Claudia led him through the courtyard to the Brassey front door. Joe could see the curtains part at the window of one of the upstairs bedrooms. A silhouette of a young man stood in the center of the wooden-framed pane of glass. A cheery Karen opened the door before Claudia could ring the bell.

"You must be Mr. Smith," Karen said.

"Joe."

"Welcome, Joe."

She ushered them into the house, but Frank and Claudia demurred.

"Come on in for a drink, you two," Karen said.

"Thanks, Mrs. Brassey, but we're having dinner with Claudia's mother this evening."

Joe sensed that their excuse was spontaneous bullshit. There appeared to be some kind of class struggle in play here, as the mechanics looked mighty uncomfortable amidst the opulent surroundings of the Brassey's residence.

The door to Lon's study opened, and he emerged with a glass of ice and whiskey sweating in his right hand.

"Your things are up in the spare bedroom at the end of the hall. Honey, why don't you get Mr. Smith situated. I want to have a word with Frank and Claudia," Lon said.

"You can call me Joe."

"What?"

"He wants you to call him Joe, dear. Come on, Joe, let's get you squared away before dinner," Karen said.

She and Joe headed for the stairs. Lon stepped out onto the front porch with Frank and Claudia.

"What do you think?" Lon asked.

"Too early to tell, Captain. But he had no problem with what we attempted to accomplish in the short time we had. We'll know more in a couple of days," Frank said.

"He's not afraid, Cap, that's for sure," Claudia said.

They left out the details of the afternoon's excursion. Lon would only need to know this man's progress as it related to his duties as a mercenary driver. There would be nothing forthcoming about his swift action in dumping the Mustang thug on the ground, or the perceived flirtation he seemed to be having with the Mustang bitch.

"Good," Lon said, and he turned to go.

"We've got two days until our next appointment at the museum. Maybe he could come by the shop before then. He should see a detailed map of the course as soon as possible."

"Yeah, okay, we can make that happen," Lon said.

Maybe it *was* a class thing, because Lon left the two mechanics standing on the doorstep without even offering anything resembling a "so long" or "good-bye." Frank and Claudia stood there as the door closed in their faces.

"This room used to be for guests, but then I got this crazy idea that I would start a business," Karen said with the hint of a pessimistic giggle.

Joe looked around at the remnants of Karen's hope for a life of industriousness. Two sewing machines, with the bulk of the room's clutter stacked atop them, occupied the corner of the room.

"Were you making dresses?"

"Kids clothing. Onesies. Overalls. Anything I could imagine for the under-five set."

"My mother made the latest fashions for the women of Big D back in the day."

"You're kidding," Karen said.

"No. When I came into this world, my crib shared the room with two sewing machines. I've been told that when I was really cranky, my mom would sew and the white noise would put me to sleep," Joe said, amazed by the sheer quantity and quality of the instance of kismet.

"Well, I don't know how your mother fared, but my endeavor was a colossal bust. People here in Motor City actually preferred the junk from China. Couture is not a word that people want to lend to children's clothes."

Joe could hear her disappointment linger only for a nanosecond, as her subtle scowl became an alabaster smile.

"Okay, Joe, there are towels in the bathroom down the hall. Dinner will ready in about an hour. After you've freshened up, I'm sure Lon would like you to join him for a cocktail on the terrace."

"Thank you."

"I think this gambit is going to work out for everyone involved," Karen said on her exit.

As the door opened, Joe could see a figure standing farther down the hall. To Joe's eyes, it appeared to be a boy in the middle of his teenage years. Joe gave the person a discreet wave, and the reciprocation came swiftly in the form of a nod from the youngster's head.

Joe slowly shut the door; they had plenty of time for introductions later. He opened his single bag to reveal just two changes of clean clothes. He laid a pair of khakis and a plaid shirt on the bed. He made a mental note to use the alms that the city had given him in the form of the money card to purchase a couple of alternate items to fill out his wardrobe.

He moved back out to the now-empty hall, entered the bathroom, and turned on the shower. Within two minutes, he was allowing his body to be spattered by a deluge of near-scalding water. As he reached for the fragrant bar of soap nestled in a brightly tiled alcove, he noticed that there was a lack of steadiness in his hands. Once perceived and studied, he noticed that it was more than just a slight tremor brought on by the lack of sustenance or fatigue—he was actually shaking uncontrollably.

TWENTY-FOUR

FIRST IMPRESSIONS

JOHN WATCHED THE thin figure—this supposed future hero of Impala—close the door to his suite before he reentered his room. Later, he heard the water rushing up through the pipes and mused on the force of the pressure fighting to overcome gravity. He thought about the energy that would be required for this paladin to find clarity amidst all of the bullshit that his father would endeavor to perpetrate on him. The crap that his father was conjuring was the constant, gravity. This guy would need to be pretty special to countermand the forces, John calculated.

John walked over to his dictionary. The moment cried out for a word to describe the emotions that he'd been dealing with since they temporarily kicked him out of school after they said he attacked Rebecca Leeann Voss. He wasn't sure why, but he felt a kindred existence with that fellow who was washing off the sins of the day in the bathroom down the hall. Maybe it was because, like him, an assessment of the effort applied could end up being the only result that carried with it any meaning.

Even though he would be turning sixteen in three weeks and would be eligible to try out for the punch-out squad, even though he had kissed Rebecca Leeann Voss to prove to her that his desire carried with it a decision to be more than just friends, and even though his father would attempt to thwart him from stepping beyond the bonds of his condition, he knew that if he never dared to try, he would be forever lost.

He thought he had a word that would fit this paradigm. It was one that he had found some years before, but he never really felt that he had the necessary context to truly understand its meaning.

As he began to page through the dictionary, he became frustrated. Searching for a word with only the basic constraints of a definition was like trying to find a single pebble on the moon—on the dark side of the moon. It was a word that would encapsulate the struggles he was going through. It would also include the warrior patsy down the hall. And in the end it would all come back to their relationship with his father—one life-long, one not a day old.

There it was, "vicegerent." He read the definition and felt that, for now, the word would have to suffice. A vicegerent is a person who has been deputized by a person of authority to carry out some deed in lieu of the deputizer. Now there was some truth, John thought, since his father was not the type of person who would ever get his hands or pants dirty.

TWENTY-FIVE

SLEEPER AWAKE

Udo Lewandoski (aka Clarence Rigney) had told the lawyer, Leo Rascone, that he would not need to be provided with lodging for his visit to Motor City. He would be bunking with some old friends in the part of the town that traditionally housed the Un-coms.

The entrance requirements had been met; there appeared to be nothing in the available records that would restrict a visa. Udo had made sure that he looked stellar on his resume by co-opting the background information from the first man he had killed in his desire to maintain a sense of piety to his messiah.

The man, Clarence Rigney, Udo's neighbor, was a one-time postal worker from Upper Sandusky, Ohio. He had been a member of the congregation of a pastor by the name of Reverend Ollie Brown, who was part of the cadre of five religious leaders that had set a date for the world's demise some thirty years ago.

Udo, all of six years old when the predicted end days were drawing nigh, had watched the old man from across the street diligently prepare for meeting his maker by selling his car, his furniture, and anything else of material worth on his perfectly manicured front lawn. It was the late fall before that predicted fateful day to come the following March, and the rye seedlings had taken root, completely masking the brown of the Bermuda carpet underneath.

A faction of Redeemers killed his church's leader the same day that he'd sold his Kia to a man from down the street, but Mr. Rigney soldiered on in his preparations. To Clarence, old Ollie Brown just got to move the schedule up a bit. He was like that guy in Kentucky, the Reverend Jack Clark, another member of the predictor group, having succumbed to a heart attack three months before, and the Reverend Bob Gibson, the one-time leader of the effort, who lost his battle to cancer eight months after the announcement of the date via a worldwide broadcast from his Colorado compound.

When that March 15 came and went, and the world still existed, Mr. Rigney withdrew into his domicile, angry and resistant to the entreaties from the neighborhood folks who attempted to bade him to move on with his life. Instead, he loaded his Remington twelve-gauge with hand-packed cartridges containing rock salt. When the noise level became too great, a stray ball was plopped into his yard, or one of the neighborhood dogs crapped on his now-deteriorating lawn, he laid down the law with both barrels aimed at the ankles of the perpetrators of the various slights.

Young Udo took a load of the ersatz ammunition when he was ten. By that time, Mr. Rigney had become a gargoyle to most of the neighborhood kids, where wagers lost were sometimes paid in full by provoking the wrathful shut-in. Udo's comeuppance for having lost a coin-pitching contest was to brodie the back wheel of his bicycle in Clarence's front yard until the old man opened the door.

Unfortunately for Udo, the door opened when he had his back to Mr. Rigney and his trusty shotgun. The shards of rock salt blew out his front tire and also kicked up a medium-sized stone that had been laying dormant in the rubble-strewn yard. That same stone struck Udo in the torso and cracked one of his ribs. He rode away on the bare rim of his purple Huffy, the jeers and cheers of his compatriots providing a dramatic soundtrack, while he desperately tried to re-inflate his collapsed left lung.

Six years later, at just sixteen years old, fully indoctrinated as a Redeemer through a man tied to the organization's origins, Udo killed Clarence Rigney on a quiet Sunday afternoon. He tore the cover off the Bible that the old postman kept parked next to his living room chair and scrawled the words "New Testament for Now" on the page that listed the edition. His weapon of choice was an eight-inch chef's knife that he'd liberated from Mr. Rigney's kitchen drawer.

The Upper Sandusky Police Department investigated the case. They found only partial prints, and they followed a blood trail that disappeared somewhere into the grove of trees out back. The rapidly cooling case was marked unsolvable within a year of Mr. Rigney's murder. A note was placed in the file that suggested that the killing was ritualistic and possibly motivated by revenge. Speculation was that the murderer or murderers were transients connected to this group that called themselves Redeemers, and Rigney's death was payback for an incident that had occurred two years before.

Mr. Rigney's house was sold to a young attorney and his wife, and in a very short amount of time, the memory of his existence was relegated to another chapter in the tome that chronicled the neighborhood's folklore.

How Udo came to be a member of the Redeemer movement could be explained by some of the details of his upbringing combined with the forces of natural selection.

Udo was an only child, raised by a single mother with a penchant for bringing numerous men of a dubious nature into their home and lives. His birth father had run off prior to his birth and naming. He had caught his wife, Anna, orally copulating with a man she had met in a bar during the sixth month of gestation of the child that would turn out to be Udo.

Udo's preschool-years' experiences were remembered for being a time where he existed in a constant state of fear that one of his mother's multiple boyfriends would beat or maim him because of the attention he would naturally draw away from them due to his blood connection with Anna.

As Udo approached adolescence, his mother took in a boarder by the name of Craig Bellows. Mysterious and murky, Craig Bellows came into their life under circumstances that Udo was not fully able to comprehend at the outset.

The whole of the story he had been told is that Craig was related to a cousin his mother had in Oklahoma. A drifter, Craig had only the name and address of the mid-thirties blonde Anna at his disposal as he wandered through north central Ohio on his way to hook up with a group of individuals that shared his belief that the Son of God had recently been on earth. Craig fervently believed that Russell Reading, aka the Redeemer, was that messiah.

When Craig first showed up to flop at their ratty two-bedroom clapboard, Udo was convinced that his mother had brought the devil into their lives. Craig was dirty and bearded, and he sported one tattoo on his forearm and one under his right eyelid.

As was his nature, Udo searched through the newcomer's belongings and found some interesting but disturbing clues. In the rucksack that contained Craig's earthly goods were items that would have brought alarm to any twelve-year-old. Beyond only a couple of changes of clothes, there was a tattered book with the title *The New Testament for Now*, a nicked but lethal-looking machete, an electronic storage device, and a filthy orange prison jumpsuit with a patch that looked like an upside down crown of thorns ironed onto the area that would cover the left breast. The jumpsuit was stained with what looked like a combination of clay, dirt, and/or blood.

When Udo heard the clomp of Craig's heavy boots in the hall, he got nervous and searched for a place to hide, even though he was in his own room and he had every right to be in there at that particular moment. The large hulking man entered and found Udo sitting at the desk, reading the first book he could put his hands on. It was the Holy Bible that had been passed down through his father's family—the father he had never known. Craig strode over and snatched it out of his hand.

"What is this?"

"The Bible."

"Hah. The hallowed, though outdated text. There is very little meaning left in this here book, kid," Craig said.

Udo said nothing in response. What was he to say? He wasn't really reading it, just using it as a diversion. The fact was that even though he had attended school for the required number of years, Udo could barely read. Craig rummaged through his bag, ignorant to the fact that it had recently been rifled through by the inquisitive kid sitting—trying desperately to disguise his quaking—at the desk in the corner.

"You want to read something that actually has real value?" Craig asked.

"That's okay. I wasn't really reading it. I was just looking at the front part of the book where it listed my father's family."

Craig sat on the edge of the bed and paged to the part of the bible that had lines and spaces for the Lewandoski family tree. Everything had been filled in up to and including the marriage between Udo's father, Viktor, and his mother, Anna.

"Tell me about your dad," Craig said.

"Nothing to tell. I've never met him."

Craig right eye slowly blinked and revealed the blue tattoo that had been etched onto his eyelid.

"What's that?" Udo asked.

"What?"

"That thing on your eye."

"It's my life. It's my reason for being."

"Can I see it?"

Craig closed the eye, and Udo could see that the indelible mark had the characteristics of a two-dimensional section of tangled tumbleweed. There was cross-hatching with spikes pointing downward, and he figured that, whatever the hell it was, the image had been put there upside down.

"Did they make a mistake?"

"What do you mean?"

"It looks like it's upside down," Udo stated.

"It is."

Craig could see that this was confusing to the boy. *He must not have a lot of education*, Craig realized. *He doesn't understand the original iconography or its classic orientation.*

"You know about a Jesus?"

"Just what I learned in Sunday school once."

"Well, when they killed him, they paraded him around the town with a crown of thorns on his head," Craig said.

"Why?"

"They were making fun of him. They called him the "King of the Jews." And then they hung him up on a cross, banged nails into his hands, and left him there to slowly bleed to death in the desert heat."

Craig could see that as Udo processed this new information, he began to lean toward him—emanating an intellectual hunger that he probably didn't experience very often. Craig also saw the glint in the young boy's eye when he mentioned the nails and the blood.

"Anyway, I believe that Jesus was the first Son of God and that the Redeemer is his brother. The image is reversed because the legend is reversed."

"The Redeemer?"

"You ever get out of the house, boy?" Craig asked.

"Sure."

Craig nodded. Maybe this was enough for now. He was hungry and began to wonder if they would be having dinner soon. When did the mother say she would be home from work? He rose from the bed and began to head for the door.

"Tell me about the Redeemer. I want to know."

Craig stopped.

"You got anything to eat?"

"Sure."

During the meal of boxed macaroni and cheese, Craig related the facts of the Redeemer's time on earth: his revelation, his direct action of taking the lives of the wicked, and his incarceration and condemnation at the hands of the corrupt government. He contrasted the Redeemer to the only other person he thought might be the Son of God, Jesus Christ.

"You've read the Old Testament?" Craig asked with a full mouth.

"Sure. Some of it."

Craig knew that this response was most likely a fib, but he pressed on as if the kid was familiar with the material.

"God set the rules in that first book, and Jesus deviated from them. Because Jesus softened those rules, he gained a big following. Nobody wants things to be tough and hard. And where did that get us? Nowhere. We have failed God by not living up to the standards of his original writings."

This was the basis of the concept that drew Craig to the movement. People will follow anyone who makes things easier, he thought at the time. The rejection of the path of the sublime became the basis for his personal creed that stated: One had to be willing to sacrifice everything to adhere to God's word, and not try to diminish its litany by looking for comfort or an easy way out. This whole idea of confession of sins resulting in mythical absolution was a farce. When one sinned, there should be consequences.

Craig continued on, outlining the narrative that would offer some of the details of the rise of the Redeemer.

"The Redeemer believes that lessons in the Old Testament—and some of the work of the apostles who weren't total butt-kissers like St. Matthew—are the only words of God. A follower, St. Horace, wrote *The New Testament for Now* to bring these precepts forward into the new era."

He saw Udo nodding.

"When we finish here, I want you to go upstairs, take your father's Bible, and read the passage that is in St. Matthew, chapter 13, verse 41," Craig said.

"I will."

"That's where we're going to start."

Udo needed a little help from his new instructor to read and comprehend the essence of the Bible passage. It read, "The Son of man will send out his angels and they will weed out of his kingdom everything that causes sin and all who do evil."

"I am one of those angels," Craig said.

He rolled up the sleeve of his shirt and offered the inside of his forearm for Udo to inspect. Tattooed in black ink was the numerical sequence 7/81341.

"Matthew is either the seventh or eighth apostle, and the other numbers are for the chapter and verse," Craig said.

Udo touched the skin and, for the first time, felt an emotion that could only be described as jealousy.

This vagabond who had happened upon them was nothing less than a huge inconvenience to Udo's mother. With the presence of this large man in her house, the already wanting square footage seemed to contract to the point that Anna felt alone only when she was in the bathroom behind a locked door. In the coming days and weeks, she made some nuanced sexual advances to the stranger. This was possibly intended as a ploy to attain some power in the situation, but Craig responded as if he were repulsed by her wanton desire.

Craig consistently offered her his counsel as to why she seemed pathologically consumed by this focus on her libido. In their discussions, Craig seemed to suggest that she wasn't really cursed by an insatiable need to be sexually satisfied, but was trying to fill a hole in her life, a thirst that could easily be slaked by letting God into her being. Her snorts of derision in response to his suggestions could be heard down the block.

Anna took to leaving the house in the evening and seeing where the night might take her. The early part of the evening's drinking in any bar in town almost always led to a place to sleep somewhere.

She didn't worry after her child. The kid seemed to like the burly man, and even when she was around, they barely paid attention to her, so consumed were they with their studies.

After four months she tried to get a message to her cousin, Charles, requesting advice on how she might get his friend to move on. There was no response. When she broached the subject directly with the freeloader, her son flew into a rage. At one point, her child threatened her with the handled end of a mop. She disarmed him and slapped him across the face, and the two did not exchange a single word for the next two months.

Something had definitely changed for the better, though. Her son's grades suddenly advanced up two levels from C's and D's to A's and B's. He began to take a more active role in keeping the house clean and providing the meals. He spent hours alone in his room reading and writing in an essay notebook.

Through the ethanol haze, Anna had few moments of clarity, but the light of an epiphany appeared to be trying to illuminate its way through her fog. This Craig, this unkempt religious fanatic, had become the first father figure that her son had ever known. She had no specific knowledge of his background; she only had her cataloged ob-

servances of his behavior, and the effect he had on her son, but something was beginning to tug on the outer sheath of her hardened heart.
She stopped taking her nightly excursions, cut way down on her imbibing, and began to assume a more traditional role as the woman of
the house. She took over the duties of the cooking and the cleaning.
As the year came to a close, she realized she might actually be falling in
love with Craig Bellows.

TWENTY-SIX

LIKE ADAM'S FALL

Young Udo advanced his understanding and comprehension of Craig's fanaticism at a rapid pace. Dinner table conversations—of which Anna was decidedly not a verbal participant—were represented by a continuous, almost Jesuit-style, dialog centered on the literal interpretations of the passages of *The New Testament for Now* that Craig had assigned Udo to read.

Anna found many of these sessions to be wearying. Both of them had taught themselves the art of being able to argue from either side of the conflict. To her, there was never any resolution, just a constant stream of babble. She had no idea that the purpose of these tête-à-têtes was to develop Udo's formally dormant mind. The effects were tangible, though. Her son was now a student of high quality.

Had Anna been fully capable of seeing the world beyond her own experiences, she would have witnessed the devious nature of the man who had come into their lives in a more defined light. Unbeknownst to her, Craig had taken the empty yet fertile brain of her child and filled all of that open space not with knowledge, but with his craziness.

Udo's main goal in life had distilled into a simple, straightforward idea: to impress his teacher/father figure.

She didn't know it at the time, but her burgeoning love interest in Craig was the culmination of more than just her need to have someone share her bed. Looking back, she realized that the reasons behind her desire to couple with him included the effect the man was having on her son. She was jealous that he had replaced her as a parent. She was envious of the way that Craig could get her son to perform a task by simply asking that said task should be completed. She was livid that she had become a ghost in her own house. All of the inward expressions of these vibrant emotions became more florid now that she was no longer drinking heavily. Without the numbing effects of the alcohol, she began to pay attention to feelings that had been nonexistent for as long as her son had been alive.

Still, she couldn't find the key to unlock Craig's heart (or his dick) to see if he might feel, even slightly, similar.

She remembered how she had been rebuffed when she first came onto him some eighteen months before. The fear of rejection a second time had the effect of rendering her tentative. This was not a quality that anyone who knew her would remotely consider as being part of her makeup. She needed something other than the base desires of her own loneliness or horniness to motivate her to take the next step with him. Perhaps she would have to hatch a plot to ensnare him. More months elapsed, and she continued to be flummoxed by the situation.

For Craig's part, he was aware that he'd been a positive influence on the household. The previous dour situation had surely changed since his arrival. The woman had stopped drinking and screwing around. The son seemed to finally be on a track of usefulness.

It had been almost two years now, and his original intention to hook up with some like-minded colleagues in the area south of Toledo had dissipated. The plan was to begin to establish roots in the corridor that fronted Lake Erie, so that eventually a northern Redeemer presence could confront the Jesus-loving idiots—as Craig saw them—that populated the state. The state of Ohio was littered with many Christian denominations from Unitarian to Catholic, and everything in between.

The original rough sketch of the plan set forth by his buddy, Charles, was to wreak havoc by eventually killing as many of the infidels as they could. Charles had hoped that Craig could bring together the small Redeemer following that he knew existed in the areas around Columbus and Cleveland, and begin the job of recruiting a greater, more potent force that would begin the task of extermination.

But Craig had gotten slack ever since he set foot in the Lewandowski household. When he had first arrived, he was only two weeks removed from the massacre that had taken place down in Kentucky.

Craig Bellows had been one of the leaders of the assault on Mercyville. By his own count, he had personally killed over forty people. Bathed in the blood of what he believed to be the wicked, he had been transformed to a status beyond that of believer. No doubt, by virtue of his deeds in the Christian compound that was once connected to the Jack Clark congregation, Craig believed that there would be a place in heaven for him, hopefully next to the Redeemer almighty himself.

This was what the movement was all about: Russell Reading had killed many people to prove that the laws that the Lord had written were literal and sacrosanct. The government awarded him a sentence of death, but on the supposed last day of earth, Russell Reading was raptured to heaven to be with his father. He was the only one known to have experienced the return home on that fateful day. Like Craig, the warriors of the faith wore orange prison jumpsuits in homage to the one that was left, bodiless, on the floor of Russell Reading's death row prison cell.

This was the twisted myth that propelled the followers of the Redeemer. They clung to the absolute belief that the only way a ticket would be issued for travel to God's kingdom was to emulate the actions of his true Son.

Anna was never really privy to the depth of the commitment that her son was making in fealty to this newfound religious figure. For the longest time, she was just grateful that her son seemed to have gotten on a path that would lead to some place other than enfeebling drug use or extended jail time.

She did not like the fact that she had been left out of the equation that should have included three residents in the house, not two, and that perceived slight may have been one of the motivating forces in concocting the plan to coerce Craig Bellows to become her sex slave.

Anna needed to change the dynamic, to drive a wedge into the union to see if she could insert herself into the present hierarchy. She needed to no longer be a subatomic particle imparting little or no effect on the nucleus that the two of them had created.

She knew that Craig Bellows was heterosexual and experienced something akin to yearning. She had noticed him slyly checking to see if he could spy a nipple when she bent over the sink to unclog the drain in one of her loose-fitting low-cut tops. She had peripherally observed him staring at her vaginal area when she wore the tight jeans that accentuated the shape of her *labia majora*. She even noticed the indication of an erection one evening when she innocently allowed him to see her recently coiffed strip of ash-blond pubic hair after the nightgown she was wearing inadvertently opened as she rose from the couch. Feigning horror that she had exposed herself, she embarrassingly ran off to the bathroom only to reemerge to find that there was a significant bulge in his pants.

She had no idea that a serious and debilitating addiction to thoughts concerning sex had been the compelling force behind Craig's desire to seek spiritual fulfillment from a higher power. In his early twenties, Craig had divested himself from all of the money that had found its way into his wallet on hookers, pornography, and fake affection from the women who removed their clothes for a living.

Seeking out the one man in his circle of acquaintances who had professed a zeal for religious commitment—Anna's cousin Charles—Craig confessed to him the sins related to his preoccupation with prurience.

Charles immediately set about bringing Craig into the congregation of the Church of the Redeemer. The two shared the cost of transportation to attend services at the chapel in El Dorado, Kansas, from their home base in Oklahoma City, a nearly 300-mile round trip each and every Sunday morning.

Charles had been attending services since the church's opening. He also authored a weblog on the church's activities, replete with videos of the sermons, under the pseudonym "Peter T." Quickly, he built an online following that continued to expand during the five years between the opening of the chapel and the rapture of the Redeemer. It was Charles—as "Peter T."—who inspired the first killings that took the lives of the Reverend Ollie Brown and another of the doomsday predictors, the Reverend Alvin Sampson.

In the Redeemer faith, Craig found his salvation. As he learned to give over his addiction to carnality to this Son of God, he had a long-hoped for spiritual awakening. The excitement generated by the release of his demons became the kick-start that put him on the road to zealotry. Following in the footsteps of his deity, he began to activate the primordial forces that would eventually lead to actualizing a desire to kill another human being. It was an effort tied to his need to emulate his master. The act of taking a life became the substitute for his previous fascinations, and he approached the task with the same unrelenting ferventness.

Now ensconced within the Lewandowski household, it had been nearly two years since he had fulfilled that notion that every life he ended meant another step on the ladder toward salvation with his Redeemer. During this prolonged period of expressive dormancy, the old thoughts and patterns of his past began to reemerge. At the time, he had wondered if his two-year stay in the Lewandowski residence had effectively weakened his resolve to carry on his work as a loyal servant to his Redeemer.

Yes, he had begun to notice the sexuality represented by the female in the house, and it was starting to cause problems as he vacillated between the points spanning the extremes of the gratification centers that existed in his brain. The issue was limbic in origin, and it centered on the emotive instincts that laymen like to label "fuck or fight."

On noticing that something had awakened in him in deference to an old desire based in hysteria libidinosa, his first thought was to remove the impediment that was appearing to entreat him to veer from his chosen path. Killing Anna would have been an easy and effective way of keeping his distance from the evils of his past. The act could be easily validated on multiple levels, including the fact that through her boozing and fucking around, she was a sinner of the first degree, and thus warranted removal.

He was fully aware that the simmering of the pot that contained his sexual fantasies could not be allowed to come to a full boil. He would surely see any capitulation as a transgression in its own right—a transgression that would make him no better than the average non-believer. In the moments just after he caught sight of the area between her legs and he felt the ensuing rigidity in his own genitalia, he vowed to take this tack and end the source of the temptation. This entire event was obviously an important test being administered by his Redeemer.

He did not immediately carry out the act, though. There were other very important storylines competing for rationalization space when it came to the need to swiftly end the association with the devil's handiwork that this vixen represented.

Anna was also the mother of the growing young man who acquired his intellectual sustenance from the time spent under Craig's wing. Their work over the last two years took precedence over all of the petty lusts and false detours into deviance. The boy was maturing physically, and the day would soon be coming that he would have to test himself within the limits of his training. Craig felt that removal of the mother—especially if the snatcher of the life was he—could confuse the young man to the point that all of the work they had accomplished might have been for naught.

For whatever purpose, Craig began to see that the act of killing Anna to satisfy his own need to maintain righteousness would have represented more than a hiccup in the seamless educational program that was developing her child into a special entity for the Redeemer movement.

Still, how was he going to control the rapidly accumulating images of her body, her smell, and the tactile warmth she emanated when they awkwardly brushed against each other? How was he going to repress the sudden existence of the erotic pictures of her that spontaneously erupted in his mind? As much as he tried to restrain himself, every incident led to consequences in that area of his body that he had kept dormant for so long. He would have to bring his extraordinary power in the form of boundless will to remain sinless. He had brought down this beast before. He would have to muster the power to resist it again. With the Redeemer's help, it was possible.

Anna could sense that the man was weakening. It wasn't only the outward manifestation of arousal she had observed; this man now appeared to be continually distracted in her presence. She decided to increase the pressure. The two males shared the bedroom upstairs, but the only bathroom in the house was located downstairs, just off the living room, next to her room. Often, Craig would be forced to relieve his bladder at night. She rarely heard his tiptoes on the stairs on most nights, but recently, because her bloodstream had a lower concentration of the foreign substances that used to bring on a nightly coma, she would hear him quietly enter the john and sit upon the toilet so that the noise of his urine stream would not disturb her.

One night, after hearing his stocking feet padding by her door, she began to moan softly as if she were in the midst of an act of masturbation. She heard him hesitate outside her door, obviously drawn by the noises coming from within. She feigned the sounds of ecstasy—discreetly muffled by her pillow—as if she had reached culmination. Fulfilled, she sighed and rolled over like a daughter of Bacchus returning to slumber. There was a long pause before she heard the sound of his retreating from her closed door.

She knew then that she was closing in on executing the transformation that would change the way the three people coexisted under the roof of the bungalow.

On ensuing nights, she heard him slow as he passed her bedroom, possibly dejected that he had missed what he thought (or maybe hoped) might be a nightly event.

On a warm summer evening, a week after her initial performance, she left her bedroom door slightly ajar and noticed him stop and peer briefly into the darkness of her room. From that day forward, she made it point to keep her bedroom door open at night.

After a couple of weeks in which she slept through the night, or missed the times he ventured downstairs, she knew that the level of Craig Bellow's curiosity had reached a breaking point. He became restless, prickly, having to will himself to leave the room if she was in attendance. Her son had noticed the change in his behavior and commented on it more than once during dinner, or when the three of them whiled away the evening watching the Chinese comedies or Russian soap operas on the streaming satellite screen. His responses were usually cryptic—something about the need to understand a religious concept that had baffled him.

And then it happened. Late one evening, her son away on an overnight camping trip with his summer school class, Anna retired to her bedroom early, ostensibly to read from the bodice-ripper paperbacks that made up the bulk of her entertainment.

As Craig cleaned the dinner dishes, she lay atop her bed, naked, and began to pleasure herself. She was fully illuminated by the stream of light from the bedside lamp. The bedroom door had been left half-open, as if she'd simply forgotten to close it. When she heard the water in the kitchen shut off, the dried dishes being stacked and put away, she started to feel the increase of anticipation that he might wander past her threshold and catch her. She decided to roll over to her side, away from the door. She did not want him to think that he was supposed to see this; it would simply be an accident, and if it bothered him, he could simply walk on by or reach out and shut the door.

When he did saunter by with the sole intention of using the bathroom, he saw her from behind. He couldn't help himself from following the curve of her spine down to the taut half moons that bulged at her center. She was beginning to rock her body in a series of small convulsions. He did not look away. Deep down, even as he knew that restraint was his ultimate priority, he had been hoping for moment like this. He maintained a bearing of absolute quietude, and his breathing became nothing more than a faint whisper.

And that is when she rolled onto her back and achieved full release. When she noticed him standing at the door, his vision focused on her, she did not act startled. She held out her beckoning arms and simply said, "Please."

It was over quickly. The sacred fluids that had been dogmatically held in abeyance for nearly eight years were unleashed just moments after he entered her.

The memory that she would always have, the one that would always haunt her, was the moment that he completed his paroxysms and closed his eyes. It was her first, and only, close-up view of the inverted blue crown of thorns that had been etched into his eyelid. There was a swirling contrast of colors between the Bic ink blue of the design and the swollen red capillaries and vessels snaking throughout the surface of the lid. In her post-orgasmic haze—the climax that she had provided for herself—her docile mind warped briefly into a hallucination. For just a couple of moments she witnessed the vessels of the eyelid bursting and bathing the crown's image with a river of blood.

The eyes of the man snapped open. The whites were now also doused in crimson, and she could see into the blackness of his irises, deep into the recesses of his brain.

She had no idea, though. She had no idea of what this act meant to him. She hadn't really grasped the substance of the ongoing dialogs this man was having with her son. Maybe if she had heard and comprehended even ten percent of their conversations, she would have been somewhat prepared for what was to happen next.

The scream came from somewhere deep inside of him. It was a plaintive wail. It was the cry of a mortally injured animal. He withdrew his penis and stood before her, every muscle clenching with a supernatural tension.

"It's okay, honey. You probably haven't done this in a long time. The first time back can sometimes be funky. We can give it another go after you recover," she said, totally misreading the reason for his outburst.

"You're the devil!" he screamed at her.

The look of disgust on his face could not possibly be misinterpreted. She knew it wasn't about her at that point. This guy was going through something that was unrelated to her charms. She momentarily felt a wave of fear as if she were about to be subjected to an act of violence, but he turned away and began to run. He got up to speed as he almost crashed into the front door. He nearly ripped the barrier off the hinges as he swung it open and headed out into the street, his penis still fully engorged, preceding his progress like a bowsprit of a tall ship.

She heard the scream again, but this time it was prolonged and inconceivably louder. A couple more moments passed before she heard the thunder of an unbaffled firearm from across the street. *Boom!*

She jumped up from the bed, rushed to the curtained bay window, and peeked through the sliver of space where the drapes met. Standing on his porch, his Remington still belching smoke from both barrels, was Clarence Rigney. In the weeds at his feet lay Craig Bellows with most of his internal organs scattered about the yard. They were just a minor addition to all of the other crap that had littered the Rigney property for the last eight years.

When the police arrived on the scene, Clarence Rigney was sitting in a decrepit rocking chair cradling his reloaded burglar deterrent. A crowd of neighbors had gathered on the sidewalk, but no one was willing to trespass onto the property to check the condition of the man lying in the yard. He hadn't produced even a twitch since the first person's arrival, and everyone assumed that he was dead.

Clarence told the cops his side of the story. Dozing on the couch, he had been startled awake by the sound of a loud, screaming maniac. He went to the window and saw a naked male, his penis fully erect, walking around his yard, bellowing some religious gibberish. He loaded his 12-gauge with his alternate ammunition—000 steel buckshot—opened the door, and told the man to get off his property. When said man (who, Clarence explained, "had eyes like the devil") rushed at him, he let loose with both barrels at the man's lower torso.

When the news spread that the dead man had two distinctive tattoos on his body signifying that he was a member of the murderous Redeemer sect, Clarence Rigney was hailed a hero. His reign was brief, however. The neighborhood once again turned against him only two months later after he killed Mrs. Carpenter's Lhasa Apso. The poor little teeth-challenged canine had chased a ball into Clarence's yard only to be sent to the great beyond via a load of rock salt to the head.

TWENTY-SEVEN

AVENGING ANGEL

THE NEWS OF Craig Bellow's death had a serious impact on Udo. When he returned from his camping trip and heard the story of his mentor's demise, he was devastated. It took him many months to recover from the shock that his teacher was no longer a part of his life.

His mother told him an alternate version of the events of that night: There was no enticement to sex; Craig just went crazy, stripped off his clothes, began speaking in incomprehensible guttural tones, and ran out the front door for no apparent reason. Anna opined that the pressure of trying to solve his spiritual conundrum—the one Craig admitted had made him brittle and incorrigible—had finally caused the strange man to crack.

Since Craig rarely, if ever, ventured outside of the house, no one in the neighborhood could recall having seen him in the vicinity before the night of his death. Mother and son concurred with their neighbors that they did not know the identity of the dead man. The local cops didn't think to swab the body for DNA—the tattoos, his nudity, and Clarence Rigney's story were enough to close the casebook. This happenstance worked out well for Anna, as she would not be asked questions about why her genital mucous happened to be on the deceased man's detached penis.

Udo took the man's death as a bellwether in his own life. He doubled his efforts to understand the precepts set forth by St. Horace in the text of *The New Testament for Now*. With help of a savvy classmate, he was able to hack into the electronic storage device that was part of Craig Bellow's left behinds. In it, he found hundreds of pages of a diary and multiple files of photographs.

His mother had sent a message to her cousin, Charles, to inform him of his friend's death. There was no response, and the maternal wisdom imparted on her son suggested that her cousin may have disappeared or died as well. Udo never told his mother about her cousin Charlie's alter ego as the infamous Peter T., and he never told her about the content of information that was stored within his teacher's device.

The mother and son never reconciled after all the "I's" and "T's" were dotted and crossed on the whole affair. It only took a couple of weeks before Udo's coldness and total disregard for his mother took on the quality of cruelty. He definitely held her responsible for Craig's death, though he never had anything approaching fact to back it up. He also was not kind to himself for having been away on the evening of his mentor's demise. The mix of this, spiced with the confusion of youth, created feelings of hatred for Anna that could not be mollified. She tried—on more than one occasion—to offer anything she could to pacify her retreating son, but she found herself only imploring deaf ears. Desperate, she used the only thing her crazed mind thought might work—an offer of incestuous servitude. His reaction almost resulted in her death. She drove away one night, bruised and bloody, and Udo never heard from her again.

Even though he was now reading at grade level, it took Udo awhile to get through the diary pages. Viewing the unvarnished history of the man he idolized was not easy. The entries were unedited, contained numerous spelling and grammatical miscues, and lacked contextual foundation. Some of the essays had dates that allowed Udo to identify and create an irresolute chronology, but much of the body of work contained meanderings about philosophy and theology that were merely ejaculations of ideas with no accompanying hypotheses. There were some sections that could only be described as graphic pornography—pages and pages of coarse descriptions of various women's mouths, breasts, vaginas, and anuses. Some pages were stained with blood, and many pages were written in what Udo could only think was some form of numeric code. It was these pages that intrigued him the most, and he spent the bulk of the next year trying to discover the key.

The pictures, on the other hand, were stunning. Where the jottings in the diary came off like a jumbled mass of vertebrae without the unifying column of a spine to provide relevance, the photos told a clear, concise story of Craig Bellow's past.

There were photos depicting his childhood—fourth birthday party, Little League awards ceremony, school prom, and first car. There were photos of his parents and sibling that depicted a vacation in Florida, Christmas, a new puppy, and a family reunion barbeque. Udo arranged them in a logical order, giving him the perspective of time.

There was a file of deleted photos that were still cached in a backup file. Udo's classmate was able to resurrect these, and their content was jarring to the boy who had so admired the ethos that Craig purported to live by. The deleted files were all examples of hard-core pornographic images of Craig and a bevy of women.

This was where things went a little haywire for Udo. He experienced a serious disconnect between the image of the man he knew and the behavior displayed in the photos. The span was too great for him to comprehend, and he began to question for the first time whether his teacher was worthy of his idolatry. After viewing these panels, he debated whether to repeat the deletion commands (he chose not to), and spent a few days trying to find solace in the pages of *The New Testament for Now*. On his return to these images, he noticed that Craig's identifying tattoos did not exist during this phase of his life. Obviously, a "conversion" had taken place somewhere after these pictures were taken. He began to understand that these electronic memories must have been representative of a low point in his mentor's life, possibly the trigger for his need to find salvation through the Redeemer.

The subject heading for the last file of photos was "The Awakening." All of these images were from the massacre at Mercyville.

Udo had seen pictures like these before in the history books that detailed the atrocities in Darfur, Buchenwald, Der-el-Zor, etc. The Mercyville photos were not dissimilar in that there were plenty of images of piles of bodies—men, women, and children—in the middle of well-paved suburban streets. There were photos of Craig's blood-drenched compatriots holding their weapons aloft with a resounding sense of triumphant glee, and there were photos of the Redeemer iconography painted with the victims' blood on the garage doors of the residents of the Reverend Jack Clark's doomsday community.

But there was one photo that trumped them all: the only photo of Craig Bellows taken during the massacre. The picture showed Craig, decked out in his orange prison jumpsuit, eyes glazed over in ecstasy, holding the head of a young blond child in his left hand. Held high in his right hand was the machete, still dripping warm blood and spinal fluid moments after the decapitation. Udo noticed that the expression on Craig's face mirrored the expressions he had seen on the photos depicting the acts of sexuality, and that the same demonic intensity existed in both examples.

Udo finally figured out the numeric code that covered more than a quire or two of Craig's diary. He had spent months moving the numbers around, trying to discover the base of the system, and looking for anything resembling a repetition that he might be able to exploit as a key. He tried aligning the numbers with letters of the alphabet. He experimented with looking for sums and multiples to see if there was anything that appeared to smack of consistency. He tried dilution, fractional values, and exponentials, but there was no result that led him to anything other than one dead end after another.

If he had not been so convinced that the system had to be sophisticated and complex, he would have seen that the answer to the paradox was right in front of his eyes. He would have remembered the night of the first conversation that he had with Craig when the newcomer had rolled up the sleeve of his shirt and offered him the numbers that had been etched in ink into the layers of his skin. Those numbers pertained to a verse in the book of St. Matthew. The numbers in the diary pertained to words in the verses in *The New Testament for Now.*

The numerical sequences—usually a grouping of four or five consecutive numbers followed by a period or back slash—were grouped together to each reveal a single word. The early numbers in the sequence allowed him to plot the chapter and verse of the text. The next number would give the count of the word in the verse. For example: A numerical sequence that read 16325 would denote chapter 16, verse 32, the fifth word in the verse. In this specific case, the word was "way." This word would be added to a sentence that grew into a paragraph that eventually grew into a grouping of secret messages passed between only the most highly regarded members of the Redeemer organization.

The transcription was a long and painful process that took many more months. Udo began to notice that most of the entries were messages sent by his elusive and infamous second cousin Charles, aka Peter T. Many of the missives gave the names and locations of the burgeoning cells of Redeemers that Craig had originally been dispatched to seek out in the local region of north central Ohio.

Udo decided to conduct an experiment. He coded his own message. Using his mother's discarded address book, he sent it to the last known whereabouts of his second cousin. In the message he gave some details as to the circumstances that occurred in regards to Craig's death, and he introduced himself as a blood relative and faithful student of his friend. Many weeks elapsed with no response. Maybe his mother was right. Maybe their cousin was dead.

In a last-ditch effort to try to assert himself as someone worthy of cousin Charles's attention, Udo used his classmate's computer to post the message on the bulletin board of a site that cryptically discussed all things Redeemer.

When he checked back during the following week, there was a notation signaling that he had been forwarded a private response. The response was written in the same code. A dialog began between Udo and the writer of the message, but there was no absolute confirmation that the communicator was Charles.

Udo repeatedly tried to get the writer to divulge his identity, but to no avail. After many exchanges, Udo began to trust the encrypter—he no longer cared if they were related—and he allowed the next level of his education to commence.

The writer often quizzed Udo on his knowledge of St. Horace's text, and when it became obvious that the fifteen-year-old's scholarship was impeccable, he was given a series of tasks to complete as evidence of his devotion.

The first task was to kill the man who had taken Craig Bellow's life. He was also to leave behind some indication that the Redeemer nation was responsible for the man's death.

This accomplishment would turn out to be a watershed moment for the young acolyte, and it took him a bit of time to gather his nerve. He spent many months planning and praying to the Redeemer for guidance.

He observed that Clarence Rigney only left the house on Sunday morning, and his departure allowed for somewhere between one and two hours of vacancy in the house. Over a period of four weeks, Udo created the conditions that would make his entry easy. He spent one Sunday morning inside the walls of the house familiarizing himself with the layout. It was on that visit that he discovered the knife drawer, and he made the decision to use the biggest one as the murder weapon. The Sunday before the killing, he took the knife out of the drawer and worked its edge with a whetstone before replacing it. For all of the incursions, he donned Craig's orange prison jumpsuit and covered his hands with the dishwashing gloves that his mother once used to keep her manicure intact.

When he awoke on the Sunday that would be Clarence Rigney's last, he did not feel nervous or flustered. He ate a breakfast of instant oatmeal and took a seat in front of the window that looked out across the street. He watched Clarence Rigney leave and return, waited another hour or so, gathered the elements that made up his outfit, exited through the rear door of his house, and walked around the block.

He came through the grove of trees that was the de facto limit of the Rigney property, hopped the decrepit wooden fence, and walked up to the rear entrance of the house. Through a small port window, he could see that Clarence Rigney was sitting in an overstuffed chair, lit by a standing lamp, reading from his Bible. Somewhere in the house, a radio blared gospel music.

Having rigged the door to allow for his entry, Udo stole into the house, took the knife from the drawer, came up behind the unsuspecting old man, and plunged the blade deep into his neck. As the man struggled to rise from the chair, Udo brought the knife over the man's head and stabbed him in the chest and the stomach. Blood was everywhere. The old man did not try to move again. Udo waited until he thought that Clarence had gone a long time without breathing, then he tore off the cover of his Bible and rewrote the title to match St. Horace's text, walked back out the rear door, and retraced his steps into the grouping of black walnut trees that stood sentinel between the Rigney property and another row of houses.

It would be a week before the body was discovered—a week that Udo felt took much longer than seven days to arrive. It was the week that Udo Lewandowski turned sixteen years old.

As the incident came on the heels of Craig Bellow's death in Clarence Rigney's yard over a year before, and as the title of the Redeemer's bible was inked into the page of the King James version that sat next to the deceased and taking into account the sheer brutality of the crime, the investigators concluded that the killer (or killers) were of the same sect that had begun to terrorize the good Christian people of the Midwest.

Word filtered down to the Redeemer sympathizers on the Net, and after another couple of weeks, Udo received a coded response from the person he had been exchanging messages with. The query read: "Was this you?"

Udo's return response was, "What do you think?"

After that, the coded messages came in a flurry. One of them included the confession that the person Udo had been conversant with was, in fact, his second cousin Charles, aka Peter T., a hallowed moniker to the Redeemer nation.

Charles wanted to know what ensued in the aftermath of the murder, and when Udo mentioned the formation of a neighborhood militia, Charles suggested he sign up. The best way to gather intelligence on your enemy is to become one of them, Charles instructed.

Udo approached Devon Michaels, a former army staff sergeant, and asked to be part of the group. Sergeant Michael's first reaction was to demur, but seeing the strength, potential, and ardor that the young man displayed, changed his mind. It was not long before Udo was promoted to squad leader. Weekend exercises on the outskirts of town were filled with a combination of hands-on weapons training and treatises on the subject of combat strategy.

In the meantime, Udo began to get in contact with some fellow travelers of the Redeemer ideology—the names of whom he both culled from Bellow's files and communications via Peter T. By the time he turned eighteen, he was considered a leader in both groups.

One weekend, the Redeemer splinter group attacked and killed fourteen members of a Methodist youth group just before the end of their retreat in Findley State Park, a point equidistant between Upper Sandusky and Cleveland.

After the attack, Sergeant Michael's small militia joined forces with other groups that had sprung up in the region. The fears were real, and the intention of the consolidation was to create an overwhelming force of good. Udo was anointed as a company commander of the newly combined forces.

As a leader of the Redeemer faction, more bloodshed ensued as Udo led his orange-jumpsuit-clad maniacs on killing spree after killing spree. With each event, the citizenry became more and more jittery. Cleveland began the process of forming its enclave, and the people of means rushed into the city for protection.

Eventually, there would be clashes between the small band of Redeemers and the force militia that now numbered in the hundreds of members. The forays were short, brutal affairs in which the militia got its blessed ass kicked by the smaller guerilla force during a series of ambushes and camp overruns. Even though the militia's potential firepower reigned over the scruffy clan, they were continually defeated. It was as if the Redeemers knew every move that the militia was preparing to take. Every attempt at employing a strategy was convincingly thwarted.

As the numbers of the militia dwindled due to deaths and defections, Udo pressed his Redeemer comrades to not give up until the entire opposition was vanquished.

There was a final battle. It would be the one that would be celebrated by the entire Redeemer following, and the hero of the conflict would be venerated as the first true apostle of the blessed Redeemer.

The assault took place on a brisk windy Sunday as the remnants of the full militia trained in what was supposed to be a secret location. During their lunch period, the Redeemers came out of the east with their hand-held weapons of steel. The startled, mostly baby-faced, protectors had no time to raise their substantial weapons and repel the onslaught. One group was able to unshoulder their guns, but as they prepared to draw down on the marauders, a fragmentation grenade rolled to the ground at their feet. Its deflagration killed all four of the militiamen.

The man who had deployed the grenade was Udo. Working from the inside, he had divulged the training location to his Redeemer comrades, signaled them when his militia brothers would be at their most vulnerable, then proceeded to join in the act of their decimation.

More than one soldier, running away from the fracas, exhorted Udo to join him in retreat. Each and every one was put to death by a burst of Udo's militia-provided M4.

For Staff Sergeant Michaels, Udo used his bare hands. The look on his former commander's face as the life was squeezed out of him could only be described as supremely aghast. Udo was the last person Devon would have suspected to be a mole.

After the militia's defeat, Charles ordered Udo to penetrate the enclave of C-town. The Redeemer hierarchy was interested in developing front companies that would generate revenue along with intelligence, and Udo was tabbed to lead one of these new endeavors. He would be given seed money to find a location and open a business that specialized in providing security to those who desired to venture outside the protectorate's walls. He was twenty-four years old.

It was the perfect ploy. Because of his affiliations, there was never a chance that Redeemers would be involved in an attack on his clientele. As for any of the other terrorist organizations, well, Udo was well versed in their strategies and carried the implements needed to repel them. He also had at his beck and call a force of Redeemers that could shadow his clients and do considerable damage to anyone that wished them harm.

The company took awhile to establish itself, but eventually they became the standard bearer when Clevelanders wanted to travel into the perilous unknown of the wilderness. It didn't hurt that Udo made sure that many of his competitor's clients met their death out on the road by informing his Redeemer brothers that they were en route to points east, west, or south.

The situation involving the armory near Akron was a screw-up, though. It was not supposed to be so complicated, and he had Joe Smith to thank for the suspicions that the incident brought on his company's credibility. His decision to trump-up his resume, use a fake identity, and offer his services to the captain of the Mustangs was made to affect more than one outcome. It was a "kill two birds with one stone" kind of thing.

And so, Clarence Rigney was the name he signed on the visa form. Only the lawyer knew his actual name, and the barrister didn't blink when Udo told him that he would be using an alias for his attempt at employment in Motor City. Udo listed his actual age, thirty-six years old.

When Udo arrived at the Mugwump high-rise that housed the three individuals he had told Leo Rascone he would be staying with, he calmly rang the bell, announced into the sound system that Apostle Udo had arrived, and waited for the steel security door to be buzzed open.

Two of the three individuals had been in the city for two years, working for the crews that provided infrastructure maintenance, waiting and praying for their cell to be activated. With the arrival of one of the most important members of their community, a true legend, they knew that the thrice-daily prayers to their Redeemer had been answered.

TWENTY-EIGHT

TWO SUGGESTIONS OF RESTRAINT

WHEN JOE AWOKE on the first morning after his arrival, he had absolutely no idea where he was. As his eyes searched the interior of the room for some kind of clue to provide an orientation, he burped. The odor that exited his mouth—an acrid blend of garlic and wine—reminded him that he was in the Brassey house, and that he had consumed some kind of meat stew during the awkward dinner that had taken place the previous evening.

He rose to a seated position and put his feet on the floor. As his blood became attracted to the gravitational pull, his head began to feel as if a layer of peach fuzz was sprouting on the surface of his brain. Joe was never much of a drinker, and he knew that his consumption of a third glass of wine last night was pushing his physiological limit, but the communal table experience had been so odd that he hoped the effect of the alcohol might help him cope with the strangeness.

Finally, Joe felt stable enough to stand, but he heard some activity occurring out in the hallway. The kids must be getting ready for school. He had to pee, but he wanted to wait until the upstairs bathroom had been used by all that needed to exit the house early. He burped again and tried to figure out what kind of meat Mrs. Brassey had used in the stew. He remembered hearing Karen say something about elk.

John Brassey was ready to head downstairs and out the door to school before he remembered that there was someone else in the house besides the members of his immediate family. He stared at the closed door at the end of the hall, hoping that the visitor might show himself and give John a little more insight into his character.

This guy who his dad had brought in was not what he expected at all. This was no comic book hero, no nail-chewing gunnery sergeant, nothing like the images that John had created about the mysterious fellow who would be driving the Impala car in the race.

Last night's dinner had been a stilted affair. To outsiders, most formal gatherings of the Brassey family unit tended to carry the taint of maladroitness, but last night, all of the normal oddities seemed to be exaggerated. It was as if the old man had flashbacked to his pre-executive days as a salesman—the conversation was decidedly one way with nary a thought that he might take a moment and listen to someone else. His father nearly broke the gauge on the bombast meter. It brought a word to John's consciousness—magniloquence. The word meant to convey the quality of one who speaks pompously, and he knew his father could have been cited as an exact example of the definition.

Lon had orated on and on about the history of the race, Impala's place in that history, and the depth of his personal efforts to try to reverse their fortunes. He never once asked a question of their guest.

"John?" his mother screamed from downstairs.

The sharp level of her insistence in getting him to respond had the effect of breaking his reverie. He grabbed his book bag and headed down the stairs. It would be his first day back at school since the "kissing incident."

The suspension seemed a little draconian in regards to the time he had to serve. All he did was kiss a girl, for god sakes. Two weeks for that? It was total and utter bullshit.

The suspension would never have been this long if his dad hadn't gotten involved. His father wanted to teach him a lesson, had intervened with the principal, and had requested that his son not be dealt with leniently. As far as he knew, Rebecca's parents made no suggestions as to the term of the sentence, but they were disturbed that their daughter had to experience the trauma and the notoriety of being labeled a victim of harassment.

Victim? Were they sure? John had tried to contact Rebecca multiple times since that day, but walls of protection had been built between the two of them by her circumspect family. As he strolled toward school, he was still convinced that his impulsive act was not an intrusion on her person, and had she been aware that it was coming, she would have welcomed it.

Rebecca, though, had been dreading his return for a couple of days now. She didn't fault him for attempting to kiss her—she knew that it would eventually come to something like this in their relationship—but she didn't appreciate the time and place that he had decided the question would be raised. If they had been in a private setting, she could have found a way to explain her disinterest in their union being anything more than that of friends. But he had done it in front of everyone, including one of the guys she had determined might be a suitable beau, Denny Regan.

Now it was all screwed up. She could handle the ridicule that her classmates had dished out in the intervening days, but she couldn't handle the thought that she would always be known as the gal who got a tongue shoved down her throat by the kid they once called "penis head."

She truly believed that she didn't have a superficial bone in her body, and that she and John were alike in so many ways, given their health situations and the years they had been ostracized from the more popular groups. Due to her brief relationship with the hunky Richard, though, she had begun to gain a certain amount of desired traction in the social scene before her remission dissipated and she was compelled to endure multiple rounds of chemotherapy. She most certainly didn't want to regress back to a state of total anonymity.

John was convinced that their reunion should be organic, so he didn't look for her at her homeroom class upon his arrival on campus. He figured that they were likely to see each other during the break between second and third period when they both would be heading toward the east wing of the campus for that hour's class.

However, John didn't expect Mr. Fedder to hail him as he hurried to his first-period physical chemistry class.

"Young Brassey," the teacher said.

"Yes, sir."

"Welcome back."

"Thanks."

"I just want to give you a little heads up. I think that you should not try to speak to Rebecca for the near term," Mr. Fedder said.

"What?"

"Her parents wanted me to ask you to refrain from trying to contact their daughter."

"Really?"

"Yes."

"Well, you can tell them that you failed to get the message to me before I got a chance to speak to her, can't you?"

"Ah, but that isn't the case, John," Mr. Fedder said.

A standoff loomed. John was obviously confused by the situation. He honestly thought that Mr. Fedder may have been fucking with him, but looking at the older man—still trying to be a cool guy under all of the tweed and bestowed authority—he realized that the teacher was serious.

"I guess I don't understand. I thought her parents had no problem with me. I spent a lot of time at their house over the last year. Nobody was acting funny or telling me to leave or anything."

"You are a good friend. You gave her a tremendous amount of comfort during her recent darkness. I'm sure she carries a great deal of gratitude for you, but I don't think that she was interested in it being anything more than that," Mr. Fedder said softly, trying to cushion the landing.

"Did she tell you that, or was it her parents?"

This is where it was going to get tricky, Mr. Fedder thought. In so many words, she had told him exactly that. But one look at the kid standing shakily in front of him, and he knew that he couldn't attribute the last statement to her alone.

"I haven't spoken to her directly," he said, hoping that he could rationalize the lie as being warranted. The kid looked like he might cry.

The unobvious whiteness of the prevarication seemed to buoy young Mr. Brassey, and immediately Mr. Fedder realized that he had to create a specific boundary if the task assigned to him by his former business partner, Rebecca's father, was going to be completed.

"Here's what I know, John. The school administration was pretty freaked out by the whole thing, and they are considering placing a specific condition on you that you have no contact with her at all. So, I think you should wait until everything calms down a bit and stay away from her for the time being. Let her make the first move here."

This wasn't a lie. There had been discussions between the principal and his staff about making sure that an incident such as the one that happened could not occur again. Some type of internal restraining order had been one of the options that had been placed on the table. Mr. Fedder could see that John was mentally sorting through scenarios, trying to come up with one that could circumvent the desires of all parties that differed from his.

"Please, let time do its thing here," Mr. Fedder said.

John just nodded. It was a noncommittal response, but he could tell this whole thing had been blown out of proportion. What was once a small drop of spilled water had flooded to ocean-size in a very short time. He would heed Mr. Fedder's suggestions for now.

Joe spent the morning sharing a small breakfast with Karen Brassey. There was no mention of her husband's performance during last evening's repast, and Joe used their time together as an excuse to find what bound this particular husband and wife together. It wasn't as if Karen enabled her husband's egotistic behavior; she just seemed to disappear into a role or character that was not considered to be a principal cast member of the play. She became an extra—easily moved about and placed—to give the stage set a suggestion of some other life than just the soliloquizing lead character.

One-on-one, she was lively, knowledgeable, empathetic, and precise. In the presence of her husband, she was an absolute non-entity.

Her children spent much of their time biting their tongue, itching to get in the game, but Karen just existed in a perpetual state where the laughs that she offered in support of husband's humor sounded hollow and canned.

As Joe headed out to begin his day, he thought about how the dynamic of the Brassey's might be endemic in all marriages. To some degree, there would always have to be someone playing second chair to the concertmaster, and the trick was narrowing the gap between the two, or trading off the role on occasion. In Lon and his wife's case, the chasm seemed to be vast—he at the podium bowing his Stradivarius, she out back with the percussionists sharing a smoke during a lento movement.

Fed, showered, and a lot less wobbly, Joe picked his way across the Impala frontier to meet up with Francisco and Claudia. He was going to have to get used to the ever-present stares emanating from everyone.

"Hey, are you the guy?" a voice asked.

Joe turned to the poser of the ambiguous question. It was a woman in her fifties, trying to keep two snarling dogs from breaking their double leash. As the dogs provided an annoying alto countermelody, the woman nearly sang her feelings of dubiousness.

"It just ain't right, you know? We don't know you and we don't know where your loyalties lie. This idiot captain thinks he's being smart, but we haven't even sniffed the winner's circle in more than thirteen years. And now we're paying some Mugwump to change all that? I'm not the only one that feels this way either. There are plenty of people that think this is stupid."

Joe initially offered her a nod of equivocacy, but that was before he had any type of visceral response to her criticism. He made sure to engage her eyes as he spoke his truth.

"I understand that you don't know me. For the record, my name is Joe Smith. Believe me, I am fully apprised that there's only one outcome that will change your mind. I hope that after I've won your race, you will be so kind to come find me and apologize for not sharing the same faith that I have in regards to whether this will be a success or not," Joe said evenly.

This woman was not used to being dealt with in this fashion. Most of the people who knew her—including her often-cowering husband and children—usually chose not to respond to her constant dissertations of disapproval. She was briefly staggered by Joe's simple expression of confidence in his abilities, and he used her stunned silence as an opportunity to exit.

"Have a nice day," he said.

He did not turn around to see if she was either staring daggers at him or pondering the possibility of altering her judgmental first impression.

On his arrival at the warehouse space that adjoined Frank and Claudia's bungalow, Joe pressed the buzzer to announce his presence. A stream of lights began to cycle, and when they flashed green, he grabbed the door handle. He walked into something akin to a laboratory clean room. Through the glass partition, he could see Frank and Claudia dressed head-to-toe in white paper suits moving around what looked like a metal sculpture.

Joe began to enter the inner section.

"Not without changing into a clean-suit, cowboy," Claudia said.

"They're in the bathroom to your left," Frank explained.

Joe entered the combination bathroom/janitorial closet and found a plastic-wrapped stack of the disposable suits. He found the ones that fit Frank—marked XXL—and put the one-piece coverall on over his clothing. He took a cap from the package that contained Claudia's stock. When he reemerged, Claudia was laughing at him.

"You're not supposed to put it on over your clothes, you idiot. And you need some booties to cover those gross-looking boots."

Joe nodded and disappeared again. When he returned, she burst out laughing anew.

"Jesus, I didn't mean you should go Scottish."

Joe didn't get the reference.

"You just removed all possibilities of imagination," she continued, still laughing, half-covering her eyes with her latex-gloved hand.

"Can you translate your daughter's use of the vernacular, Frank? Scottish?" Joe pleaded.

"She's saying you can keep you underwear on, kid."

"Oh."

"Please," Claudia said.

Joe went back into the room for the third time. When he entered the clean room again, the two mechanics were up close to the sculpture, staring into what looked like a hole on the side. Getting closer, Joe saw that the thing that looked like art was actually an automobile engine.

"We'll be with you in a minute, Joe," Frank said.

They continued with their conversation about balanced compression and power output; these were just further examples of Greek to Joe's ears.

Joe wandered over to the workbench and looked at the collection of engine schematics on the wall. There were nine different blueprints. Notes had been placed over some of the blueprints that denoted the year of a specific area of modification. Other notes were warnings of potential problems that might need further study.

"Come have a look at this, Joe," Frank said.

Joe shuffled over, fully convinced that if he were asked to render an opinion, it would be worthless. Claudia backed off so Joe could peer into the open metal well at the front left side of the engine. As he had predicted, he had nothing to say since he had no idea what he was supposed to be looking for.

Frank launched into a discussion about this particular engine and detailed the tendency of the cylinders to occasionally warp on a microscopic level, altering the ability to create the perfect amount of compression when the piston slid through it on its way toward the spark that would ignite the gasoline it carried.

"If we get the Mustang, we're going to have keep an eye out for that," Frank declared.

"Harold would have to get the one with the 289, wouldn't he? Can you imagine if he had bought the '68 that came with the 428 police interceptor?" Claudia mused.

"It would certainly have changed the competitive advantage. Even the Dodges couldn't keep up with that."

"The added weight might be a form of compensation. The thing probably handled like a tank," Claudia said.

They both turned to Joe to see if he desired to add anything to the conversation. He didn't.

"This was a damn fine motor, though," Frank said.

"Shut your mouth, Mr. Concepcion. This is the enemy you are praising," Claudia said.

"I'm just saying."

Claudia shook her head in disgust and walked away. It really appeared that Frank's comment had pissed her off. Frank leaned over to Joe.

"She'll never admit that a Ford product might be worth a crap, but this little compact V-8 was an example of some serious genius."

All Joe could do was nod. This had obviously been a joust between the two mechanics for many a moon now. How anyone could get so worked up about a piece of machinery was a question that Joe could not answer.

"You know, I have no idea what you guys are talking about," Joe said.

"I figured. But, if you're going to be our driver, I want you to have an appreciation of more than just the athletic pursuit. When we practice, you will need to give me feedback about the car's performance. To do that, you're going to have to submit to a tutorial about how an internal combustion engine functions at its optimum. After that, we'll get into things like handling, strategy, and road conditions."

Joe was always open to acquiring any knowledge—even elements of the arcane—and from the look of passion that came over Frank's face when he began to list the sections of the forthcoming syllabus, Joe knew that he could have no better teacher.

"We're going to be able to simulate pretty much anything we want in Robby's beloved machine over at the museum, and my daughter and I have memory banks filled with all of our experiences, through all of the years, with all of the various cars," Frank said.

"Just do us one favor, won't you?" Claudia yelled from the area Joe would later learn was the carburetion table.

"Name it," Joe said.

"Every night, before you go to bed, get down on your knees, and pray we don't get that fucking AMX."

That one made Frank laugh.

"So, how was your night at the Brassey's?" Frank asked.

Joe wasn't sure how to answer that. He sensed that Frank and Claudia had some issues with the captain, but he didn't want to add grist to anything resembling a rumor mill. He had yet to even slightly understand his place here, and it made no sense to stir waters that he could not even see.

"It was fine."

Claudia's snort of condemnation could be heard across the room. There were lines being drawn here and, again, Joe had no desire to color in the boxes by regaling these two with any sort of gossip. The facts were these: Joe had no inclination to connect with any of the people of this enclave with anything other than an air of detached and superficial servitude. Anything that smacked of a personal connection was fraught with too much turmoil, given the state of his emotional life on arrival in their world.

He couldn't help but be curious though. There was some type of rift here between the mechanics and the hierarchy, and Joe rationalized his intention to probe the gulf by determining that all information attained would be useful in his quest.

"What's the deal with Mr. Brassey?" he asked, innocently.

"We call him 'Captain' now, friend," Frank said.

"And you better, too," Claudia added.

Frank hesitated in answering Joe's question—the reason being that he'd only known this guy for a little over a day. From Frank's reticence, Joe sensed that it was too early for the mechanics to tell if he was an ally or just another intelligence gatherer for the Impala board.

"You know, Dad, it is not as if you're going to be replaced. You've survived every one of the regime changes. Anyone that has ever tried to blame you for a loss has ended up holding a bag of shit," Claudia said.

Was Frank blushing? Maybe he was experiencing a flashback of anger from the remembrance of something long in the past. Either way, he continued to think about the consequences of divulging his personal feelings to Joe as the red color slowly ebbed from his face.

"It's complicated, you know?" Frank began. "Captain Brassey was my last boss at GM, and we didn't always see eye to eye."

"That's a bit of an understatement, Dad," Claudia chimed in.

"You be quiet, now. That is all in the past."

"What did you do at GM?" Joe asked.

"He was a VP in charge of power train development," Claudia answered.

"I was an engineer."

"Dad."

"The title thing was a bunch of crap. I was an engineer, honey."

"Dad developed super-efficient turbo-charged three-cylinder power plants that, if brought into the line, could have bridged the gap between the end of the gasoline-powered era and the onset of the full-electric line. He found a way to get over ninety miles per gallon yet provide enough torque to power a half-ton pickup towing a travel trailer. Captain Brassey was convinced that the old engines should continue for the transitional period. He thought it was stupid to build something that would likely become obsolete in a ten-year period. When the fuel sources dwindled, GM was essentially fucked. They were still equipping nearly everything with the inefficient engines that drank gas like a sailor who'd just been paid."

"It was all going to end anyway, Claudia," Frank said.

"Maybe not."

"Ancient history, dear."

Joe watched the two relatives banter. He wondered what had occurred between Frank and his wife. There was an element of femininity missing in the daughter, and he wondered if there was some lack of maternal influence during the years that the parents were together. That their split took place a long, long time ago was the logical assumption.

The chasm between Frank and Captain Brassey seemed larger than what would have been created by this type of business disagreement, but Joe decided to drop it for the time being.

TWENTY-NINE

THE COURSE

JOE KNEW IT was time to change the subject. Defining relationships in this place would come with experience. He didn't need to know all of the answers now.

"So, Captain Brassey did tell me that you had some maps that might be useful," Joe said.

"Of course. Sorry—it was the reason you were supposed to stop by today," Frank said.

He scurried to a wall that was largely taken up by a dry-erase board. Above the sheet of white, and the scribbles of mathematical formulas, hung long dowels that contained non-rigid laminated paper. Frank tugged on a piece of twine that dangled from one of the dowels, and a window shade of map unfurled from its wooden holder.

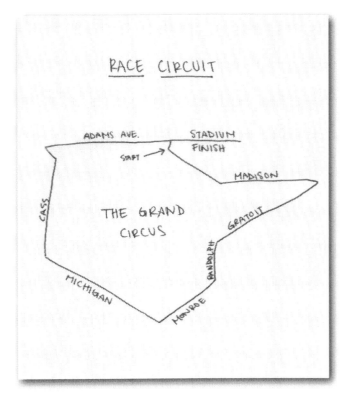

Frank removed a hand-held laser out of the tool kit on his belt and took Joe through a gross overview of the course. The race started on the grounds of what was once Ford Field, the former home to the Detroit Lions football team, and it skirted Grand Circus Park (the center of the Mugwump world) before connecting to Madison smack in the middle of the DeVille neighborhood. From there, it was a hard right onto Gratiot Avenue before they spilled left onto Randolph Street for a short time. Then, there was a right turn—at speed—that took them onto Monroe Street. As it approached the Red Wings' ward, the route made a less-than-ninety-degree turn onto Michigan Avenue, and then a similar turn onto Cass Avenue. Then it was through the gates before jogging onto First Street and that hair-raising, twisty sequence that had been built to connect to Adams Avenue West. From there it was a straight shot back into the stadium. Total distance: Just a little over six miles and slightly under ten kilometers.

Joe stepped closer to the gridded black lines on white. From what he could gather, there were a total of ten turns, nearly an equal amount of rights and lefts. Frank saw Joe calculating some of the sums of the obvious variables.

"You see ten turns, right?" Frank asked.

"That's what I counted."

"Well, you better count again, dude," Claudia said.

Joe did just that and came away with the same figure—ten turns.

"Is there something within the stadium, like the entrance, that is possibly another turn?" Joe asked.

"No."

"Okay, I give up. What am I missing here?"

Claudia smiled, but Frank looked a little disappointed that Joe's intuition appeared to rate on the lower end of some amorphous scale. He tried to offer a hint.

"There are actually twelve turns, Joe," Frank stated.

Joe moved even closer to the map and hand-traced the route, counting each time he would have to turn the wheel at least forty-five degrees. Again, he came up with the total of ten—four lefts and six rights. He turned to Frank, perplexed.

"You are missing one left and one right," Frank said.

And then it hit him. There was the memory of the simulator and that crazy turn toward the end. Hadn't the simulation taken him through some type of S-turn before the last straightaway?

"The S-turn."

Frank let out a breath to let him know that he was on the right track. "Where?" he pressed.

"It's toward the end, right?" Joe asked.

"Where?"

Joe looked again at the map and finally found the reason for his befuddlement. It was the manufactured turn at First Street and Adams Avenue West.

"Here. This is the turn where we need to go right but the road is banked to the left. To get through it, you need to do the extra two turns."

Claudia began to applaud. She explained, "It's a critical double-apex move. If you don't draw the correct line at any points on the optimum graph, you'll either spin out, wreck, or have to slow down to a point that my dead great-grandmother could pass you walking."

Frank laughed at that one.

"And from what I hear, Great-Grandma needed a cane," Claudia added.

———

John found sitting and paying attention in whatever class he was attending this first day back to be positively unbearable. He had no trouble dealing with the eyes of his fellow students that clocked his every move; he'd been the center of attention for so long because of his illness that he didn't even notice. But to be put in a box—to be told he could not have any sort of contact with the woman he loved—well, that was just plain wrong. What kind of world was this? When had this era of fascism begun? Had he been blind to it before?

His personal workout that evening was infused with a freakishly large amount of self-determination. When he finished, he felt better. The patina of sweat that coated his body had attached itself to the toxic negativity that coursed through him. Like an army of leeches, the beads of perspiration seemed to draw the bad blood from his being.

Later, under the stream of a hot shower—his troubles eddying down into the drain—he imagined all of the crap he had carried inside of him since his suspension. When he emerged from the bathroom, he was renewed. *Fuck them all*, he thought.

———

Joe was finally able to extricate himself from Frank and Claudia's dungeon after being presented with way more questions than he had answers for. Maybe he hadn't given enough consideration to the depth of responsibility that would be required to complete this particular project. Why had he accepted the task so readily? Was it the pay? Was it the adventure?

He did know that when he had seen the invitation on the kitchen counter at his parent's house, he did not hesitate. There were many reasons why he leapt at the opportunity, and foremost is that he wanted to find a way to honorably leave behind the craziness that existed in that house by White Rock Lake.

His lack of hesitation may have also been based upon the somewhat addled state of his current mind. There were a host of unsettling things that had been divulged to him over the recent weeks, and he had yet to know what effects that information might hold for his future. Issues like his genetic profile and the identity of the people who were responsible for creating it, the revelation that his teacher and mentor's earlier life furthered the goals of an organization that he had committed his life to destroy, and the dissolution of his employment after the demise of the company that he had spent the majority of his working life toiling for were all part of a growing list that needed further processing.

This adventure could have been nothing more than an excursion into a temporary state of denial—a simplistic expansion of the time frame allowing him a brief window before he would be forced to deal with all of this shit at some later date.

He pushed all of those thoughts aside again and decided that another quest was in order. He wandered out to Woodward Avenue in search of a store where he could purchase some much-needed underwear. The fund card he had been issued on his entrance resided in his front pocket, and he hoped that it contained enough purchasing power to provide for his needs.

On arriving at the main thoroughfare, Joe scanned the areas to the southeast but saw nothing that looked like the type of mercantile he required. He began traveling to the northwest, even though he would soon be leaving the Impala neighborhood and entering the outskirts of the Mustang ward. He had been informed that all of Woodward Avenue was meant to be commercial and thus was to be considered neutral territory, but he'd seen Frank and Claudia balk at dining at the restaurant owned by a Mustang proprietor, and he had no desire to put himself in jeopardy by committing any sort of mistake of manners.

A couple of blocks passed, and he came upon a haberdashery that carried the logo of a leaping lion in the window. He had not been able to glean whether acrimony existed between the Lions and Impala; he wasn't sure if his patronage of the establishment would cause any sort of problem, but they appeared to stock what he required.

Stepping into the store was like stepping back in time. He had only seen examples of these types of businesses in old movies. Those images had flickered across his screen in a technology known then as black-and-white, and he swore when he entered the shop, the color of the environment seemed to wane toward those opposing tones.

"May I help you?" a teenager asked.

"Yes, thank you. I need some underwear," he replied.

She gestured to the back of the store, over by the dressing rooms, where his quarry was hidden in the drawers of an ornate bureau.

"What size and style?"

Joe rummaged through the drawer and came up with three pairs of what he assumed were white cotton shorts.

"Those might be a little big for you," the clerk said.

Joe checked the waistband. The size was written in bold black Chinese character.

"He should try them on," a voice called out from the door.

It was a voice of a woman. And partly because of its brusqueness, did not carry a ring of familiarity. Backlit by the large bay window in the front, Joe could not make out any specific physical characteristics other than the outline of a female body. The clerk seemed bugged by the intrusion.

"I'll be with you in a moment, ma'am," the clerk said.

"What size are those?" the woman insisted.

"Bashi limi." (Eighty centimeters.)

"Ni shuo de dui. Tamen shi tai da." (You're right. They are too big.) The woman replied.

The Mandarin being spoken made Joe feel like he was five years old again. It reminded him of the time his mother got into a terrible argument with a sales person as they tried to fit him with soccer cleats before his first practice. The row was about the width of the sole, and whether the sizing the employee was pushing on them would provide her son support and not cut off his circulation. His mother ended up throwing the shoes to the ground, grabbing his hand, and storming out of the store.

The clerk heeded the advice of the woman and selected a pair that appeared to be a smaller size.

"You should try these on," she said.

"Okay."

"Please try them on over whatever you are wearing now."

"Okay."

Joe sheepishly exited the scene. When he returned, the woman who had spoken up had her back to him. She was now over by the tie rack getting assistance from the young clerk. Something told him that he had possibly met this person before, but he wouldn't be able to confirm it until he saw her face in direct light.

"These will work," he said as he wove his way around the display tables hoping the clerk would disengage from the woman, and meet him at the register.

The woman finally looked up at him.

"Better. Am I right?" she asked.

It was Cassandra, the woman from the Harold Getty Museum. All Joe could offer her was a crooked smile.

"Yeah, it would have been a big mistake to buy the wrong size," he said with an air of blandness.

"Got to have that security," she said.

Joe found himself blushing. The teenage girl looked like she was about to lose her lunch. Joe held out the fund card.

"Is this okay?"

"Is that all you have?"

"Yeah."

"We can give it a try."

She scanned the card, and the noise the machine returned registered a tone of negativity. Cassandra crossed to them.

"Is that the card they issued to you on your entrance?"

"Yeah."

"Captain Brassey didn't give you anything on your arrival?"

"Should he have?"

Cassandra shook her head and reached into her purse.

"You can put it in on this. Add this in," she said as she laid a blue plaid tie to the pile.

"My dad's birthday," she added to explain the reason she had stopped by the store.

"Wait a minute. You can't buy my underwear," Joe said.

"Well, neither can you, Mr. Smith. Not with that card. It is for food and water only. The city officials don't give a damn if you need clothing; they just don't want visitors to starve on their streets," Cassandra said.

"Thanks. I appreciate the consideration, but I'll figure something out."

Joe removed the underwear from the counter and went to return it to the bureau drawer. Before he could get too far, she grabbed his arm.

"We'll trade. I'll buy this, and you buy me a cup of coffee."

"I can't imagine the price of a cup of coffee approaches the price of such fine clothing," he parried.

"You'd be surprised. What if I promise to also get something to eat?"

Joe paused. He remembered that Frank and Claudia had warned him about her heritage. Someone would have to really explain the harm here, he thought.

"Sure. Thank you."

"My pleasure."

As coffee went, it was indeed expensive. She also ordered them some kind of confection that included a bread base with what seemed to him to be a caramel spread. That first bite rocked Joe almost as hard as the ham sandwich the day prior. His reaction to the food provoked a laugh from her.

"What were you eating before you came here, prison food?"

"Obviously."

"Let's get the formalities out of the way. You can call me Cassandra, or any shortened version. I presume I can call you Joe."

"Of course."

He took another bite of the combination bread/cookie.

"Good God, that is amazing."

She giggled again.

"Where are you from, Joe?" she asked.

"Texas territory."

"Big D?"

"Basically. I spent a lot of time near H-town, but my job had me away from home quite a bit. And you?"

She offered her hand to the mild bustle of Woodward Avenue, just fifteen feet from the outside table they occupied.

"I'm an 'innie.' I was born here."

"Someone called me a Mugwump today. What the hell is that?"

"An outsider. I still don't know who came up with that ridiculous name, but everyone uses it," she laughed.

Joe observed the ease with which she allowed herself to be so free with her expressions. She had an eerie confidence that reminded him briefly of his wife before all of the tragedies began to color her world in the darkest shades of crayon black.

"Where did you work?" she asked.

"I worked for Tynan International, Ltd."

"Oooh, cloak and dagger stuff, huh?"

"Mostly dagger," he said, trying to compete with her seamless repartee.

That statement stopped the conversation's breezy momentum. She narrowed her eyes and began to study his face. Maybe she was trying to find the vicious killer he had intimated might be inside. He felt a wave of paranoia wash over him. Was this the stuff that Frank and Claudia had warned him about? Was she probing him for information that she could take back to her ward leaders?

"I worked protecting the assets of the former government under a contract that Tynan had acquired and executed," Joe said.

"I heard about that acquisition. The payoff must have been huge to secure that deal."

"Beyond my pay grade and level of expertise. I was an operations guy, not an executive."

"And now you're a driver," she stated.

"Yep."

He wouldn't be going into his qualifications at this juncture. That kind of information would be valuable to someone seeking to collate data on him. They sat in silence for a moment.

"So, are you married?" she asked, matter-of-factly.

"I was. My wife is dead."

"I'm sorry."

There was another long pause as Cassandra tried to come up with a topic that wouldn't stall the conversation after just three volleys.

"I finally figured out why Captain Brassey is doing this," she said.

"Doing what?"

"Bringing in someone from the outside to represent the ward behind the wheel."

He got that feeling again—the one about her seeming to be fishing for particles of information.

"Why's that?"

"Mr. Brassey has a young son. He knows that eventually, like all boys, and some girls who are related to the prominent members of the ward, his son will feel a need to volunteer for the job. The pressure to succeed is so enormous—only one out of nine do every year—and I think by changing the protocol, he removes the possibility of his own flesh and blood ever having to assume that burden."

Joe had never thought that Lon Brassey had brought him in to protect his son from having to perform at some later date. The man didn't seem to give a shit about anything (or anybody) but himself.

"I think you're giving Captain Brassey a little too much credit."

"How so?"

Joe stopped the conversation again. Here was this vibrant, beautiful woman engaging in verbal banter with him, and all he could think of was the fact that she had been labeled an enemy by his benefactors.

"Okay," Joe began, "don't take this the wrong way, but did someone send you to talk to me, you know, try to gather some kind of profile?"

Cassandra nearly spit coffee in his face.

"What?"

"Are you trying to find out information about me that might be useful to the people in your ward?"

She didn't laugh, or even titter. She reached for her purse and the box that contained the tie and quickly rose to her feet.

"Our agreement was that you pay the check, am I right?" she asked in an icy monotone.

Before he could paddle the boat back up river, against this suddenly robust current, she was walking away up Woodward Avenue. He dropped his fund card on the table and followed her.

"I'm sorry," he said when he had caught up, but she didn't acknowledge him, hesitate, or break stride.

"Please. I'm new here and I don't know anything. Somebody tells me something and I take that as truth until I'm shown the difference. I really didn't mean to offend you."

She stopped.

"Just because you didn't mean to offend does not absolve you. That was a really stupid thing to say," she said.

There was a definite change in the hue of her face—a redness that didn't exist before. Joe's immediate reaction to seeing the well of her anger rising was to view her in sexual terms for the first time. Up until then, he realized he'd been intimidated by her pneumatic confidence and nonchalant attitude toward her physicality, and had given little thought to the fact that she was a woman, and he was not.

"Can we get together again soon? I'm sure the cost of the meal didn't rival your expenditure for the clothing. I feel an obligation to make good on my debt," he asked.

"I don't know."

"You've got to help me here. I'm but a lowly Mugwump, you know. Please, take pity on me."

She laughed, and the contrast to the anger she had recently exhibited entranced him further. She allowed her gaze to wander off him while she pondered whether a second meeting was worth her time. There was no doubt that she was intrigued by his character, but she understood—only too well—the complications of establishing anything that smacked of a friendship with an outsider, let alone one that was affiliated with Impala.

"You're coming into the simulator to train tomorrow, are you not?"

"I think so."

"Let me think about it."

"Okay."

Her eyes returned to the place that had her looking again over his right shoulder. There was something that had her caught her attention when she had looked there before.

"What the fuck are you looking at?" she suddenly screamed.

Joe turned to see who might be the recipient of the outburst. It was the woman he had encountered earlier—the one with the two inbred dogs. The woman was wagging her finger at them. Cassandra strode over to her.

"What is your fucking problem, lady?"

The woman cowered slightly, and the dogs began to yip and strain on the leash. The woman never answered the question as she walked back into the shadows of the trees that lined the side street.

Cassandra returned, but only briefly.

"This place is too much sometimes, you know. I'll see you tomorrow, Joe."

She spun on her heels and headed back up Woodward Avenue toward her home in Mustang.

THIRTY

TWO SUGGESTIONS OF RESTRAINT - continued

THE FAMILY DINNER that night was only slightly different from the previous evening. Lon held sway again, but his audience seemed exhausted by the events of the day. Where last night the children had tried to force their way into the conversation, this night they sat with eyes downcast toward their plates, their mouths only opening to take in the sustenance.

"So, Frank told me that you had a good work session today. What do you think of the course?" Lon asked.

All eyes turned to Joe.

"I was little confounded by the turn at First and Adams."

"It's a killer," Lon said.

"By the way, Karen, the meal is outstanding," Joe commented.

"Why thank you, Joe," Karen replied.

Lon cut off the extraneous conversation at that point.

"You know, that turn has only been in the race for the last ten years or so. The first couple of years not a single driver made three consecutive clean passes of that turn. Impala gathered a consortium of their best mathematicians, engineers, and physicists and worked out the formula that would produce the most efficient line, but one cannot account for things like adrenalin, the other competitors, and a whole host of other things that would make a driver miss his mark," Lon said.

Joe could see the rest of the family had reverted to their state of quasi-hibernation. The doorbell rang and filled the brief silence with a new sort of tension.

"Who the heck is that?" Lon asked.

Karen was already up, heading for the door.

"Everyone knows we eat at six, and I don't like to be disturbed during dinner," Lon added informatively.

When Karen returned, the expression on her face was tinged with more than its usual ponderous gravity. She leaned down at the head of the table and whispered in her husband's ear. He nodded briefly and rose from his chair. As he departed, she returned to her seat, making every effort to avoid looking at Joe.

John knew his father taking his leave during a session of oration meant that something monumental was afoot. The respite did provide him with a window to try to discover some things about their guest.

"So how old are you, Mr. Smith?" John asked.

"John, it is not polite to ask after someone's age," Karen said.

"Come on, Mom, that's intended for the folks who ask after a woman's age, not a man's," Holly said.

"No, I don't think it's gender specific," Karen said.

"It is," Holly said.

The table was alive now—the three Brasseys arguing the point. It was a wholly different experience than anything that had come before in Joe's brief time in the household. At the height of the hubbub, Joe offered to step into the fray.

"I'm thirty. I turned thirty just this past March."

The spell between Joe and the other members of the family was broken. There was a flow to the conversation that had been absent up until that moment.

"March what?" Holly asked.

"Okay, I'm going to tell you, but you have to understand that I've had to deal with odd looks, jokes, and whispers of inconceivability in regards to it for my entire life."

"The fifteenth?" Holly blurted out.

"Yeah."

"Why is that a problem?" Karen asked.

"The fifteenth, thirty years ago, Mom," Holly said.

"Oh, of course. Oh my. Well, that is unique," Karen stammered.

"Wow. That must be kind of a burden to carry, isn't it?" John asked.

"I get weary of the attention, but it doesn't come up as much as it used to when I was young and filling out job applications or school forms. I got razzed a lot when I was a kid."

"Like an invisible helmet," Holly said under her breath.

John reacted sharply at the comparison being drawn by his sister's sarcastic comment.

"Shut up."

"John, do not tell your sister to shut up."

"I thought my comment was extremely witty," Holly said.

"It was a bullshit comment," John said.

"John!" his mother screamed.

Joe had no context to explain what had just happened. He didn't know a thing about the family history. When Lon appeared at the threshold to the dining room, Karen remembered the conditions that were present after she'd answered the door. She became flustered and looked to her husband for assurance that everything was all right.

"Joe, could I have a word with you in private?" Lon asked.

"Sure."

Joe rose from the table and followed Lon out of the room. Karen pensively watched them exit before picking up her fork and searching for something on her plate that she could qualify as appetizing. The fork shook slightly between her slender fingers.

"Who was at the door, Mom?" John asked.

"Holly, apologize to your brother," Karen deflected.

"Mom?" John asked again.

Karen held her ground and stared at her daughter.

"Okay, fine, I'm sorry," Holly said without a gram of contriteness.

"And John, you apologize to your sister, please."

"For what?"

The ensuing silence told him that the reasons for the apology were supposedly tacit.

"Fine, I'm sorry for telling you to shut up."

"So, who was at the door, Mom?" Holly asked.

"Kevin Gatz and Billy Klock."

"What did they want?" John asked.

"They wanted to speak to you father," Karen said in the most non-committal fashion she could muster.

Lon was by the credenza in his office, surveying his collection of after-dinner libations. Joe was seated on the couch that sat parallel to Lon's large antique desk.

"What's your pleasure, Joe?"

"I'm fine. Alcohol and I aren't the best of friends."

Lon pulled out a crystal snifter and poured three fingers of amber colored syrup into the bell of the glass.

"There is something that I am forced to bring to your attention. My subordinates have informed me that you spent time this afternoon with the woman who curates the Getty Museum. Is this true?"

"It is. I was in kind of a bind, and she offered a helping hand. To compensate her, I bought her a cup of coffee."

"I don't need to know the specifics, Joe. What I need to tell you is this: You are not to be seen in her company again. Unfortunately, appearances are very important here. Someone spotted you and has subsequently told a great many people about your indiscretion."

"We had a cup of coffee."

"I don't give a shit if you just waved at her from across the street. I must be very firm on this subject. If I have to make it contractual, I will."

Joe shifted his weight. These were the kind of situations that had always undermined him in the past. He never reacted well to any hint of authoritarianism, unless the source was his master. He thought about his training, took an exceptionally deep gulp of air into his lungs, and exhaled a smile.

"Captain Brassey, it is obviously going to take me more than thirty-six hours to get my feet even damp here. The knowledge that you have imparted to me in the short amount of time I've been here has been extremely valuable, but you can't expect me to know every bit of protocol that is practiced here, can you?"

Lon showed immediate signs of relenting. Joe's comment was not meant to engender any pity, but Lon could not help but place himself in the shoes of his employee at that moment. It must be as confusing as a non-illuminated labyrinth.

"You're right. We'll try to get you up to speed as expeditiously as possible, and if you have any questions, feel free to ask me. No one will think that you're stupid."

That last statement struck Joe as odd. Why would he use the word "stupid"? Something clicked in his mind. It was a warning that there were layers of information about his role here that awaited further discovery.

Lon covered his nose with the glass of cognac and created condensation on its walls by exhaling. As the fog began to evaporate, he took a long sip before standing and assuming a position by the hearth.

"I guess I should have a little sensitivity to your situation. As an older man, issues like these things are no longer taking up much space in my consciousness. There was a time, though. What I'm trying to say is that you . . . you might have some needs. It would be better if you provided for them in a place where there can be no possibility of confusion. I have an address in the Grand Circus where the Un-committed reside. There is a proprietress there that can satisfy any desires that you might have. My understanding is that there is a vastness in the variety. I will make sure to open an account tomorrow."

Lon had that "we're both men, I understand" look on his face. It was one of the creepiest things Joe had ever had the horror of experiencing.

"No. Don't do that. I'm cool," Joe said.

"It's not a big deal. The ward has an expense fund."

"I appreciate the generosity, but I am not interested, Captain Brassey."

Lon shrugged. "Let me know if you change your mind."

"I won't change my mind."

"So be it. We're clear on the other thing, are we not?"

"Yes, sir. We're clear."

"Good."

Lon sat down at his desk, giving every indication that the meeting was over and Joe should depart forthwith.

The subject—like Lon's span of attention—had now been shuttered like slats on a window treatment being cranked closed to squeeze out any light. Joe turned and headed for the door. He was starting to form an opinion about the quality of this man, and it appeared to be dovetailing with the negative impression espoused by others who had known Lon Brassey for many a year.

THIRTY-ONE

ROADWORK

UDO HAD TO spend the first few days of his Motor City residency returning the awed cell members to a real-world understanding of the effects of the earth's gravitational energy. One of the minions actually swooned when the door opened and he was revealed to be the surprise visitor.

The sleepers had infiltrated the community over the last three years and had only reached their full complement as a triad in the last nine months. That they were now being activated—and by someone of the stature of Udo to boot—was more fantasy realization than they could handle.

Udo's primary tack was to remind them that he was not to be worshiped. The Redeemer was their messiah, not him. They still took a while to settle into their new paradigm with an actual apostle leading them.

Udo's fame had preceded him, as it did in most of his dealings with the Redeemer rank and file. The cell members had heard all of the stories of his vicious heroics, knew the appraisal of the kill statistics that had elevated him to such an elite status, and carried with them the myths and rumors that circulated about his personal history.

When he stripped off his shirt and they saw the infamous dent in the side of his torso—the resultant scar from his run-in with the stone that had been propelled by the rock salt of Clarence Rigney's shotgun—they marveled at the feature as if they were being afforded a personal view of the stigmata.

Another item they had heard about was the special tattoo—the one on the upper part of Udo's right arm. They knew the data that only two or three people in the whole world had been authorized to sport this particular skin art, and even though they were ignorant to its meaning, they knew that getting to view it was a once-in-a-lifetime experience. These particular Redeemers were not likely to ever come in contact with a man of the level of Udo's prestige again, and on that first night, they begged him to allow them to examine it.

As opposed to the tattoo that his teacher, Craig Bellows, carried on his right forearm—the crude one that contained the numbers 7/81341—Udo's tattoo was a true marvel of artistic expression. Meticulously placed in the muscular quadrant that contained the protrusion of his massive deltoid, the etchings were written in gothic black script—no character larger than 4 millimeters in height. From any sort of distance it appeared as non-descript as a birthmark.

Up close though, one could see what had been indelibly written in excruciating detail into the skin—a sequence of numbers spaced by periods on two parallel lines. From left to right, the top line read: 931.1263.3145. Using the secret system of decoding the numerical values by finding the appropriate link to the chapter, verse, and word in St. Horace's *New Testament for Now* produced a fairly simple phrase for this grouping: "The Redeemer Lives."

The bottom line was a conundrum, however. From left to right, it read: 2215.412.381-2154.354.322. Udo had not been given the key to this sequence and it did not appear to follow the rules of the first line, or any of the coded transmissions he had received over the years. He had been told at the time that there was some amorphous level to be passed before the hidden message in this second line would be made known to him. He was told that when the time was right, all would be revealed.

When he first had the tattoo applied, he feared that there had been a mistake in the text. He had pored over the directed items in *The New Testament for Now* and came up with a sequence of words he thought were given in the bottom line. From left to right they read: constant, me, sick, in, ladle, and brother.

He tried every possible combination in the ordering of the words—720 in all—and found only the most tenuous of connections. The best he could come up with was "The Redeemer lives in me constant brother," or the alternate, "The Redeemer lives constant in me brother," but there was no place to graft the other words—sick and ladle—onto any of the combinations that would create anything resembling a coherent sentence or phrase.

He tried breaking each word down into syllables and reordering them, he tried stringing all of the letters together and trying to unravel any possible anagrams, and he tried reversing the flow by assigning numbers to the letters in the words, and then looking up the corresponding passages in the text. Every avenue was a cul-de-sac.

The dash was a new symbol in the Redeemer's cryptography, and it signified to him that perhaps the six words were broken down into two three-word phrases. Every combination, including any possible anagrams, still maintained the impregnability of the cipher.

Time passed and so did his obsession with having to unriddle the opaque translation. Acceding to show the cell members the design briefly reminded him that the puzzle had yet to be solved. But there were things now that would have to take precedent. There was so little time to get things in order.

Udo hoped that the cell members had been hard at work in preparation. In any case, if they pulled it off, maybe the hierarchy would grace him with the key to his vexation, or maybe he could make himself comfortable with the thought that he would never have to know.

The three slightly built cell members were all in their late-twenties and went by the names Ned, Jay, and Kip. Per the overall plan, they all held employment in the infrastructure department of the city—particularly the reconstruction of the streets and roadways.

Ned and Jay had been in the city for nearly three years now and had been handed the task of preparing the way. Kip had only joined them recently, but the addition of a third hand had been a boon as it allowed them to accelerate their pace. They had existed in their current state of readiness for three months now. All they lacked was for someone to arrive and flip the switch that would allow them to proceed to the next level. That someone, by the Redeemer's grace, had arrived in the personage of Udo the apostle.

The specific type of avocation that the three practiced had been chosen long before they arrived, and the original entrants, Ned and Jay, had a few years of experience in the discipline before they applied for their visas through the Motor City "need program."

At the time, Motor City had put out a call to the wilderness looking for experienced outsiders with expertise in asphalt preparation and application. With the dearth of sources that could provide new raw material to repair the streets and avenues, the enclave was forced into a situation that had them recycling their road surfaces by subjecting preexisting pavement to a rejuvenation process.

The process to accomplish this task was a fairly complicated chemical procedure that involved emulsification of the shards and pieces that the team collected from the undermined roads of the city, as well as some of the derelict roads outside the walls. Once emulsified, the asphalt could be refortified, heated to the correct temperature, and reapplied to the road surface.

As the logistics people affiliated with the Redeemer movement knew, the process of asphalt production begins with crude oil. Tars left over from the fractionalization—the refining process that produces everything from gasoline to diesel fuel and kerosene—are incorporated into many applications including asphalt manufacture.

As the prospects of acquiring oil bordered on nil, someone in the Redeemer brain trust had speculated that more and more of the walled cities would eventually have to resort to recycling as the only avenue to maintain even a modicum of road quality. Plans were drawn up, and over the course of the previous five years, sleeper cells of Redeemers were inserted into most of the major enclaves and bade to find employment with the various road-services departments.

All of the groups were at varying levels of preparedness, but the Motor City cell was widely known to be the furthest along. It was the paramount reason that Udo jumped at the opportunity to get to visit the city for an extended period of time.

———

The first few days of Udo's visit were annoyingly crowded with introductions to the members of his benefactor's ward. There was also simulation training on Robby's machine in the event that he should be called on to represent Mustang in the race. In typical Titus O'Keefe fashion, there had been no definitive declaration that Mustang would be using a driver from the outside, just the suggestion that they would be maintaining their right to make the determination at some point in the future.

Besides Udo, the possible pilot candidates included the ward's driver of the last three races, Roger Burnham, and two rookies, Colin Masters and Christopher Willard. In all of his previous efforts, Roger had performed admirably, but many felt that a change was in order for the coming year.

It wasn't that Roger lacked nerve. The collective thought running through the ward was that he might have been cursed with a boatload of bad luck. His endeavors always seemed to end with either a mechanical failure or a situation where he was in the wrong place at the wrong time when another ward's driver made a costly error. No one would blame him for his effort two years ago because Mustang happened to pull that blasted AMX during the lottery. Roger was actually applauded for getting the car through two laps before it broke down, as usual.

Udo's presence in the mix was a wild card, for sure.

His early simulation trials were a little ragged, and when the results were posted on the board at ward headquarters, the odds associated with the possibility of his winning a seat in the car began to climb steadily. After the first week's work, Udo (known to all as Clarence Rigney) was definitively pegged as a long shot. This was the result he was trying to achieve, because by virtue of his mediocre performances, his time commitment was minimal. It was only May, but he needed every extraneous second to bring the Redeemer plans to fruition, and the lack of competitiveness he exhibited helped give him that extra time.

Because of their experience, Ned and Jay had enjoyed a great deal of freedom in how they scheduled the multitude of work orders that cluttered their calendar. Every May, there was a distinctive acceleration in their efforts as the more brutal weather eased and the race date loomed. It was de rigueur that any patching along the course take priority, and that often meant abandoning jobs in other sectors of the city.

Because there was a finite amount of product available and a certain amount of loss associated with the rejuvenation process, the tail end of spring usually involved time spent outside the walls tearing up roads to restock their needs. Currently, they had just completed the destruction of a section of streets that encircled the Elmwood Cemetery in the northeast sector of no-man's-land.

The electric lorry that was used in the transportation of the broken asphalt was always temperamental, so there was a certain amount of leeway given by the road-services department higher-ups in the time schedules associated with tasks performed extra-enclave. This allowed Ned, Jay, and, later, Kip as well to not only to complete their assigned tasks of road destruction but also to gather the other items on their scavenger list.

Unbeknownst to any but the three, they had been successful in gathering large stocks of young pines trees, pilfered sheet metal, derelict automobile batteries, and the all-important distillation apparatuses needed to capture the wispy petroleum ethers that were emitted during the asphalt revivification procedure. By the time of the apostle's arrival, they had completed all of their initial preparations.

In retrospect, the higher-ups should have known that something smelled fishy. Not once during all of the instances when they were out in the wilds was there an occurrence of any sort of nastiness. At the very least, the desperate souls that lived outside their community—affiliated with an organized effort or not—should have threatened this small group of unarmed workers, but that event never came to pass.

At the time, the higher-ups just assumed that this particular group was exceptionally lucky and had dodged their share of proverbial (and actual) bullets. What they didn't know was that this group was inoculated against ever having to deal with the presence of all of the dangerous elements that existed in the nether lands.

Obviously, they were immune to the viciousness of their brother Redeemers. They were also afforded the advantage that their excursions were always shadowed by an ever-increasing band of Redeemer scouts. Plenty of times they were forced to confront highwaymen and other thieves, and plenty of times those that endeavored to relieve them of their truck and/or valuables were left headless by the side of the road.

As the spring ended, a huge force of the Redeemer nation had begun to occupy many of the abandoned houses due north of the city in the Motor City exurb of Hamtramck. Scattering themselves amongst the impoverished residents, they went about recruiting new members and gathering their forces in anticipation of an important mission.

After a week of glad-handing the Mustang elite, Udo got down to the business of trying to realize one of the Redeemers' ultimate goals— a devastation of an entire protected city. This was just another step in their overall plan to defeat the infidel. An event like this would further their ultimate aim by bringing a condition to the populous that signified that their options were severely limited. It would be the harbinger of the next period of Redeemer power. It would produce the era where the citizenry's choices were narrowed to two alternatives: "join or die."

It was sure to be a continuous diet of sleepless nights for the apostle as he tried to balance his duties with his sponsors with the after-hours manufacturing facility that he and the three cell members had yet to construct.

The overall goal for the four who were operating on the inside was to create the mythical substance known as "Greek fire." The recipe, a tightly kept secret—known to only the most worthy when it was first observed in the Peloponnesian War and for a thousand years after— involved the deployment of a mélange of some form of inflammable liquid, evergreen tar pitch, and sulfur.

The group's goal was to combine the elements into two immense packages, strategically embed them into the walls at the extreme northwestern part of the city, and hope that the detonation would open the barriers and allow the gathering force encamped in Hamtramck to enter.

The sulfur and the tar pitch had already been rounded up. The decrepit car batteries had been drained of their remnants of sulfuric acid, and the pitch had been extracted from the evergreens. The only crucial item left—except for the exact titers of the formulation—was the production of the inflammable liquid. Though no one could be sure, the thought was that the fluid part of the recipe used by the Greek warriors could have been what is known today to be naphthalene—one of the early by-products of crude oil fractionalization.

The theoretical hope was that during the emulsification of the asphalt, ethers would be released that could be cooled and then distilled into this liquid. The liquid was very similar in composition to lighter fluid—highly flammable and only moderately stable.

Ned and Jay had observed fumes being released through the venting that led to the outer atmosphere and had rigged some of their sheet metal to see if they could produce a bit of condensation before testing the resulting drops of liquid for its incendiary properties. All they knew was that the stuff, when ignited, burned like the sun.

Only Udo knew that for it to take on the qualities of the liquid required, it would need further refinement.

So, the four men built an ersatz cooling tower on the roof of the asphalt rejuvenation facility and attached a distillation device that they had fashioned from some pilfered plumbing fixtures.

It took a couple of nights before they saw a product that they felt might be considered utile for their purposes. Modifications were eventually made, and in the space of a couple of weeks, as the asphalt rejuvenation process was in full swing, they were able to produce more of what they believed to be naphthalene than would ever be needed.

They had all of the components now.

By this time, it was early June. Ned, Jay, and Kip were hard at work patching the streets that were used on the racecourse. Udo's duties to Mustang became more arduous as the competition for the seat behind the wheel of the ward's car began in earnest.

Little by little, Clarence Rigney began to make himself a viable contender for the coveted spot. Each week, his simulations improved. This was becoming a problem for him, but he had been assured that he had to perform up to a level of competence to remain within the walls. If he was worthless, immediate banishment was certain. At least, that's how the lawyer, Leo Rascone, put it.

In all of the physical tasks, Udo had no equal. As the first week of June came to a close, the other two rookies, Masters and Willard, appeared to be out of the competition. The possibility that he might actually have to be the driver was not something Udo relished. It certainly did not fit into his plans. His growing hope that he would be spared was buoyed by the resurgence of the hangdog Roger Burnham, who had used his veteran wiles to remain on top of the heap in every category except for those that involved brute strength. As Titus noted on viewing the simulation reports that were released at the week's end, the Mugwump Clarence Rigney was gaining, but he hadn't performed anything resembling a negotiation of the hurdle that was required to unseat Roger just yet.

As far as Udo was concerned—the Redeemer willing—that is how the competition would end. Roger Burnham would, once again, be driving for Mustang, Clarence Rigney's talents would not be required, and Udo could place his focus where it was needed.

THIRTY-TWO

EXPOSURES

JOHN FIDGETED AS he waited to take his place in the first of two rows of chairs that were arrayed on the brightly lit stage of the Impala auditorium. It would all be over in an hour, and he would finally be consecrated along with his fellow sixteen-year-olds as a Man of Impala. The event was part of the ward's yearly calendar, and its annual occurrence was on the first Saturday of every June.

As a de facto member of the ward, Joe was expected to attend the ceremony that included a cocktail meet-and-greet, dinner, a fashion show put on by the sixteen-year-old girls, the actual Rite of Installation, and a cake and coffee reception.

As social events went, it was the only one of the year that could be considered formal. There was the Christmas party and the New Year's Eve gala, but the attire for those tended to be more toward what is considered cocktail wear. This here thing was the pull-out-all-the-stops, wear-only-once, make-your-significant-other-jealous, infect-your-neighbors-with-verdant-envy, get-wasted (but not too wasted, lest you risk a lifetime of humiliation), and blow-out-the-pipes real deal.

Karen was kind enough to alter one of Lon's old tuxedos for the event, and the blasted thing actually fit Joe quite well. It was hardly comfortable, though it did provide him with a small amount of anonymity amongst the identically dressed Impala men—something that he'd had little occasion to treasure during the entire time he had been intra-enclave.

He'd regaled the group that hovered around him during the cocktail hour with stories of his race training. He'd allowed his dinner companions, Frank and Claudia, to do the same amongst the eight at their pre-assigned table. Now, he had found a space, just off the stage, camouflaged by the light scaffolding, to observe John Brassey complete the Rite of Installation.

Joe and the kid, John, had spent a lot of time together over the last couple of weeks. School had ended for the year, and John had become Joe's shadow during the periods of time he worked in the simulator or brushed up on his mechanical knowledge in Frank and Claudia's garage.

At first, Joe was wary of the constant looming presence of the younger Brassey. Was there a design here? Was John the conduit to providing eyes, ears, and memory about what he experienced in Joe's company to his father?

Claudia made a fairly strong effort to enhance Joe's level of paranoia by intimating as much during the times that John was present. She had a very large bug up her ass that appeared to possess a great deal of venom when it came to expressing her opinion of the captain, but the silence she displayed when John was in their environment was of the type that could only be described as consciously suppressed.

There had been a couple of occasions when Joe and John had been left alone, and during those interludes, Joe had discovered the young man to be anything but an agent of duplicity. In fact, this kid had his own sort of insect gnawing at the tissue of his lower intestine about the old man, and in those moments when it was just the two of them, John did not need prodding to express the depth of his anger toward his father.

From what Joe could gather, John's father had obviously been disappointed that his male heir was far from perfect due to the medical condition that had rendered John as handicapped in the old man's eyes.

None of this seemed to get the youngster down, though. The kid had gone to great lengths to develop many of his talents. The story of the disappearing medication showed Joe the kid displayed perseverance and game. The strict training regimen informed Joe that John understood the ethics of commitment to a goal. It didn't take a whole hell of a lot for Joe to see that the kid was special. Even factoring in the small amount of time he had spent in the presence of the young man, Joe had come to view him with a certain quantity of awe.

Their life experiences were different, though. By the time Joe turned sixteen, he was physically and emotionally a man. He certainly didn't need a formal ceremony to inform him, or the rest of the world, that he had been advanced to the state of adulthood.

Standing in the wings, watching the boys file onto the stage to sit in their assigned seats, Joe wondered whether his accelerated development, coupled with the litany of tragedies that had happened in his short life, had contributed to his recent feelings that all of his good days were behind him.

John was a little pissed that the seating chart had him sitting in the first row. He intrinsically knew it was because his last name began with the letter B and the boys had been arranged in classical alphabetical order. It wasn't that he feared the exposure; it was that a boy named Denny Regan would be occupying the seat directly behind him. This was the same Denny Regan that his love, Rebecca Leeann Voss, was confirmed to be dating. The overall effect of this particular configuration would have Rebecca looking in his direction because the person sitting behind him was the focal point of her interests.

John knew Denny pretty well and liked him for the most part. There was a part of him that could see why Rebecca might be attracted to him. Denny had a masculine physicality, but he had little or no prowess in the areas of academics and reasoning. John assumed that a future with Denny would eventually lead to disappointment for his love, as she became more aware of his intellectual limitations. Those thoughts gave him some comfort but also instructed him that the woman he cared so mightily for might lack some ability to reason as well.

"Ni hao ma?" John asked Denny.

"Fucking hot in this suit, bro," Denny said.

John nodded and turned back to face the crowd. Rebecca was in the middle of the audience with her family, staring in his direction. He confirmed his earlier suspicion that she was not looking at him, but through him, trying to comfort that boy sitting behind him. He saw a familiar look on her face, the one she had when she was trying to provide support to one less confident than herself. Currently, she was trying to spiritually blow a cooling breeze in Denny's direction, hoping that an arid zephyr might evaporate the flop sweat that was beginning to accumulate on Denny's chiseled face.

John's heart began to beat more slowly, more athletically, as he tried to use some of the rudimentary tools that his new friend Joe had given him to combat any ill-timed emergence of stress.

It had only been a couple of weeks, but he had learned more techniques about how to control his body from Joe than he had learned from any parent, doctor, teacher, or peer. They had worked out together a few times, and John could swear that he had gotten qualitatively stronger since those sessions.

John had never had access to the elements that made up the mental components that related to strength. This was the area on which Joe placed his focus. Much of their work centered on pain tolerance, and Joe had been very clear that most of the signals that suggested the onset of suffering did not originate in the muscle tissue, but in the mind.

There had been a pithy line that Joe had delivered at one point: "Pain is cowardice leaving the body." That sentiment reverberated within John now as he tried to avoid allowing his gaze to fall on Rebecca.

———

Joe thought that the ceremony was a little over-the-top, what with the extinguishment of the candles that were supposed to suggest the termination of childhood, the stern lecture by the elder of the community about responsibilities and loyalty, and the sometimes sappy recitations of historical precedents and ward-deifying bullshit by various members of the present and former regimes. It was finally, mercifully, coming to a close when one of the kids headed to the podium.

Joe would find out later that this boy was selected to represent the group not because he excelled, but because his father had called in every favor that he could count as a credit in his relationships with Lon and the other dads.

The boy, Mickey Cleaver, had not desired to be placed in this position—had argued vehemently with his father for months—but was eventually forced to be the one to deliver the speech. It was pretty obvious to Joe that he had not written it himself.

In quavering waves, just a blip above a whispered monotone, Mickey said, "This is a pretty big night for all of us. For me, it is probably the most important night in my life to this point. I've thought about what this means to me almost every day that I've had the pleasure to live amongst my brothers and my sisters in this glorious place. Tonight means that I have arrived at a place in my life—a crossroads, if you will—where the road I take from here on out is one that is ultimately my responsibility. I and the other men sitting here are ready, willing, and able to adhere to that simple tenet. Thank you."

Mickey sat down accompanied by an eruption of partisan applause led by his family of three. To Joe, it looked like Mickey's eyes were crossing, and he could see a protruding vein pounding on the side of his head.

Joe was trying to figure out if anything of value had been imparted during Mickey's speech. The reaction of the crowd told him it was worthy, but to Joe it was just a bunch of hollow words strung together for the purpose of completing a task. There was nothing in the bombastic pomp of this exercise that these boys could use to enhance their advancement into manhood.

The final part of the rite involved the distribution of Impala lapel pins to the forty-nine youths who had gathered on the stage. As each one accepted his trinket from Captain Brassey, Joe paid special attention to John. He'd been doing his best to avoid focusing on that girl he talked so much about, but his best efforts to act cool and composed were showing the first signs of cracking apart. The back row had headed up to the dais first, and as luck would have it, John was positioned directly behind his benign nemesis, Denny Regan, in the queue.

When Lon handed Denny his pin and shook his hand, a squeal erupted from the area of the crowd where Rebecca was stationed. Joe could see that John did not take having to be regaled by this outburst with any sort of enthusiasm—the pressure on his right mandibular bone increased to the point where some of the enamel may have been chipped off of one of his back molars.

There was a distinct contrast in the crowd's level of pleasure when John received his pin. Karen and Holly's response—a "yeah" from his mother and a whistle from his sister—accentuated the polite applause offered by the rest of the gathered.

Joe pitied the poor kid in that moment. He had gone through so much to get to this supposed monumental point in his life, and there was no acknowledgement of his triumph over the trials that none of the other kids were ever forced to confront. What pissed Joe off the most was the way John's father reacted to the muted response of his constituents. Joe could see the continuation of the emotions that this father felt for his son—embarrassment and enmity. This was expressed by Lon's near mortification when the tepid applause for John quickly withered into total silence.

Joe knew John was not blind to it all and thought that he would have to find a way to give the kid some perspective in how much attention should be paid to events such as these. He wanted to tell the kid that there would be many more moments that would take precedence over something as petty as this garish display. Tomorrow, when they were going through their exercise routine, he would bring up some of these concepts.

THIRTY-THREE

PRACTICE MAKES SOMETHING

JOE HAD PRETTY much done everything that he could within the limited parameters of experience offered by Robby's simulator. Even the veteran driver's scores could not hold a candle to his performances when all of the achievement metrics were applied.

Frank and Claudia were dutifully impressed. By all accounts, this guy was everything that the captain had promised and more.

Even Robby was forced to admit that he'd never seen anything like it. Where he had once been pompous and vocally orotund in his dealings with Joe, he now looked forward to watching the mercenary demon, strapped into the cockpit, turning record-lap speeds on nearly every foray around the track.

With nearly a month to go before race day, Joe was getting bored. He asked Robby if they could quit making the full circuit for awhile and concentrate on a couple of the areas of the course that Joe knew would be the most challenging on the day.

By now, Robby was up for whatever Joe wanted to try. So they spent one day concentrating on the turn at First and Adams—trying to better the optimum line and speed that the Impala engineers had determined was not improvable. By the end of the session, Joe was able to achieve an increase of eight miles per hour above what the experts had determined was the absolute maximum.

On another day, they dealt with the gates. With the gates positioned to only allow one car to pass, Joe attained the highest speed ever recorded in his approach to the steel barriers.

Joe had inquired about the actual aperture of the gates in their most closed position and was told that they were set at a tolerance that would give the widest vehicle in the race—the Plymouth Roadrunner—six inches of clearance on each side of the driver's and passenger's side-view mirrors. This gave some of the thinner-bodied cars, like the Mustang, the Barracuda, and the Camaro, a little extra space. Joe felt that if they were lucky enough to select one of those cars, he should be able to be near the top end of the car's capabilities as he passed through the heavy metal walls.

John then offered Joe a challenge. What if the gates were closed further, so the available space was only five inches of extra width per side? Joe smiled devilishly and asked Robby if he could dial the thing in and give him a space that would provide only two extra inches beyond the breadth of the vehicle.

One of the janitors overheard the boastful request, and the news spread quickly around the building. A crowd began to gather outside the window to Robby's control booth.

Teller, the security guard, heard the news over his rover and joined members of the office and cleaning staff just as the wagering between the spectators began in earnest.

———

Cassandra stepped out of her office to find her administrative staff absent without leave. Her curiosity in regards to their whereabouts led her out into the vacant hall, down the empty corridor, and finally to the simulator hangar.

She was fully aware of which ward happened to be doing their training during that period of time. She felt her heartbeat pick up pace as she approached the massed group of museum employees. She knew Joe wouldn't be able to see her if he was strapped into the cockpit, and no one would be the wiser as to why she was coming down to the hangar at this specific time.

"What's going on?" she asked Teller.

"The Mugwump is going to try to make it through the gates at speed, but he's having Robby narrow the width to a total of four inches of clearance."

"He ain't gonna make it," said the custodian.

"What's normal?" somebody asked.

"Normal is twelve inches of clearance," Cassandra stated.

"He ain't gonna make it," someone else said.

"I'll take that action," one of the janitors said.

Many took him up on it.

"What about you, boss?" Teller asked Cassandra.

"I don't know. But you all know that what you see here cannot be talked about with anyone. Everyone's clear on that, right?"

All in attendance nodded, but Cassandra knew the word would probably get out anyway. Every ward offered sop to the museum employees to get them to disclose anything that could be considered inside information. It had been notoriously hard for Cassandra to keep control of it all, and many of the Uncommitted that worked there had—in the past—availed themselves of the bribes to supplement their meager earnings.

There were significant risks, though. If caught, you were immediately deported from Motor City, and under no circumstances could you ever reenter.

There had already been a couple of security breeches, and they were still only in the second week of June. Teller had recently focused his suspicions on two of the janitors who maintained the areas around the simulation hangar. At Cassandra's request, he had even attempted to plant disinformation in hopes—should it alight out in the world—that he might be able to root out the squealers, but to this point his efforts were for naught.

Robby had things ready to go. He checked and rechecked the new virtual width that Joe had requested they attempt. It took him awhile to figure out how to override the default systems on his race programs, but now he was pretty sure that he'd gotten it right.

"Okay, Joe, I want you to drive up to the threshold and see if we've gotten the tolerances right," Robby said into the microphone poised over his right cheek.

"Roger that."

Joe put the car in gear and slowly advanced toward the gates. From the watching mob's perspective, there appeared to be no clearance at all as he approached the barrier at no more than five miles per hour.

Just for kicks, Joe acted as if he'd suddenly lost his nerve. During the approach, he corrected the steering multiple times. They were just minute modifications, but with so little leeway the changes had huge ramifications.

"Oh crap," he screamed before crashing the left front quarter panel into the edge of the gate.

All of the watchers gasped. Cassandra knew better and only allowed the thinnest, most discreet of smiles—Joe was just messing around.

"Okay, are we done playing?" Robby asked.

"Sorry," Joe said.

He depressed the clutch and grabbed the gearshift. He threw the car into reverse and began to back down the representation of Cass Avenue at a fairly rapid rate. Robby grimaced as he saw the needle on the tachometer begin to push toward the red line. Joe was approaching thirty miles an hour in reverse.

Now nearly a quarter of a mile away, Joe braked and took the car out of gear. Robby noticed the group gawking at his window, and he reached over to switch on the external speakers. The onlookers were graced to the simulated sound of a finely tuned combustion engine idling at just under two thousand revolutions per minute.

"He ain't gonna make it," another naysayer said.

"Shut up."

"I'm just saying."

John moved in close to the monitor and shared the space with Frank and Claudia in front of the big screen. This was exciting stuff. Claudia noticed John lurking close to her, but she was going through a thawing period in regards to her rigid insistence that the kid should bug off.

"It's all yours," Robby said.

Joe didn't hesitate after that. He put the car in first, spun the tires briefly, and sped off for his goal. Through second gear, he kept the point that he'd been focusing on centered in his field of vision. The only corrections he made were slight and related to the small lapses in concentration that occurred when he shifted from one gear to the next. Hearing the whine of the eight cylinders reach the correct frequency, he dropped the shifter down into fourth gear position and stole a glance at the speedometer. It recorded a figure of eighty miles per hour and was creeping higher as it fanned across the dial in a clockwise fashion. The gates were just ahead.

Cassandra found herself watching the group that seemed so entranced with the spectacle. The collective tension that this group generated had the potential to power the entire building, she mused.

Joe hit ninety-two miles per hour at the final speed check—ten yards short of the walls—before he blew through the gates without even nicking one of the side-view mirrors. He did not hear the cheers from the onlookers. He did not even know that they were there.

Cassandra could see immediately that the details of what everyone had just seen would not remain in-house for very long. On someone's payroll or not, there was no way these employees would be able to keep mum about the feat that had just been performed for them.

Back inside the simulator, Frank, Claudia, and John cheered before dissolving into uncontrollable laughter. When the cockpit door hissed open and Joe emerged, they had composed themselves, acting as if the whole thing was only mildly impressive.

"Come on, you got to give it up here," Joe said.

"I don't see what the big deal is," Claudia said dryly.

"Now if you had done it with only two inches of clearance total, maybe I would be impressed," Frank said.

Their stern facades began to weaken, and when John proclaimed, "That was so fucking cool," they gathered around their driver and slapped him on the back.

Cassandra watched the employees settle their debts and shuffle back to their stations. She knocked on the window, and Robby turned to her with a rare smile on his face. When he shook his head in disbelief, she knew that he was acknowledging that he was not likely to see anything akin to that type of exploit again for many, many moons.

She passed the door to the simulator unit just as the Impala mechanics, the captain's son, and their driver emerged in a celebratory mood.

"Did you see that?" the kid asked her.

"Yeah. You know this thing is not a toy," she said tersely before continuing down the hall. She never once made eye contact with Joe.

"She's such a fucking bitch," Claudia said.

The silence expressed by the other three confirmed to Claudia that their agreement was tacit.

Outside the museum, the group split up. Frank and Claudia were headed back to their shop. John had some type of appointment, and Joe voiced a desire to grab a cup of coffee at his favorite café.

It was the same joint where Joe and Cassandra had shared their one and only public meal together. The tinkle of the little bell announced his arrival, and the barista swiftly moved to the espresso machine to make Joe's café Americano. When they met at the register, he handed her his new money card, and she handed him his coffee with a bloodred napkin wrapped around the mug.

It would've taken an incredibly detail-oriented person to see what had happened in that moment where legal tender and steaming java had been exchanged. They really would have had to notice only one anomaly: All of the other napkins that were given to customers were white. Joe sat at the table by the window and blew into the meniscus of the opaque liquid. The ripples moved to the outer edges of the cup and lapped at the porcelain shore.

THIRTY-FOUR

THE RUSE

THE BARISTA HAD the entire color spectrum of napkins stored in the drawer below the register. Red meant that Cassandra wanted to meet in the usual place, within the hour if possible. If Joe returned the napkin with his empty coffee cup, the message implied was that he intended to accede to her wish. Cassandra would be informed by a quick telephone call from the barista that their assignation was on. As soon as she heard the bell tinkle his exit, the barista would pick up the phone and call Cassandra's private line. When she answered, the barista would say an innocuous word that began with the letter "y"—like *yellow* or *yacht*—before hanging up. If the communication were meant to convey a negative response, the word would begin with the letter "n."

───────

"I didn't know you were such a grandstander," Cassandra said, teasing him.

"I'm not egoless," Joe responded.

"No, I'm well aware of that."

She climbed atop him, straddled his stomach, and looked down at his face. There was something detached in the way that he looked at her. It was something that was starting to become an issue for her. She felt something oozing down the inside of her thigh, and she realized that some of his seed was leaving her and dripping onto him.

The lovemaking had been as glorious as it had ever been. Though today, she'd entered into it with a great deal more anticipation than she had ever had in her life. She knew it was foolish—possibly immature—to get so turned on by his act of derring-do just an hour or so before. She felt like the head cheerleader, so excited to get to fuck the quarterback after he'd single-handedly delivered victory. She'd even changed into a short skirt—something in the vein of girl's school uniform—before she caught the pedicab that brought her down Woodward Avenue to their love nest.

When her climax arrived, it reverberated through her like no other she could recall. This had been happening to her a lot with him, and she was at a loss when it came to describing the why of it all.

Maybe it was because he was so vastly different from the other men living inside the city walls. Maybe it was related to the uber-clandestine nature of their relationship. Either way, at this point, she really wasn't that interested in doing the analysis—she just wanted it to continue.

She wasn't exactly sure if the feelings were mutual, and that could have been the source of her constantly rampant feelings of super-anticipation. He was so detached sometimes that she wondered whether he even knew that she was there.

She was careful not to apply any sort of reasoning that he was in any way reticent about their coupling. The overwhelming evidence would not support that. It did frustrate her that—in the long periods where they found themselves apart—she found herself rationalizing his behavior, not trying to adjust it.

"Where are you?" she asked.

"I'm here. In this apartment. In Motor City. With, huh . . . What was your name again?" he said with a wee bit of sarcasm.

She rose from the bed and crossed to the bathroom. Leaving the door ajar as she urinated, she caught sight of him in the full-length mirror that was attached to the face of the door. He was just staring blankly at the ceiling. She suddenly felt angry—like a child being left behind in daycare by a distracted, tardy parent.

"Tell me about your wife," she blurted out.

Cassandra could see that this startled him, and he shifted his position on the bed to one side of the mattress. She flushed the toilet, returned to the edge of the bed, pulled a blood orange out of her bag, and began to peel away the rind.

"Come on, you can give me the boring version. I don't need any enhancements," she said.

"We were married when we were twenty. I suspect that we were still a long way from being fully-formed people when we got hitched, and that fact might have contributed to the demise of the relationship over time," he said tersely.

"I thought you said that she died."

She knew immediately that any statements he had made along those lines—that his wife was deceased—were nothing more than prevarications.

"Where is she?" Cassandra asked.

"I don't know. She probably is dead by now."

"But you have no specific information to make that claim."

"No, I do not. But the odds are that she's no longer of this earth."

"But you're not sure?"

"There has been no funeral, no black car pulling up at the house to offer any confirmation, but if I had to bet my life on it, I would say that she's dead."

Cassandra watched him stare at the ceiling again. She could tell that he was relating his truth. There was little doubt that he was convinced that she was deceased.

She chose, in the immediate, to not continue her probe. She sensed that he might decide to fill the silence with a few more details without her having to urge him forward. She bit into a segment of the orange and allowed the crimson juice to play on her tongue.

"She wasn't the same after our boys died. Nothing was the same," Joe stated.

The silence that ensued seemed to last forever, and it compelled her to break her earlier promise.

"They got the flu?" she asked.

His nod was nearly imperceptible. *Okay, that's enough.* She vowed to stop asking for any other clarifications. She could tell that this was difficult for him. He hardened his stare on the amorphous white perforated tile looming six and a half feet above where he lay.

"I would say that she wasn't strong enough, though weakness was not a trait that I would have ever ascribed to her. She fell apart so completely. Her dissembling led her to attempt some outrageous acts," Joe whispered.

Cassandra thought that statement intimated that she had tried to commit suicide to quell her grief, and that was why Joe had determined that she was probably dead by now. She couldn't have been more wrong.

"She tried to steal someone else's child once. Luckily my father knew the family, explained the situation, and saved her from being charged with kidnapping. I can still conjure the look on her face when the kid's mother took back her daughter. Cynthia had completely lost any sense of compassion—any thoughts that the child's mother had a right to what she thought was her own flesh and blood. She was just maniacally pissed off that this child—even though it was not hers—was being taken from her."

Joe shuddered then. The memory represented only one ounce out of the veritable ton of crazy shit that Cynthia had gone on to do in the months after the deaths of her sons.

Cassandra now regretted having brought the subject up. She knew now that she had been petty and capricious in trying to effect some definition in their relationship. But the cap was off and the deep well—suppressed for so long now—was verging on becoming a full-blown gusher. She tried to put a finger in it.

"It's okay. I'm sorry I asked. I don't really care about the past. I'm only interested in the present," she said in an attempt to bring the subject to a fitful close.

"There was a year of therapies and medications. But nothing worked. I was beginning to take more jobs out of town, and every time I returned, I oddly expected that she might have gotten better in my absence, but it was not to be. One day I woke up, and she was gone."

Cassandra knew she wouldn't be able to get the lid back on the box, so she didn't try again. She started to blame herself and her selfish nature, for now she felt a creeping desire to hear how it all ended. She laid the rest of the orange on the bedside table and tentatively crawled onto the empty side of the bed.

"I did some investigating and found out that the last place anyone had seen her was at a storefront in downtown Houston. This was four years or so ago, and Redeemers were using places like these in an attempt to recruit new members under the guise of some other spiritual organization. I think this particular group was called The Faithkeepers or some shit like that. They had a sign in the window that asked: 'Are your children suffering because of your sin?' So many children had died during the epidemic, and these assholes were using that fact to infect a lot of people with a noxious dose of guilt. They blatantly said things like 'You killed your kids' and 'Had you believed, they would still be alive,' and all kinds of other horrible stuff. Now you take a person that is so vulnerable, so sick with grief that their disease has mutated into a florid state of mental illness, and you give them an opportunity to view the whole thing as their fault; they will jump at a chance to lay it all on themselves. I knew that she'd spent time there, but I had no idea about the true identity of the progenitors of this group until much later. After she disappeared, I asked them if they had seen her, and they had no response. I followed them to their flophouses or campgrounds at night, but she wasn't there. She'd just vanished. Within a couple of weeks the storefront had a For Lease sign on it, and every one of The Faithkeepers had disappeared. I never saw or heard from her again."

Cassandra nestled into him. She was instantly relieved that he did not resist her.

"I'm sorry," she reiterated.

"For getting me to talk about it, or for what transpired?"

"Both."

"You know, it could have been me."

"Could have been you what?"

"I swear I had all of the same feelings that she had—the anger, the immense grief, the utter sense of failure—but she saved me from tumbling into the abyss."

"How so?"

"By default, she made me take on the role of the strong one. All of her insane actions defined me as qualitatively sane in a strange way. Because of her utter debilitation, I was forced into taking all the responsibility, and in the end, it was a benefit to me. The evidence exists in the facts that I'm alive and somewhat stable."

This abstract point of view was confusing to Cassandra. How could he find anything positive in what had transpired during the end of his time with this woman? It was if he was intimating that Cynthia had suddenly become some kind of shaman instead of the totally narcissistic bitch that Cassandra had judged her to be from his recollection of the events. Were there not traces of venom in his voice as he related this history? She found herself staring at him with a quizzical look on her face.

"You take issue with the assessment of stability, I see," he said playfully.

And just like that, the melancholy that had hovered in the room like a visible cloud of wood smoke dissipated in an instant.

"Can you stay longer?" she asked.

"Until the dinner bell rings at the Brassey's."

"Good."

How these two came to be in this modest apartment overlooking the Detroit River on this sweltering June afternoon was not by chance. Once they both became aware that the spontaneous chemical reaction that arced between them during their early meetings was fissionable, they were forced to institute a carefully crafted level of subterfuge to progress their desires beyond the theoretical to the practical.

All of the tiers of security were conceived and created by Cassandra. Even though he was an expert in the area, Joe was clueless as to how the environment functioned and was amazed by all of the steps that would be required to make up the completed diversionary tactic.

Their napkin semaphore dance at the cafe was only a very small part of the process. There were many bogies that needed to be dodged as they endeavored to arrive at the location of their trysting, and the countermeasures were numerous and detailed.

A few trips would have to be abandoned, but there was a protocol for every eventuality. If one of them should have been spotted headed for the river, or should they be waylaid by a sudden change in plans, there were interim stops along the preferred route where a message could be conveyed detailing possible tardiness or cancellation.

A rearrangement of advertisements at a kiosk, the purchase of a specific item at a certain bodega, or a street vendor's flower laid inside a garbage receptacle were part of the possible signals. The first to arrive at the apartment would wait for the proscribed one hour before eventually seeking out the message signifying that the other had not been able to complete his or her journey.

The apartment had been sublet from a third party—a close friend of Cassandra's in the area—who Joe had never had the pleasure to meet. Its location in the district that encompassed the Red Wings' ward was intentional, as few ventured there because of the proclivity of its inhabitants to be uncivil toward strangers. Joe and Cassandra did their utmost to appear invisible by disguising themselves with a variety of caps and other accoutrements, usually bearing the local neighborhood's logos.

So far, there had been few glitches, and once inside the apartment—keyed in by sequenced buzzes on the intercom and coded knocks on the door—they felt as safe and secure as a slumbering flannel-swathed child clutching a stuffed animal.

The exits were always timed with one party departing thirty minutes before the other. The system worked.

Now that John was sixteen and officially consecrated, there were no regulatory impediments to his trying out for the punch-out squad. His intent was to proceed with the process even though he knew that younger men rarely made it through the initial cuts. He had transformed his once scrawny frame into one that was nearly absent of body fat but also noticeably devoid of any type of bulging muscular definition. Again, he found himself cursing his fate in regards to his genetics. Why hadn't he grown? Where was the presence of the extra hormones that should have been coursing through his body at this point, making his strenuous efforts more apparent to everything other than the mirror in his bathroom?

He felt there was one crucial hurdle to be transcended before he could declare himself ready to enter the competition. When he arrived at Cass Park to meet a group of his friends, he was still feeling the elevation of his adrenalin levels after witnessing Joe's daring escapade in the simulator.

John found his three buddies gathered near the Roger Smith fountain. As instructed, one of them had brought along a couple of pairs of oversized boxing gloves.

That youth, Keith Picker, had four brothers, and the gloves had been a present from their father. They were intended to solve disputes between the siblings, but after a physical hierarchy had been established—within their first two days of deployment—they'd been banished to a closet for many years.

John could see the evidence of mold and the unconditioned nature of the leather when Keith presented them to him on his arrival.

To John, this was the most profound of the steps in his development. Yes, he had done all of the rigorous physical training, had worked on his endurance and strength, but he had never laid a hand on another individual nor absorbed a shot himself. This was the moment that was sure to make him the most anxious, as he honestly had no idea how his body would react to the reception of any type of blow, especially to the head.

Over the last couple of weeks he had lain in bed thinking that it would be fine, but he had no recent experiences to draw upon to know for sure.

The last time he had been on the receiving end of any kind of contact was when he banged heads with that older boy in the jumping tent at his fifth birthday. That incident had proven to be costly, and it directly led to the perceived need for endless precaution and debilitating medication.

The assumption all along was that anything paralleling a blunt-force trauma to his head must be avoided at all costs. He was still familiar with the doctor's insistence that he sport a helmet to protect him from the possibility of seizures that might result from a blow to his bean. But he was eleven years down the road from that damning diagnosis, and his belief (or hope) was that he had grown out of the condition. Hell, due to his illusionist abilities, it had been four years since he had taken any medication at all, and he had been just fine during that span, thank you.

As his hands were plunged into the gloves, John was nearly overcome by the stench that exuded from the inside of the leather and cotton digit protectors. A hefty dose of residual sweat and mildew had mingled together through winter dank and summer swelter for nearly a half a decade. The resulting mutated biomass contained a pestiferous brew of bacterial fungus, and the resulting new species emitted a reek that could have stopped traffic.

"My god, Picker, did one of your brothers piss in here?"

"Wo zuzhou ni," Picker shot back.

"Fuck you very much, too, Keith."

One of the other boys, Chris Reckert, drew the drawstrings tight, and John turned to face his opponent—the third boy, Buddy Belasco.

"Let's see what you got," Chris said.

"Yeah, bring it on, penis-head," Buddy goaded him.

The two boys squared off and began to tentatively circle each other. Buddy struck first, a wild swing with his dominant right arm. John saw it coming from a mile away and easily ducked the blow. He countered with a quick right of his own and the glove compressed against Buddy's nose.

"Owww!"

Buddy's nose immediately turned red as a spate of blood rushed in—an obvious overreaction of his fragile circulatory system.

Chris and Keith began to laugh uproariously as Buddy's nose quickly doubled in size. John was angling for another shot, but Buddy dropped his arms and signaled with a helpless look that he'd had enough.

"Who's next?" John said triumphantly.

"Me," Chris said.

Keith stripped the gloves off Buddy's now-rubbery arms and went about installing them on Chris's large hands.

"Young Brassey?" a voice asked from across the park.

John spun around to find Kevin Gatz descending the knoll that they had cozied up against to hide their activity.

"Hey, Mr. Gatz," John said in the most noncommittal of fashions.

"What are doing?"

"Messing around."

"Really?"

The other three boys were studying this exchange between the captain's son and the chief lieutenant. Nothing easy and breezy was being passed between the two—that was for damn sure.

"Seems to me, young Brassey, that you taking a blow to the head might not be such a good thing," Kevin said with one of his patented twisted grins.

"And you know this because you've read some recent medical reports?"

"I wasn't aware that there had been a change in your condition."

The boys could see the pent-up anger—fueled by a coursing rush of adrenalin—rising in John as he took a step toward Lieutenant Gatz. Keith reached out and grabbed John's left arm.

"Bie jinzhang," Keith whispered.

"Yeah, John, take it easy," Chris added.

Kevin just kept grinning his grin. He knew he had something on the kid that was as good as currency. These were the kinds of things that Kevin held in his personal bank of psychological assets. He only disbursed the funds when it was most advantageous during whatever human transaction he was involved with at the time.

"You don't have to run to my house and tell my dad. I'll get there before and save you the trouble," John seethed.

"Why would you think I would tell your dad anything?"

"Because you're a fucking asshole, that's why."

Buddy Belasco gasped at the sheer level of insolence that John had displayed. He certainly didn't want to be lumped into the same schism that John seemed to be creating between himself and the lieutenant.

"None of us were going to hit him, Mr. Gatz. We made a pact."

Chris and Keith picked up on the ad-lib and nodded in agreement. They too wished to separate themselves from John and his belligerent attitude.

Kevin just held his grin, nodded once, and headed out of the park. John shook his head and held up the gloves to Keith Picker.

"Help me get these off," he said.

"Are we in trouble?" Keith asked.

"No."

"Are you in trouble?"

"Maybe," John said.

They wriggled the gloves off and John was once again assaulted by the smell from inside. He knew he would have to wash his hands with scalding water and a fragrant soap before he told his father what had transpired that afternoon.

THIRTY-FIVE

PUTTING THE BRAKES ON A TRANSFORMATION

IT WAS NOT yet dark when Joe walked out onto Atwater Street. He could smell and feel the moistness of the river as he watched his shadow elongating in the dying light. It had been a somewhat glorious afternoon.

He couldn't call what he felt for the fair Cassandra love. In the moment, he wasn't sure if that word could be used to describe any emotion that might emanate from him. And what was love to him anyway? Other than his parents, anything or anyone that he had applied that standard to had either died or disappeared. Best that he just define their union as one of affection. He definitely had that particular quality in abundance for her.

He felt a little lighter on his feet as he crossed by the Mariner's Church and began the walk up Woodward Avenue. Cassandra had taken her leave a good hour before him, and the only thing between him and a leisurely pace was the precision regimen represented by the Brassey dinnertime—six thirty on the dot. He would miss the cocktail hour, but that was not an odd occurrence. He would often shun Lon's invitation on the grounds that he was in training and needed to keep every possible whit operating at its fullest capacity.

Something had definitely shifted in him this day. He knew it wasn't his conquest of the simulator. He supposed there may have been some seeds of transformation rooted in the conversation he'd had with his mistress about grieving and loss. He had never discussed this part of his personal history with anyone to this point, though many knew most of the details and had gone on to form their own opinions. The last time he had allowed himself to be that open with another individual was in the early days of his marriage. That seemed to him to be from another life, from another person than the one who was coursing north up the avenue.

Before he had a chance to gather any sort of perspective in regards to the state of his development, to start laying out the flowchart of his past and allow his internal banter to debate its relative importance to his future, he sensed that something was amiss in his immediate surroundings.

He was approaching the Mugwump center in the Grand Circus region when he noticed—through a combination of reflections from all of the various examples of window glass—that someone was tailing him.

It was a stout, bearish man dressed in some kind of neutral-colored clothing. The man had affected something of a disguise that consisted of a blue ball cap and dark shades. These were some of the elements that had initially piqued Joe's interest: the stalker's desire to camouflage himself by screaming to anyone around him that he was doing just that.

The man kept his distance. He seemed to insist on keeping a buffer that measured at least a good block to the rear. As Joe indirectly clocked the follower's progress, he used the fiery light of the setting sun to his advantage. Since he was walking northwest, he would have the edge in that he could use the light source as an effective blinding implement to the left-hand periphery of the pursuer. This service paid dividends in short order. Joe made a sudden move toward due west, crossing the street to use the arced spur of Clifford Road. This maneuver allowed for further observation, and Joe gained a certain measure of confirmation when he'd seen the man crane his bulbous head above a sudden, frustrating instance of congestion to make sure that his subject had not eluded him.

All of these observations were just part of the freakishly high level of intuition that Joe had been blessed with by birth and subsequently allowed to be nurtured by his training.

He looked again at the angle of the sun and feared that he was going to be late for dinner. He doubled back onto a vector that would return him to Woodward Avenue. Once there, he hailed a pedicab. As he boarded, he looked back to find that his pursuer no longer appeared to be in the vicinity.

PART TWO

THIRTY-SIX

MONDAY

"Could you please come over here and provide some much-needed narration for this extravaganza?"

Joe was standing on the balcony of his and Cassandra's love nest looking east at the crowd gathering down by the banks of the river. It seemed to him that every artery that fed into the pilgrim's destination was clogged up as far as his eyes could see.

"Do you think you should be out there? If you're being followed as you say, whoever it is can probably see you right now," Cassandra said from inside the bedroom.

"This is my last week here anyway. Not a lot is going to change between now and Saturday. Besides, I haven't seen any recent evidence that anyone is shadowing me. Nothing since that first time."

Cassandra heard a tendril of finality in his statement, and the sadness that suddenly gripped her was palpable. Maybe it was her sometimes-fatalistic nature that caused her to spin his words toward the negative, but once he said that he was likely to be moving on after the race, she could only start the clock counting down until all this would end.

"Come on, help me out here. Who are those people that are gathering at the base of that refinery?"

Cassandra rose from the thin layer of their sweat that had formed a cooling barrier between her body and the cotton sheets, slipped on a sheer robe, and joined him out on the terrace. There were tears now that mingled with the perspiration on her face, and she didn't really give a shit whether he noticed them or not.

"Okay, here's the deal: This is the Red Wings' turf, so the entire event is under their control," she said.

Joe could see that a man with a megaphone and a red cap was addressing the huge crowd. Even Joe could hear that the din created by the revelers would never be usurped by the voice of the screaming man. The sounds that met his ears—even from this distant perch—consisted of coordinated yells, voices singing, and the occasional hurled insult.

"Nobody's listening to the guy."

"Wait. This happens every year."

She held up her arm like the conductor of an orchestra, smiled at him, and waved it down as if she wanted the first movement of a symphony to commence. As if on cue, the entire group seemed to jump out of their skins. A second later Joe understood why. An explosion had rocked the senses of the gathered. The echoes traversed through the canyon of high-rises, making the noise appear much louder than the force of its initial source.

"Dynamite?"

"No, silly. It was just a really big firecracker. Those goofballs do this every year to settle the people down before the big moment when they unveil the precious liquid. There!" she exclaimed, pointing at an area of the crowd that was beginning to part.

Joe saw another group of people, decked out in red hats and shirts, pushing an old wooden cart. Atop the cart was an object that appeared to be a large black steel barrel. A comely twenty-something sat atop that vessel, dispensing her pertness via a constant wave of her right hand.

The cart and its occupant withstood the onslaught of a mass of flowers and greenery being flung at them from the people that were lining the parade route. The cart rolled on and disappeared through a door at the base of the refinery.

"That's it?" Joe asked.

"For now. Everybody stuffs their gut and drinks an ocean of whatever they've brought with them before the cracking ceremony continues."

Joe could see groups beginning to disperse for other locations. The migration of the masses afforded him a more delineated view of the geography. There were tents set up everywhere, steam and smoke rising from cooking apparatuses, and lines of the famished taking their places in front of the facilities provided by their respective wards.

Cassandra returned to the interior of the apartment and began to gather up her clothing. Joe finally figured out that the weather had been altered in the room, but he was confused as to the reasons that might have triggered the change in pressure.

"You're leaving?" he asked.

"It's race week," she said as if he were a child.

Now Joe knew that the forces of her nature had been stirred, but he still couldn't reckon why.

"Did something happen here?"

"Yeah, we fucked, and now I'm leaving," she said.

She made a move for the bathroom. Joe reached out and bade her to stop.

"Cassandra? I'll ask again. What happened?"

"Apparently, not much. You came to town, we had a moment, and now you're leaving."

She disengaged from him and continued on her trek to the bathroom. Joe sat on the edge of the bed and stared at the now-closed door. His first thought was to flee. He certainly didn't want to get into a whole thing about some amorphous future. He was a guest here, and when his usefulness was no longer welcome, his assumption was that he would be asked to leave. When he heard the water in the shower come on, he returned to the balcony and watched the proceedings surrounding the cracking festival.

He could see that the people's attention was intermittently being taken away from their libations and sustenance as many started to look up toward the towers of the refinery. Joe followed the trajectory of their gazes and saw that there were people making their way up to the catwalks that crisscrossed all of the vertical piping. Once emplaced at the correct level, one of the men was outfitted with a full asbestos fire suit, replete with a respirator and helmet.

As the man in the bulky accoutrements walked gingerly into view, the crowd uniformly rose and cheered. At the end of the scaffolding, he removed a chrome implement from his front pocket and held it aloft. The crowd suddenly became frenzied and rhythmically clapped and chanted, "Fire and fraction, fire and fraction . . ."

The man twisted open a valve, once again held the tool aloft, and then reached over and offered it to the altar that was represented by a vent pipe. Joe knew now that the tool was a spark wrench, and when the man clicked it once, a steady consistent flame began to pursue a path for the heavens. The chant disintegrated into a storm of applause, whistles, and yelps.

"Wow. That was crazy," Joe said toward the interior of the apartment.

There was no answer.

"Cassie?"

Nothing.

He walked inside to find that she had departed. He put on what constituted his disguise—a ball cap and clear-lens horn-rimmed glasses—and left the apartment.

Joe knew that he had violated their protocol by not waiting the requisite amount of time before venturing out, but at this point, he was more interested in trying to resolve the contentions between them than following any rules.

As he hit the street, his hopes of finding her were buoyed by the reality that the entire area was devoid of people. He immediately assumed that she would be forced to make the trip uptown on foot—all of the mechanical conveyances seemed to have disappeared. Joe knew that they must have mustered over to an area close to the festivities in hopes of cashing in on the wealth of business that would emerge when the event ended.

He made his way across Hart Plaza, skirted the Mariner's Church, and hustled himself onto Woodward Avenue. Looking to the northwest, he saw no one else heading up the street. He picked up his pace, breaking into a light jog, hoping that she had not taken an alternate route.

As he approached the Grand Circus area, the Mugwump commercial and residential center, he saw more people on the street. Obviously, the Independents had no stake in the jamboree that was taking place down by the river. As he wove around all of the sudden busyness, he was struck by the realization that this day would likely end without a conciliatory conversation with his girlfriend. This took the wind out of his sails and he slowed down. What would he tell her anyway?

He hadn't given a whit of thought as to what his life would be after he completed his duties here. That had been liberating in the moment, but now he knew he would have to turn his attention toward it to provide explanations for her, and the fact was that he just hadn't processed things that far.

A figure flashed in the side-view mirror of the lone pedicab that was parked on the street. Something clicked in Joe's mind, and he became aware that the hue of the clothing was similar to that worn by his former pursuer. He feinted as if to cross the street. It was a pretense to look directly at the person. The person had the same physical makeup as the man he had identified before, but he couldn't be sure. He continued up the avenue, his brain pinging red alert.

He ducked into one of the shops that the Mugwumps patronized when they were in need of tobacco, alcohol, and/or legal stimulants, and he moved toward the back of the establishment. He wanted to avail himself of the full breadth of the tinted glass windows and perhaps get a detailed look at his tail.

"Hey, you're the guy," a male voice stated from behind him.

Joe did not immediately turn to acknowledge the person who was speaking to him. He had already spent nearly his entire tenure in this place having to withstand being engaged by that exact same greeting, and frankly, he had become weary of it.

"You're Josiah Smith, am I right?" the voice asked.

Joe couldn't ignore the voice now. He hadn't heard anyone use his real first name since his soles first met the unyielding pavement of Motor City. He tried to angle the interested man into a position so the window would be just over the man's shoulder.

"I'm the guy who found you," the man said.

"Oh, hey."

"You were one elusive son-of-a-bitch."

"How is that?" Joe asked with his attention firmly placed on the people gliding past his field of vision. To that point, no man with neutral colored clothing had deigned to walk by or stop and peer into the shop.

"I had you tracked all the way to H-town, and then you just fucking disappeared on me. I see you got the letter I left for you at your folks'."

"Yeah."

"Caught holy hell from your captain for not delivering it to you personally, but I guess things are supposed to work out the way they do, you know? Word is you are some kind of kick-ass driver. I should ask the lawyer to ask your boss for a bonus."

"That sounds about right," Joe said, sure that the man could hear the aura of distraction oozing out of him like blood from a small caliber gutshot.

"Just a word to the wise: You have enemies here," the tracker said in an effort to be familiar.

"No shit."

"I'm serious; the lawyer had me contact one of my interviewees and bring him in as a possible driver for Mustang. This guy was not your biggest fan."

Joe dropped his focus on the window and looked his tracker in the eyes. This new information immediately grasped his attention.

"And I know him? Personally?"

"I think you do. Look, everyone I interviewed told me you were some type of god or something, but this guy was not up for giving you any consideration. It didn't strike me as odd at the time because I was just getting started, but later—as my journey progressed—there wasn't a single person who didn't hold you in some kind of esteem, except this guy. I mean, some feared you, some gave me nothing but glossy reviews of your abilities, but this guy was just plain dismissive. When I put two and two together, I figured he must be covering something, and that the two of you might have some kind of history that he wasn't interested in discussing."

"Who was he?"

"Some guy named Udo something."

It was like a solitary lightning bolt from a thunderstorm cell—one that coded black on the radar screen—and it struck Joe squarely in that vulnerable spot between his eyes. He didn't need the tracker to clarify the surname.

"Where is he?" Joe asked with an even, trained voice.

"He's locked away in Mustang territory, as far as I know."

"Can you find out where?"

The tracker shrugged. Joe took that response to be a suggestion that a negotiation was required.

"How much for the information?" Joe asked.

"It isn't about any money, brother. I just don't know if I have the authorization, you know? I got to protect my position in this burg. I don't work for Mugwumps, that's for sure. I work for the lawyer, and that's it. If I fuck up, like offered up something that might be classified as confidential, I could find my ass fighting for my survival out in the wilderness. I've been out there, and every time I return, I make damn sure to kiss the ground of this place no matter how oppressive it can be at times."

"Can you give me your employer's name?"

"Ask your captain. He's the one that contacted the lawyer to have me find you."

"Okay."

"And if you do, could you do me the favor of not mentioning any of the stuff I told you? I had no idea it was that big of a deal, you know?"

"I'll keep you out of it."

"Thanks, friend."

Joe reached out and offered his hand. The tracker just held up a finger in acknowledgement. He knew he shouldn't have said anything, and this subject, this guy he had found down in Texas, was not a friend, just an entity associated with his work.

When Joe came back out on the street, there was no man who fit the description of his shadow awaiting his exit. If there had been, Joe would have waved him over, found out his connection, and asked him for the name of his employer. He would ask the follower to help him locate where Udo Lewandowski was currently holed up. He would have done this because he was pretty sure that it must have been someone from Mustang who was following him. They seemed to be the only organized entity that might have a stake in his movements. He'd heard stories about the ruthless tactics employed by the Mustang captain, Titus O'Keefe, and this seemed to fit the profile.

He had come to the conclusion that the motivation for this other ward in keeping tabs on him was so they could use this intelligence as leverage if they felt threatened by his presence at some point. No doubt, the accounts of his accomplishments in the simulator were sure to have had a hand in stimulating a response from Impala's archenemy.

As Joe saw it, they would most likely contact him after the lottery and tell him that they knew of his dalliance with the museum curator, and if he didn't want his captain to find out, he was either requested to pay some fee or take a dive in the race. He would do neither.

Joe did not follow his normal stress-relief protocol: a long, centering inhalation followed by a excruciatingly slow exhalation, during which all of the possible scenarios would appear in his analytical mind. He lit out for the environs of Impala at a pace just shy of an all-out sprint.

When he arrived at the Brassey townhouse, he found only Karen in the residence.

"Lon headed over to the clubhouse with Kevin about twenty minutes ago."

"Okay," Joe said before hustling up the stairs to his room.

"Is everything all right?" Karen asked on his departure.

Joe didn't answer her. He changed out of his sweat-stained clothing and contemplated whether he should search the house for implements that might serve as possible weapons. Finally, he decided to deal with the ramifications of all this by first seeking out his employer. Surely Captain Brassey would be able to understand the seriousness of the news that a Redeemer had made his way into Motor City.

THIRTY-SEVEN

JOHN MADE IT through the first three cuts of the strength tests that were used to whittle down the field of hopefuls trying out for the punch-out squad. The initial one hundred and six entrants had already passed through the sit-ups, push-ups, and pull-ups, with twenty percent being eliminated after each specific exercise. John had finished in the middle of the advancing pack for the first two and had gone on to set a new record for pull-ups by raising his body to the horizontal bar seventy-one times, by far tops among the remaining sixty-eight contestants. Up next for the fifty-four survivors was the endurance portion of the program. Those who passed through this trial would move onto the combat phase of the selection process. There were two endurance tests: first, continuous jumping jacks, and second, suspension of a weight held out parallel to the floor in front of the aspirant. The amount of weight that each contestant was required to hold was equivalent to roughly eighteen percent of the hopeful's body weight.

The last forty-three still standing after the first of the endurance tests would move forward, and at the end of the second examination, only thirty-four would remain.

The eleven who would be eliminated during the jumping jack phase departed quickly, within five minutes after the whistle had blown to commence.

John easily made it through and had little desire to try to set the bar for the most, as the ensuing test was sure to be the toughest. He took the respite to recover before he was to be handed the twenty-seven pounds he would have to hold directly in front of him until enough people (nine) dropped out.

Through the years, there had been much dispute about how the competition for determining the team had been set up and whether this format really did identify the best candidates for the squad. Many argued that a big fucker who might be slow afoot would never be able to make the team because his endurance or nimbleness was not considered his forte. John knew that many tough bastards, guys who could knock you into next week, were often eliminated before they ever got to the combat part of the test.

After much back and forth, and even though there had been decades of poor showings by Impala, the committee responsible decided to continue to rely on this specific sort of evaluation. Their reasoning was that tests such as these had definite metrics and would eliminate any charges of cronyism or favoritism in the selection process.

John's dad was maneuvering behind the scenes to change the procedures. He couldn't understand the correlation between fitness and raw power. There were some Goliaths in their ward, and those brutes never seemed to have a shot at being allowed to smash their bare fists into a Mustang face.

John wobbled a little at the outset of the weight-holding test, but he made it to the next level by eventually finishing in fourth place overall. It helped that at one hundred fifty pounds of body weight, he was required to hold far less than most of his other competitors.

To say that no one expected him to last this long would be a total exaggeration. No greater than zero people ever thought he would make it through the first test. Each and every observer, official, and contestant had been uniformly amazed by the feats displayed by the newly consecrated sixteen-year-old.

Though the punch-out extravaganza was a weapons-free, bare-knuckles event, the tryout committee employed a gladiator-style contest utilizing pugil sticks to determine the final pool.

A pugil stick measured roughly five and half feet in length and was padded on each end. Heavily armored contestants, randomly chosen, would battle each other, and a bout would end only after one had been felled. With thirty-four left, there would be seventeen winners. Subjectivity would be used to select the fifteen members of the squad and two alternates from the champions of the tryout. Previous experience and overall impression were important factors used in the final determination.

As the lots were being chosen, John finally began to get a little nervous about his prospects. Again he was placing himself in a situation that would require him to accept a blow of force. Finally his name came out of the hat, and he was paired against a man he knew fairly well, Jody Springer. Jody was in his mid-twenties, had participated in three punch-outs, and was generally considered to be a lock to make the team from the outset.

The hastily assembled schedule informed him that they would be the fifth bout on the docket.

———

Lon Brassey and Kevin Gatz were deep in argument as they passed through Cass Park on their way to the Temple Street clubhouse. The random citizens of Impala rubbernecked toward the loud voices that their captain and his chief lieutenant were using to get their points across.

"No, goddammit. We will wait," Lon snarled, his voice degrading from a yell to a seething whisper when he noticed the stares of his constituents.

"This is going to come back to bite you in the ass," Kevin said with a forceful shake of his head.

"What do you base your supposition on? This is wholly new territory for us, and you have no experience to call upon to make your case."

"I have my intuition."

"No offense, Kevin, but you tend to color everyone with the same hue of blackness. When was the last time you ever said anything nice about anyone?"

Kevin just looked off to the right. His eyeballs nearly disappeared behind their sockets. He didn't feel that he had to explain himself to Lon; he should have taken immediate action in deference to the intelligence they'd been steadily gathering for the last couple of weeks.

"I'm just saying this could be a bigger problem than you think. Why take the chance?" Kevin asked quietly.

"Your dissent is duly noted. Now, shut up about it."

The anger rose up in Kevin again. Would this be the time that he divulged something from his arsenal of secrets that would set his superior straight? He contemplated whether to extend the confrontation. It wouldn't take much.

As they neared the temple, a large crowd was milling around the outdoor garden. The group contained a mixture of rejects from the punch-out competition, relatives and friends consoling them, and a cadre of Impala insiders who were taking a break from the proceedings while the ballroom was being readied for the bouts. Billy Klock broke away from a small caucus when he saw Lon and Kevin advancing up the block.

"You are not going to believe it, Cap," Billy exclaimed upon his arrival.

"I told you," Kevin said, harkening back to the substance of their original argument.

"Kevin? Enough," Lon warned.

"What did you see?" Kevin asked Billy.

"What do you mean?" Billy asked.

"Did he meet up with that Mustang slut again?" Kevin asked Billy.

This was not at the core of the exciting news that Billy wanted to impart to his captain. Billy was overcome, once again, by a stultifying look of confusion. Kevin just shook his head and spat on the ground—a release of the same carbonated bile that Lon had agitated by disagreeing with his assessment of the situation that had made up the subject of their previous conversation.

Kevin stared at Billy, his counterpart. Effectively, they were on the same level in the overall hierarchy of the ward, but there was no way that this dolt was an equal. Look at the fucking clothes he chose for his surveillance duties: tan shirt and pants, ball cap, and oversize blue sunglasses. Only an idiot would choose an outfit that would make one stand out from the crowd like a splotch of dried blood under an ultraviolet light.

"Just start talking and we'll see what comes out, Bill," Lon said softly.

"Your kid," Billy began.

"What about my kid?" Lon asked.

"He's made it all way through to the bouts."

Lon's eyes nearly spontaneously combusted.

"What?" Lon screamed.

"He's the talk of the whole competition. Apparently he did something like a hundred pull-ups, someone told me."

Billy wanted to go into more detail, but Lon had already left the two standing on the sidewalk.

When Lon entered the ballroom, he didn't notice the stench of nervous sweat that was now a predominant part of the interior atmosphere. He didn't notice the noise of the witnesses as they assessed the combatants in the forthcoming tilt and engaged in friendly wagering. He didn't notice the outstretched hands of the plebes of his realm, straining to offer their congratulations to him on his son's astonishing success.

He walked straight over to the staging area just as John was being outfitted with his suit of armor for the pugil stick contests.

"Stop," Lon said to the attendant.

"Hey, Dad," John said as nonchalantly as possible.

"Take it off," Lon said in the same even tone.

"But . . ."

"Take that shit off of him. He won't be fighting. He has withdrawn from the competition," Lon said to the attendant.

"Wait a minute," John pleaded.

"Do it now," Lon demanded.

The attendant reached for the set of Velcro straps on the suspenders that were responsible for keeping the fortified trousers up. John slapped his hand away just as one of the officials sidled up.

"Congratulations, Captain Brassey, your son's achievements today have been nothing short of monumental," the faceless official said in his best toady speak.

"That's great, but he's done. He will not be fighting. He has a medical condition that requires medication. People in this room are aware of that. My question is, how was he even allowed to compete?"

The official just sputtered incoherently like the motor on a toy boat.

"I lied," John said defiantly.

"There," Lon said, "he doesn't have to formally withdraw. He is disqualified, am I right?"

The official concurred with a steady nodding of the head. John knew he was finished. He removed the armored clothing himself. Jody Springer crossed to him from the other corner of the room.

"I just wanted to say good luck, kid," Jody said, extending his now-gloved mitt in a display of mutual knighthood.

"I'm out," John informed him.

"What?"

"I'm a fucking epileptic and I'm not cleared to do this. Congratulations, you win in a walkover."

Jody's response did not contain any elements of joy or relief. Like the gallant he was, he felt sad that he couldn't battle for his place.

"I'm sorry, kid. Watching your exploits leading up to the fight made me look forward to testing myself against you."

"Thanks. Me too."

John was finally out of the protective getup. He reached down for his gym bag and walked out of the building. Lon followed the official over to the scoring table to make sure that the withdrawal was recorded, and forthwith, his son would be forever banned from attempting this sort of thing again.

————

As Joe approached the temple, he could see that almost the entire perimeter was ringed with crowds trying to get inside. Obviously, those who had attended the cracking festival were just returning to the ward and wanted to see how the competition was progressing.

Of course, Joe knew that John was going to offer himself to the selection process that day and he had promised the youngster that he would steer clear of the event.

Because of the fact that they'd been nearly inseparable for the last month or so, John thought that Joe might suffer some of the blowback should he be caught in his lie. As Joe was arriving, he had no idea that John had performed admirably and had been disqualified for his prevarication.

There was only one figure walking away from the Temple as Joe came upon the outer satellites of the crowds that were in near-synchronous orbit. It was John. Joe could see the purposefulness in his steps, and he sensed by the kid's gait and sway that he was supremely disappointed in his effort.

"Hey," Joe said gently as John walked past him.

John looked up briefly. The sun's reflection produced a glint that exaggerated the amount of tears that had stained his reddened cheeks.

"Fuck him," John said as he continued to walk away from the building.

"Whoa, kid. What happened?"

"Ask him."

"I'm asking you."

Joe grabbed his elbow and tilted him so that they were face-to-face.

"I'd made it to the final. I fucking kicked ass. And then he showed up and shut me down. God forbid there should be more than one special person representing the Brassey family."

Joe knew that the kid wasn't idly boasting. It wasn't in his nature to crow. He had tried to make his own mark this day and by his account had come close.

"Your dad . . ." Joe said.

"He's going to make it so I can never try again."

"Obviously, he's afraid that you're going to get hurt. That has to be his motivation."

"You can side with him if you want, but he only seems interested in humiliating me at every opportunity."

"Oh, I don't think that's it."

"Yeah, it is," John declared.

John pulled away and continued his retreat from the building. Joe wanted to go with him, try to help him deal with his pain, but it was a different agenda that had called him here, and he was compelled to see it through to completion. He was pretty sure that repairing the damage that had been paternally foisted on his young friend could be handled at some future time, and maybe with the kid fully engulfed with irrational emotion, now was not it.

The crowd that had caused the entrances to the building to swell into an impenetrable human blockade could not be parted, so Joe searched for a place that would allow him to scale up to someplace other than the congested ground floor. At the western end of the building stood an old elm tree. Spring having sprung awhile ago, the now dense foliage on the limbs would provide him with good cover from the mobs below, and hopefully no one would glom onto the idea that this was the only reasonable way to get inside.

Joe took a small running start and jumped up toward the trunk's central point, accessing the knot that allowed for a slight indentation in the otherwise flat verticality. His boot found brief purchase on the tiny ledge as his forward momentum straightened him into a parallel position to the spire that was the trunk. A quick bending and unbending of his knee joints shot him rocket-like upward, where the lowest of the branches that would support his weight jutted out like the steel awnings of the Big D downtown buildings he used to swing on as child. He clambered onto the limb, crossed back toward the center, and searched for the strongest arm of the grand tree that tapered toward the parapet on the building.

A group of men who were catching the sunset on the balcony saw him emerge from the tree, jump across the divide, and drop down onto the terrace. They had no time to comment, as he was suddenly past them and into the hallways of the third floor. He sprinted down the four flights of stairs to the ballroom and emerged into the crowd of spectators who were watching the commencement of the first of the pugil stick bouts. He saw Captain Brassey, over by the official's area, screaming at a group of men in white short-sleeved shirts that supported identical green bow ties.

Brassey had finished with the verbal portion of his tirade by the time Joe reached him, but his face was still crimson, and his eyes were still lit up like an exploding howitzer shell. Seeing Joe, he immediately shifted the thrust of his fury onto him.

"Did you know about this?"

Joe was never desirous of being put in a position of feeling that he had to be anything less than relentlessly truthful, but his young friend had been seriously wounded by his father's lack of understanding—if not outright cruelty—and Joe felt obliged to back the kid in this particular situation.

"About what?" Joe asked in deflection.

"John and his harebrained scheme," Lon said as clarification.

"You are going to have to be more specific," Joe said.

"Forget it. It doesn't matter now. It's over."

"I wonder if we could find some privacy?" Joe asked.

"What's up?"

"A matter that needs to be brought to your attention. Suffice it to say, it cannot wait."

Lon cocked his head toward the stairs.

"I have an office on the fourth floor. Room 415. I'll meet you there in fifteen minutes."

Joe nodded and made for the western stairwell. Lon disappeared into the crowd.

———

Tradition held that the Impala captain's office door was never locked to his constituency. Joe twisted the crystal knob of the darkly stained oak door and entered a world that appeared to be frozen in time.

In the whole of the anteroom, not twenty feet from the main office door, a collection of old photographs covered the burnished wood walls. Joe found himself entranced by a photo that was marked with the date 4/22/1922. The picture depicted the laying of the cornerstone of the building he was standing in, and special attention—by way of point of focus—was made of the trowel that held the mortar.

"That is George Washington's own trowel that he used to lay the cornerstone of the Capitol Building in Washington D.C. They had it shipped in from his archive in Virginia for the event," Lon said, silently entering and acknowledging the image that had caught Joe's eye.

Joe had heard the stories of the fledging democracy's first chief executive, but now, in this time and place, Lon might as well have been talking about Greek or Roman history—so thin were the memories of what was once a vital empire.

Two other men entered the room, Kevin Gatz and Billy Klock. Seeing Billy's get-up gave Joe instant confirmation that his pursuer was not of the ilk that fit with his original conclusion. This was the man who had followed him, and Joe was initially at a loss in trying to explain the reasoning behind the subterfuge.

"What's on your mind, Mr. Smith?" Lon asked.

Joe could see the interest the question engendered in the two lieutenants.

"It's private matter," Joe said.

Joe caught a glimpse of Kevin as he curled his lip, signaling the onset of a knowing smile of self-satisfaction.

"Anything that you have to say can be said in front of these two men. They are as dense as marble in their ability to maintain confidence," Lon said.

"No," Joe said simply.

He fixed his gaze on the two underlings. Everyone in the room now knew that the point was non-negotiable.

"Very well. Please, come inside," Lon said as he crossed in front of Joe and opened the door to his office proper.

The only word to describe Lon's office was "majestic." Joe had read many books in his youth about various kings, tsars, emirs, and presidents. Lon's space gave him a visceral interpretation to supplant the images that had once been only an author's nudging to his imagination.

The desk alone was so impressive that Joe could only stare at its heft and beauty.

"This was the desk that was once used by the man who created General Motors, William C. Durant. Funny thing about him: He started the company, and then he got kicked out. So he took over another company that made the Chevrolet, bought out that partner, and made so much money he was able to buy enough shares of GM in the stock market to gain back full control. Then he merged Chevrolet into the company, and they nearly took over the entire industry," Lon said.

"What happened?" Joe asked.

"Henry Ford and Teddy Roosevelt happened," Lon said derisively.

Joe didn't know the history, and he really wasn't interested in learning about it. He did notice that Lon's demeanor, when he spit out those last two names, darkened. It was an expression that Joe had witnessed from him many times, and it always carried with it the suggestion that Lon was infused with a certain amount of ingrained paranoia. Joe assumed that because of this specific personality defect, Lon would react to the news with interest. It was why he chose to seek out the captain as a first step.

"You've got a problem," Joe said.

"And what is that?"

"Mustang has brought in a driver from the outside."

"That's not news, my friend. We're on top of it. At this point, our information tells us that he's only a backup."

"Do you know who he is?" Joe asked.

Lon rummaged through some papers on his desk and pulled out a file.

"Yeah, his name is Clarence Rigney. He ran a security company in C-town."

"That is not his name."

Lon looked back down at the dossier that his intelligence squad had created for the ward. He held it up so Joe could see the information it contained. Joe quickly read the scant amount of information that Impala had on the guy.

"These guys who do these things are pretty thorough," Lon said.

"His name is Udo Lewandowski. He is a Redeemer apostle. If you want confirmation in regards to his allegiances, you should ask your brother. This is the guy that almost got him killed."

Lon's initial reaction lacked anything that could be qualified as surprise, and instead he offered a simple nod of acknowledgement. He followed that with pursed lips and a shake of his head that inferred a languid resignation.

"And what do you want me to do?" Lon asked.

"The lawyer who found me found him for Mustang. I need to speak with him and find out where this Udo is holing up."

"And then what?"

"I'm going to take him out before he can hurt anyone."

"I don't know, Joe. We've got a lot more important things on our plate this week."

Joe paused for the briefest moment. He couldn't understand why Captain Brassey was reacting in this manner. "Wait a minute, you do understand what's going on here, right?" Joe asked incredulously.

"Yeah, you've had some kind of flashback or something. I get it. I know the pressure to perform can be overwhelming sometimes, but I certainly didn't expect you to start crumbling now."

Joe held his ground, but his first instinct was to rap Lon in the temple with an open hand. It would carry with it a multitude of intentions, not the least of which was to knock some fucking sense into him. For now, he commanded his right arm to stay at his side.

"I don't think you understand what this means."

"No, I do. Kevin, Billy, you can come in now!" Lon yelled out.

It was as if they had been listening at the door—the warp speed with which they turned the gathering into a foursome was impressive.

Joe tried to appeal to the other minds in the room.

"Kevin, help me out here. I've just told your boss about a realistic threat that's lurking here, and I don't think he comprehends the seriousness," Joe said.

"What threat would that be?" Kevin asked.

"You have a Redeemer living in your city."

"Huh." Kevin replied.

"Really?" Billy asked.

"You do understand that his presence puts the entire city at mortal risk?" Joe asked.

"One guy?" Billy asked.

Joe could see that nothing he was saying was penetrating this lot. He was appealing to nothing more than three statues. His boss had been right—dense marble.

Joe began to see Lon clearly in the glaring, abrasive light of his son's descriptions. This guy didn't give a shit about anything that didn't pertain to him personally, and the fate of his walled city was not part of his purview at this time.

"All right," Joe said, "sorry to bother you."

There was nothing sarcastic in the statement, but all three men interpreted it as such. Joe headed for the door.

"Where are you going?" Kevin asked.

Before Joe could answer, Lon grabbed Kevin's arm and signaled him to stand down.

"But . . ." Kevin uttered.

Joe was gone, and Lon sat down in his chair.

"I'm telling you, Cap, we've got to deal with this thing he's got going on with the Mustang bitch. It makes us all look bad," Kevin pleaded.

"Look, goddammit, I told you before, we will deal with that when we need to," Lon said, his voice tightening.

"When is that, Cap?" Billy asked.

Kevin didn't pile on; he allowed Billy's question to hang in the air.

"Nobody outside of the three of us knows about it. Do you want it to get out to the whole fucking ward? We don't need the kind of chaos that something like that would bring, do we? And another thing: Tomorrow is the lottery. When we know we have a competitive car, other contingencies obviously come into play. Let's say we draw the AMX; what good is it to put our thumb on this guy if that happens?" Lon asked.

Neither one of them had an answer to that one.

"Use your fucking heads," Lon said, exasperated.

"Do you want me to still follow him?" Billy asked.

"No, we've got what we need. I just hope he doesn't completely lose his shit over this whole Redeemer thing. That would be a problem."

THIRTY-EIGHT

EVEN THOUGH IT appeared that he was stymied by Lon Brassey's complete dismissal of his dire warning, Joe was not about to just go on as if he didn't know that Udo Lewandowski was somewhere in the city. Yeah, he had the duty he had sworn to fulfill and he sure wasn't going to abdicate his responsibility, but he knew that the majority of his thoughts would be centered on this butcher and his evil intentions. He needed to expunge the distraction as soon as possible.

So focused was he to find his quarry that he did not process that tidbit of information revealed to him when he noticed the achromatic textiles that Billy sported—that his shadow was actually one of the Impala lieutenants.

This was curious, in and of itself, but he had pushed aside any immediate need to answer all of those questions because this other issue had claimed the number one ranking on his priority list.

He covered the length of the Impala ward and made his way to the café that linked him to the woman who he had obviously pissed off earlier in the day. Luckily, the barista who served as their medium was still behind the bar. It was near closing time, and the only patrons were those who were lonely or had a reason to avoid going home. Joe waited for a hairline-challenged stick of a man to accept his order before moving in close to the barista.

"I need for you to call her," Joe said.

The barista looked around. How big were the ears of the customers?

"This is not how it's done," she whispered harshly.

"I know. It's an emergency. Could you, please?"

"This is not what I agreed to."

But she could see in Joe's normally placid eyes that something was different. She disappeared briefly before returning with a dour expression on her face.

"She doesn't want to talk to you."

Joe's only response was akin to a shrug. This was done for the benefit of this intermediary; he had no need to explain the whole situation to her. His hope was that he could just handle this swiftly and get back to the task that lay ahead for him at the end of week.

"Okay. That's okay. Could you do me another favor?" Joe asked.

The barista just wanted to total up the day's receipts before the street powered down, but she nevertheless offered him a look of possible compliance.

"Could I borrow that hat?" he asked.

She had on a motorman's cap that functioned in the dual capacity of fashion statement and hair net.

"I'll return it tomorrow," he added.

The request registered as a disarming non sequitur, and her first instinct was to remove the cap and hand it to him.

"Thank you. You'll have it back tomorrow. I promise."

Before she could figure out what had just happened, he was past the loitering customers and out the door.

This was a first for him, traversing the Mustang neighborhood solo. There were some innocent revelers on the streets still stoking their fires of inebriation in homage to the venting torch, burning steadily at the refinery down by the river. There were families out on a post-supper stroll, connecting with the neighbors while trying to stay out of the way of the most wasted individuals. And there were members of an inter-ward blue-coated security detail that had been tasked with making sure there were no fuck-ups by the citizens lest someone from the committee should be trolling the area looking for any infraction on the eve of the festivities.

Joe picked his way through all of these hazards as he made his way to the environs of the museum. It helped that the power had already been diminished and most of the sources of light had been doused for the evening. Up ahead though, he could see that wasn't the case. The entire breadth of the area in and around the museum was awash in illuminated brilliance. It still seemed a good distance away—this oasis of light—and there were many pogues to avoid before he could arrive at his destination unscathed.

Out of whim or nervousness, Joe decided to project a quality of intoxication so he could blend in with the majority of the people in the street. He allowed his gait to become wobbly, and he added heft to his eyelids in an effort to mimic the drunken Mustangs on the road.

His choice to sport headwear had been inspired, if not prescient, as pretty much everyone had something adorning his or her head. Most of the coverings were of the novelty variety and included intricate foam recreations of cars and engines. Joe recognized one of them as the small Ford V8 that Frank had fawned over the first day he visited his shop.

He was bearing down on the museum when he noticed a different sort of individual mixed in with all of the Mustang folk. These others were dressed in identical suits of a grayish tone. They carried tablets with them and were gathered in groups of twos and threes, fifty meters from Harold Getty's building.

Joe knew immediately that he would have to find a way to penetrate this group that appeared to be perpetrating nothing less than a siege of the museum. None of the neighborhood crowd stood inside of the perimeter that these people had created, and many of the Mustangers who had been occupying the street began to line the thruway on the other side of the officials as if they had burgeoning expectations of a coming parade. Now Joe was caught between the army of officials and a growing group of drunken locals.

Joe spied Teller, the museum's daytime security guard, walking a beat near the rear doors of the loading dock. He removed his cap, straightened his posture, and approached one of the officials.

"Excuse me, I wonder if I could have a word with Teller over there?" Joe asked.

"We're trying to keep this area clear, sir."

"I understand. I left some of my notes behind, and I'm assuming that the museum will be closed for the next couple of days, and, well, I'm really going to be lost without my training journal."

"And you are?"

"Joe Smith, I'm driving for Impala."

"Oh, you're the one."

"Yes."

"You either got a lot of balls or a shitload of ignorance to be lurking around this neighborhood at night."

"I think it's probably the latter," Joe said with an impish smile.

"Well, you understand that no one other than museum personnel and the laborers are allowed in the museum this evening."

"Yeah, I can see that the security is heightened. I thought that maybe I could get Teller to enter the facility and bring out my notebook."

The request seemed reasonable. Joe's intimation of a casual familiarity with the security guard convinced the official that Joe was no impostor. The official waved to a nearby colleague that he was intending to advance from his position and move closer to the museum. A thumbs-up from his buddy cleared him, and he led Joe over to the area of the loading dock. As they approached, Joe took a shot at separating himself from the official by jogging up to the platform that supported Teller.

"Hey, Teller," Joe called out.

Teller jumped at the sound of the voice ringing out his name.

"Who's that?" Teller asked.

"Joe Smith."

"What are you doing here, Mr. Smith? The simulator is closed."

"I know. I need to speak to your boss."

"Not a good time, Mr. Smith."

"It's urgent," Joe pressed.

The official was closing the gap that Joe had created. Teller wasn't a big fan of this group of functionaries, and he took the opportunity to express his disdain by thumbing his nose at any of the power that they felt they had in the moment.

"Come on," Teller said, waving him up to his level.

"Whoa, friend, he's not allowed to enter," the official said, suddenly panicked.

"He'll be in my custody, 'friend,' and we won't be in any sensitive areas," Teller said.

"I want him returned to this exit."

"Copy that."

Teller grabbed Joe by the arm and led him through the side door adjacent to the loading dock bays. Once inside, he spoke into his rover and requested that Cassandra switch to a private channel.

"You know, those idiots out there think they own this place. One day a year I have to put up with those chumps, and I got to tell you, one day is too much," Teller said as he waited for Cassandra to respond.

"I know I must sound stupid, but what is actually going on? Has there been a break-in or something?" Joe asked.

Teller laughed.

"It's moving day. The lottery is tomorrow and all the cars go over to the stadium for the night."

"Oh, of course."

Cassandra's voice squawked over the receiver imbedded in Teller's ear.

"Yes ma'am, sorry ma'am, but Mr. Joe Smith is here, and he says he has something urgent to discuss with you," Teller said into the small microphone that jutted out from the receiver.

The response was completely unintelligible to Joe, but it made Teller wince. Why was she so pissed off? He knew that the pressure of the evening was getting to everyone, but they were still in the preparation phase, for chrissakes.

———

Cassandra wasn't in over her head; she was fully confident of her abilities. Putting the caravan together was always chaotic. Each vehicle had to go through the pre-delivery inspection by a team of non-partial engineers. There always seemed to be at least one car that was missing something from the vast and detailed inventory that the engineers used for their checklists. That this kind of thing still happened—especially on the night of delivery—always shocked her. How could this stuff linger for an entire year?

Often cars would be returned from ward custody with missing or damaged parts. Usually, all of these situations would be resolved during the fall months when most of the repairs were performed.

There were instances of vandalism where the damage was maliciously intended. This was certainly effected by a mount's less-than-stellar performance in that particular year. The most egregious example occurred when the people of Marquis, supremely frustrated when their car crapped out a hundred meters from the finish line, descended on the machine and literally beat on it until it was nearly unrecognizable. Their subsequent five-year suspension included a clause, as well as a caveat, that should any other ward perpetrate anything of similar nature on their granted vehicle, they would receive the death penalty and be banned forever from the competition.

Yet, here they were still missing the spark plug wire set on the Chevelle. Also, the water hoses for the Gran Torino had been reconfigured to bypass a leaky heater coil, and that had never been set right, even though an entire year had lapsed.

When Teller broadcasted that she should go to an internal channel on her radio, it was just at the point that a determination had been made to requisition the wire set from the parts warehouse for the Chevelle and to let the bypass on the Gran Torino remain. With temperatures expected to be in the nineties for the coming week, it seemed ludicrous to demand that the heater be reconnected.

Cassandra disengaged from the squadron of the non-partials and moved over to a corner of the room. She changed her receiver to the requested channel.

"What the hell do you want? It's kind of hectic over here right now, Teller," she explained.

When Teller responded that Joe Smith had some type of emergency that she needed to be made aware of, she lost it. This was not the time. This was certainly not the place.

Cassandra could see out of the corner of her eye that she was drawing a curious audience that seemed to be obsessed on observing her tirade. Many folks were waiting on her to conduct the symphony that was about to commence. Besides the non-partials, there was an army of Mugwumps that were to be split into teams and were ultimately responsible for providing the requisite muscle needed to accomplish the conveyance portion of the evening's agenda. She so didn't want to deal with what she believed to be the substance of Joe Smith's "emergency."

"Goddammit!" she screamed as she clicked off the transmission.

She held up a solitary finger to the masses, a signal that she would return forthwith. She saw that all of the workers and engineers had suddenly become inert. Their potential was arrested and could only be released if she stated her next instruction. Hopefully these idiots could get themselves motivated to start on their own. She scurried away.

They met in the hallway that led to the simulator. As Joe crossed to meet her halfway, Teller shadowed his rear flank.

"Go back to your post, Teller," she said through the tiny space created by her clenched jaw.

"But, ma'am, he is not to be allowed in here prior to the . . ." Teller tried to get out.

"We will not be leaving this hallway, I assure you," she barked.

Teller was reticent to move, but he eventually headed back up the hall that led to the doorway near the loading dock.

Cassandra knew that every detail of Teller's contact with her, with Joe, with everything that would happen this evening would eventually be related to members of the Mustang hierarchy. That was only one in the litanies of reasons why Joe's presence in the facility at this particular time reeked of awkwardness and inappropriateness.

She had finally figured out that somewhere in the last couple months, Teller had given into the temptations offered by Titus O'Keefe and/or his minions and had been reporting all of the doings within the walls of the museum, including all of the heroics that Joe had displayed in his dominance of the simulator. She knew this because she had planted unique false information with him that had returned to her through her own Mustang contacts.

She had no idea whether Teller suspected that she and Joe had become involved romantically; he would be hard-pressed to draw conclusions based upon their behavior toward each other up to this point. But Joe's appearance this evening, the familiarity he displayed with her, and her agreement to see him had to start the cogs in motion and the gears meshing in Teller's mind.

"What is wrong with you?" Cassandra began, waiting for the apology that was sure to spill out of his mouth once she gave him the opportunity to talk.

"I'll be quick. What is name and location of the lawyer that Lon Brassey used to summon me here?"

This might have been the last question she expected him to ask. Truth be told, it wasn't even in the top one hundred.

"Uh, I'm sure he must have used Leo Rascone. He has an office in the Grand Circus. It's next door to the State Theater."

"Thanks."

"That's it?"

"Yeah. I know you're busy. I'll get out of here now."

"What the hell, Joe?"

"I'm sorry."

There it was. Now he was going to want to get into the whole thing, and she really didn't have the time or the inclination.

"I needed this particular information. I had our contact call you, but she said that you didn't want to talk to me," Joe continued.

"That's right."

"You're busy, I know."

Cassandra just stared at him. Was he really that daft? Now *she* wanted to get into it, but her earpiece began to squawk. The amassed workforce was waking from their stupor and ready to begin the load out. All they needed to begin was her authorization.

"Thanks for info," he said as he turned to leave.

She muttered something, but he didn't hear her. Stunned, she turned on her heels and headed back for the exhibition hall. She knew now it was over, and as the reality began to set in, she started to weep softly. It would take her the entire span of her return to reassume her professional bearing.

───────

Joe exited the building and found himself confronted by the angry disposition of the guy in the gray suit who had escorted him over to Teller.

"This is highly irregular," the official grunted.

The official knew that a superior would most likely ream him out for his gaff, and he wanted the person responsible for his future lambasting to understand how much he had harmed him.

"I'm so sorry. Apparently Robby took my journal home with him and forgot to tell me," Joe lied.

"Well that explanation is not going to save my ass. You were not supposed to enter the facility under any circumstances."

"Blame it on me," Teller said with his chest puffed out.

The official weighed whether the prospect of this ploy was prudent.

"Okay. That'll work," the official said quickly.

Teller caught Joe's eye and gave him a look that indicated he retained a vast superiority over these fops who were clad in the hues of abject monotony.

"Am I free to go?" Joe asked.

"No," the official said.

Joe wondered for a moment if he was being detained.

"No one can leave the area until the cars have passed," the official added.

No one heard Joe groan as he advanced toward the boundary that had been set up by the other officials. He peered over the heads of the men lining the street and saw an identical group ordered on the opposite curb. Mustang folk had crammed in five deep behind the officials on both sides.

A smattering of applause began to ripple through the crowd, and in short order, it transformed into a loud ovation replete with eardrum-piercing whistles and screams. The first car was beginning its journey through the street on the way to the vault at the stadium. The route would take them northeast on Selden Street, southeast on Woodward Avenue before making a left onto Adams, and straight into the bowels of the stadium.

Each vehicle was pushed by a minimum of ten members of the Mugwump labor force, clad in black T-shirts and white shorts. One by one they passed. As they did, the gray suits moved also, creating a centipede-like buffer between the fans and the priceless machines.

In deference to the neighborhood of origin, the Mustang led the procession. The Chevelle, the Plymouth Barracuda, the Dodge Challenger, the Impala SS, the Gran Torino, the Plymouth Roadrunner, the Pontiac GTO, and finally the American Motors AMX followed it in that order. After the Mustang passed from view, the cheers dissipated slightly, but the locals were careful not to be too dismissive of the rest lest they be presented with one of the other models during the lottery. The appearance of the AMX caused the gathered to completely lose their manners, though. Flying phlegm joined the verbal insults as the cursed car was wrestled past the crowd.

Joe folded into the group that trailed the parade as it made its way to Woodward Avenue. He could see Cassandra up ahead, fully ensconced in her official capacity, marching with a group of men that looked like nerdy engineers. He made no effort to let it be known to her that he was nearby. His intention was to continue his mission this evening, locate the lawyer's office—break in if he had to—and find out the location of Udo Lewandowski.

Joe briefly followed the march as they left the Mustang neighborhood and diverted onto Woodward Avenue. There the sidewalks were clogged with people from all the various wards who had come out after dinner to watch their metallic beacons of hope being humanly propelled toward their resting place for the night.

Joe skirted up a side street and used the neighborhood of the Lions' ward to traverse back down to the Grand Circus. The whole dynamic surrounding his relationship with Cassandra never crossed his mind. He had a mission at the moment, and absolutely nothing was going to cause him to veer away from its completion.

THIRTY-NINE

TUESDAY

J OHN STOOD LIKE a bewildered sentinel outside the closed door of the room that Joe had been using during his stay. The window to his left was open, and he heard nothing but the sound of the wind and some occasional tweets and honks from the random fowl that sparsely (and only temporarily) populated the enclave from time to time.

It was still fairly early in the morning, and most of the people of Impala were busy sleeping off the effects of their skylarking from the night before. *It is only Tuesday morning*, John thought. *Didn't they know they had to pace themselves?*

To him, it seemed to get more frenetic each year. The only reasonable explanation would be that this resultant wanton behavior could only come from the reaction to the citizens having to restrain themselves for a full cycle of the calendar. When the shackles and strictures were removed and the beasts were allowed to roam free, they did not lie down in their cage and take a nap.

John had not slept much. The exhaustion he felt from the effort he had expended during the competition could not overcome the anger that he felt for his father. He had lain atop his bed, his muscles pleading for an opportunity to recover, but his mind could not approach the silence needed for slumber. He had tried to focus on something other than the paternal rancor that consumed him, and in doing so his mind drifted toward worriment about Joe.

Joe had not returned for dinner, had not been present during the powering-down phase of the evening, and had not entered the house by the time John had taken to his bed. Being the first instance of this since Joe's arrival, John began to create a pile of bleak scenarios in an effort to explain his new friend's tardiness.

One of the librettos had Joe being kidnapped by some Mustang assholes, tortured, and being told to throw the race or face certain death. The implements of lancination included rusty blades of carbon steel and muddy multi-pronged gardening tools.

Now with the heart of the outside world beating unusually faintly, John listened for the rise and fall of Joe's breath, hoping that he had stealthily entered their domicile at some point in the evening and that his fears could be allayed.

His sister Holly was the first to disrupt his vigil.

"Are you crazy?" she asked him.

"What?"

"When I got home last night, Mom told me what you tried to do. Did you really think you could get away with it?"

"I did get away with it."

"Until Dad showed up."

"I would have made the team."

"You would have ended up in the hospital the first time someone bopped you on the head."

John shrugged. There was no sense explaining to her about his nearly four-year abstinence from his medication and the fact that no pathology had presented during that span. He was not going to let her goad him into divulging that secret, so he took the tack of allowing her to think that her last point had merit.

"What do you want for breakfast?" she asked, brimming with confidence that she had assessed yesterday's situation correctly.

"Where's Mom?"

"She's out with the woman's auxiliary decorating our section for the lottery."

John nodded.

"Dad?" he asked nonchalantly.

"I think he's still asleep."

John continued to keep an eye on the door to Joe's room.

"What did Dad say to you when he got home last night?" Holly asked.

"Nothing."

"Typical. Come on, let's eat," Holly said.

"Should we wake up Mr. Smith?"

"No. He came in pretty late. He's going to have a big day today, you know. Come on, I'm hungry," she said as she headed for the stairs.

As she made French toast, his favorite, he probed her for information on Joe's possible whereabouts the previous evening.

"I don't know. He was here and asleep when I came home," she said.

"What time was that?"

"Late. We went to this party over in DeVille. They had two bands and a lot of beer. I keep forgetting that this thing goes all week. I've got to learn to start slowly," she said, echoing John's earlier admonition for the rest of the ward.

John left the house before either his father or Joe awoke. He saw his departure as the smart play. He didn't want to face his father's wrath or silence. He knew that if confronted with either, his reaction would be tainted by his lack of sleep along with the multitude of blind fury that his father's part in yesterday's debacle had provoked.

Joe had taught him a precept of his training that stated: "Seek not to harm others, but only to protect the self from the violation of others." John's act of leaving the house was following that tenet to a T.

John didn't really have a destination in mind, but he found himself taking a route that would eventually lead him to Frank and Claudia's shop. He was a couple of blocks from his goal when he saw Kevin Gatz strolling toward him. Kevin's left hand held a cup of freshly brewed coffee that was releasing a steady stream of vapor. *Fuck this guy*, was John's instinctual reaction. *All of the emotions I feel for my father could easily be transferred to this fucking weasel*, John thought. But again, he listened to the precept, put his head down, and acted like he didn't notice Lon's lieutenant was in the area.

"Hey, kid," Kevin called out.

John restrained himself from charging the fucker like a bull that had been prodded with an overwhelming dose of electricity. He half-nodded at the prick and kept walking.

"Hey, kid," Kevin repeated in a louder voice, but John never turned around.

Cassandra's night had roughly started with the issues surrounding the missing part, and the hive of inspectors, race officials, and Mugwump muscle constantly buzzing about in need of her attention. Finally, as the practiced protocol asserted itself, the events of the evening reverted to rote procedure, and the rest of the process went off as smooth as a glass mirror.

After the cars were tucked in and all of the paperwork was signed and checked off, the clock had struck twelve, and she had a moment to reflect on her encounter with Joe earlier in the evening. She could not imagine that he could be that insensitive—to show up in the midst of the cacophony of the load out and ask her for the name of the lawyer who Captain Brassey had used to locate him. She really thought that he had come to apologize for the lack of consideration he had displayed earlier in the day when he, ever-so nonchalantly, mentioned that he would be leaving after his contracted task was fulfilled.

When those sentiments were left behind in lieu of this other pressing question, she was sure that she had misjudged this man. It pissed her off that she could have been so blind in regards to assessing his character. It pissed her off that he could have been so blind as not to see how his callousness had affected her. And it really pissed her off that she knew—deep down—that this was how it would all come apart in the end. And yet, she had allowed herself to deny that probability and eventually fall in love.

She knew that he was dealing with issues related to prior traumas, but still, in their most tender moments when it was just the two of them, she saw something behind the mask, behind his training, that informed her that what they had was real.

One of the most confounding things to her was that their union was not a relationship that had sex as a foundation. It was something they did, but she was certain it was not the reason they were compelled to see each other. In fact, she often sensed that—at least, from his point of view—the act was never an imperative when they had the opportunity to steal some time to be together.

From the moment they met in the lobby of the museum, she knew that this foreigner was unlike any other man she had ever met. Of course he noticed her superficial assets, but he also seemed to allow himself to see the parts of her that were veiled in nuance. This was a man, not a freakish child with the features of an adult like so many others she had dated before.

The coincidental encounter inside the clothing store that had led to a communion over coffee allowed for a quality of insight that had been unexpected. Though seemingly shy, Joe possessed qualities that she had only seen in men with much more life experience. These others had acquired their fruits of knowledge by simply existing chronologically. Joe was still young, vibrant, and curious.

The fact that he seemed to enjoy her company—even with her clothes on—was confounding to her at first. This was a complete re-orientation, a nearly uncontrollable spin away from the norm. As she began to expose herself without the pressure of consequence, the initial fear that she could put her trust in him dissipated.

She started to want him more than anything she had ever wanted in her life. She projected on him many of her hopes and dreams and infused him with an importance in her existence that approached necessity. She speculated on things that portended a future together. All of this happened within just a handful of weeks on the calendar.

Now it was over, or soon to be over. Just like that. This was not going to be an easy row to hoe. Of this she was convinced.

———————

Joe awoke with a feeling that his neck was supporting a sodden-filled skull that may or may not have been his. As his eyes opened and he looked around the room, he began to flashback to his first night here and the tremors of the body that he was powerless to control. Had he heard someone knocking at the door?

His previous night's search for the lawyer had resulted in the acquisition of nothing more than a big bowl of void. The building that housed the barrister's office turned out to be impenetrable, and though similar stumbling blocks were normally nothing other than momentary setbacks, Joe had been unable to solve the equation that would allow him entry. He had circled the building so many times that he knew every scratch on every window, the location of every instance of dried, putrefied bird shit that stained the exterior, and all of the various security devices that the tenants had used to secure their cubicles of toil.

He would have to ask someone why there were so many precautions taken with just this one building. It seemed so out of place with the rest of the city—this incongruous need to create such a fortress in an environment where there was no acknowledgement of anything resembling a threat.

Another knock at the door had the effect of reactivating his brain, informing him that he was here, in this room, and today was the day of the thing they called the lottery. It also served as a reminder of the pressing need to eradicate the danger that was lurking—not within these four walls—but somewhere out there among the unsuspecting.

"Come in," Joe said to the door.

He supposed he expected either John or his mother, Karen, to slowly open the door and to peak his or her head inside, but the visitor turned out to be his boss, Captain Brassey.

"Rise and shine," Lon said.

"I'm up."

Lon entered the room and sniffed the air. The aroma was a direct contrast to Lon's recently bathed self, and he began to become concerned that if he lingered, he might have to start his morning hygiene practices all over again.

"Big day, Mr. Smith," Lon stated.

"So I've been told."

"After you get yourself cleaned up, meet me downstairs for breakfast."

"Yes, sir."

"Don't dally."

"I won't, sir."

Lon made his exit.

As Joe stepped into the shower, he came to realize that he had not washed himself since the morning before. A scent clung to him that he knew immediately was that of Cassandra. Actually, the fragrance was an alloy of him and her, and its presence inspired him to begin to piece together the events of the previous day. Something informed him with the persistent recollection that she had been extremely unhappy with him when last they spoke.

The impulsive act of her lone escape from their love nest and her frigid, angry demeanor when he queried her at the museum should have made it clear to him that he had fucked up somehow, but he had been so blinded by the knowledge that an unleashed Redeemer was lurking inside the walls of Motor City that he had lost the ability to see beyond his conditioned response to avenge.

As he washed, he began to gain some perspective on his behavior. Was his reaction to the news of Udo Lewandowski's presence personal, or was it meant to serve the greater good of this unsuspecting community?

And what of this community? Was this really a re-creation of some sort of quasi-Avalon, or an internment camp for the rich and privileged? Maybe they should all reap from the ripened stalks of ill will since they seemed to have sown the seeds of hate for each other.

He shut off the water, dried himself, and reentered the room in search of clean clothes. Karen had recently washed the sum total of his wardrobe, and from that collection he chose the items that showed the least amount of wear.

When he arrived at the breakfast table, Lon was pouring the coffee. Karen had baked some pastries the night before, and the aromatic combination of cinnamon and almonds drew Joe to his regular station.

"Have we reprioritized, Mr. Smith?" Lon asked cryptically.

"What do you mean, sir?"

"We need your focus to be on the task at hand, son."

"My focus has never wavered, sir."

Joe's hands remained in his lap. He was waiting patiently for Lon to take his standard place at the end of the table.

"Eat up, Mr. Smith."

"I'll wait."

"Don't be silly. I've already eaten," Lon said.

Joe reached for one of the hot pastries. It tasted as good as it smelled and looked.

"Terrific," he exclaimed, mid-bite.

"Yeah, the little lady knows her way around the kitchen," Lon said with a smug smile.

Fuck you, Captain Brassey, Joe thought. *You have no idea of the multitude of talents that your wife possesses. As with your children, you only view her as an appendage.* Joe superficially smiled at him as his teeth ground through the sweet roll.

"So tell me, what do you need from me today?" Joe asked flatly.

"You'll be with Frank and Claudia on stage during the lottery. You three are the designees for the ward."

"So all of the drivers are designees?" Joe asked.

"Yes. Drivers and mechanics only."

Well, there it was. Hopefully he'd be sharing the stage with his quarry, the butcher Apostle Udo. Okay, this is something he could work with. The eel was going to have to come out of its nook, and Joe hoped that he could begin to gain some access to him. It was a start. Joe wouldn't need the lawyer to point out his whereabouts after all.

"So should I head over to Frank's?"

"When you finish your breakfast."

"And where are you going?"

"This is always one of the busiest mornings of the year for a captain. There is the flesh of my constituent's hands that I need to enthusiastically press. There are the ongoing preliminary negotiations related to the race. There are always issues related to the ward dinner, inspection of the punch-out team . . . It never ends."

"What negotiations?" Joe asked.

"You don't need to worry about that stuff. You need to get your training in with Frank and Claudia. Make sure you eat and sleep."

He placed the slightest bit of emphasis on the word "sleep." It was a not-so-subtle indication that an air of disapproval was in the wind. Joe could not hold his most compelling question at bay any longer.

"Why were you having me followed?" he asked.

"Excuse me?" Lon asked.

Lon's mouth contained a sloshing of coffee, but not enough to do a full spit take. The question was a complete diversion from the thread of the conversation they were having, and Lon was not prepared for the abrupt segue.

"Let's not get into some kind of game where you act as if you don't know. You're the captain, are you not? You are privy to all that transpires under your command."

Lon nodded and set his cup down.

"I take exception to the context with which you qualified the act as 'following you.' It suggested to me that you think that there is some type of malice afoot."

Joe continued to wait for him to provide the answer to the direct question he had posed.

"You weren't supposed to notice Billy," Lon admitted.

"A blind person could have noticed him."

Lon laughed at that one. The outburst wasn't meant to disarm Joe and suggest that Lon was in the process of committing an admission; the laugh was genuine. Billy was, and would always be, a dork, is how Lon saw it.

"Back to my point that you may have misinterpreted the intent in regards to his presence," Lon said. "We had Billy keeping an eye on you for your protection."

"Do you think I need to be protected?"

"You're a source of fascination to many people here. We just wanted to make sure that you were safe," Lon said in a reassuring fashion.

Joe let the man's prepared bullshit create an ebbing to this particular topic. He wasn't in the mood for a circular conversation anyway. He did want to ask about Lon's son, but he figured that if he did, he would be confronted with an amplitude of similar obfuscation. Joe rose from the table.

"I'm heading over to Frank's," Joe said as he carried his dish and cup to the sink.

"Good. I'll see you all at the stadium," Lon said.

As Joe made a move for the door, the bell rang. He could see Kevin and Billy standing on the stoop through the frosted glass. He opened the door, and as he passed over the threshold, he made sure to smile directly at them.

"Good morning, gentleman," Joe said.

He was gone before they could respond in kind.

FORTY

WITH THE SIMULATOR having been closed for the entire week before the lottery, Frank and Claudia spent their extra hours preparing their shop for the arrival of the Impala entrant. Every contingency was allowed for as they inventoried all of the spare parts, tools, and diagnostic equipment.

These two always had a few tricks up their sleeves, including different carburetors for the various engines that could be swapped in during training for purposes like decreased fuel consumption. Now, with everything ready and in its place, all they could do was sit and fret about how their fortunes might turn after a vehicle was assigned to the ward in the coming sweepstakes.

That was exactly what they were in the midst of doing when John knocked on their door.

Maybe it was the fact that Joe had accepted this lad as a comrade. Maybe it was the commitment that John had made to assist the two mechanics when they needed something. But either way, the enmity that Claudia and—to a lesser extent—Frank felt for the captain's son had silently evaporated in the intervening weeks.

When it was John who was revealed to be at the door, he was greeted with a combination of enthusiasm and concern over the debacle of the day before.

"Sorry you didn't get a chance to prove yourself yesterday," Claudia offered in commiseration.

"Yeah, kid, that must have been a tough one," Frank said.

John nodded with the same resignation that he'd displayed with everyone else who had offered condolences. He would get over it, he knew, but in the present, he could still feel a persistent pain pulsating in the sheaths of his heart.

John changed into a clean-suit and got busy sweeping the floor, though it was already spot free. Frank and Claudia returned to their game of speculation. The pall that hung around the room like a wraith was the one-in-nine possibility that they would draw the AMX. Claudia was the first to give a half-muted voice to this disastrous scenario.

"Do we know where the problems originate? I mean, is it the fuel system? Is it along the lines of an electrical malfunction?" she asked as if it would be prudent to try to get a head start on any potential problems.

"Take the most rat-fucked situation, and then flush it down a toilet. What empties into the sewer is that fucking car," Frank said.

The imagery that Frank presented made John laugh.

"It ain't funny, John," Claudia said.

"I know," John said.

"What ain't funny?" Joe asked in a booming cartoonish voice as he entered.

"Us pulling the AMX," Frank said.

"Ah, the ubiquitous nightmare scenario," Joe said.

He proceeded to pull his shirt over his head and bare his teeth like a vampire trying to hide the sudden protrusion of his fangs.

"I vant to drink your oil, and in the process reduce the friction coefficient to a number that will blow up the engine . . . or whatever might cause something like that to happen," Joe said in his best Transylvanian accent.

That put them at ease for the moment, but the trepidation continued to build as the event neared, and it was pretty obvious to Joe and John that Frank and Claudia's nerves were on the verge of being shot.

"You've got to change," Frank said.

"Hey, I just showered. I'm not carrying any dust. What could I possibly soil anyway?"

"No, silly, you've got to put on your outfit," Claudia said.

"Outfit?"

Frank pointed to the door of the bathroom. Joe crossed to the room to find a fire-retardant, skin-tight, one-piece racing suit balancing on a hook on the back of the door. The suit was bone white with black epaulets, a tuxedo-like black stripe down the sides of the legs, and a large green Impala logo on the back. There was a similar, though much smaller, Impala logo above the right breast pocket, and his name, "Joe Smith," embroidered in black thread above the left breast pocket.

"See if it fits," Frank said.

"Oh yeah, and this time, you can eighty-six the clothes," Claudia said, recalling the first time he came into the shop having retained his clothing before donning the protective clean-suit.

Joe shut the bathroom door and stripped down to his underwear. He had questions: How did they know his size? Was the uniform altered from a pre-existing one? He began to slip into it and was grateful that the garment was not too sheer to his body. He wasn't really up for wearing something that might look like a costume for the male lead in a ballet.

He thought that the measurements might have been taken from the clothing he had recently purchased—all items that he had purposely bought in larger sizes assuming that his weight would return to his previous standard.

He stepped out into the light of the shop. The three occupants broke into a round of applause. Somewhere, he'd seen phototypes of what were once called "male models," and for the benefit of the assembled, he struck a pose.

"Oh, God, you are not going to do that on stage, are you?" Claudia squeaked.

"Maybe," Joe said, "This thing looks pretty good, I think."

"Just make sure you have the necessary flexibility," Frank said soberly.

"It'll be fine," Joe said.

The excitement over, Frank and Claudia went back to their default state of high anxiety. Joe felt the tension in the room rising and signaled John to meet him outside.

They found some shade under the umbrella that stretched over the picnic table in the yard.

"You want to talk about what happened yesterday?" Joe asked John when they had settled on the benches.

"There is nothing really left to talk about," John said.

"Oh, I don't know about that," Joe said softly.

Joe waited to see if John had processed any of the feelings of disappointment about not getting an opportunity to fight it out for a spot on the punch-out squad. He didn't have to wait long for a response. John's eyes got misty, his face contorted slightly, and his voice started to stammer.

"The only thing I've learned is that I will forever be seen as nothing more than a fucking cripple," John said.

All of the defensive effort that was keeping his emotion under the surface began to crack. His first reaction was to cover his offending face with his hands.

Joe sat quietly and watched as it all came tumbling out. There was no need or desire from Joe to dissuade John from this cleansing expression. Joe's main hope was that Frank and/or Claudia did not have a reason to leave the shop and disrupt the scene.

For John, it was a battle of two overwhelming forces: the breadth of emotion that had been building up inside of him for most of his short life, and the complications that surrounded his need to prove that he was a man. He needed to cry, but an opposite energy was working pretty hard to try to get him to cease.

Joe could see the armies of the internal struggles inside John becoming entrenched as the opponents lobbed their most sophisticated weaponry at each other. Neither side gained more than a momentary advantage.

The young man began to shake, and Joe's immediate fear was that the kid was about to experience one of his mythic seizures.

"Hey, kid," Joe interjected.

As if he was a hypnotist and had just snapped his fingers to end a trance, Joe's words of attention caused John's body to cease shaking. The young man looked up to Joe. The figure he now presented was tear-streaked and slightly embarrassed for his outburst.

"I think I'm going to need your help," Joe said.

"With what?" John said through the sniffles.

"I've become aware of a problem that needs to be solved."

John straightened his posture.

"What?"

"Obviously, when I tell you, you'll realize that the subject matter is sensitive, so I'll need you to swear that you can maintain my confidence."

"Of course."

"There is at least one Redeemer running around the city. My best guess is that he is not the only one."

"How do you know this?" John gasped.

"The guy that tracked me down for your father said he did the same thing for the Mustang captain. The man that Mustang brought in as a driver is the one."

"You're sure?"

"Yeah. He's the one that almost got your uncle killed."

"And what is this guy capable of?"

"You name it: mayhem, mass destruction, and everything in between. The timing of his visit is not coincidental."

"We've got to tell my dad," John said.

Joe smiled.

"You already did?" John asked.

"Last night," Joe said.

"He blew it off?"

Joe nodded in assent.

"Why wouldn't he listen to you?" John asked.

"I suppose there are a lot of reasons not to find me credible: I'm new. I'm sure I'm perceived as a zealot, etc. But your old man was simply uninterested in knowing anything about it."

John sat back on the bench and took a knowing breath.

"Yeah. Anything that might fuck him up immediately gets tossed in the denial file," John said.

"I've noticed."

"What do you want me to do?" John asked.

"Nothing yet. But when the time comes, I might need your help."

"Anything."

"Thanks.

They sat in the shade, but both could feel the oppressiveness of the summer heat trying to invade their place in the garden. Joe felt as if the reinforced aramid fiber suit with the Lycra details was trying to epoxy itself to his skin.

"Someone once told me a fact that I've always thought was pretty interesting," Joe began. "You know, when the human body is burned during cremation, everything goes up pretty quickly. The flesh, the muscle tissue, the bones—it doesn't take much to turn it into ash. But the process can take a long time because of one, simple factor: There is a part of the body that is stubborn and refuses to be easily degraded by the heat and the flame. Do you know what part of the body I'm referring to?"

John had an idea, but he let Joe finish.

"The heart. The muscle is so dense that it requires repeated exposure in the pyre to turn it into dust. I want you to remember that, kid, when you ponder the wonder of the results of what you were able to accomplish yesterday. It was never about the brain, John. It's about this lump of a pump in the middle of your chest. When they're preparing your shell for the bone yard, they're going to have to throw a couple extra logs on the fire to turn that bastard into cinders."

This wasn't some facile attempt to elevate the kid's spirits. It actually worked. The pall of John's disappointment—his utter frustration—lifted. It took to the ether and altered his demeanor immediately.

"You let me know what you need," he said.

"I surely will, kid," Joe said.

FORTY-ONE

LIKE PILGRIMS TO a religious shrine, the citizens of Motor City were drawn to the stadium just as the sun began to approach its highest point in the sky. Joe, John, Frank, and Claudia folded into the teeming masses as they approached the decaying structure. All of the entrants displayed a certain quantity of fortified joviality.

Joe could hear the singing of the wards' songs in the small groups of the like-minded as they filtered onto the ramps and breezeways that led to each group's section. Though it was still an hour away from straight-up noon, the lower tiers were already at about eighty percent of capacity.

Joe's eyes panned the colosseum. The element that jumped out at him was the vibrancy of all the color displayed by the flags, pennants, and clothing specific to each assemblage. It evoked memories of his younger days—high school sporting events and civic celebrations.

John sidled up next to him.

"You and Frank and Claudia need to head down to the tunnels."

Joe nodded. He finally was able to pick out the Impala section by the array of similar colors represented by the racing suit that identified him as the ward's driver.

"Where's the Mustang section?" Joe asked.

John pointed to an area that was diametrically opposed to the section that the Impalans occupied.

Joe drew his focus to the zone that blared nothing but baby blue and white. He did a cursory search of the gathered hoping he might get lucky in locating either Cassandra or Udo Lewandowski. As he methodically scanned groups of ten at time, he began to realize that the odds of finding his quarry bordered on nil. By all rights, Cassandra would be tending to her duties with the cars and Udo would be down in the tunnels with the Mustang designees waiting to take his place on stage. What was that name that Captain Brassey said that Udo used to gain entrance?

Frank tapped Joe on the back, and he turned to join the two mechanics as they departed for the downstairs holding area. John would be heading over to join his family in the Impala section, though he dreaded having to sit with his father.

Frank, Claudia, and Joe had to fight the steady stream of spectators as they made their way upriver toward the internal stairways that would take them down to the Impala waiting room, many floors below the field level. As they walked along the cracked and unevenly patched cement, they resembled a group of spawning salmon attempting to negotiate their way through stones imbedded in the rushing water.

Up ahead, a group of Mustang youth could be seen approaching them. Five-wide, the young toughs immediately noticed Joe in his enemy uniform and began to close ranks for the purpose of creating a confrontation. Claudia saw what was happening and moved quickly ahead of Joe.

"Make way," she barked at the group.

"Fuck you, bitch."

One of the thugs shoved her out of their path. That was the wrong thing to do. Joe stopped and began stretching his neck before taking a wide stance and staring at the oncoming mob. Just the sight of this fearless man, clad in his one-piece, patiently awaiting their arrival, caused three of the boys to stop and reconsider their options.

The other two, unaware that their quorum had shrunk by sixty percent, motored forward with their bad intentions intact. Joe held his ground. His spread legs took up nearly the width of three of them. This was intended to cause them to divert from their course and assume a wide berth, or be perilously close to the man who could drop them to the pavement before they could open their vulgar mouths again. When they didn't yield, Joe got their attention by bringing his arms slightly out in front of him, stepping forward, and placing his face not two inches from theirs.

"Move, asshole," the older of the two said.

"After you apologize to the lady for your rudeness," Joe said in an even tone.

Frank moved up to them.

"It's a ruse, Joe. They're hoping to provoke you so you'll get disqualified before the race," Frank said with a slight amount of panic in his voice.

"Is that what this is about?" Joe asked the two Mustangs.

Neither of the two deigned to answer him.

"Tell you what: I will promise to commit an act that will probably get me thrown out of your city, get me banned forever, but the price for this transaction is that at least one of you will forever lose your ability to see," Joe said.

The other three boys who had now formed a quasi-perimeter backed off even further from the center of the confabulation. The younger of the two that were directly facing Joe began to waver.

"Forget it, Stan," he said to his comrade, "let's just get to our seats."

"Listen to your friend, friend," Joe said.

"No, I think I'll have to teach the Mugwump a lesson. Motor City does not need outsiders driving—Impala fuckbrain or not," the older one, Stan, said with continued defiance.

"There is no honor in being blinded, young man. Everyone in your ward will know that the cost was too great for the effort. You'll be labeled a fool, not a hero. Wise up. Apologize to the lady so you can peacefully leave with your buddies here, and you can spend the rest of this beautiful day whooping it up with the rest of your clan."

The Greek chorus represented by the three who were standing out of the way began to agree with Joe. They took it upon themselves to offer their apologies to Claudia. After the tough guy's partner did the same, the recalcitrant member of the fivesome appeared to relent. He stepped out of the way so that Joe and Frank might pass.

But Joe did not move.

"Be a sport and make your apologies," Joe told him.

"C'mon Stan, just do it," one of the kids said.

The chorus echoed his pleas. Stan had already made enough concessions in his mind; he wasn't about to allow himself to be humiliated as well. Claudia could see that this could all end if the Impalans simply walked away.

"I'm good," she said. "Good luck with the lottery, boys." She gave them her most patronizing smile.

Joe did not budge. Stan began to take his retreat, and Joe reached out and grabbed his arm. He stared into the young man's eyes for a long moment.

"You can only enlighten yourself," Joe said, only for Stan's benefit.

Finally he released him to his own remorse. Frank ushered Joe away before there could be even a hint of a second round.

"You're fucking crazy, you know that?" Frank said.

"You think so?"

"Maybe not crazy, just from another time perhaps."

"Not another time, Frank, but definitely from another place."

The statement was not meant to be flippant; it was meant to be truthful. Joe felt a rush of nervous energy and tried to determine why it would present itself now. Immediately, he knew it wasn't related to his task of being the driver for the ward, though he had yet to tell any of his benefactors that his heroics in the simulator would probably not be repeated when the real thing happened. In fact, on that account, he could almost assure it, since he had virtually no real experience driving a flesh-and-blood automobile.

He knew his angst and the need to mitigate it was about this impending threat exemplified by the Redeemer. He flashed back to when he had surveyed the crowd, and he now noticed how vulnerable the citizens were to an evil someone bent on their mortal destruction. The thought of the possibility of being a witness to that kind of carnage made him shudder, and the effect of the spasm snapped some random neurons into their correct firing order. He remembered the assumed name of his target, Clarence Rigney.

The Impala waiting room was little more than a janitor's closet. Frank and Claudia explained that the big dressing room—the one that the former football home team, the Detroit Lions, once used—was always reserved for the winner of the previous year's race.

Joe had no quibbles with the space; he'd loitered in far worse in his life.

There was no doubt that the location of the enemy Mustang holding area was on the opposite end of the clockface, somewhere around a corner in the corridors that encircled the bowels of the arena. As much as Joe wished to explore the area to confront the butcher before he could unleash whatever hell he had planned for the people of Motor City, he knew that now was not the time. He'd been informed that the lottery, though usually well attended, did not draw all of the people of the city. Over the years, the proceeding's rowdiness had turned off the meeker members of the society. Likewise, the event known as the punch-out only drew the real diehards, frenzied to satiate their annually repressed bloodlust.

The actual event of the race was the key. Then the stadium would be at capacity, and Joe knew that was when the Redeemer apostle was most likely to plan his strike.

Joe was convinced that Udo had no way of knowing that anyone had even sniffed the possibility that he might be strategizing a course of mayhem, and this fact presented Joe with a dilemma that he knew required an exacting resolution. To assess the inconstants necessary to answer the conundrum required factoring in a couple of variables.

The first: Would Udo believe that Joe was savvy enough to remember who he was and what he looked like? The slim probability existed that Joe might have forgotten the incident back in Akron, and Udo may have thought that there would be no notice of his presence by anyone who could call him out for what he was. Joe wanted to go with a strategy that encouraged that premise. When they took their place on the stage, Joe's aim was to appear as disinterested as possible and to seemingly fail in any effort of recognition.

Second: If Udo believed that he retained a quality of invisibility, wouldn't he seek to maintain that stature throughout all of the days leading up to the event? Joe would have to be careful in his pursuit so as not to spook him into moving up the timetable of what was sure to be an attempt of a massacre. Joe also wanted to limit the possibility of Udo having to ad-lib in case he had other members of his organization in the city. If there were others, they would have to be removed as well.

Even with all of this existential preparation, Joe could not honestly tell anyone how he would react when he actually had the man in his sights, probably not more than twenty feet away from him. He did not possess a weapon at this time, but he had his training, and many times that was all that was afforded him when a killing was in the offing.

There was a forceful knock on the door.

"We're up," Frank said.

───────────

Like gladiators entering a hippodrome of yore, the various drivers and their mechanics began to form a line in the tunnel that led to the stadium floor. Leading the procession would be last year's winners, Marquis. After them, the order was random except for the de rigueur separation of the Impala and Mustang camps.

To accomplish the differentiation, one of the enemies immediately followed the most recent victors, and the other brought up the rear. Impala had been placed in the forward position, which required Joe to try to peer into the darkness of the tunnel to locate Udo. Before Joe could get a fix on him, the entire retinue was moving up the ramp and onto the compacted dirt field.

The roar of the crowd hit him in the face like a haymaker. The squeals and the screams assaulted his ears, making him feel as if he had been standing within a couple inches of a large jet turbine. The rabid fans hurled a combination of insults and cheers depending on their allegiances. As they marched toward the stage, Joe heard every possible combination of curse word directed at him. Some of the compositions were so obtuse that Joe found himself unable to suppress a smile or a brief chuckle. After someone yelled out, "Hey motherfucker cock ball shit-for-brains turd head," Joe caught Frank's eye and noticed that he wasn't the only one amused by the profane serenade.

As they mounted the stage, Joe finally got a chance to view the Mustang entourage. Their two mechanics flanked a man who was not Udo Lewandowski/Clarence Rigney, but a much slighter gentleman.

"Who's the Mustang driver?" Joe asked Claudia.

"Same guy that they've used for awhile now, Roger Burnham," she replied.

Shit. This was the proverbial monkey wrench that got tossed into the gears of his mind. His simple strategy suddenly became a non-starter. It was as if someone had taken his blueprint and dipped the painstakingly created document in a vat of black ink.

Joe wondered whether Udo was even in the stadium at this time or if he had been shipped away when his usefulness was determined to be less than adequate.

"Get ready," Frank screamed into his ear.

Joe began to hear some of the songs specific to each ward competitively being sung. The lyrics came at him like a jumble—multiple tracks bleeding into each other like a spate of incoherent static.

Then Joe saw why Frank was trying to get his attention. At the end of the field a group of black-shirted men began to swarm. Joe knew that this was the same group that had manually moved the cars over from the museum the evening before.

The mood shifted in the crowd, and the first strains of unison began with a chorus of rhythmic clapping. When the first car appeared, cheers and whistles joined the paradiddles of applause.

One by one, each vehicle was pushed into position, and the lot were arrayed like a fan in front of the stage. The nose of each car pointed toward the center, where the commissioner, Carter Pleasant, stood with his arms crossed in front of his wilted white dress shirt.

Joe saw Cassandra at the gates directing her minions to maintain order and keep up with the pace of the car in front of them.

Carter Pleasant stepped to the front of the stage and motioned to the wings. Two large drums—obviously made from old oil barrels—were wheeled into the space between the platform and the perfectly arranged vehicles. Joe could see that the horizontal drums had handles welded to one end and hinged doors on their sides, and they sat atop a blackened steel frame that allowed them to spin freely.

When Carter began to march in front of the assembled designees like a stick-up-his-ass general inspecting his troops, one could feel the anticipation building among all those that had a stake in the proceedings.

John was seated with his parents in the Impala captain's box. His mother and her fellow auxiliarians had done a masterful job of adding elements of taste and color to the eroding facade that symbolized the decrepit facility in its usually naked state. Framed by green, black, and white bunting, the family presented a picture of unity.

Holly was trying to keep it together—the debilitating effects of her hangover had yet to abate—and Karen was waving to her friends like the prom queen she had been. Lon sat back in his seat projecting an air of confidence, but if one could get just under the surface of his outer layer, they would see the tremendous effort he had called upon to tamp down his nervousness.

For Lon, there was a great deal on the line here, and the trajectory that he and his fellow Impalans were about to take would be determined by how the contents of the two drums came together.

John toggled his view between two distinct destinations. Both venues held the possibility of disaster for him. There was the natural draw of the events down on the field and the car that Impala would be awarded or saddled with, and how that affected the fate of his new friends Joe, Claudia, and Frank. His other focal point was the presence of Rebecca Leann Voss, cuddled up to her boyfriend Denny Regan, three rows down on a direct line from John's seat. As much as he tried to keep his eyes on the doings on the field, part of him felt compelled to lower his gaze and submit to being a tortured witness to the cooing intimacy displayed by this couple.

Carter Pleasant approached the barrel on his right, rotated the cylinder, opened the hatched door, and withdrew a piece of paper. He opened the folded-up note, confirmed the findings with another, and beckoned one of the Mugwumps to place an enumerated plastic hat atop the first vehicle in the line, the '69 Plymouth Barracuda. The numbers appeared to be random, as the digits that now identified this first car in the automobile array read "24." Slowly and with a marshaled precision of each and every movement, Carter and his helpers completed the numerical assignations of all of the vehicles on display.

Under the watchful eyes of his underlings and the entire stadium crowd, he refolded the nine pieces of paper and returned them to the drum from whence they had been drawn.

A viral silence began to overtake the patrons as Carter crossed from the drum on his right to its opposite number on the left. After multiple rotations, he halted the drum's momentum, opened the hatch, and withdrew a swatch of colored fabric that appeared to have been fashioned into the shape of an isosceles triangle. He stretched the pennant between his hands and displayed its symbols to the crowd. It was the flag of the Pistons. The entire Piston nation began to sing their song:

Bounce, bounce, bounce, can you feel it?
We're Motor City's own bad boys,
The baddest in the land,
We'll wipe the floor with anyone,
Kiss the trophy before you realize that you've lost,
We'll be victorious, no matter what the cost,
Eight-nine, Ninety, Oh-four,
That's what we're here for.

Carter Pleasant handed the flag to one of the attendants, called the Piston designees to the front of the stage, and beckoned them down to the area where the other drum that contained the numbered pieces of paper existed. He gave this one another couple of spins, brought the gimbal to a stop, reached through the opening, and withdrew a solitary piece of paper. The Piston section collectively held their breath until they saw the joy become infused onto the faces of their driver and mechanics. They had drawn the number 47, and that corresponded to the identity of their entry for this year's contest.

Their driver, Marlon Brickle, turned to the crowd and offered an ecstatic thumbs-up. He grabbed the flag from the attendant, walked over to the '69 Chevrolet Chevelle SS, and draped the piece of cloth over the waxed and polished hood. He removed the service hat with the number 47 and handed it to the Mugwump attendant. The Piston faithful exploded into a state of exuberance run amok. Other wards groaned because everyone knew that one of the truly competitive cars was now gone.

"Fuck them!" John heard one of his fellow Impalans yell.

The Mustang flag was the next to be pulled from the drum, and John could see their entire congregation rise as one.

Carter Pleasant had a little trouble securing just one of the pieces of paper from the drum that held the car designations, and that was met with a resounding blast of jeers and screamed implications that the fix was in. He paid no attention to the noise and handed the separated single slip to Roger Burnham.

For only the second time in the history of the race, the Mustang ward was awarded the car that bore their namesake. If the reaction of the Pistons' good fortune seemed a little over-the-top, the subsequent response from the Mustang crew would have bordered on the limits of insanity.

John sat back in his seat and silently cursed. The reasons for his muted response were rooted in the tradition that had always demanded that the son of the captain was supposed to maintain his cool. It was getting agonizingly uncomfortable for everyone in the section. The only blessing—at least from John's point of view—was that he hadn't looked down at the canoodlers since the selection process had commenced.

As the base nature of luck would have it, every time Carter Pleasant reached into the drum to pull a ward's flag, he came out with something other than the Impala colors.

Marquis got the Plymouth Roadrunner, DeVille was given the boat-like Ford Gran Torino, the Tigers assumed the equally girthed Chevrolet Impala SS, the Red Wings were presented with the Dodge Challenger, and the Lions received the' '68 Pontiac GTO.

There were two flags left in the barrel—Ram and Impala—and two cars not designated for assignment. Both wards were vying for either the '69 Plymouth Barracuda or the dreaded AMX.

The entire Impala section had slipped into an abyss of apoplexy. They held their faces in their hands and could not bring themselves to look at the proceedings, even for the briefest of moments.

When the Ram flag was the next to be pulled, the only words that were spoken by the Impala folk were those of mumbled prayers.

Carter Pleasant crossed back to the number drum. His hand disappeared into the opening in the vat, and a single, folded-up piece of paper was removed.

John could hear the laughter building from the Mustang section. If Ram got the Barracuda, their ultimate dream would be coming true: Mustang's hated enemy Impala would not be a factor this year. John knew that Titus O'Keefe and Tom Cobble were probably calculating how much money they would be able to save if they didn't have to pay the other wards to screw over Impala during the race.

The Ram driver, Kent Dornan, slowly opened the wad of paper that would determine his fate. When he hung his head in anguish, John knew that the worst-case scenario had not come to pass.

"Fuck yeah!" John screamed before anyone else caught onto what he knew to be true.

Lon nearly snapped his neck as he swiveled it to the left with the full intention of rebuking his son for the outburst, but before he could get the words out, he saw what John's passionate eruption had pre-lapped—the dejected Ram delegation was moving to the AMX to lay their flag on the cursed car's hood.

———————

As was customary, the ward's driver was given the honor of piloting the vehicle back to the neighborhood. Thirty of Impala's strongest alternated pushing the car as it wound its way out of the stadium onto Adams Avenue and made a hard right on Woodward before the left on Temple that would take them into the bosom of the Impala ward. Its final destination for the night was to be the pristine floor of Frank and Claudia's shop.

As Joe sat in the leather-wrapped bucket seat of the Barracuda, he began to panic slightly. From the moment that he released the brake, depressed the clutch, and maneuvered the pearl white shifter into the neutral position, he had the sinking feeling that he just might be in over his head.

Nothing about the real thing felt remotely similar to the sensations he had felt while strapped into the cockpit of the simulator. The steering wheel felt sluggish and only intermittently responsive. The sight lines appeared to be compromisingly obscured, as there were no port windows. And the ride seemed relentlessly bumpy, even at a pace that couldn't have exceeded five miles per hour.

Joe began to have serious doubts on whether he could make himself one with this machine.

The Impala faithful certainly did not share his concerns. They were positively exhilarated by the outcome of the lottery. As they pushed their prize toward its resting place, they allowed themselves to dream of breaking the years-long streak that had found them somewhere short of victory year after frustrating year.

They had the car. And by all reports, they had the driver.

Throughout the entire journey, they sang at the top of their lungs:

See . . . the . . . way we play,
We're the Kings today,
Impala is the reason you will fail.
That's why we all say,
She's the only way,
We are the Motor City's Holy Grail.
When you see us, you will want to holla',
Nothing is sweeter, nothing can beat her,

Life is completer in Impala!

Each rendition ended with anticipatory smiles. All the mothers covered their youngsters' ears before the current squad that was responsible for the pushing screamed out in a unified tone of cascading baritones, "Fuck Mustang!"

FORTY-TWO

WEDNESDAY

F RANK AND CLAUDIA spent the entire day and night tearing down the engine of the '69 Plymouth Barracuda. Joe and John hung around until well after the Brassey dinner bell had rung, but as the clock edged toward its vertical limits, the two men returned to the homestead to get their rest. Wednesday would be the first sanctioned day of practice.

On the walk home, they both admitted to being bored to tears by the mind-numbing dialogue that was exchanged between Frank and Claudia. As each part of the motor was disassembled, dissected, documented, disseminated, distinguished, and discussed in the most minute detail, both Joe and John's eyes starting bugging out of their orbits. That first breath of fresh air—uncontaminated by the fumes of lubricants and solvents—was one of sweet relief.

Frank and Claudia knew they would be fighting the clock right up until the time that the fuel was delivered. They were acutely aware that the time for practice was limited and therefore extremely precious, but they had a tough job on their hands making sure they could squeeze every last bit of horsepower out of the 'Cuda's massive V8.

So they checked for any anomalies, honed out the cylinders, ground the parts that might have even the slightest burrs of metal protruding from them, and put the whole thing back together in roughly eleven hours.

Schematics for the engine covered the walls and an entire workbench. They worked quickly but precisely, and they had the job finished as dawn approached.

Every joint had been lubricated, every weld checked for integrity.

They made only one modification. It was something that they would reverse before the race, as it did not meet the specifications of the original equipment. They swapped out the huge four-barrel carburetor for a smaller two-barrel aftermarket version that they took from their personal stock. The way they saw it, they would use the smaller fuel regulation unit for just the initial practice sessions, when speed wasn't as important as trying to achieve intimacy with the contours of the course. Its purpose was strictly to provide a reduction in fuel consumption as their neophyte driver got his feet wet.

The fuel wasn't usually delivered on practice Wednesday until sometime after 11 A.M. The reasons for this were related to nothing more than the reality of the situation: a delivery made any earlier would put too high a price on the mechanics' speed to prepare the car. Swifter mechanics or wards that deployed teams early might have an unfair advantage. Also, it was festival week after all, and no one wanted their sleep disturbed by the sounds of nine roaring behemoths racing around the streets in the hours well before the cock had an opportunity to savor his first sip of coffee.

With their work done, Frank and Claudia could probably get at least a good five hours of shuteye. This was a luxury on the eve of the first practice. It was a testament to their efficiency and vast wealth of knowledge that gave them this unexpected gift.

Frank looked up to a large schoolroom clock on the wall. It read 4:45.

"Let's hit it. Set your alarm for ten. We'll have something to eat when we get up, and then we can see how good a job we did," Frank said.

Claudia knew that sleep wouldn't come easily for her this night. She was currently debating whether it made any sense to even attempt it.

"I want to start her up now," she blurted out.

Frank smiled at his daughter. If he had made a habit of prayer, he would've laid his head on the pillow every night and thanked God for the gift of this particular child.

"Do we want to risk it?" he asked.

"Come on, we're soundproof in here. Who's going to know?"

Frank was beginning to become slightly intoxicated by his daughter's enthusiasm. His normal response would have been a flat-out "no," but this time he decided to take a moment to think it through.

What only the two of them were secretly aware of was that they had a personal stockpile of fuel that they had been hoarding for nearly their entire tenure as the mechanics for Impala. Each year they would amass whatever ounces or drops were left over from the previous year and store them in a plastic container in a space that was accessible only by a trap door in the floor. They rotated through older crops as each degraded with time.

The amount of subterfuge required to acquire their illicit pool depended on many factors. Some of the entrants devoured the precious liquid at much higher rates than others. The Gran Torino, the Challenger, and the Roadrunner had markedly lower miles-per-gallon ratios compared with the lighter cars that made up the field. During the years that Impala was awarded those vehicles, pretty much every drop of the requisitioned fuel was used over the span of the week.

Switching to the stingier carburetors always helped in their quest, but sometimes that would only end up extending the practice time. Since they were the only two who ever knew of their ploy, they never limited any fuel use out of fear that their brazen tactic might come to light.

Frank pondered the consequences should race officials determine that they had run the car at some point before the fuel delivery. They had protections: the sound insulation that Claudia had alluded to and an ingenious filtering system to vent the exhaust.

"Okay, let's do it," Frank said.

Claudia screamed something along the lines of "Yippee."

Both of them knew that to expend any of their precious fuel this capriciously was probably stupid, but they also knew that if she started up and ran like a dream, they might actually be able to grab ten to twenty winks of moderately peaceful slumber.

Frank pulled the gas can out of its subterranean spot and held the red plastic vessel up to the light. The volume registered at about one-eighth of the five-gallon capacity.

He poured no more than a quarter gallon into the tank, grabbed a corroded aerosol can of benzene-based accelerant, sprayed some into the chambers of the carburetor, and gave his daughter a high thumbs-up.

The engine kicked over immediately and began to run as smoothly as the surface of a newborn's skin. Frank messed with the air/fuel flow mixture until he heard the rhythm of the pistons begin to oscillate at a frequency that pleased him.

Claudia dismounted from the driver's seat and crossed to a place next to her father. They spent the next couple of minutes in silence, their arms around each other, listening to their opus. It was the debut performance of an orchestra comprised of eight cylinders of forged steel.

Joe slept no more than six hours and was out of the house before the rest of the Brassey family rose to greet the day.

John had practiced his script. When his father queried him as to the whereabouts of Joe, he replied in a fashion that was both natural and rehearsed.

"He told me that he wouldn't be at breakfast. He said that he planned to walk down to First and Adams. Something about feeling the contours of the road with his feet before he committed tires to it. He said he'd be over at the shop around ten."

Lon bought it. John knew that his father had probably swatted away the gnat of a memory that represented Joe's warning, so excited was he about the prospects of his ward's chances given that they had an ultra-competitive car.

John also supposed that the lack of suspicion could be due to his father's participation in the multiple raucous celebrations that sprung up after the lottery. He did not seem his usual sharp self at breakfast. If there was one day where the captain did not have to be a ubiquitous figure among the community, it was the Wednesday of race week.

It wasn't as if the captain had the day off—far from it. It was just that his presence within the community would be diminished due to the other duties that would certainly preoccupy him on this day. There would be no need for him to form his mouth into a smile or raise his upright thumb ninety degrees from his body because nearly all of his responsibilities today would take place extra-ward.

Of course, John had been briefed on where Joe was headed that morning, and it was not the corner of First and Adams.

Joe had only a couple of hours for his reconnaissance mission. He would start in the exact place he had finished the previous Monday night—the office building that housed Leo Rascone, Esq.

On his arrival, he was struck by the fact that the Mugwump section of town was inordinately quiet. Joe surmised that the Independents were getting their rest in where they could. They had the punchout to deal with tomorrow, and today was as close to having a day off as they could claim over the ensuing seventy-two hours. Crews would be heading to the stadium in the afternoon to prepare for the coming days, but for now they could put their feet up and attempt to recover from the mounting exhaustion they had accumulated during the week.

Joe arrived at the lawyer's building to find a skeleton crew assuming the normal security day shift. When he asked the man at the door if he could see the barrister, he was rebuffed and told that most of the offices were closed for the week. When he inquired as to whether there was any of the lawyer's staff on the premises, the guard shrugged and said he didn't know.

"Might I go up and knock on the door?" Joe asked.

"No."

"I'm kind of in a desperate situation," Joe offered as a plea.

"I don't really give a shit," the guard said.

The other guard in attendance was munching on a commercial sugar-based treat and eavesdropping on the conversation. Joe's use of the word "desperate" caused some additional pricking of his ears.

"What's going on, brother?" the other guard said between chews.

Joe hadn't really thought of the lie he would tell in this situation. He quickly scanned his short-term memory, searching for some type of commonality of fear that he could lay on these two. He knew he couldn't use the truth—that there was a Redeemer roaming free in the city. This information was still too sensitive a topic for laymen, and he didn't want to provide the answers to the questions that these two would pose, as a lot of verification would have to be passed on to establish his credibility. Also, he was afraid that once the alarm was sounded, he would lose complete control of all of the scenarios he had formulated to deal with the issue.

"It's a deportation issue," Joe said.

Both of the guards perked up. Joe had remembered something that Cassandra had once explained to him: that the looming threat of deportation was the hammer the city held over these Mugwumps to keep them in line.

"You're getting deported?"

"No. Not yet. But I'm under contract only until Sunday, and well, you know, I've met someone special, and I'm afraid that I will be gone before we can figure out what we're going to do."

The demeanor of both of the guards transitioned rather quickly. They had known others who had experienced similar tales, and once the split was made and someone was returned to wilderness, they tended to never return.

"What's your specialty, brother?" the cupcake-eater asked.

"My name is Joe Smith. I'm the driver for Impala," Joe said.

This revelation caused the conversation to come to an abrupt halt. Everyone in this part of town had heard about this change to the normal protocol. In the Mugwump world, the myth of Joe Smith, the outsider, had grown into something that might someday be the basis of future lore.

"Let him go knock on the door," the eavesdropper said to his partner.

The partner was wavering now. Joe could see that he was leaning and just needed a little nudge to be tipped completely over.

"The lawyer knows me. He's the one who brought me here," Joe said.

"Okay, go ahead. Fourth floor."

Joe sprinted for the stairs before the guard could change his mind. He took the steps two at a time with the intention of giving himself as much time as possible before the guards might feel a need to come looking for him.

Because the building tapered up to its complement of four stories, the fourth floor had the smallest square footage of any of the other tiers and could just as easily have been called the penthouse. From what Joe could see, Leo Rascone was the only tenant on this level.

As promised, he knocked on the door, though he had already assumed that no one was inside. Joe's assumption was that Leo and his staff had gone the way of the rest of the Independent community and were probably taking the day off as well.

Joe had the ingrained skills to easily break into the office, but some unfamiliar wiring by the door spooked him into thinking that there had to be some type of alarm attached to the main entrance. He prowled the halls looking for another way inside.

He stopped at a random door at the end of the hall. Hoping that he hadn't just found the conduit to the janitorial closet, he compromised the lock and found himself standing in what appeared to be a private bathroom. It was Leo's bathroom. Every towel had the letters L and R scripted somewhere on the dyed cotton.

Once inside the office, he set out on a hard target search, looking for the files that contained the most recent transactions. His initial fear that this might be a paperless enterprise was unfounded. Leo wasn't stupid enough to ever permit all of his records to be wiped out by someone with a powerful magnet, or for his valuables to be ravaged by a natural catastrophe like a common serial power surge.

Tick. Tick. Tick. The clock on the secretary's desk kept reminding him that he had to find something indicating the Redeemer's location now. The rhythmic noise contained the elements of duality: the need to find something that might lead him to the man, and the countdown sequence that would determine the fate of Motor City.

The voice came out of nowhere.

"May I help you?"

Joe turned to find the face of a weasel of a man peering through a crack in the door that led to the inner offices.

"Are you Leo Rascone?"

"Yes, and who might you be?"

"Joe Smith."

"Oh, hey, how's it going? Are you enjoying your stay in our fair city?" Rascone said as he opened the door and fully revealed himself.

Leo was cradling an old snub-nosed pistol in his right hand. Joe's eyes were drawn immediately to the weapon.

"I need your help." Joe said.

"From the looks of your actions, it appears you might have needed it quite quickly. You obviously couldn't wait long enough to make an appointment."

Joe could see that the lawyer was clad in blue silk pajamas. Leo also appeared to have possibly been asleep not more than a couple of minutes before he cracked open the door and came out with the gun at his side because the mane of dyed hair that usually covered his bald pate hung down over the top of his left ear. Joe heard the voice of a female calling him from somewhere inside one of the other rooms of the suite.

"Should I call downstairs, Leo?" the voice asked.

Leo weighed her suggestion before turning his head to the direction of her voice.

"No, my dear. Go back to sleep."

Leo grinned sheepishly before manipulating his shoulders into an obvious shrug.

"Sometimes I've got to work late. I've got a little apartment in the back here. Just an efficiency really, but it's cozy," Leo said.

Joe was pretty sure that his mention of the numbing burden of having to get his work done was the lie he told his wife. Joe was equally sure that the woman who was offering her help from within the living quarters was not his betrothed. The two men stared at each other for beat.

"So what can I do for you, Mr. Smith?"

Joe decided to ask the question straight out.

"I need to know the whereabouts of Udo Lewandowski," he said.

"Who?"

"Clarence Rigney."

"Ah. And do you have any reasonable explanation as to why you are trying to locate Mr. Rigney?"

Joe tried to read Rascone's face in an effort to determine whether anything he offered in regards to Clarence Rigney's affiliations might spark a fire of recognition. He did not think Rascone was aware that Udo Lewandoski/Clarence Rigney was a Redeemer apostle. Before he could blow the guy's mind with his knowledge of the hell this man could unleash on his precious enclave, Leo's lips twisted into a queer grin.

"Actually, I don't really need to know the why, Mr. Smith. I have

Mr. Rigney's location, and will give it to you for a price," Leo said.

"This is not a negotiation," Joe stated firmly.

"In my business, everything is a negotiation. What world do you live in?"

Joe's answer to his question was wordless. He strode over to where Leo was standing, disarmed him, and punched him in the nose.

"That's the world I live in, Mr. Rascone."

Joe unlatched the cylindrical chamber of the snub-nose and removed all six of the .38 caliber bullets. He held one of the projectiles up to the skylight.

"This ammunition is old. You could really hurt yourself."

If Leo responded to his admonition, Joe did not hear him. Rascone had clamped his hand over his deviated proboscis, and tears began to well in his eyes.

"I'd like the address now, Mr. Rascone, please."

Leo crossed to one of the file cabinets in the outer office and began rifling through the folders.

"I could fucking have you disqualified, you know that?" Rascone said through the fingers that now covered his mouth.

"Look, Mr. Rascone, I won't tell you why I need to locate Clarence Rigney, but I will tell you that it is for your own protection."

Rascone handed him a manila folder.

"For my own protection? You mean he also wants to punch me in the face? And what, you're going to stop him?"

"Something like that," Joe said as he scanned the document that had been tucked into the folder.

"You understand the meaning of the word irony, don't you?" Leo asked.

"I do."

"I'm referring to the irony inherent in your statement that you are looking out for my wellbeing after you have just assaulted me."

"I know it sounds odd."

"I'm glad we're on the same page here," Leo said sarcastically.

"Do not discuss our encounter with anyone, Mr. Rascone."

"Or what? You'll come back here, and offer me protection by punching me in the face again?"

"Something like that," Joe said as he exited.

Back in the lobby, the two guards had not changed their positions.

"Did you get what you need?" one of them asked.

"I did, thanks," Joe said on his exit.

Joe did not see Kevin Gatz lurking around the corner of the building as he headed back up Woodward Avenue on his way to the Impala mechanic's garage. And he did not see Kevin veer off from his surveillance to access a shortcut that would get him to the Brassey townhouse at pace.

FORTY-THREE

IT DID NOT take long for Leo Rascone to get dressed, send his mistress off, and head out in search of Titus O'Keefe—swollen, throbbing face and all. As he hailed a pedi-cab at the apex of Adams Avenue, he cursed himself for bringing up the whole thing involving a negotiation. His emerging bruise informed him that his notion had provoked the maniac to strike him, but that was not why he was ruing his attempt to make the offer.

"Fucking idiot," he said, directed at himself, just as a cab pulled to the curb.

"What did I do?" the man perched on the pedals asked.

"Nothing, I was referring to myself," Leo said.

"Well, things are looking up for you, my friend. You just made a genius selection in opting to have me ferry you on this fine day."

This was the last thing that Leo needed—dull repartee with a Mugwump transpo slave. He pulled out his money card.

"Twenty percent gratuity if you take me where I want to go without opening your fucking mouth again," Leo said as he climbed aboard.

The driver mimed a zipper being drawn determinedly across his lips. For a twenty percent bump he would carry this unctuous, offensive asshole to another planet.

Leo reclined on the seat and tried to formulate how he could implement the new information he had been granted by Joe Smith's spontaneous visit. There were angles to play here. He was going to have to be more intelligent than he was with the Impala driver, and he silently vowed that he would not allow his off-the-cuff nature to enter into any future discussions on this particular matter. But one thing was for sure: Titus was going to have concrete proof that the retainer he was paying was a worthy investment.

John heard the doorbell ring. When nobody yelled, "I've got it," he put down his tablet and crossed to the door. Standing in the threshold was an out-of-breath Kevin Gatz.

"Where's your dad?" Kevin panted.

"Probably upstairs."

Kevin nearly shoved him aside as he entered and began a determined search for his captain. John trailed behind him, but not so close that he would be noticed as doing anything other than transiting from one room to another. There was a certain fervor bubbling in Kevin's eyes that had usurped his usual look of cynical abstention, and seeing it piqued John's curiosity.

John trailed Kevin toward the door under the guise of needing his father's immediate attention before Kevin could be given his solo hearing.

"Dad?" he asked.

Kevin cut in with, "Not now, kid."

All Lon could say was "What?"

John and Kevin began speaking at the same time. Kevin, who venomously stated something about having just seen Joe exit the building where the lawyer had his office, overlapped John's innocuous question about which ward they would be visiting for their first deal meeting.

When Lon's face took on a look as if one unit of gravity was no longer the standard for Earth, John shut his trap in hopes that Kevin would elaborate.

"Don't you have somewhere you have to be?" Lon asked John.

Lon was visibly beginning to shake. John began to look for the wisps of smoke that he was sure were going to come shooting out of his father's ears in due time.

"I was going to help with practice," John said.

"Well, then go to it," Lon said.

"Okay."

John crossed for the door.

"Shut the door," Lon added.

John tried to comprehend words from the muffled sounds that were emanating from beyond the oak barrier. He heard a couple of key words or phrases like "Redeemer," "Mustang whore," and something referred to as "the final option." When he sensed that the conversation was completed and the men were headed out of the study, he hustled into the hall and concealed himself behind the doorway of the laundry room.

"No, I'll meet you at the DeVille clubhouse at eleven thirty. Tell Billy to get the thing built and make it quick. I have a feeling we're going to need it tonight," Lon said to Kevin as they traversed the hall leading to the front door.

"Yes, sir. I think it is the only thing we can do at this point," Kevin said before his exit.

"Just tell Billy to get it built," Lon reiterated.

"Yes, sir."

"And, Kevin?"

"Sir?"

"I appreciate that you didn't say anything along the lines of 'I told you so.'"

"Of course not, sir. I would never . . ."

Kevin didn't finish the thought. He headed straight out the front door. From his hiding place, John saw his father slowly pull the door so that it latched, turn away, and curse under his breath. Lon crossed back into his office and shut that door with more than his usual amount of force.

———

Joe showed up at the appointed hour and quickly became aware that Frank and Claudia were beyond elated. Having witnessed their normal mien of dour pragmatism for many weeks now, it was jarring to him to see them acting with an almost eerie concoction of giddiness and excitation.

"She's a fucking dream," Claudia proclaimed on Joe's arrival.

"You can tell that just by looking at it? Don't you have to get it running before you can make a declaration like that?"

"It just a feeling we have," Frank said as he winked at his daughter.

"Yeah, we know what the fuck we're doing here, Joe," Claudia stated with a smile.

Joe shuffled off to the bathroom to put on his suit. When he returned, the two seemed to have put a cork in their bottles of bubbling exhilaration. They were now affecting an air of sobriety, but Joe could see that their newly dispassionate expressions were falsely conceived. He could see this by the effort being expended to keep their effervescence in abeyance.

"So what do I need to know?" Joe asked.

"Well, we swapped out the carburetor, so your power today will be diminished somewhat," Frank said.

"It's no big deal; you'll have plenty of time to wind her out tomorrow and Friday," Claudia said.

"What are your expectations?" Joe asked.

"We'll just tool around the track, let you get a feel for the turns and the straightaways and such. We have you scheduled for the flag drill at one, so we'll maybe make one full circuit before then," Frank said.

"The flag drill?"

Claudia giggled.

"We didn't tell you about that?" she asked sheepishly.

"About what?"

"The race isn't over until you scale a fence, grab our ward's flag, and run it up the flagpole," Claudia explained.

"Nobody told me about this."

Frank jumped in with, "It's an addition that's been part of the race for only a decade or so. It used to be that the first car to enter the stadium was the winner. You see, for the last quarter of a mile, there is only about a car width and a half of road, and whoever entered that part of the track off Adams Avenue never got passed. The race was actually being won out of the view of the spectators, and over time, that became dissatisfying to the fans. So, they added this wrinkle. You pull into the stadium, stop, get out of your car, race over to the wall, scale a fence, and pull down your flag. You then sprint over to the flagpole and send the flag up the lanyard. Sometimes two guys make it to the flagpole at the exact same time, and the physical battle can get ferocious. No one in this room is worried about whether you'd be successful should that circumstance arise."

"We also don't feel as if the physical demands of the driving are going to have much of an effect on you. Some guys get out of the car, and the best they can do is half-wobble to the wall as if they threw back a bottle of Scotch on their way around the track," Claudia added.

"It was one of the reasons the captain picked you. He knew what he was doing on that account," Frank said.

It was odd to see the two of them in such a good mood. Joe began to get a bit nervous about the coming practice session. He was hoping that the transition from the simulator to the real thing was not as abrupt as he feared.

John entered the room and brought with him a demeanor akin to a sky full of ominous black clouds, recently seeded to produce a spate of torrential rain.

"Can I talk to you for a moment?" John asked Joe.

Joe checked with his keepers. They nodded their assent, and John and Joe slipped out the side door.

"I'm pretty sure Kevin saw you either coming or going from the lawyer's office this morning," John said.

"So what else is new?" Joe asked with resignation.

"My dad is really pissed off."

"So what else is new?" Joe echoed in attempt to lighten the kid's mood. It helped a little.

"Did you find out where this guy is staying?"

"I've got an address. I can only hope that it's the right one."

Joe recited the number and street that he had easily committed to memory.

"Well, if that's it, he's not staying in Mustang."

"He's not?"

"No. That's in the Grand Circus. That's Independent territory."

Joe let that information work its way through his mind.

"You know what that could mean?" Joe asked.

"That he's staying with someone he knows."

Joe nodded. They were startled by a tantara of loud horns honking from out in the street. Claudia came to the door.

"The fuel has arrived," she said.

―――――――

It initially pissed Leo Rascone off that he had to wait before he could meet with Titus O'Keefe. Tom Cobble explained that without an appointment, on this busiest of days, Rascone was lucky even to get the opportunity to cool his heels. Nobody got an unscheduled audience with Titus, especially on the Wednesday of race week, but they would make an exception for one of their trusted friends.

Looking back on it, Leo had to admit that having to submit to the interlude did him some good. The time allowed him to distill his plan and the intention to demonstrate to Captain O'Keefe that he was more than just one of the run-of-a-mill assets in his ledger book. He even allowed himself to dream momentarily about the ultimate prize of permanent residency and eventual appointment as a full-fledged member of the Mustang ward.

Titus finally did pay deference to his mole by venturing out from his inner sanctum to meet Leo in the waiting room.

"I'm sorry to keep you waiting, counselor," Titus said.

Titus's act of conciliation disarmed Leo to the point that he found himself apologizing to the captain for taking up his precious time.

"It's my fault for not securing an appointment. I know you are very busy today," Leo said.

"Busy is not the word, Leo. We're swamped. We've got the 'Stang, as you know, so the pressure is on to win this thing. My constituents will accept nothing less," Titus said.

Leo used Titus's statement as a way into the conversation.

"Well, maybe I can help you with that," Leo said.

"Well come on in. Tom? You want to rustle us up some coffee?" Titus asked his lieutenant.

Once settled, the pleasantries dissipated into the empty corners of the room, and Leo got right to the point. He detailed the nature of his experience with the Impala driver that had taken place only an hour or so before. When he mentioned the punch to the face, Titus snapped his fingers in sudden recognition.

"I thought there was something different about your mug," Titus remarked.

Leo wrapped the story up with a retelling of Joe Smith's warning that he should not talk to anyone about what had just transpired.

Tom entered on cue, steaming cups of coffee in each hand. Leo was pretty sure he had listened to the complete exchange via some type of extra-chamber listening device because when the discussion began about how to disseminate and apply this new information, no one had to get Tom up to speed.

"Well, the first question we have to ask is why would he do this?"

"Might there be some previous relationship between these two that we are not aware of?" Leo posed.

"That's plausible." Titus said.

"You said that you thought you might know of a way to use this information," Tom said to Leo.

"Well, my first thought was you should switch drivers. Put Clarence Rigney in the car," Leo said.

Titus and Tom shared a look of dubiousness. They were much more comfortable with the known element that was Roger Burnham. Besides, this Clarence Rigney had not really hit the charts when it came to competing for the job. In fact, if one were to add up the numbers, the guy finished dead last among the field of hopefuls. In Titus's mind the whole gambit to bring him in had turned out to be a bust.

"You'll have to explain to me what that does for us. We've got a good car. We plan on making some killer deals this afternoon. We're going to need the driver that gives us the best chance. And this guy is not that," Titus explained.

"I'm not the only one who has heard that the Impala hired gun is some kind of hotshot pro. There might be a psychological advantage to putting a true rival up against him. I mean, any way to get this asshole off his game would be a positive, wouldn't it?" Leo offered.

Titus was having trouble sifting through all of this to find any specks of logic. If the guy was a pro—as he had also been made aware of via intel supplied by Teller—nothing like what Leo Rascone was suggesting would have much of an effect on him.

The suggestion from the lawyer reeked of lameness. But Titus didn't retain his position by negating possibilities. Maybe there was something in this that was in need of further refinement.

Titus knew whom he had to talk to next about this situation, but he didn't feel a need to give Leo any of that information.

"This is all very interesting, counselor. We'll keep it under advisement. Are you reachable, should we find out anything further?" Titus asked.

"Of course, Captain O'Keefe."

"Splendid."

The meeting was over from the Mustang standpoint. Tom rose with the intention of escorting Leo from the office. To hasten the process, Titus stood and extended his hand to the lawyer.

"We really appreciate all of your help, Mr. Rascone. There is a reward for you when all of this over, I promise you," Titus said with a rare smile.

Leo beamed. When Tom led him away, he felt like he was floating across the room. He no longer felt any pain in his face.

When Tom returned, Titus was trying to reschedule the afternoon.

"We need to speak to her," he said to his lieutenant.

"You want me to find her and bring her here?"

"No. We need to catch her off guard. Not give her any time to develop a story. We need to get at the truth here."

"When do you want to do this?"

"Now," Titus said.

"But we've got the Pistons in twenty minutes."

"Yeah, I know. It appears that we are going to have to push."

It was Claudia who actually turned the key on the car. Joe was grateful that he got the opportunity to observe this simple task because there was nothing like an ignition switch in the simulator. At that point, everyone took his or her places in the vehicle. Frank grabbed the co-pilot's seat, and Claudia and John crammed into the tiny bench seat that spanned the back of the coupe.

Joe drew in a deep breath and examined his surroundings. He identified the pedals: accelerator, brake, and clutch. He located the different gauges: temperature, oil pressure, electrical charge, speedometer, and tachometer. He caressed the shift knob and noted the H-pattern of the gear sequences. The only thing holding him back at this point was fear, and he reminded himself that he had been trained to have the power to overcome that.

He depressed the clutch, found first gear, gave the car a little gas, and slowly released the pressure on his left foot. The Barracuda jerked forward two feet, and the engine immediately stalled. No one in the car made a peep.

"Well, that was a good start," Joe said breezily.

He reached for the ignition key and turned it to the start position, but he had not depressed the clutch. Since the car was already in gear, it began to jerk forward as the engaged motor tried to turn over.

"Put in the clutch," Frank said calmly.

Joe did as he was told. The car stopped its forward movement, and the engine, once again, sprung to life.

"You all right up there?" Claudia asked suspiciously.

"Been awhile since I've been in the real thing," Joe said.

"Don't worry. You know what to do. Give a little gas, and slowly let out the clutch," Frank said.

Joe did just that, and the car began to jerk again. He pushed the accelerator to the floor and the car bolted forward. Joe could see the RPM indicator jump clockwise like the opening of a lady's fan. He depressed the clutch again and pulled hard on the gearshift. Everyone could hear the grinding noises as he fought to get the car into second gear.

That accomplished, he popped the clutch again and the car nearly got airborne as it bucked forward. With all of the distractions going on inside—the gauges, pedals, and the gearshift—he had paid scant attention to what was coming at them from out the front windshield. He was about to barrel into a large garbage dumpster when Claudia screamed from the backseat.

"Look out!" she cried.

He reacted quickly by jamming on the brakes and maneuvering the steering wheel to the right, but he did not depress the clutch, and the car began to rattle again before abruptly shuddering to a stop as the engine died.

"What the fuck?" Claudia screamed.

"What's going on?" Frank asked.

"Look. I've never really driven a car like this before. I thought it would be just like the simulator, but obviously that is not the case. I think we are going to have to start from the top here."

Claudia groaned. John sat stunned next to her. This was the last thing he had expected to hear his hero admit. Frank, on the other hand, was flat-water calm.

"Okay. We can do that," Frank said as he opened the passenger door.

"This is a fucking disaster," Claudia said.

"I'll get it," Joe promised as he began to get out of the car.

"Did you know about this?" she asked John accusingly.

John just shook his head in the negative.

"We are fucked," she said.

"Please be quiet, Claudia. You are not helping right now," Frank said as he slid behind the wheel.

When Joe assumed the seat that Frank had once occupied, Claudia punched him on the shoulder.

"You lied to us," she said.

"I did not," Joe pleaded with her.

"He's right, dear. He never said that he could do this. We are at fault for assuming that he could," Frank said.

"I thought your dad checked him out," she said.

"He did," John replied.

"Well, what the fuck?" Claudia asked again.

"Okay, everyone just stop it," Joe said firmly. "Everything is going to be fine. We've got two days, right?"

Though it was a tight space in the backseat, Claudia was still able to bend over and bury her face in her hands.

Frank started up the car and began to drive it down the street, making a verbal note of everything that he was doing. Because they were not scheduled to be at the stadium for nearly another hour, they made one full circuit of the track. The only part of the course that he avoided was the turn at First and Adams. With the carburetion providing less power and the car at maximum occupancy, he didn't think that they could ever get to a speed that would make the turn possible.

Many of the people of Impala had ventured out to the course to see their entrant make its practice passes. When they didn't see the "man of myth" behind the wheel, they began to react with looks of disbelief if not outright alarm.

Joe hoped that they would find a way to rationalize this oddity. Maybe their reconciliation would include his unfamiliarity with the track and the need for his mechanic to teach him the nuances before he went at it himself.

Joe absorbed the minute details of every movement that his instructor performed. He even began to mime Frank's gestures and rhythm. In his mind, this would be the extent of his tenure in the passenger seat. As soon as they finished with the stuff at the stadium, he would get back in the cockpit and get on with it.

FORTY-FOUR

Cassandra awoke with a different attitude than the pervasive negativity that had seemed to pursue her for the last couple of days. She had been plagued by the confusion she experienced the last time she had seen Joe. She had no idea why he would need that information about the lawyer, and up until her eyes opened and she rose to greet the day, she had never fully analyzed why he might make such a request.

She was aware that she had reacted offensively to his insistent demeanor at the time. She also couldn't seem to shake the anger that she felt when it was determined that he had not come to her that night to make amends for his faux pas earlier in the day. She reacted as if he had casually informed her that her presence in his life was not worthy of strong consideration. No matter how diligently she tried to process whether this could actually be possible, she honestly felt there was no real truth in her evaluation that he did not care for her.

There was no way that could ever be the case.

But why had he approached her for the lawyer's particulars? That was the question that had moved to the forefront of her consciousness as she lay in bed, betwixt wakefulness and aestivation, feeling the heat of the morning begin to creep into her small split-level townhouse.

Oh, shit, she thought. *That's it. He wants to see if he can stay here.* Why else would he need the name and whereabouts of the lawyer who brought him into their world? Wasn't that the lawyer's specialty, immigration?

She sprung out of bed, showered, ate, and dressed for the day. She had duties at the museum, as she did every Wednesday of race week. There were a lot of fires to put out when the cars finally hit the streets for practice. After sitting idle for a year, cars often broke down during their initial test runs, and the wards that had custody would often come looking for a replacement part.

Harold Getty had not sat idle during the years that he retained ownership of his fleet. To protect his precious children, he had spent much of his time securing original backup parts for all of his vehicles. Except for the rare AMX, he had acquired at least two full sets of replacement parts for all of the other vehicles. Through the years, many other parts were fabricated by the various mechanics out of necessity.

On Wednesday of race week, an authority representing every one of the levels of approval needed for part replacement was stationed in the museum. Requests were not accepted before twelve noon.

Cassandra arrived an hour and a half before the doors opened. She and the members of her staff who toiled in the warehouse set up a station to accommodate each and every entreaty.

Though no one was waiting outside the facility, Cassandra had Teller unlock the doors at exactly 11 A.M.

When Teller asked her why Joe Smith had materialized out of the blue on the Monday they were transferring the cars, Cassandra became wary. Subjects like her personal life were never on the table for discussion with anyone but her closest friends. Other than the facilitator at the coffee house, no one knew of her affair with the foreigner from the wilderness.

"He was just confused. He thought the drivers were supposed to be present when the cars were moved," she said, walking away in wonderment that he had the balls to even bring something like that up.

Could he be trolling for information for the benefactor who she had recently discovered he was beholden to? When Tom Cobble suddenly showed up and asked her if she was available to come outside and have a chat with Titus O'Keefe, she knew that Teller had told them that Joe had showed up two nights before asking for her.

Titus was dressed for the weather and affiliation—Mustang blue linen suit and a white shirt.

"I know you're busy, Cassandra, but I wonder if I could ask you a couple of questions?" Titus began.

"I've got a minute. No one has broken down yet," she said with a teasing smile.

Titus looked at his watch.

"Well, they're just delivering the fuel, so you should have a little time before all hell breaks loose," Titus said.

Tom Cobble stood off to the side. He would not be offering anything to the conversation.

"What do you know about this guy that Impala brought in to drive for them?" Titus asked.

"Not much. Why?"

"I'm just curious. I know that you are supposed to maintain a mien of neutrality given your position here, but we both know that, deep down, Mustang blood runs in your veins."

"That it does, Titus."

She let that statement hang in the air. He would need to bait the hook again if he wanted her to add anything else.

"Do you have a personal relationship with this man?"

Cassandra knew that when she silently reacted to this question—especially the bluntness aspect—she told him everything he needed to know.

"Why are you asking me this?" she asked as she struggled to maintain a sense of total ambiguity.

"Oh, you know me. I'm looking for any and all advantages for the ward. I was hoping that you might have some worthwhile information on him that we can use. The way I understand it, your professional neutrality wouldn't really be compromised if you were seeing this man, other than the filial conflict of interest, and that would signify to me that there is nothing unseemly taking place. Of course, one would have to wonder if you imparted any of the ward's secrets during a moment of vulnerability, but I know that you are loyal to your people and you would never do anything to the contrary."

She attacked. When he had asked his initial inappropriate question, she had experienced a flood of adrenalin, and now that he had paused amidst the spouting of his fountain's worth of bullshit, she used the catalyzing effect of the endorphins to rip into him.

"You are a fucking piece of work, Titus—a slimy backstabbing cocksucker who would sell out anyone including a close relative for the tiniest leg up. You know that I would never place myself in a situation that would jeopardize my career or my affiliation, yet I can't help but think that—in an effort to gain leverage—you would execute some plan to destroy everything I've built if it served you in any way."

"Not me, sweetie. Our people."

"Fuck you," she muttered as she spun around on her heels and headed back into the museum.

"Wait. Can you tell me why he burst in on a lawyer and physically assaulted him this morning?" Titus asked.

She stopped and turned back to him. Her eyes were on fire now, and she seriously thought about striding over to him and punting his testicles over onto the next street.

"Where did you hear that?"

"From the man with the newly disjointed nose, dear," he said.

"Did the lawyer tell you why he wanted to see him?"

"Yes."

"And?"

"Well, if you don't know, I guess that can be the topic of your next conversation with him."

Titus looked over at Tom Cobble.

"Conversation? Should I have said pillow talk?" he asked his lieutenant with a ghostly grin.

Cassandra charged him, but Tom quickly stepped in and diverted her. She relented soon after and backed away from the two of them before walking briskly back to the museum.

As she arrived at the door, she saw Teller loitering not far from the entrance. He had obviously observed the entire exchange.

"You're fired," Cassandra said to him as she breezed past him.

"What?"

"Get your stuff, and get out."

"Why are you doing this?" Teller asked, his voice a good two octaves higher than normal.

"You know why. Get out now, or I will have a commissioner come over and escort you out. If you make me do that, I will see to it that the authorities initiate deportation hearings."

She gave him zero opportunity to respond, as she bolted toward her office. The chief mechanic and the other functionaries in the lobby found themselves staring at the small area where their shoes met the carpet.

———

There were at least a couple hundred Impalans in the stadium when the Barracuda pulled up onto the field for the flag drill. To a person, they had no explanation as to why Frank was behind the wheel of the Barracuda when it came to a stop atop the sun-baked earth on the stadium's floor.

Joe was determined to limit their questions and dispose of what he rightly assumed might be a burgeoning paranoid curiosity. He sprung from the passenger seat and walked over to the wall where the Impala flag was loosely attached, the lower half waving in the breezes spawned from the stadium's many tunnels and ramps.

In front of the wall was a chain-link fence that rose up nearly fifteen feet. The protocol had the drivers climbing the fence to a level that allowed them to extend their arms and grab the flag, but Joe had another idea about how this could be accomplished. It involved the deployment of his natural talents and training; the technique that had recently allowed him to enter the Impala clubhouse from the overhanging elm branches could also be employed in this setup.

To add to the drama, he began to gauge the angles and planes he needed to target in order to be successful. As the Impala crowd sought to gather at the lower levels, Frank and John noticed that the Tigers' supporters who had been there for their driver's training run were lingering to see what this outlander was up to. Additionally, the Rams who had arrived early for the next time slot were also being drawn to what everyone thought might turn out to be a spectacle.

Joe allowed the level of tension to rise further as he made numerous false run-ups toward the fence. On the fourth or fifth trial run, he added a slight hop at the end of the sprint. Murmurs of anticipation spread throughout the crowd.

In a final act of theatricality, Joe scavenged a strip of discarded paper from the ground and wrapped it around one of the diamond-shaped openings in the fence about seven feet from the ground. As he returned to where the vehicle was parked, he saw Frank, Claudia, and John standing just in front of the hood. He offered them a private wink before settling himself in the driver's seat and closing the door.

He waited another beat or two before he burst out of the car, sprinted toward the fence, broad-jumped up, placed his boot in the exact portal where the piece of paper rested, and vaulted vertically the balance of the distance to where a corner of his quarry was Velcroed to the wall. He snatched the flag and paused in mid-air before allowing gravity to grab his body and return him to the ground. A quick sprint to the flagpole was followed by the colored cloth's attachment to the lanyard and it's rapid ascent to the top of the pole, Joe's arms pulling on the line like a timpanist playing at superhuman speed.

The spectators had never seen anything like it. When the act was completed, there was a lag in their response that bordered on eerie. Collection achieved, they exploded into a chorus of cheers and applause. Joe acted as if there were no need for the accolades. Instead, he returned to the fence and adjusted the piece of paper so that it rested two diamonds higher than his first go. His second pass returned the flag to its resting place, whereupon he curtly waved to the fans, climbed into the driver's seat, beckoned his entourage inside, and calmly drove the car out of the stadium. The car did not jerk, stall, or veer from a steady path as it cruised through the gates and out of the sight of the delirious crowd.

———————

Cassandra got to the stadium five minutes after Joe had left the scene. She cursed herself for not getting there sooner, but it had taken her longer than she had hoped to extricate herself from her duties at the museum.

Right after she fired Teller, the place began to swarm with a bevy of discontented mechanics looking for replacement parts.

She dealt with the first couple of wrench heads but was finding herself lacking focus and verve; her distractions were too immense to handle all of the complexities associated with the requisitions. Three times she sent over to the warehouse requests that returned the wrong parts. Finally, she handed off her responsibilities to one of her seconds, apologized to the chief mechanic and his staff, gathered her things, and left. She told everyone she would be no more than an hour, though the bulk of that time had nearly been used up when she arrived at the stadium.

On the way, she stopped at their café to see if Joe had left any messages. Finding none, she left her own missive in case they missed each other and then struck out for Ford Field. A pedi-cab could only get her to the blockade on Adams Street. She was forced to walk the rest of the way.

The schedule told her that Impala was scheduled for the half-hour that began at 1 P.M. It was one-fifteen when she arrived at the stadium, and Joe had already performed his stunt and disappeared. Frustrated and bewildered, she sat down in one of the stadium seats and burst into tears.

She didn't really know why she had begun to sob, but she did know everything in her world appeared to be totally fucked up.

The balance of the afternoon for the Impala team produced the exact opposite result from the morning. Though not closely approaching anything resembling race speed, Joe's handling of the car was markedly improved. Even Claudia seemed to quit her bitching from the backseat.

As the practice session's time waned, Joe asked Frank if they could attempt their first pass at the turn at First and Adams. To this point, they had avoided the test as Joe continued to get a handle on the nuances of the car's performance. With the shakedown cruise coming to an end, he wanted to dip his toes into the waters of what he had been told was the most crucial part of the course.

As the car idled one hundred meters from the curve's entrance, Claudia and John abdicated from their positions in the backseat. As Frank returned to the passenger position, Joe held up his hand.

"I want to go it alone," Joe said.

Frank began to balk.

"Look, Joe, I'm really impressed with the growth you've made since this morning, but the ultimate responsibility for this car is with me. If anything were to happen, you can just leave the city. I can't. I live here, and the consequences I would have to deal with are of astronomical proportions. This is about my daughter's and my survival. We would like to continue to have a future."

It was an impassioned plea, and Joe immediately acceded to his wishes.

With Frank's coaching, Joe made two marginal passes through the turn. John commented to Claudia that the second was decidedly better than the first.

"Let's get this horse back to the barn," Frank said as they returned to where Claudia and John had stationed themselves.

Joe slowly drove over to the blockade on Adams Street and Woodward Avenue. Mugwumps were removing the barrier as they arrived. They passed through and headed back toward the shop.

On the way, both Joe and John could see a confrontation developing between Frank and Claudia. They had both been witnesses to a brief argument during an earlier break in the action. Whatever was discussed had yet to be resolved.

At the shop, Joe changed back into his street clothes, thanked the father and daughter Rodriguez for their help and understanding, and hustled out the door. The last thing he said to John was, "I'll be back at the house for dinner."

———————

The building in the Grand Circus that matched the address that Leo Rascone had given Joe did not have the same security the lawyer's office had. Joe walked right into the lobby from the street without anyone asking for identification. He wasn't here to do anything other than to get the lay of the land. He had brought no weapons with him.

The lobby was packed with a mob of raucous Mugwumps returning from their festival duties. Joe tried to blend in as best he could, but it was immediately obvious to him that all these people knew each other, and it wouldn't be long before someone identified him as an outsider. In the corners of a large cavernous room, buddies had busted out bottles of booze, and toasts were being made to celebrate the survival of another day of the festival week.

He had no idea what floor or room number housed Udo and his friends, and he became aware that he could go no further in his investigation without the help of a guide, an incidence of supreme luck, or both.

As he exited the building, he saw what he assumed were a couple of Impala operatives loitering just up the block. He kept his eye on them as he began the trek back to the Brassey's. Because his focus was on tracking his pursuers, he did not see Udo Lewandowski and one of his acolytes cross behind him and enter the building.

Joe might not have recognized him anyway. Udo, like his compatriot, was covered head to toe with multiple layers of dirt and black oily grime. They resembled a pair of troubadours decked out in the accoutrements of minstrelsy.

———

The battery-powered lighting equipment was functioning at full capacity in the greenroom area of the basement of the Impala headquarters. The room had once been a staging area for brides, honorees, theatrical performers, and their ilk back in the days when the Masonic Temple played host to every conceivable type of affair.

Tonight it was being reconfigured to perform another task. As the afternoon gave way to the evening, swing gangs of local artisans, under the direction of Billy Klock, were nearly halfway through with their transformation.

All day the deliveries had been accepted at the loading dock and carted to this room. The materials had been sorted and laid out across the floor. Most of the frame had been welded into place, and there had been a brief discussion on whether the walls should go all the way to the ceiling or if a roof should be built to complete the enclosure. The latter choice seemed to be preferred, and as the batteries began to die, and the light dimmed, Billy proclaimed that everyone should pat themselves on the back for a job well done. Other than Billy Klock, not a single soul in attendance had any clue as to the end use of the structure they had just erected.

FORTY-FIVE

THURSDAY

Frank and Claudia ate their breakfast in silence. It had taken a good deal of arm-twisting on Frank's part to convince her that he was right. Some things had been said that both of them regretted, but they would get past this, just like all of the other times they had come to loggerheads.

The silence wasn't symbolic of any lingering animosity. If a state of enmity still existed between them, there would only have been yelling. The quiescence meant that the battle had been fought and decided. It was the first step in moving beyond the disagreement.

The issue that had caused the displacement between them was fuel. Frank was insistent that they use their hoarded supply to get Joe Smith as much practice time as possible. Claudia felt that they might as well just pour it into the gutter—they would never have enough to get the imposter ready for the actual race. The debate came down to the particulars of the situation and Frank's point that they might not see as competitive a car as the Barracuda for a long, long time.

None of this moved her off her position that Joe was a total and utter fraud. She also held a great deal of virulent contempt for Captain Brassey and the responsibility he should share for foisting this flim-flammer on them and their community. Joe's trick with the flag drill only confirmed to her that he was an empty suit—all hat, no cattle; all sizzle, no steak.

The tide only turned when Frank offered up that he was seriously thinking of making this year's race his last. At his mention of this possibility, Claudia immediately halted her all-out attack on his ruinous idea.

"What do you mean?" she asked.

"I'm getting too old for this. There have been too many years of frustrations. I'm sick of dealing with guys like Brassey and his asshole sycophants. When this Smith guy came along, I thought, well, this is something new. He's not one of the same old losers that have been in the car year after blasted year. And then came those crazy, fun days in the simulator, the drawing of the Barracuda—I really got excited again. I felt rejuvenated, like I did when I was your age. Hell, when I was younger than you are now. As much as you're bothered about what you saw yesterday, I'm not thrown by his performance at all. This guy is an extraordinary athlete. He doesn't place limits on himself, and he will get this as long as we stand by him and help him along. Of that, I am convinced."

That was when the silence began to hover over them like a spectral cloud. During the meal, Claudia was still mulling whether she would fully participate in this boondoggle, but she eventually decided that she would not hinder Frank's quest. If he wanted to use up their valuable stockpile, she would not stand in his way.

———

The breakfast table at the Brassey's had a quorum of four: Joe, John, Karen, and Holly. Lon had taken his morning sustenance alone, in his study, surrounded by an ever-growing pile of notes that registered and recorded the results of his meetings with the other ward's captains the day before.

Holly and Karen had heard about their houseguest's exploits during the flag drill, and they both had questions regarding the physics involved in accomplishing such a deft move.

"It's like most things. Momentum does not always dictate direction. With the right practice and training, direction achieved by momentum can be bent to the will of the user. Much of what is achievable is controlled by the mind and not the body," Joe said.

John took special note of this statement. It was something he needed to remember. It was not the first time that he'd heard Joe espouse a similar hypothesis, but because it sounded like new information, he knew he had yet to incorporate it into his persona.

Joe stood and conveyed his plate over to the sink.

"That was absolutely delicious, Karen," he said on his move away from the table.

"I'm glad you enjoyed it," she replied.

"You've put on some weight," Holly remarked.

"I'm figuring at least ten pounds, and I have your mother to thank for that. Another ten would get me back to where I was about a year ago. I'm afraid that with my time here drawing to a close, I will have to be content that I got halfway there," Joe said.

"Leave the dishes in the sink," Karen said.

John rose from the table and crossed to Joe.

"You heading over now?" John asked.

"Yeah, I hear the track is only open until eleven, and then not again until three," Joe said.

"They have to remove the barriers so that people can get to the punch-out at the stadium," John said.

"I guess I'll see you there," Joe said, having recently been informed that all drivers were expected to be present for the pugilistic free-for-all.

The two locked eyes briefly and passed a coded message between themselves.

"Yeah, I'll see you there," John said before heading back upstairs to brush his teeth.

Joe and John had decided that the younger would perform the task of finding the specific location of Udo Lewandowski. There was no way that Joe could entirely trust that the lawyer would keep his mouth shut, and he had to factor in the possibility that, by now, Udo knew that Joe was looking for him. It was possible that Udo had already vacated the digs he had used in the two-odd months he had been here. John was optimistic that this was not the case; housing space was scarce in the Mugwump's zone of inhabitance, and if Udo had compatriots with him, finding an abode that could house multiple tenants would be a serious chore, especially on short notice.

Joe decided to run the half-mile to Frank and Claudia's. It wasn't just maintenance of fitness level he was looking to achieve; he also wanted to dissuade anyone on the street from trying to engage him in conversation. He thought if he kept his head down and his pace high, no one would think of disturbing him as he voyaged across the ward's turf.

The stratagem appeared to be successful as he made it to the shop in a little over four minutes, and though passersby took notice of his presence, no one tried to stop him. As he rounded the corner of the street, his hopes that he would be spared from having to deal with the Impala homers were dashed.

Loitering around the shop, awaiting his arrival, was a crowd of fifty or so partisans. A loud cheer and the first verses of the Impala song began to fill the morning air as he approached the door.

Joe waded into the group of fans, shyly waving as they parted for his passage like the zipper on a ragged jacket. There was a steady stream of encouraging words to accompany the percussive backslaps as well as the tentacle-like invitations from the people to have him touch their outstretched hands.

As Joe struggled to make his way through the horde, Frank appeared at the threshold of the shop door.

"Let him through, goddammit. Time is running short today," Frank yelled at his neighbors.

Frank grabbed him by the front of his shirt and yanked him inside. The crowd started up the Impala song again as Claudia shut the door.

"We're going to have to get you some bodyguards," Frank said.

"Yeah, to protect me from the mob that is going to want to beat the shit out of me when I stall the car before I can get out of the stadium."

"You are not going to stall," Frank said.

Joe glanced at Claudia. She did not respond to his attempt at humor.

While changing, he heard a muffled conversation between the two of them on the subject of carburetion. Frank seemed to be proposing that they would make the change to the gas-guzzling four-barrel for the afternoon session, and Claudia was just as adamant that the sipping two-barrel should be employed for the whole day. He waited in the bathroom until he felt that a resolution had been reached.

As Joe reentered the room, he felt the need to diffuse some of the underlying tension by announcing, "I'll be ready for the big one before we finish this morning."

The sheer vitriol that was behind the emanation of the scoffing noise from Claudia did nothing but make him more determined.

Joe knew that acceding to the wishes of another in matters that involved craft and art was a dangerous path to venture down; he had survived this life to this point by adhering to his training. As the master had told him repeatedly, "The opinions and judgments of others are nothing more than hollow words intended to stifle one's full expression."

Yet he had let Claudia's disregard for his potential get under his skin, and his response had been, for him, oddly emotional.

"Let's go," Joe said.

He helped Frank push the car off the shop floor and out onto the patio area. Like a row of ducks in a boardwalk arcade, there was a continuous line of children perched atop their father's shoulders peering over the wall. When Joe appeared, they began to scream with glee.

John had a rough strategy for trying to locate the apartment that housed Udo and his comrades, but it required at least a few of the tenants and hopefully some management types to be present. Considering that this was the morning of the punch-out, the pickings could be slim.

He checked a couple of times to make sure that none of Kevin Gatz's operatives had followed him as he took the roundabout way toward the Grand Circus through the Ram neighborhood. He jumped the barriers that were protecting the southwestern side of Cass Avenue, hooked onto Washington Boulevard, and headed for the area the Mugwumps called home.

At the door of the building that housed the Redeemers, he could see that the current was definitely moving away from the interior of the high rise. To John's right there was a long line of uniformed Mugwumps standing at some form of attention. Each submitted to the inspection required prior to their sanctioned release to the destinations of their servitude.

John knew he wouldn't find Udo in this line because his duties as the backup driver would not place him in the same category as the vast majority of the residents. He wondered whether the Redeemer's acolytes had obligations that would call them to the stadium, or if their station was to toil at a different location.

John found one of the apartment managers quarrelling with a resident over whether he should be charged extra for the arrival of a woman who was to become his wife. John knew that this was a shakedown, and there was ethical leverage to be had over this manager if he played his cards carefully.

The whole protocol around the situation that involved a Mugwump acquiring a spouse—either from intra or extra enclave—was very tricky, and it involved a thick volume of conditions that had to be met, including an oath that there would be no progeny. It was risk to take that step, as there was zero tolerance when it came to enforcing any of the innumerable precepts. One slipup always resulted in banishment for the couple.

Yet it was not uncommon for a union to occur, and Mugwump men had their pick of the litter when they ventured into the wilderness in search of love. If they survived the excursion, their success in acquiring a fetching partner was a fait accompli. Every eligible woman wanted a ticket to the inside.

The manager was begrudgingly paid, and the Mugwump shuffled over to take his place in the inspection line. John stepped into the space that he vacated.

"Excuse me, I wonder if you can help me?" John asked.

"With what?" the manager barked.

"I'm wondering if you have any space in this building?"

"Full up. The waiting list is close to six months."

"Anyone ready to move out?"

"Didn't you hear me? If someone is on the move, there are people to fill the vacancy."

John nodded. This subtle attempt at manipulating this man to give him an answer wasn't working.

"Okay, look, I need to know if a certain person is staying here," John said.

The manager stopped and turned back to him. He took a moment to look his inquisitor up and down.

"What's up with you? You ain't no Independent."

"Yeah, okay, you're right, but I'm looking out for someone who is."

"Well, you have them come with their contract of employment, and talk to me. There are ways to be moved up the list," the manager said with a furtive smile.

John wanted to call one of the inspectors over from the door and have this man punished for his display of axiological deprivation, but that would only move him farther away from his goal.

"Let me ask you a question. Do you have people that are not on your manifest staying here illegally?" John asked.

The manager screwed up his face in response to this sudden diversion.

"What are you saying, kid?" the manager asked.

"Well, if my friend knew someone who was living here, could he just move in with them, and bypass you completely?"

"I know everyone in the building," he stated.

"Do you?"

"Yes."

"Well, I happen to know that there is at least one person who is staying here that is not on your list."

"And who would that be?"

"Go get your list and we'll see if I'm right."

"Look, I don't have time for this. Why don't you go back to your cushy ward, and quit bothering me. Have pity on a man who works for a living," the manager said before again turning away from him.

"I know what you do. I know that you take bribes and extort people. My father is the Impala captain, and I swear that I will tell him about your nefarious practices as soon as the festival week is over."

The manager heard the determination in John's threat and he began to make the calculations that would put the odds in his favor. It wasn't as simple as telling this youngster to go fuck a duck. This kid could really hurt him.

"You would do that?" the manager asked, wheezing now.

"I absolutely would."

The standoff ended quickly.

"Okay, come to my office. I'll show you what you want. I'll prove to you that I am right, but there will have to be some ground rules set."

"Here's the deal. I promise to never say anything about your business dealings if you show me your list of tenants. Is that the kind of rules you had in mind?"

"You'll swear to that?" the manager asked.

"I will," John said.

In the office, the manager pulled up the data on his tablet.

"What's the name?"

"Udo Lewandowski."

"What?"

"Wait, try Clarence Rigney first."

"Is it two guys or one?"

"One guy, two names."

"You are really confusing me, kid."

"Sorry."

He scanned through his alphabetical list and came away with nothing resembling the last name Rigney. He handed the tablet to John for confirmation. John subsequently scrolled through the L names and also came up empty.

"He's here," John said.

"Not according to this."

John was stumped. The only thing he could do was wander the hallways and hope that he came face-to-face with a man that he had never seen—someone who would kill him before he could finish inquiring about his identity.

"This doesn't queer the deal, am I right?" the manager asked.

"No, you held up your end. Sorry that it had to come to that. Besides, if I'm right, his name was never going to come up anyway."

"So, what's going on here? Why are you looking for this guy?" the manager asked.

"I can't tell you that."

"What's he look like?"

"Big guy, tall, strong, blond hair."

"That's all you got?"

"Yeah."

"You just described about a hundred guys that live here."

"I figured."

John was ready to give up. He was pretty sure he was just chasing his tail now.

"I've got another favor to ask you," he said to the manager.

FORTY-SIX

Someone once said that the race through the streets of Motor City is the fairest competition because it is the most fixed competition. Before they fire the gun and the race commences, every ward has made some kind of deal with their allies to try to affect the outcome of the race. These agreements might involve a friendly ward helping out by blocking their enemy's car as it tries to get out of the stadium, putting an enemy's car on the defensive by driving erratically, or deliberately crashing into someone for a reward.

The reality, though, is that every ward is looking to perform at their best. The unwanted distractions that abound when responsibilities are added to an agenda that involves doing anything other than trying to win the race usually end up causing any promises made to be swiftly broken.

Even though that theory was proven over and over again, it did not stop each and every ward from plotting for the demise of their foes by enlisting others to help.

With Billy Klock supervising the construction at the headquarters, Lon and Kevin were left to make the rounds of the wards that were the most likely to be amenable to the thought of doing business with them.

Because of their inherent wealth, Impala often got invitations from some of the less fortunate wards to make an offer for the more penurious ward's services. The Red Wings were always willing listeners, and depending on their level of confidence for the particular race, usually agreed to forgo their own ambitions to do the bidding of the richer Impala.

The accepted protocol was that no contracts would be exercised unless the team that made the deal won the race. A ward could create a master plan of chaos by agreeing to pay multiple neighborhoods to do something specific during the race, but if that ward was to not be victorious, all agreements to extend treasure to those who had agreed to aid them would be voided.

Only the winner had to pay off all of its conscribed helpers regardless of whether or not they actually ended up performing what was asked of them. This made up the basis for a lot of accusations, but in the end there was no debate because the winner had to open their purse strings lest they be labeled a pariah.

Many years ago, the ward known as the Tigers won the race and then refused to compensate all of the other wards that they had fashioned deals with. To this day, collusion forever keeps the Tigers on the sideline when business deals are being negotiated. Also, it would not be an aberration if the entire community ganged up on the Tigers' vehicle and drove it from the race early in the contest.

The preliminary meetings that had taken place the previous morning had provided Impala with a trove of information that they could use to craft an overall strategy. They knew that everyone was aware of the competitiveness of their car because it became a recurring theme continuously brought up at the onset of every discussion about a proposed transaction.

Because the expectations for Impala appeared to be high, the opening price for another ward's promise of cooperation was exorbitant. The Red Wings went so far as to guarantee to be in cahoots with Impala, but they had the temerity to suggest that they be paid upfront and would be giving no regard to outcome. Lon and Kevin rejected them, but they also knew that this was just the opening salvo tossed out in this particular negotiation.

Today, during the morning at the various clubhouses and in clandestine meetings at the stadium amidst the punch-out, they would revisit their discussions with all of the neighborhoods they had contacted yesterday.

It was common for most deals to close on Friday, though some would have to wait until Saturday morning for the ceremonial handshake as counteroffers were weighed and agreements were massaged into something of mutual benefit for the parties involved.

In the Red Wings' case, they were sure to make the same demands from Mustang for their services. If during a second discussion with Impala they were still in the mood to negotiate, Lon and Kevin could infer that Mustang had also said no to their arrogant demand of prepayment.

Of course, there was never surety. Occasionally a ward would make separate deals with each of two warring entities, but that tactic was risky, and if unmasked, the double-dealers could go the way of the Tigers and be shunned in the future for their reckless attempt to deceive.

What no one would have guessed was that Lon had secretly begun discussions to enlist the aid of the disowned Tigers many months before. The Tigers were only too happy to even be considered in anyone's plans and had been fervently hoping that someday, some entity would slip the city's bounds and approach them for their help.

Shortly after his election, Lon had approached their captain, Tim Rizzo, and proposed that they discuss the possibility of creating a working relationship. Tim did not hesitate in his affirmative response. The Tigers needed to pull themselves out of the bottomless pit they had fallen into, and it was Tim Rizzo's hope that they could build relationships one ward at a time. Why not start with one of the most powerful, Impala?

For Lon and Kevin, it would be a realization of a dream—having a recondite ally willing to commit suicide to further your cause, and no one but the two parties would know the truth.

———

There was a moment between Frank and Joe where they independently examined whether a foundation of trust existed between them. It happened as they were all piling into the car and Joe portrayed virtually no hesitation in staking his claim to the pilot's seat.

With the crowds still milling outside the walls of the garden, Frank had made a not-so-resolute move to relieve Joe of the burden of possibly failing in front of the passel of massing Impalans. Seeing Joe bolt for the driver's side, Frank found himself being robustly impressed with the neophyte's moxie, and it lent credence to his belief that he had been on the righteous side of the prior argument he had with his daughter.

Claudia opened the gate as Joe fired up the Barracuda. He slowly drove toward the opening without a single jerk or quaver. *Well, thank god for that*, she thought. She climbed into the backseat, and the trio left the cheers of the crowd behind.

As Joe cruised down Temple Street toward the Woodward Avenue artery, he kept his mind on the business of synchronizing his body parts with the pedals and the gear shifter. He did not see the lines and lines of people standing on the curb as the 'Cuda proceeded past them.

A sentry allowed them through the barrier that had been erected at the corner of Woodward and Adams. Joe hung a hard left turn onto Adams, drove the short distance to Witherell, took a right, and skirted the Grand Circus before making the left that would put them back onto Woodward for the first long straightaway—a foot-to-the-floor quarter-mile blast down Madison.

Just up ahead of him, Joe saw the Plymouth Roadrunner, hood up, idling by the side of the road as one of the mechanics from Marquis made an adjustment.

"Pull up alongside them," Frank said.

Joe sidled the car up close to the Roadrunner. Frank rolled down the window.

"Everything all right?" Frank asked.

The Marquis mechanics shot Frank a look of defensiveness. Obviously, whatever problem they were experiencing was turning out to be a much bigger deal than they had initially thought. When they noticed that the questioner was Frank, they relaxed a little.

"We're way up in temperature here. Hoses look good; water pump appears to be fine," the older mechanic said.

"We had that car three years ago, and I thought then the thermostat was going. You might want to get yourself another, just to be safe. We're pretty well stocked on Chrysler stuff if they don't have one in warehouse at the museum," Frank said.

"Okay, thanks, Francisco. Good luck to you."

"You too, Bubba."

Frank motioned Joe forward. Both of the men up front could sense Claudia squirming in the backseat.

"Why do you do that shit, Dad?" she asked.

"What?"

"You know what I mean."

"It's a little thing called professional courtesy, dear. Someday you might need something that they have squirreled away. We banked a little gratitude back there."

"I'll never understand why you always willfully reach out to help someone that could beat you in the end," Claudia said.

"You don't see me helping Mustang, do you sweetie? We're neutral with Marquis. Besides, ain't no one beating this 'Cuda this year. Right, Joe?"

Joe nodded in assent before turning to Frank.

"I'm going to let her rip," Joe stated.

"The dance floor is wide open, kid."

Joe hit the gas, and the car jumped forward. Everyone in the car heard a faint squeal from the tires as the clutch disengaged during the shift into second.

"That could be a little smoother," Frank instructed.

Joe kept Frank's mild admonishment in the back of his mind as he flipped the shifter into third and wound that gear out before slamming it into fourth.

"Better," Frank said.

"Turn?" Claudia asked from the back with seeds of panic beginning to germinate in her voice.

Joe did not comprehend that she was voicing a warning. He was fully concentrating and trying to attain the top speed that the restricted carburetion would allow.

"Okay, back off," Frank said calmly.

"Why?" Joe asked.

"Because you aren't going to make this curve if you don't," Frank said in the same monotone.

Turn? Oh, that turn. It was the nearly 120-degree-curve to the right that took the course onto Gratiot Avenue. He took his foot off the gas, braked slightly, depressed the clutch and downshifted into third, but it was all happening way too slowly. There was no way they were going to make it.

"Jesus Christ!" Claudia screamed.

Joe pushed his lower back into the seat and laid a heavy foot on the brakes, but the car continued across the intersection, jumped the curb, and narrowly missed a bench before coming to rest not five feet from a gurgling fountain. A couple of kids, using the tepid water to cool off, stared at the Barracuda with eyes as wide as a harvest moon. Having forgotten to depress the clutch through all of this, the car stalled and died.

"What the fuck?" Claudia said.

"Take it easy," Frank said.

"Let me out, goddammit," she said as she scrambled to climb out of the claustrophobic backseat.

The favor John had asked the manager to grant was to allow him to roam the halls of the building to see if he could narrow down the possibilities of which apartment held Udo Lewandowski and his demented disciples.

Though the prospects were slim, the logic was not all that flawed. With almost all of the Mugwumps who resided in the building bound to their duties for the festival, the only people who remained in the structure would be those who had not been assigned specific tasks, or like Udo, had responsibilities that would not have them showing up to work at this hour.

As the backup driver, Udo might be out on the racecourse observing Roger Burnham practicing, or he could just be hanging out waiting to join his employers at the punch-out later in the day.

John walked each of the twenty-eight floors, listening at the door of each apartment for any signs of present life, be it random movement or noise. The entire trek took him nearly two hours, but at its completion, he had narrowed the possibilities down to four different domiciles.

Two of the four seemed to be occupied by only one person. One's resident was clearly female. The fourth, and the most intriguing, was a room on the twenty-second floor. John listened at the door to what sounded like three distinct voices. That none of the occupants had headed off to start his workday was definitely not normal behavior. He noted the number, but as he turned to continue his search, he heard the sound of a fourth voice in the room. The only intelligible phrases he could make out were "final preparation," "command structure contact," and a response that sounded like, "Not until the end. Not until it's full."

As he moved away from the door, an acrid smell lingered briefly in his nostrils before diminishing with each step that took him away from the apartment. He couldn't put his finger on it, but the odor did not carry the aroma of food.

———

Frank wanted to make sure that Joe had not produced any type of insult to the car's front suspension. If the forward axle happened to be bent, that would be a huge problem for the team to have to overcome.

Frank rolled off the ground with a grunt—an oral recognition that the years of his life had been many.

"It's all right. We'll check the springs and shocks tonight, but everything else appears to be intact," he said.

"Sorry," Joe offered.

"I'm going to wait here until you come around again," Claudia said.

It was a subtle form of protest—a manipulation meant to convey to her father and his protégé her overall discontent with this whole enterprise.

"Suit yourself," Frank said.

Back in the car, cruising away at slow speed, Frank gave Joe the barest indication that the line in the sand that he'd drawn regarding his expectations for Joe's performance might be getting smoothed over by the size-eight boot of his daughter.

"Are you going to be able to do this?" Frank asked with a bit of exasperation.

"Yes," Joe stated.

"Okay. We've got the little jog onto Randolph before we hit the straightaway on Michigan. Then we'll turn onto Cass, the long straight road with the gates at the end. I was hoping you would be able to recreate what you did in the simulator, but that isn't happening. So, we are going to have to get into some measure of a remedial mode. You are going drive the car, but you will follow every one of my commands."

"Okay."

"We're going start at the next curve," Frank said.

And that is how the rest of the morning developed, with Joe responding to every order voiced by Frank. If there had been a recording device in the vehicle, the playback would have sounded something like this: "Gas, clutch, shift, gas, clutch, shift, gas, brake, clutch, downshift, brake, right turn, gas, clutch, shift, gas, clutch, shift . . ."

By the time Frank and Joe had made a complete circuit of the track and neared the corner where they had left Claudia, silence had started to reign in the vehicle. Frank had been mute since they had gotten back onto Madison Street, just below the stadium. His quietude was not borne out of frustration. Frank could see that he no longer needed to yank on the reins of his thoroughbred.

Claudia, on the other hand, had not been in the car, so when she saw the Barracuda barreling confidently toward her, she assumed that it was her father driving. As she heard the car slow with the revs increasing after the downshift and watched the turn made with the perfect apex, she was shocked to see that it was Joe behind the wheel.

The ride back to the barriers at the corner of Woodward and Adams was a revelation to her. Joe seemed to be a different person than the one who had vaulted the curb and nearly crashed them into the fountain a little over an hour ago. His driving was smooth, the turns flawlessly executed, and he nearly always achieved the maximum speed available to him given the lesser limits of the smaller carburetor that they had installed.

Joe gave a pretty good showing of himself on the frightful turn at First and Adams before they were forced to slow down their approach to the temporary barriers at the Woodward intersection.

Joe offered to walk the remaining quarter-mile to the stadium. When Frank hopped into the driver's seat to take the car back to the shop, he didn't hesitate informing his daughter that they would be putting the 4-barrel carburetor back on as soon as they arrived. It was time for Joe to be introduced to the fully toothed Barracuda—all three hundred and thirty horsepower.

FORTY-SEVEN

THERE WAS A steady stream of Motor City residents weaving their way toward the stadium. Even from a couple of hundred yards away, Joe could hear the noise building.

He felt conspicuous—maybe even a little vulnerable—clad in the vestments of his racing colors, but in the moment, no one seemed interested in threatening him. There were a few sideways glances, a nod of acknowledgement or two, but the patrons hustling to their assigned sections seemed to be more intent on getting to their seats than gawking at the outsider.

Once inside, seated in the Impala VIP section next to Kevin Gatz and Billy Klock, he felt differently. He could sense there was something in the air. Neither Billy nor Kevin would look him in the eye when he asked them to explain the rules associated with the event that was about to take place.

He noticed that John was fidgeting in his seat one row back and to the right of him. It was obvious that the kid wanted to impart something of importance to him but was hamstrung by the presence of the Impala officers, including his father.

"It's pretty simple, Joe," Billy was saying. "Each ward brings fifteen team members to the field. The object is to get all of the other teams off the field in whatever way possible. The team with members, or even one member, still standing when everyone else is off the field is the winner."

"So all you have to do is push your opponents to the sidelines?" Joe asked.

"There isn't a lot of pushing going on," Kevin said.

"Has Impala ever won?" Joe asked.

Both Kevin and Billy burst into laughter. Joe did not feel affected by their childish response, which was nothing more than a blatant attempt to point out to him that his question was stupid. He sat patiently and waited for their juvenile hilarity to subside.

"We have only one aim here, Smith, and that is to beat the everliving shit out of the Mustang scum," Kevin said.

Joe nodded absently. He was pretty sure that he could figure out the etiquette just by observing. He had not expected worthy commentary; he was only interested in engaging them to see if they might spill the reasons why they appeared so detached.

Joe looked out to the field as each team made their entrances from different tunnels. As each team stretched or went over a last-minute strategy, he saw the genius of the founders who conceived this event.

This would be the only instance during an entire year's span when any sort of violence was licit. All of the pent-up rage that had been kept in abeyance—like a vast pool of molten lava in the base of a volcano on the verge of eruption—would be released only during this sanctioned event. After the consummation of these orgiastic desires to rip the body parts off one another, the moratorium would be imposed again, and the cone spewing the liquid rock would be sealed.

That a ward could find themselves disqualified from both this competition and the race by not adhering to the laws was tremendous incentive to be nice for fifty-one weeks, six days, and twenty-two or so hours of the year.

Joe had been told once that the last time a neighborhood had screwed up and been sentenced to a year's penalty was many, many moons ago—such was the level of disincentive.

Joe felt the people in the stands move subtly toward the edge of their seats as he saw Carter Pleasant appear from the darkness of one of the tunnels and move toward the center of the field.

There was no amplification to be had, so the scene that unfolded on the field as Carter gave his pre-punch-out speech to the team leaders took on the essence of a theatrical expression.

Joe kept his eye on the two leaders who sported the Impala and Mustang colors. Like their teams, these two men stood at twelve and six in the clock circle that formed around Grand Commissioner Pleasant. Where the other team leaders had cast their eyes toward the ground, on Carter, or up to the crowd, these two enemy combatants leveled stares of certain death at each other.

Carter scattered the team leaders back to their squads, but neither the Impala representative nor his Mustang counterpart moved. Quickly, the rest of their team members joined the two. As the other teams entered onto the field and began milling around in anticipation of the pealing of the start bell, the two groupings of mortal enemies began to gesture and point.

There was a cataclysm-to-be swirling in the atmosphere that encompassed the playing field. Up in the stands, the members of fandom that were pulling for their favorite sons sang and cheered. Joe heard the Impala section break into a loud rendition of the ward's song, accompanied by a bugle and a marching-band bass drum.

When the bell finally rang, it did nothing to quell the stored-up violence deep within the belly of the people in the stands. There were clenched fists and gritted teeth being displayed by all of the patrons encircling Joe.

Down on the field, the other teams put their game plans into effect. The Lions spread out across an even line and advanced. Some of the boys from Marquis went at their left flank—multiples of three guys ganging up on each of the suddenly isolated Lions.

The Ram squad joined up with DeVille with the intention of taking out those welchers, the perennially persecuted Tigers. Nearby, there was a dust-up that included half squads of Marquis, and the smaller-in-stature Pistons.

Circling the entire affair, like an earthbound group of ravenous vultures, were the wicked Red Wings. Their strategy seemed to be that they would stand down for such a time as it took everyone to be softened up a little.

Joe only saw these actions taking place in his periphery as he focused on the doings taking up center stage on the field.

Impala and Mustang had completely ignored the activity going on around them. They ripped into each other with a force of viciousness supported by the power inherent in their years-long blood feud. Fists were smashed into faces, kicks were aimed at testicles, and death grips on free limbs were leveled with the sole intention of causing fracture.

As the people sitting around him rose in unison to exhort their brothers, Joe caught sight of John. The young man seemed distraught—his dream of being a participant and affecting the outcome on the field having been dashed by his overbearing patriarch. It was almost as if he had become uninterested in the spectacle.

On the field, the Impala boys were getting in their shots, but it was obvious to everyone in the section that when they picked up the teeth that sprung from the struck mouths, more of them would have had their origins in the oral cavities of the Impala team than in their abhorred counterparts in the baby blue.

As more of the Impala team was scattered to the hard pan, bloodied or losing consciousness, the fans from both neighborhoods moved toward the railings, clogging the aisles and creating a second wall of support.

It seemed to Joe that more than a few of them had it in their minds to jump onto the field and really show those Mustang fuckers what kind of pain the entire ward could dish out. Mugwump security tried to disabuse the mob from entertaining the possibility and screamed at the frenzied Impalans that they were putting at risk everything they had spent the last year trying to achieve.

Over in the Mustang section, there was also the potential for a donnybrook. Though the Impalans were generally getting their asses kicked, some of the stronger members of the Impala team—including the inimitable Jody Springer—had isolated some of their counterparts in an area just below the tiers that held the bloodthirsty Mustang fanatics.

Impala was down to three functioning combatants. Mustang had maybe nine still waling away, but by now, some of the other wards had made their way over to the part of the stadium that had become the personal battle theater of Mustang and Impala. The Red Wings began to pick off one or two of the Mustang fighters who had been nudged outside of the circle of pain that had previously held only those dressed in the green, black, and white of Impala.

The possibility that the Mustang strongmen might be taken out of the fight before they could fully waste Impala began to register with the Mustang faithful in the stands. They were screaming at the Red Wings, and the encroaching Lions, to let their men finish the job on their hated enemy before they engaged with them.

With their circulatory systems pumping high concentrations of adrenalin and testosterone through every vein and artery, the gladiators were not able to comprehend anything as mundane as a command or a suggestion from the crowd. With all that was taking place in the moment, they couldn't hear a thing except the instances where bone met bone in close proximity to their ears.

And then it happened. Someone in the Mustang section got punched by either an interloper or one of their own, and the activity in the area escalated into a war zone. It was over quickly as the Mustang people realized the severity of the consequences that could be administered for such a mistake. An immediate plea for calm rang out amongst the attendees.

There was only one casualty, and he was being escorted out of the stadium before he could point out the person who had broken his jaw.

After the incident, the activity on the field became nothing more than an afterthought. Commissioners hovered over the Mustang section, attempting to find a reason for the altercation. Joe could see a screaming match break out between Mustang Captain Titus O'Keefe and the lead investigator.

Out of the corner of his eye, Joe saw Lon get up and begin climbing the steps to the walkway that would take him on a trek around the stadium. Kevin and Billy fell in at his side.

Released from their prying eyes and ears, Joe slid over to the seat next to John.

"What'd you find out?" Joe asked John.

John was preoccupied with the goings-on across the way. He nodded toward the Mustang section.

"Did you get a look at the guy they carried out of there?" John asked.

"No."

Joe didn't care about what had transpired across the stadium. He had only a finite amount of time to get a briefing from his scout.

"Forget that. What did you find out?"

"I think he was in the building when I was there. I checked the names of the people that were legally registered for the room I identified as the most likely with the manager. They were all Mugwumps that worked for the road crew."

"How many?"

"Three."

"Plus Udo?"

"Yeah. I'm pretty sure I heard four distinct voices."

"I'm going to take them tonight."

"What do you want me to do?"

"Nothing. Run interference with your Dad and his toadies if they inquire about my whereabouts."

"I could help you."

"No, no. I need you to do exactly what I ask."

John hesitated.

"You have to listen now, John," Joe said as he swiveled the boy's face so their eyes could connect. "I am trained to do this. Your presence can only make things more complicated. I cannot take on the responsibility of minding you and do the job with the effort that will be required. Do you understand me?"

John wasn't ready to be dismissed.

"Do you understand me?" Joe said evenly.

"Yes."

As usual, the Red Wings ended up having their flag raised in victory. They had stuck to their plan: When the other wards' energy levels dissipated through pain or exhaustion, they stepped in and busted heads with their customary ruthlessness. The distraction produced by the craziness in the stands gave them an advantage, as the commitment from the other teams wavered.

———————

Leo Rascone watched the Red Wing flag ascend the pole as if he were interested in the outcome, but what he was really intent on accomplishing was keeping himself from peeing in his pants. His plan had worked perfectly.

The Independent section that housed the Mugwump elite had only one other ward—the Red Wings—as a buffer between them and the area that confined the Mustangs, so Leo had a crystal-clear view of the incident that he had surreptitiously provoked. He could see the escalation of the argument between Captain O'Keefe and a group of commissioners. He could see an out-of-breath Carter Pleasant, accompanied by his entourage of the Uncommitted, approaching from the north. He could see Captain Brassey along with his weasels forming a peanut gallery with some of the other captains. He could even hear them calling out for serious sanctions to be levied for the infraction.

Leo was sure that the ward would only be issued a warning by the swarm of administrators; there would be no way they would ever be able to discover the origins of the machinations that led to what Captain O'Keefe and Tom Cobble were proclaiming was nothing more than an accident.

Leo imagined that Titus would be able to back up his theory by pronouncing that no one in his ward was stupid enough to do anything intentional to the sole victim—the ward's designated driver, Roger Burnham.

The Greek chorus of dissenters—fronted by Captain Brassey— was not likely to influence Carter's ultimate decision. That group was predisposed to show zero empathy for Mustang's predicament and was only viewed as an annoying drone of discontent by the administration staff. Their influence was immaterial and would not be part of the considerations when it came to rendering a verdict.

Carter reached a decision, informed Titus of his findings, and invoked the other administrators, the Mugwump security people, and everyone else in the vicinity to disperse. There would be no sanction since no other wards were involved and the incident had been confined to just that section of the stands.

Leo saw Captain Brassey continue to lodge his complaints, but the energy surrounding the situation ebbed. In mere seconds, the exiting patrons engulfed him and the other protesters.

Leo wouldn't feel a need to set the record straight; he was perfectly content to go with the whole inadvertent elbow hypothesis that Titus would have proffered. The truth: The balled-up fist to the kisser of Roger Burnham was deliberately delivered by a man named Dyk, the smaller of the two Nordic bodyguards Leo had employed that morning for just this purpose.

In exchange for assuming the risk and creating the ruckus that would result in the blow to the Mustang's driver's mandible bone, Leo would use his expertise to transition the assailant from his current temporary status as a freelance dayworker to that of a fully employed Mugwump.

Dyk had made his excursion over to the Mustang section during the interlude that preceded the throwing of the first punch on the field. He waited for the mania to build, and when the bulk of the Mustang fans began to crowd down toward the railing, he waded into the morass of bodies with his safety off. He found Roger Burnham in the crowd, screaming obscenities at both the Impala lowlifes as well as the other squads that were going after his own.

A frustrated stratum of Mustang people who had lost sight of the action caused a chain reaction; they began to push into the people at the rail, and as critical mass was achieved, Dyk drew back his right hand, and drove it down into Roger Burnham's face.

Mere seconds later, Dyk withdrew back up the aisle and retreated back to the Independent section. No one had a clue as to what had happened, especially Roger Burnham. And if he had, he would not have been able to communicate it orally with his jigsaw jaw in desperate need of wiring.

It had worked like a dream. Leo waited another couple of minutes—until most of the crowd had cleared—before crossing over to Titus O'Keefe and offering his condolences.

"How fucked up is that?" Leo asked rhetorically.

Titus had already moved on. He was reformulating his strategies now and thinking about more than just the driver-replacement issue. As was his way, he would use the predicament as an opportunity, not as an impediment. He pulled Leo to the side, seeking at least the illusion of a private venue.

"I need your help," he said to Leo.

"You got it."

"I need you to make contact with someone within the Tigers' organization. Do you know anyone who might be of use to us?"

"How about Tim Rizzo?" Leo said with a grin, invoking the name of the ranking member of the Tigers' hierarchy, their captain.

"That'll work. See if you can set up a meeting for tonight. Maybe we can do it at your office," Titus said.

"It will be done," Leo said.

Titus began to move away from their little confabulation, but Leo beckoned him back with a final question.

"Who's the new driver?" Leo asked.

"It's gonna have to be your boy. The import," Titus responded.

Leo concealed his smile of satisfaction. He had work to do. Not only did he have to arrange the meeting with the Tigers, but he also had to find the most advantageous mode to unleash Clarence Rigney on an unsuspecting Joe Smith.

FORTY-EIGHT

JOE WAS ABLE to compartmentalize his priorities like few mortals could, and the afternoon's task of practicing with the unbound Barracuda was completed without the distractions associated with Udo Lewandowski.

Strangely, the increases in the torque and performance of the vehicle actually enhanced his abilities, and he sailed through the paces of Frank's regimen with relative ease.

They spent a majority of the time working out the kinks of the turn at First and Adams. Joe had been dubious that he would have the skills required to make it through the turn unscathed, but he realized that his reticence was due to the balkiness of an underpowered car, not because he lacked adeptness.

As the sun began to set and the barriers were removed, they slowly rode back to Frank and Claudia's shop, all a bit exhausted, though subtle feelings of exhilaration existed just under the surface of each of the principles.

At the shop, Joe quickly changed back into his civilian garb as Frank and Claudia inspected the vehicle. Claudia was on the verge of conceding Frank's point that everything was going to work out just fine when Joe emerged from the bathroom.

"I thought you did real good today, Joe," she admitted.

"Thanks. Thanks for sticking by me," Joe said sincerely.

She left it at that. She would later tell Frank that she was sorry she had been so doubtful and would thank him for being so steadfast in his support of Joe. Frank would accept her mea culpa with his customary graciousness and would never remind her that she had been on the wrong side of the debate.

Joe wanted to pilfer something from the shop that would serve as a weapon, but everything he saw lying out in the open required too much modification to be utile. As Frank efficiently settled on a schedule for the morrow, Joe thought of a place where he might be able to acquire a killing implement. He left the shop in a hurry and headed straight over to the café.

When he entered, the barista nearly went into shock. There had been many minutes of commiseration with her friend Cassandra over her feelings about this rogue, and she had assumed that their thing was mercifully over. She was pretty sure that her duties as the conveyor of information between the two had come to the point of termination as well.

"Hey," he said.

"Hey."

"Uh, I wonder if you'd let me rifle through your knife drawer and maybe borrow one for a couple of days?" he asked in an upbeat fashion.

She didn't quite know how to take his request.

"What do you need a knife for?"

"I have to kill someone," he said jokingly.

She laughed, though she knew not why.

"Actually, it's a long story, but I have this uniform that they are making me wear, and it tapers down by the ankles to the point that I feel my circulation is being cut off. I've asked them to let me cut it, but they gave me the impression that they think I would somehow be defiling the thing. I'm going to go with it for now, but once I am in the car, right before the race starts, I'm going to slit that fabric up to my shin bone, and I need something sharp to do that. I promise to return it on Sunday with your hat that I seem to have forgotten."

She bought it and leisurely stepped aside, allowing him passage to the back room. She pointed out the correct enclosure, and he began his search.

"You know, she's left a couple of messages for you," she said.

"Yeah. I've been busy and haven't been able to stop by. Could you tell her that we'll get together as soon as all of this is over?"

"Okay."

"Could you tell her that I miss her?"

"Sure."

"Thanks."

The stew that the two of these people produced was not balanced, the barista thought. How could their thing be over, and yet he was professing this obtuse point about missing her?

Joe found what he was looking for—a six-inch boning knife. The blade was thin but sturdy. He deemed it to be the sharpest one in the drawer.

"You got a whetstone or something similar?"

She reached around him and pulled out a rusty sharpening steel from the open drawer.

"That will work," he said as he set about honing the blade.

Forty strokes of steel sliding across steel and he was finished. He borrowed an old kitchen towel, wrapped it around the business end of the knife, and shoved it, blade down, into his boot.

"You think I could get a coffee, before I go?"

"You want your regular drink?"

"Yeah, thanks," Joe said.

"Don't' forget my hat."

"I won't. I promise."

————————

John was physically present at the dinner table, but his mind was all the way across town at the apartment building that rose above the Grand Circus.

His mother had inquired about Joe's absence, and John had made up some excuse about having to debrief with Frank and Claudia about the day's practice session. Holly commented on the dismal performance of the Impala punch-out team, which caused Karen to flinch; she was still sensitive about the contention between father and son over John's participation in the tryouts.

"I thought they did better than last year," Karen said.

"I wonder how we would have done if you'd been on the team," Holly said to John.

This quasi-question caused their father to lift his head out of his plate of food and look at his daughter. Before he offered to rebut her, he stole a glance at his wife. She was using her eyes to exhort him to stand down. Surprisingly, he did just that.

"You certainly wouldn't have hurt the cause if you could have been part of it," Lon said with a tone of uncommitted reconciliation.

Karen knew it was the best he could do, and she smiled at him to validate his effort. John let the comment zoom past him. He wasn't taking in anything that his father had to say. Not anymore.

Lon took a look at his watch. John immediately suspected that something was up, as his father looked a bit angst-ridden. He wondered whether the pressure of it all was beginning to cause his stoic demeanor to fray.

"Everything all right, Dad?" John asked with a concealed mischievousness.

"Yeah. Why wouldn't it be?"

"I don't know."

————————

Joe was not entirely sure if the other members of Udo's cell would try to fight back. He was going with the plot that had him quickly killing

Udo and then seeing if the will to fight still existed in his cadre once their chief had been dispensed with.

As he headed down a nearly deserted Woodward Avenue, he felt the cold steel of the blade against the skin of his ankle. The contrast between the outside air temperature and piece of metal was indelible, though he knew that his body temperature would warm the stainless in due time.

His reverie was broken by the sudden appearance of Billy Klock. Billy had stepped out of an alcove and positioned himself directly in Joe's path.

"Captain Brassey would like you to meet him at the clubhouse. He needs to go over a few things," Billy said.

"I can't right now. Tell him I'll see him at the house later," Joe said as he made a move to sidestep the large lieutenant.

"It has to be now," Billy said, shifting his weight to obstruct him.

"Or what?"

"Come on, Joe, you know the drill. When the captain calls, you obey."

"Not tonight."

"You got other plans?"

"Yes. Now, if you will excuse me."

"He warned you about that girl," Billy said.

Joe could see now that his actions to not obey Lon had been hurtful to Billy. The big man was in a pet about Joe's flagrant disregard for his captain's authority. Billy wanted to like Joe, but it was hard when the mercenary showed that much disrespect to people who Billy loved and admired.

Joe tried to sidestep Billy again, but this time the bigger man wrapped his viselike grip around Joe's right bicep. In a single continuous motion, Joe stripped Billy's hand from his body, spun around, and punched him in the throat. Billy fell to his knees and clutched his sprained windpipe. This reaction was counterproductive to his most pressing need: restoring his ability to inhale a life-affirming breath.

As Billy wheezed, eye bulging in fear that he was going to be self-strangled on the spot, Joe felt pity for the man who Lon had relied on to provide muscle. The poor guy was just not cut out for the job.

He reached down to offer Billy a hand to help him to his feet. Billy reached out in acceptance, but Joe could see that his focus was on something beyond the two of them. He did not alight on the possibility that there was someone else in the immediate vicinity.

He only felt the prick of the needle on his neck before he swiftly ventured into a void of blackness.

FORTY-NINE

FRIDAY

W HEN JOE WOKE, darkness still prevailed where he lay, on his back, supported by what felt like a mattress. It was the quality of darkness that he found himself trying to assess because the recognition that the sun had yet to rise was the first connection that his muddled brain was able to process.

His eyes were set on the opposite wall of the room, high up toward the ceiling where a full-moon night sky could be seen through the gap in the butcher paper that had been shoddily taped over the transom window. His view was obscured by something that stood in the foreground—galvanized steel wire diamonds. He wondered whether he had been here for hours or for days.

He closed his eyes again and tried to orient himself. There was a definite smell to the place. He sifted through his memory trying to recall when he had experienced something similar. The source wasn't environmental, it was distinct, and it was food. His body began to react to the stimulus, and he heard and felt his stomach growl. When had he last eaten?

He attempted to move his toes and fingers and was relieved to find out that his digits responded to his commands.

He decided to see whether he could move his legs or not. He moved his right leg to his right, felt the support of the platform disappear, and experienced the sensation of gravitational forces pulling it down.

"Are you awake?" a disembodied voice asked.

It was youthful voice, decidedly male in its tonal quality.

"Where am I?" Joe croaked.

"Oh, shit," the voice said before its maker ran out of the room.

In the two seconds of light that was afforded him by the opening and closing of the door, Joe was able to get a preliminary fix on his surroundings. He was in some kind of anteroom, the appointments seemed vintage, and he was encircled by what looked like five sides of chain-link fence—four walls and a roof. That there was light in this building—the security lamp from the hall—meant that the location retained some power during the hours of the area's standard shutdown schedule. Okay, he had some facts, but no discernible conclusion. What was that smell, and where had he smelled it before?

John was distraught. He had stayed up most of the night listening for the door to open and close—the signal that Joe had returned. In the hours that he had remained alert enough to maintain his vigil, he heard nothing resembling that sound. He heard no footsteps on the stairs, saw no battery-powered light bleeding under Joe's bedroom door, and heard no water running in the shower down the hall. When morning came, he tried to convince himself that he had just missed all of those indicators.

There was another battle taking place in John's mind. It was an equally valid reason for his transient insomnia, and it revolved around the topic of death. He had been so glib earlier in his offer to help Joe, but he had done so only because he trusted his friend and had been swept up in the wake of Joe's momentum to get the job done. He hadn't really thought about what it meant to end another's life on either practical or existential terms.

Through his studies, he had become familiar with the words used to describe killing. Words like "slaughter" and "extermination." In a quest for specificity, he tried to find the term associated with the death of an enemy or undesirable. There were words for the killing of a relative—"patricide," "sororicide," etc. There were words for the killing of figures of authority—"tyrannicide," "regicide," etc. What was the word for killing an opponent? Was it simply "war"?

He ventured into his reference books for the Latin word for "enemy" and found two distinct possibilities that fit the bill. The first, "hostilis," was defined as an armed enemy. The second, and the one he determined to be most apt, was the word "inimicus." Its definition was listed as opponent or personal foe. There was no word like inimacide in his dictionary, so he wrote it in the margins on the corresponding page.

He began to realize that the time taken up in resolving that technicality was nothing more than a dodge. He was just avoiding the real issue: the moral consequences associated with the slaying of another human being.

He had been taught that the act of killing one's fellow man was a sin in the eyes of God. It was certainly a punishable offense in Motor City. Offenders were not banished, but executed in public. Any kin who were genetically connected to the killer—ascendants, descendants, and all of those with tangential status including brothers, sisters, uncles, aunts, cousins, nieces and nephews—were subsequently banished to the wilderness.

The deterrent was so effective that no one had been accused, convicted, or sentenced during John's entire lifetime. There was lore: cautionary tales about the early days of the city when disagreements were often settled by the willful termination of one of the parties by the other, but since the institution of the festival and the race, no one had been suspected of intentionally causing the death of another, and that period had spanned John's entire time on earth.

John tried to imagine the circumstances that would make the act licit for him. Avenging a family member's death seemed like a credible reason. Saving another individual from being killed or maimed by someone else also could be validated as acceptable behavior. Repelling an attacker who put one's own mortality in jeopardy would qualify as toeing the fine line of the righteous.

He could see himself carrying out a slaying in every one of these situations, but only within the realm of the intellectual. The actual application was something far more daunting than just thinking about it.

John knew that for Joe, this was part of his everyday existence. John had marveled at Joe's lack of hesitation in his determination that Udo Lewandowski must be dispatched to another plane. He saw that Joe's perception of necessity had cancelled out any debate on the subject. There was no emotion in Joe Smith's affirmation, just relentless, uncompromising resolve. John had to take that for what it was—reason enough.

He had faith that Joe would not enter into an altercation without calculating that there was a high probability he would be successful and return alive. He couldn't imagine the specificities of what Joe would find once he got into the Redeemer's lair, but he had faith that there would be enough to exonerate him from being charged with any sort of crime. He had convinced himself there would be no repercussions for the man for doing nothing less than saving the entire city from unleashed evil. Yet there was no sign that he had returned. No sign that he had been triumphant.

It was light outside now, and when he heard some movement occurring downstairs, he climbed out of his bed and rushed to its source with the plaintive hopes that Joe had finally returned. He found his mother and sister drinking coffee and filling out a seating chart for the all-Impala dinner that would take place that evening. It reminded him that today was the race's eve, and he had duties to fulfill.

"Did you see Joe?" John asked.

"No, dear. I figured he got up with your father. Big day today," his mother said.

John sidled over to the sink to discover that there was only one used coffee cup in the basin, his father's personal mug.

"What time did Dad leave?" he asked.

"Before I woke up, dear. Don't you have to help over at the club-house this morning?"

"Yeah. Not until ten or so."

"I'll make you some breakfast," Karen said.

"He's a big boy, Mom; he can make his own breakfast," Holly shot back.

She went back to adjusting some slips of paper that were meant to represent people. She shuffled them around the schematic that denoted the static table positions.

"I'm just going to head out," John said.

"Eat something, dear," Karen said.

"They'll have food at the clubhouse, Mom," he said as he moved toward the door.

John's ultimate destination was the clubhouse, but first he thought he'd stop by the Grand Circus. His inherent curiosity was pinching his brain; it had become a noose, and he felt like he was the next of the condemned to take his place on the gallows.

When the word filtered down that Udo would be awarded the pilot's seat for Mustang, he was with his crew at the outer edges of Motor City in the extreme northeast corner of the enclave. Being so close to the wall, near some of the security personnel who walked the rim of the enclosure, was an intentional act. They had been laboring in the area for over a week at this point, and it was important that their legitimacy be maintained.

Most of their work had been done at night. The security personnel who spent the graveyard hours on patrol had come to recognize them and their rig. The first night when they showed up out of the blue, Udo explained to one of the officers that they preferred to work at night be-cause the days had been so infernally hot. He started discussing things like the beauty of the flex schedule that the road department offered and other mundane observations before the officer—visibly bored to tears—shuffled back to his guard shack.

While two of the acolytes crept through the banality of repairing a worn section of the road, Udo and the other completed the task that they had begun the day after he arrived at their doorstep two months before. Udo figured that the day guards had read the reports of their night shift brethren because no one ventured out to inquire after them.

Udo had waived his invitation to the punch-out. He knew that it was ballsy to try to finish this in the daylight hours, but there wasn't likely to be many prying eyes—what with the focus of the city being solely on the combat at the stadium.

No one had been keeping tabs on him from the ward, and after the competition to determine the pilot ended and Roger Burnham had been awarded the gig as driver, Udo had just drifted away. His half-hearted effort to win the job had been part of the plan. He knew that the people who had hired him had expected more, but he didn't really care. He needed the time to whip his helpers into shape and get this job done on time.

Two weeks ago, he would have said that they wouldn't make it. But now, with two days left, they were pretty much done.

When he returned to his squat with his compatriots, the manager singled him out on his entrance to the building.

"Are you Clarence Rigney?" the manager asked.

"Who?"

"Okay, wise guy, let's just say that if you come across this Rigney fellow, tell him he's gotten quite popular."

"He has?"

"The lawyer was here. Some kid was here yesterday. And now the Mustang captain has sent his lieutenant over to find you . . . I mean him. Look, pal, I don't need this type of aggravation."

"How much?" Udo asked.

"How much? How much? What the fuck are you talking about?" the manager asked with a perplexed lilt.

"How much to relieve your aggravation?" Udo asked.

Udo could see the nervousness in the eyes of his followers; they seemed sure that the whole thing could come apart at any moment. He saw one of them fingering a knife in his front pocket, and he reached out to put his hand on his comrade's shoulder to calm him.

Udo's offer of sop titillated the manager briefly, but he was treading on precarious ground here; he'd already accepted payments from Leo Rascone and Tom Cobble in lieu of notifying them on Mr. Rigney's arrival. Could he get away with going for the trifecta and actually take some funds from the reverse side of this crazy equation? And what was the payment meant to assure—that he didn't tell them where the object of their interest was?

"See the payment as compensation for Mr. Rigney's unpaid rent. Do you know why they are trying to contact Mr. Rigney?" Udo asked.

"You don't know?"

"How could I if I'm asking you?" Udo said with a sly smile.

"Roger Burnham, the Mustang driver, got his jaw broken today, and Mr. Rigney has been appointed as his replacement."

One of the acolytes gasped. This was the sudden rockslide that none of them had predicted.

Udo knew he would have to make himself available to his patrons as there were only two days left, and they needed the ploy to remain a secret. It sure did add a whole host of complications.

He went upstairs, gave each of the cell members a specific set of new tasks, packed his gear, and headed out for the Mustang clubhouse. He spent the entire trek to their neighborhood thinking about the contingencies that this twist had either robbed them of or possibly provided. By the time he arrived at Titus O'Keefe's office, he had completely reformulated his plan. This was going to turn out to be a boon, he thought. This was a gift that could have only come from the Redeemer.

That was yesterday. Udo arrived at the Mustang clubhouse just short of the dinner bell—about the same time that Joe Smith had left the café to hunt him down.

———

As Joe came to his senses, he started to notice details. The first was that he was shoeless. That meant that the weapon that he had acquired had gone the way of his footwear.

He sat in the dark and tried to recreate his last moments of consciousness. He remembered leaving the café, and he remembered the altercation with Billy Klock that ended when he punched him in the throat, but the next memory he could conjure was the moment he awoke.

The door creaked open, and a pair of flashlights raked the walls. One landed on the area that he heard the kid's voice come from, and he saw a chair and what looked like some kind of sandwich on the floor next to it. That was the smell. It was a ham sandwich from Mimsy's, the establishment that had provided him with complete satiation on his first day in the city.

The other light snapped into his eyes. Because his pupils had been fully dilated by virtue of the darkness, his retinas felt as if they were on fire. In a swirl of concentric halos, Joe could make out the form of man standing behind the flashlight. He was pretty sure that the figure carried the stature of Kevin Gatz.

"Well, well, well," Kevin said.

Joe remained silent. He was only interested in knowing where Kevin would go after offering his clichéd preamble.

"You probably think this is a little extreme, don't you?" Kevin asked.

"What is this?"

"Just a little protection of our investment. I know it might be viewed as somewhat draconian, but this is intended to have precautionary benefits for you as well."

"How so?" Joe asked.

Joe decided to see if he could stand. He used his arms to initiate the act, and he made it to his feet. He couldn't help the slight wobbliness that accompanied the sudden rush of blood to his head.

"Well, Mr. Smith, the word is out on you. You have been deemed to be formidable, and that tends to make the other wards a little nervous. Because of this, it would not be strange for someone to wish you harm. It would be nothing overt, of course. But, there have been incidences in the past where a food-borne illness has befallen a driver just before the race. Often these circumstances are labeled as merely coincidental, but personally I believe that not to be the case. The possibility of sabotage is everywhere when victory is uncertain."

Joe took a step toward the light, and Kevin jumped back in response.

"You don't trust the integrity of your enclosure, Kevin?"

"I'm sure it's sound. It took them awhile to gather the materials and construct it. In fact, why don't you test whether it is possible to compromise it," Kevin said.

Joe walked over to the section of the chain link that appeared to be a door. Three chains, each supporting a separate lock, were looped around the supports.

"This looks pretty tight, Kev," Joe said.

"You will be let out for practice and the race, but all of your other time will be spent in the coziness of these confines."

Joe felt a rare instance of panic creeping upon him. He knew that if they were letting him out, they must have a high degree of confidence that he would willingly return to this ersatz cell. And that was the causal element that immediately gripped him with fear.

They must have created their leverage by using something that would expose his vulnerability. He swiftly went through all of the possibilities, but sadly, he knew in his heart there was only one. The realization of this caused his balance, once again, to become undermined. This time it wasn't caused by the metabolic degradation of whatever preparation they had used to knock him out. He struggled to find a place to stabilize himself and just made it back to the edge of the bed before his legs gave way.

Kevin snapped the light off.

"Fuck, we gave you too much," Kevin said, equating Joe's unsteadiness with his belief that there remained a lingering titer of the drug in his bloodstream.

Before Kevin could invoke a litany of curses aimed at the apothecary who had prepared the sedative, Joe regained his sense of footing and sprung out for the limits of the cage.

"Where is she?" he screamed.

Kevin knew that Joe was bright, but he was utterly amazed that he had put it together so quickly.

"She's safe," Kevin said calmly.

"I swear if you hurt her, I will kill you. And it will not be quick, Kevin. I will make you suffer far worse than any of the nightmares that your sick brain creates."

Kevin nodded, but Joe could see behind his eyes that the threat had made an impact.

"Nothing's going to happen to her if you do what you were hired to do. All of these other distractions—your dalliance with her, this whole fixation on some mythical Redeemer—are counterproductive to our goals. This is why we had to do this. We didn't want to, but you drove us to it. You are responsible for this, Mr. Smith. Not us."

The door opened again, and Lon entered. With light from the hall providing the illumination, he took the temperature of the fever in the room, saw a smug Kevin squared off against a supremely pissed-off Joe, and assessed that he had timed his entrance perfectly.

"Kevin? Go fetch Mr. Smith's breakfast," Lon said in a neutral tone.

As Kevin departed, Lon also banished the kid guard for the moment. The door closed again on the kid's exit, and the darkness returned.

"I'm sorry it had to come to this, Mr. Smith," Lon said.

"You didn't need to do this, Lon."

"Oh, I beg to differ. Where were you headed yesterday evening with the concealed weapon that we found on your person? Do you realize the repercussions that we would have had to endure should you have been successful in committing murder?"

"Are you ready for the repercussions associated with a couple of thousand people in your city dying?"

"That's not going to happen. Thank God Billy and Kevin were able to stop you. Do you know how bad that would look? That we were the responsible party involved in bringing a murderer into our paradise? Our ward would have been disgraced. You put the wellbeing of my family at risk, Joe."

"Your ward? Your family? You mean you, don't you? You don't care about anything else but yourself, Lon. Your family, your city, these are not things you consider priorities. If you did, you would heed my warning. I have no agenda here, no reason to fabricate anything."

"Well, now you are insulting me, Mr. Smith."

Joe's eyes were adjusting again to the absence of light. He began to make out the face of Lon Brassey through steel cage as the nigrescence abated. Was that a self-satisfied smile on his face?

"Have you ever come face-to-face with a Redeemer, Mr. Brassey?" Joe asked.

"Can't say that I have."

"There is no quarter given for the human experience. One is not viewed as anything other than chattel to them. There is nothing resembling empathy. They kill, and they don't give a shit if they die in the process."

"Sounds ominous. I'm certainly glad that I and mine live within the sanctuary of these walls."

"How can I convince you that this threat is real?"

"You obviously can't, so why don't we just table the whole issue until after the race tomorrow. You'll produce your heroic effort, we'll be victorious, and everything will return to normal."

"If normal is blood and body parts strewn about your city."

"Oh, for godsakes, don't be so dramatic. I'm curious: Have you ever been diagnosed as suffering from paranoid delusions?

Joe just stared at the face of this superficial being. Lon had really convinced himself over time that everything he believed was right. Any new information or knowledge that he acquired rarely altered the basic nature of the previously held opinion. Joe moved back to the bed and sat.

"Look, Joe, it is fewer than thirty hours from now that all of this will be over. Think about your girl," Lon said.

"I've already informed Kevin that if anything happens to her, I will be as merciless as any Redeemer," Joe replied calmly.

"Who do you think we are? We're civilized men, Joe. The only thing that is going to happen is that you are going to kick ass in the race. Now, Kevin will be here soon with your breakfast, then a group will escort you over to Frank and Claudia's, and you will get on with your final practice day. It should be exciting for you. The gates go up today."

With that, Lon exited the room. Joe rose, walked to the perimeter of his cell, grabbed handfuls of the steel wire mesh, and tried to lift the structure from its moorings. The workers had done their job well. The cage did not move a millimeter from its previous position—the six-inch bolts drilled into the floor would not allow it to yield at all.

FIFTY

JOHN FOUND THE apartment manager out behind the building smoking tobacco from an antique meerschaum pipe. As he neared, he noticed that there was a relief carving on the bowl of the pipe—two entangled asps trying to bite the other's head off. Perfect.

"Hey," John said.

"Here and gone, kid," the manager said as he removed the pipe from his mouth, tamped down the leaves of tobacco with his index finger, and struck a match.

John wondered what that statement meant. Had Joe been successful?

"I'm assuming you're referring to the disposition of Clarence Rigney," John said.

"Disposition? I don't even know what that word means. You sure talk funny, kid. But fine, I dispose he's out practicing now. Big day tomorrow, am I right?"

"Practicing?"

"Yeah, your friend—Mr. Rigney or whatever the hell you call him—is now driving for Mustang. Left here last night."

Now John was really confused. If this scumbag had seen Udo leave last night, then Joe had either never gotten to him or had somehow missed the opportunity. He wasn't even entertaining the alternative— that the battle had been fought and Joe was upstairs bleeding out on the floor of the apartment.

"What about the others?"

"You mean the paying tenants?"

John knew that the manager was implying that the others had achieved legitimacy and did not merit an outsider's scrutiny.

"Are they still living here?" John asked.

"Why wouldn't they be?"

John could only nod to the rhetorical question with an expression of amorphous concern and the realization that his narrative required revision. Seeing the manager reload the pipe, he knew he had a couple of minutes inside the building before this prick would return to his desk to idle away the rest of the day.

"Okay, thanks for your help," John said before slipping inside.

He went straight for the manager's office in hopes that he could lay his hands on a passkey or something else that might allow him entry into the room on the twenty-second floor. All he could come up with was the pipe utility tool that the manager had left behind. Its absence had created the condition that caused the manager to tamp down the tobacco with his fingers.

Exploiting his expertise with sleight of hand, John palmed the chrome instrument, waded through the sea of loitering residents, and headed for the elevators.

On the ride up, he began to get nervous. He had never examined the locking mechanisms on doors before and had no idea if they were mechanical or electronic. The pipe tool was not likely to be utile in either case, and he started to think that his mission was sunk before it had ever begun.

As the elevator car ascended and deposited other passengers on the various landings, he adjusted the parameters of his operation. Where before he wanted to enter the room and either gather intelligence or—in some crazy hero fantasy—create a confrontation with the occupants, he now just wanted confirmation that Joe had not been killed or maimed within the confines of the sub-divided space.

The lighted indicators that signified the floors no longer functioned, so the only way to determine the level was to look for the large spray painted number on the interior wall opposite the elevator doors. He was alone in the car when the doors slammed open and the number twenty-two—the twin digits slightly offset with the right numeral decidedly lower than the left—stared back at him. He hesitated just long enough that the doors began to close. He thrust his leg into the decreasing gap, pried open the insistent jaws, and tumbled out into the hallway. The horizontal guillotine snapped shut behind him, and he heard the car begin its plunge back to ground level.

As he approached the room at the end of the hall, he noted the types of locks that the other apartment doors sported. All were of varying types; he knew that his hypothesis that a passkey might have existed was sure to remain unproved.

At Udo's door, he listened for the indication of any movement inside. Did he hear footsteps? A quick examination of the lock left him crestfallen—he had no idea how to breech it. He had come to another cul-de-sac.

He stood in the hallway facing the door fully certain that his only option available was an unobtrusive exit. At the precise moment that his brain had instructed his legs to turn and head back to the elevator, he reached out with his balled-up fist and knocked four times on the solid wood.

"Who is it?" a voice asked from inside.

John's thought processes had not caught up to his physical ad-lib, and he fumbled out an unintelligible response.

"Who is it?" the voice asked again.

John was choking; he had lost any ability to riff. The door swung open quickly, and the man standing in the threshold had a scowl on his face.

"What?" the man barked.

John mumbled something about being at the wrong door, but in the moments where the room was exposed, he saw nothing like a dead body in the immediate environs. From what he could tell, the main room contained nothing but a table, a chair, and four mattresses on the floor. He whispered something along the lines of an apology as the door slammed in his face.

Until he had more information, Joe was willing to accede to Lon's prescribed protocol. He allowed himself to be escorted to the mechanic's shop by a group of henchmen he had never met before. He gave every indication that he was intimidated by this force and would give them no trouble whatsoever.

Frank was mildly surprised by the show of force, but protecting a ward's pilot on the eve of the event was part of the normal procedure. He had no idea—and Joe did not inform him—that the platoon's job description was not solely focused on repelling outside threats. Frank and Claudia would not know at this point that the troops were there to make sure that Joe followed every instruction that had been handed down by the captain.

As the morning practice wore on, he only had a handful of instances where his mounting concern about Cassandra crested to the point that he lost his concentration. The results were exemplified by a couple of bad turns, and one too many ill-timed shifts.

Frank wasn't worried about the occasional lapses. The previous day had been so glorious that he had expected some regression to occur during the morning session.

"Look who's up ahead," Frank said at some point during their tour.

Joe could see another car taking the oncoming turn with the wrong attitude.

"Who's that?" Joe asked.

"It's the goddamn Mustang," Frank said.

They both watched the driver take the curve with a late apex. It was a technique that would likely result in the car having to slow substantially to make it through the corner.

"You think he's just screwing around for our benefit?" Joe asked.

"Has to be. Roger Burnham is a pretty fine pilot. Nothing spectacular, mind you, but real solid. Catch up to them," Frank exhorted.

Joe laid a heavy foot to the pedal and the 'Cuda made up ground quickly. As he approached the same right-hand curve, he shifted down, swung out to the extreme left side of the road, touched the brakes briefly, and whipped the steering wheel to the right. He then drifted past the corner and drew a dangerously close line to the curb before stomping on the throttle, rocketing to the other side of the street, and eventually shifting into fourth gear. In the couple of seconds it took to accomplish that, they closed to within ten yards of the Mustang.

"Let's see if Roger wants to play," Frank said.

Joe blew past the other car not knowing what to expect. Frank was confident there would be some type of reaction from the Mustang, and that they might bend the rules a little by jousting along the long stretch of straight road that would lead them onto Cass Avenue and the gates.

"Jesus Christ."

"What?" Joe asked.

"That wasn't Roger Burnham."

"Who was it?"

"Beats the shit out of me. Must be one of their mechanics shaking the thing out."

Joe never gave the anomaly another thought. There were so many other things to consider, and the identity of the man practicing in the Mustang car was not even a faint blip on his radar.

They made a decent turn onto Cass Avenue and Joe got his first look at the gates, a quarter of a mile away. Coming out of the turn he was certain that they must be at their most closed position; the opening appeared extremely narrow to him.

"They already have them closed?" Joe asked.

"What are you saying? They are at their widest—three car widths' worth."

As he closed in on the barrier, he knew Frank was telling the truth. The Barracuda passed through the barriers easily and at a good rate of speed, but he'd been so concerned about the maneuvers required to safely make it through that he failed to set up for the next turn—the harrowing route through the corner of First Street and Adams Avenue.

He entered the turn on too low a line. As he tried to execute the S pattern that would allow for the maximum amount of speed, he realized that he wasn't going to make it. There was no S to be had; he had squashed the two arcs into a straight line.

Instead of trying to make it through and possibly rolling the car in the process, he braked hard, turned, and angled for the low part of the bank. The bottom of the incline was only the option available to come to a complete stop while in transit of this obstacle. From there, he could crawl along the trough before trying to rise up the slope and get around the corner.

"What have we learned?" Frank asked with smile.

"If you don't take the high line, you're dead."

"Exactly."

———

It was the Redeemer named Kip who had answered the apartment door when John announced his arrival with the four knocks. Kip never thought anything other than the incident had been a mistake on the part of the visitor. He had not put John's face to the revelations from the manager that people were looking for Udo.

His partners, Ned and Jay, had already reported for work, but Kip had called in sick because he had been tasked by the apostle to handle a duty that Udo was now unable to do.

Kip was the member of the cell with the shortest tenure in Motor City, and Udo had taken that fact into account when he had given him the responsibility of meeting with the Redeemer command structure at their headquarters.

For the better part of the month, Redeemers—both seasoned and raw—had been pouring into the city of Hamtramck and its surroundings in preparation for an onslaught on Motor City. Word had been sent to every camp in the wilderness that Apostle Udo had infiltrated the Godless community, and the siren call to be part of the event could only be ignored by those who had no knowledge or appreciation for history.

As every single Redeemer had been taught, the most important episode in Redeemer lore—other than the rapture of the man himself—was the Mercyville massacre. If anyone of the perpetrators of that transcendent experience was still living, no one was aware of their existence, yet they lived on as icons of the highest order. Not a single believer wanted to go forward as a member of this movement without the mantle of being part of the carnage to come.

To coordinate planning and provide status updates, Udo had been sending coded messages using the extra-enclave work detail of Ned, Jay, and Kip as the delivery conduit. Today, on the eve of the invasion, Apostle Udo was scheduled to meet with one of the supreme commanders at a prearranged location to discuss the final plan. With Udo's new duties requiring that he be stationed elsewhere, Kip had been appointed as his proxy.

Kip had access to one of the small electric vehicles that the road department used to scout available pavement troves, and he exited the confines of Motor City through the river gate a good hour before the appointment time.

He would have to skirt the rough patches of road that had already been harvested while making his way in a counter-clockwise fashion around the outer walls of the city.

To the security personnel who walked the top of the earthen perimeter, he was just a city employee sacrificing his own self-interest (and perhaps his health) for the purpose of doing his job.

At the point that was denoted the northern-most part of the enclave, Kip veered off and headed for the outskirts of Hamtramck. The meeting would take place at the ruins of the old Cadillac assembly facility; beyond the exchange of schedules there would be a request from Kip for the addition of some material that had not been previously discussed.

After an opening explanation detailing the reasons for Udo's absence, Kip asked the commander if the order could be filled. Kip's petition was for a reasonable quantity of either C-4 or PETN—high explosive substances that Udo felt could be used to aid the effort from the inside.

The commander had never met Kip—did not know him from Adam—and initially scoffed at the proposal. Kip handed the commander a private coded missive from Udo. A minion translated the numerical sequences using *The New Testament for Now* cipher system and returned the note to the commander.

All present could see the sudden appearance of tremors in the hand of the plebe as he presented the decoded message to his superior. All assumed it was because he had been privy to the content of the now-realized memo and that the experience had somehow altered his behavior.

It took the commander many moments to digest the designs of the text. It wasn't a short note. He reread the communiqué multiple times to make sure that he understood the thrust of Udo's intentions.

When Kip left the meeting and embarked upon his return to Motor City, he was carrying a package that had been wedged into the spare-tire container. It held thirty pounds of plastic explosive and the necessary detonation accoutrements. He had no clue as to the circumstances with which they would be used. All he cared about was staying on the smoothest parts of the rutted track he was traveling lest he become the first casualty of the battle on the eve of its commencement.

FIFTY-ONE

Tᴵᴹ Rɪᴢᴢᴏ ᴡᴀꜱ understandably nervous. The Tigers captain's emotional barometer normally functioned within strict limits—a stable baseline that very rarely ever indicated either despair or excitement.

This was similar to the way his ward was perceived by the others in the city—a non-entity, an afterthought, or a big bucket of gray. But in the last twenty-four hours, his forlorn ward was being asked to get into the game. And a rusty and stiff Tim Rizzo was more than a little freaked out that his number was being called inside the huddle.

The meeting with Impala earlier in the week had been a high point. It had been nearly thirteen years since anyone from any of the other eight had ventured to talk to them. It was a crack in the door that might possibly allow them to get back their status as equals. The way Tim figured it at the time, they would do whatever Impala needed this year, help someone else next year, and eventually find their way back into the circle. It might take a decade, but at least it was a start; they had been out in the cold for too damn long.

The eventual agreement that Tim struck with Lon was that they would be responsible for a solitary undertaking. They were to get ahead of the Mustang entrant and do everything to keep Impala's enemy boxed in for the entire race. The Tigers had been awarded a decent car, the '69 Impala SS. Lon had said something about the whole thing being divinatory given that their entrant shared the same name as the ward that was providing their salvation.

"If need be, run the motherfucker off the road," Kevin Gatz had said at the close of the negotiation.

Of course, Tim knew that any overt action like that would put them back in the cooler for real.

Tim certainly hoped his driver would be able to complete the task that Impala demanded, though he would have to do it while fending off the hateful who would be trying to do the same thing to them. That happened every year and was just the reality of being a Tiger, but maybe, just maybe, the sun was finally going to rise on them again.

Tim had fewer than twenty-four hours to enjoy the intoxicating effects of this high of hopefulness.

When Leo Rascone and his two blonde goons knocked on the Tigers' clubhouse door, Tim and his lieutenants were in the middle of briefing their driver, Ricky Longacre, on the narrow parameters associated with his duties as prescribed by the Impala captain. Tim only accepted Leo's invitation for a private meeting at the lawyer's office because he had to. Saying no to anyone was impossible and either implied reckless disrespect or confirmation that something nefarious was in play.

Leo Rascone had not specified the names of the attendees of the secret conference, and when they were revealed on Tim's arrival to be Titus O'Keefe and Tom Cobble, it was if he had been snake bit by a black mamba. He could feel the toxins flowing through his veins, a river of poison intent on silencing his heart.

Tim Rizzo could conjure the essence of what he was going to be asked to do by Titus from the moment the handshake terminated. The realization that he had no way out of this situation saddened him to no end.

He obviously couldn't tell the Mustang officials that he had already struck a deal with their adversaries, and he couldn't say no when they made a nearly identical offer to him to have his driver intentionally hinder Impala. For the record, there was no offer of compensation for carrying out the requested tasks. The currency being spent here was of the relationship type—just having anyone speak to them was worth all of the credits that ebbed and flowed through the city's monetary system.

There was one twist, however. With the loss of Roger Burnham, the odds of Mustang being competitive had dramatically decreased. Titus intimated that both Mustang and the Tigers would be attempting to accomplish the same result—keep Impala from winning—and that Mustang, unless a miracle was in the offing, would not concern itself with trying to achieve victory.

All Tim Rizzo could do was smile and say he would attempt to do his best. The way he saw it, he was supremely fucked no matter what. He couldn't help them both. He couldn't even fake it.

The assessments would be brutal on both sides, and the Tigers would be back where they started. In all likelihood, whatever the outcome, they would end up suffering an even greater undermining of the already shaky perch they currently teetered upon.

Lon and Kevin's deal-making tour took them to all of the wards except their rivals, and in the end the best arrangements they could make were nowhere near anything that suggested the existence of any rock-solid compacts.

DeVille was their natural ally, and they offered to do whatever they could but only if it didn't conflict with their own self-interest. They had a marginal car, the Gran Torino—a hulking boat of a vehicle with a huge fuel-sucking engine—but they believed that if they didn't run out of gas they could be there at the end.

As the clock continued to tick toward the start of the race, Lon and Kevin found that every ward seemed to think that Impala had a reasonable shot at claiming the crown and were wary about dealing with anyone who wasn't personally linked to either their own history or their own needs. No one, save the Red Wings, was looking for just a payday should Impala succeed. They all thought they had a chance to win themselves.

The justification for Lon and Kevin being consistently rebuffed was based on the belief that they had broken some unwritten rule, namely that they had brought in a professional driver. The expressions of resentment from the others were apparent in every conversation they arranged.

Every other ward had heard of Joe Smith's exploits, be it his dynamic simulator sessions or the gravity-defying technique he employed during the flag-pulling rehearsal.

When approached, most of the captains opened the discussion with a question along the lines of, "You got Superman behind the wheel, what do you need us for?" The negotiations usually went downhill soon after and were peppered with unrealistic demands that the Impala contingent had no interest in entertaining.

When all was said and done, Lon, Kevin, and Billy ended up feeling a sense of accomplishment anyway. To celebrate the closing of their first-ever deal-making period—as weak as it was—they opened a bottle of sixty-year-old Scotch in the anteroom of Lon's office at the clubhouse.

The prerace dinner would be held downstairs in a couple of hours, but for now they would sip from their crystal glasses and bullshit each other that they were royalty and couldn't lose.

No one mentioned anything about the incarceration or the kidnapping, and no one brought up their previously quoted treatise that stated that if they lose, they win. They had come a long way from that type of thinking.

Joe finished off the afternoon's practice session with a flourish, making multiple passes through the gates at their most closed position and tracing expert lines through the mocked-up turn at First and Adams.

As he and Frank pulled up to the barriers, two large contingents of men—the escort detail for Joe and fifteen strong Impalans that Claudia had called in to push the car back home—descended on them. Always worried about fuel consumption, she had made a declarative decision that there was no more to be wasted. They had used up all of their stash plus some of their allotment for this year's race. Frank knew that they had plenty to get through the race, but Claudia was not willing to flirt with the possibility that the gas tank might run dry at the most crucial moment.

The men of Impala eyed Joe's security detail with looks of fascination and overall wonderment. To a person, they had no clue as to their actual use, but the whole show of force was impressive and seemed to elevate the stature of the man who had been selected by their captain to represent them.

For his part, Joe played along just like he said he would. He exited the car to a rousing round of applause and folded into the group of keepers as if it were normal. The only time he deviated from his impersonation of an obedient soul was when an insistent John tried to break through the phalanx. While a small group surrounded Joe, the others prepared to repel the possible threat.

"It's the captain's son, you guys," Joe declared.

Only after one of the members of the detail admitted that he saw a resemblance between their boss and the kid was John permitted to approach their charge.

Joe knew that some of the Mugwumps who had been hired for this gig probably had some experience in intelligence, so he immediately curtailed John from asking any questions about the situation. John had obviously not been briefed on any of this.

Conversely, though he harbored a monologue's worth of pertinent information himself, John knew better than to open his mouth and spill anything that might be absorbed and later regurgitated by this disparate clique of unknowns.

So they strode along destined for their neighborhood and engaged in conversation that could not be considered the slightest bit controversial.

When they came upon Cass Park and the unit continued on a path toward the clubhouse and not the Brassey townhouse, John could no longer bear his sense of discomfiture.

"Where are we going?" John asked Joe.

"Back to the clubhouse. I'm being sequestered," Joe said nonchalantly.

"Why?"

"I was told it was tradition," Joe said pointedly.

John got the inference that Joe was being kept against his will. Why hadn't he heard any rumors about this? After the whole affair at the Mugwump apartment building, he'd spent the better part of the day at the clubhouse setting up for the dinner, and no one had said anything about them holding their driver on the premises.

"Where are you staying?" John asked.

"A room close to the ballroom," Joe informed him.

"Well, maybe I'll see you later," John said.

"Yeah," Joe said.

When they had reached the limits of the park, John veered off toward his home. He knew that he had to arrive at the big dinner with his family in a ceremonial fashion, but maybe once everyone got drunk, he could slip away and get to the bottom of all the shit that was going down.

———

The expansive back patio and the adjoining outdoor area sparkled from the illumination of over a thousand candles. When Holly was in preschool, she had pronounced the experience akin to traveling to the stars for an up-close view.

Because the taper wicks only produced halos of light and not directed incandescence, there was always a certain muted tone to the annual Impala dinner on the race's eve.

To Karen, it was her favorite night of the year. Everyone was at his or her most polite and civil, and she honestly believed that it had something to do with the absence of any fluorescence.

As always, the food was spectacular. There was aged Alberta steer, purple potatoes from Saskatchewan, and bitter greens that had their origins from somewhere out in the far west. There was champagne and red wine from the ward's cellar. This had been stocked during Impala's formation and still retained nearly a hundred years' worth of inventory. There was aged Scotch whiskey, rye whiskey, and bottles of chilled Russian vodka. And there were homemade ice cream sundaes for dessert. For some of the children, the dinner in July was like a second Christmas, and sleep did not come easily for the little ones on the night before the gala.

John sat on the dais with his family and counted the minutes until he could reasonably disappear for a longer time than it would take to visit the bathroom. He had already withstood the constant parade of ass-kissers that queued up to clink their glasses with his father, a perennial preamble to the meal.

When the food had been consumed, it was time for his father to make the ceremonial prerace toast. John knew that his father saw this as the most important experience of his life to date.

Glasses began to clink as silver met crystal. John saw his mother and sister take on the miens of anticipatory tension by immediately reaching for their wine glasses at exactly the same time and knocking back a substantial gulp.

John did the same with his requisite water. He had been forbidden from imbibing any alcohol due to the fact that he was believed to be on a medication that carried a contraindication with any sort of firewater. When he thought about that imposed prohibition—considering that he hadn't taken a single pill in over four years—he began to laugh at the absurdity. It was the wrong time to express any hilarity. His father snapped his head around and attempted to stare him into silence.

John wanted to scream obscenities at him. He wanted the entire ward to know what they had elected—this man who would easily qualify this moment as the pinnacle of his existence. All of the other milestones—his marriage to a saint, the birth of his children—all paled for him in comparison to the moment he was about to have.

Lon rose to a hearty round of applause.

"Thank you so much," Lon began. "I hope that is not just for me—there are so many more deserving than myself. Once again, the meal was terrific, and we have to thank Kerry Whitehead for doing another outstanding job. I also would like to express my gratitude to the youngsters that worked so hard this morning decorating. You did the best job ever, just beautiful. I'd also like to thank and praise my trusted lieutenants, Kevin Gatz and Billy Klock, for their yeoman efforts in carrying out my orders."

John looked down the table at the two minions. They were nodding as if they were deserving of any and all recognition. John thought that Billy must have been coming down with a cold because when he heard him speak earlier, he seemed only to be able to converse in a raspy whisper.

"Now, let's raise a glass to all that I've mentioned, and if I've forgotten anyone, I am heartily sorry," Lon said.

Glasses were held to the sky and everyone had a drink. John noticed Frank and Claudia sitting at a nearby table. They both sported looks of distracted impatience. They had a little over twelve hours before they had to hang their asses on the line, and John reckoned that the time couldn't come soon enough for them. The dinner was a divergence from their true desires: more time to tinker with the car. Lon's omission of their contribution was to be expected by them, and John didn't think the two gave a rat's penis about whether they deserved to be acknowledged or not.

"This has been an exciting year by any metric. We've got a killer car, a guy who knows how to drive it, and all the hope in the world. No matter what happens tomorrow—and I truly believe that we will be victorious—we have many things to be thankful for. Not the least of which is that we live in Impala, the absolute envy of all who dwell here in Motor City."

A volcanic eructation of applause and whistles pierced the air, stirring the ghosts of their predecessors who had spent their fortunes and sweat producing their neighborhood. The assembled knew that it was high time that they bring the glory back to the most deserving.

That was it for Lon's speech. John knew that Lon had a sense of showmanship by going out on high note. There was more to be said, more time to bathe in the glow of the spotlight, but his father was obviously too savvy for that. Besides, it was ice cream time, and the kids were already falling over the cliff of excitement into bug-eyed delirium.

It took another full hour for John to feel comfortable enough to make his exit. He knew that a devolution of the formality of the event had to take place before gender and age began to segregate.

Finally, the men migrated to the far wall of the property so they could juggle their spewed optimism with an increased ingestion of booze. The women found solace in the lobby inside and gabbed about their men and their children. The children played games revolving around terms like "it" and "water fowl," and the adolescent youth congregated throughout various levels of the clubhouse for short sessions of squaring off against each other in playful bouts or kissing and petting in the darkness of the labyrinthine corridors.

John bid goodbye to his parents as the conclaves formed, and he slipped away into the stairwell. It took him awhile to locate the room that was housing Joe, and he would have not found it if he hadn't witnessed two members of the security detail ravenously eating steak and ice cream while they parked their fat asses in front of one of the doors at the very end of the basement hallway.

"You enjoying the food?" John asked affably.

"It's amazing," the smaller of the two said, continuing to shovel the mess into his mouth in sudden fear that this captain's son might snatch it away from him.

"I'm sure there's more if you want seconds," John said.

"Really?" the other one asked.

"Sure, why not? You've earned it."

The two guards checked in with each other to confirm that they had definitely done what was asked of them and the kid's appraisal was right, meet, and salutary.

"I'm going to head inside and talk to Joe," John said.

Before either of them could react to John's affirmation, he reached for the door handle. It was locked. The shock of that simple fact suddenly brought on a realization that Joe wasn't being guarded for his safety, but was being held against his will.

"Do you have the key?" John asked.

"No," they answered simultaneously.

"Who does?"

The both shrugged at the same time.

John raced back up the stairs, trying to open his mind, hoping to imagine some kind of plan of action that he hadn't given himself time to contemplate yet. His primary tactic would have been to walk over to Kevin Gatz, punch him in the face, and rifle through his pockets for the key. How could they do this? This guy was on their side!

As he approached a very select group that included Kevin, Billy, and some of their cronies, he realized he was going to have to dispense with anything that smacked of directness. There wasn't a single member of the Impala hierarchy that would be able to find an appropriate context for his displaying violence toward the lieutenant. These people had no idea as to the extent of his relationship with Joe. They did not know half of what he knew, and the other half they didn't have the sense to believe.

He veered off from his direct course and searched for Frank and Claudia. He found them alone at their original table.

"I need your help," John asked.

Four minutes later they were back downstairs fitting the key into the lock. John had briefed Frank and Claudia on a need-to-know basis. He had told them that Joe was being held in the ballroom's green room by the paranoid Kevin and asked them if they could help him get access by telling Kevin they had to talk to Joe to discuss race strategy.

As shocked as Frank and Claudia were to hear that their driver was a prisoner, they didn't need to ask any other questions. Claudia just marched over to Kevin's group of revelers and asked for the key.

Alcohol might have played a factor in Kevin's easy capitulation— that or he really believed that Claudia's demand for a scheming session with their driver was required. Kevin never once questioned how she knew that they were keeping Joe veiled behind a locked door. Only a very few Impalans were privy to that knowledge. Either way, Kevin readily gave up the key, and Frank and Claudia hurriedly moved off to join John in the lobby.

The three entered to find the horror that Joe was not being held in a room, but in a chain-link cage.

"Goddammit!" John seethed.

Claudia was just as incensed.

"See if that key fits the padlocks," she said.

John made a move for the cell's door, but Joe stopped him.

"Don't waste your time. Think about it, John. Do you think a 150-year-old door key would work on those brand-new locks?" Joe asked rhetorically.

"Have you tried lifting the thing up from its base?" Frank asked.

"Yeah. It's sound. Now, everyone is just going to have to calm down here and work within the framework of what we've been given," Joe said.

His eyes sought out the two mechanics.

"I need to speak to John in private for a moment. Would you two be so kind as to allow us a couple of minutes? I would also appreciate if you could warn us should Kevin or anyone else wander down to check on me."

Frank and Claudia assented to his request and slipped back out the door.

Joe and John both began to speak first. Joe cut him off.

"There are things you don't know. Things I never told you because, well, I'm not sure that they were any of your business," Joe said.

"But you're locked in here because they think that you intend to kill Udo, right?" John asked.

"Partly. It's more complicated than that."

Before Joe could launch into his admission of the love affair with Cassandra, John blurted out, "He's driving for Mustang. Roger Burnham got hurt during the punch-out, and Titus O'Keefe designated Udo to take his place."

Joe took this new information like a haymaker to the chin. He stared at a spot on the floor as his brain sifted through the significance.

"That was why Frank couldn't figure out who was driving their car," he finally said.

"What?"

"I could have done it today," Joe said with resignation.

Joe turned and walked toward the bed. John tried to get things back on track.

"I went to the building. I knocked on the door of the apartment, and one of them answered. In the ten seconds that I had to look into the room, all I saw were four mattresses," John said.

"Three plus him," Joe said.

But John could tell that he seemed distracted; he seemed many moves beyond just the processing of this trivial information. At one point, Joe looked up at him, and he knew that this subject was in the process of being tabled. There was something more immediate that needed to be attended to.

"I need you to help me," Joe said.

"What can I do?"

Joe proceeded to tell him the other reason that John's father and his buddies had thrown Joe in the hole. He revealed in the most general way his relationship with Cassandra. John listened and tried not to react. The transgression—as he had been taught his whole life and had come to believe as canon—was on the order of a biblical betrayal.

Joe sensed that the kid's world had been significantly jostled, but he didn't have the time or the desire to try to explain his actions.

After laying out the how and the when for the boy in regards to his request for assistance, John let out a long extended exhalation. John knew he had to focus on the request and not his reaction to the backstory that was at the core of the cause of Joe's caging.

"Yeah, I can do what whatever you need," he assured Joe.

"I know you can.

FIFTY-TWO

THE NONES OF JULY[1]

PRIMA TO BETWEEN THE ROSTRA AND THE GRAECOSTASIS[2]

JOHN DID NOT shy away from a single ounce of the ton of responsibility that Joe had laid on him. He was ready to step up and take control of all the concerns that he knew were essentially out of Joe's hands. He felt edified that Joe gave little or no consideration to John's health—just the respect and confidence that occurs when one is viewed as an equal.

He now essentially functioned as Joe's avatar. The priority list had been established, and of paramount importance was securing the freedom of Cassandra.

From the moment that the task was handed to him, he had a pretty good inkling of where she was being kept. He didn't have definitive knowledge, and that precluded him from directly stating to Joe where he thought she was being held. There was a moment where he wanted to boast that he knew her location, but he had learned from his mentor that this would be an expression of ego and not pertinent to the job he had been asked to perform.

He discounted any probability that she was being kept in any of the rooms at the clubhouse. During this time of year, there was an extraordinary amount of activity at the facility. The prying eyes of the familiars or any Mugwump on the maintenance staff would easily notice the aberration.

The place of confinement would have to be in an environment where total control could be achieved. That line of thinking would

---

1   The nones of a month are a designation assigned to the time that corresponds to the first quarter moon. In July it is the seventh day of the month—eight days before the ides.

2   Specific designations of times of day in ancient Rome, "prima" being the start of the day, and "between the Rostra and the Graecostasis" referring roughly to the hour when the sun beamed down on the midway point between these two speaking platforms in and around the forum of ancient Rome.

remove possibilities such as the commercial areas around Woodward Avenue and possible safe houses in any of the other friendly wards. Somewhere in Mugwumpville was also not likely due to the dangers associated with the purchasable loyalties of the residents.

Whereas the security detail surrounding Joe was made up of Independents, John thought that would probably not be the case with those who were guarding the Mustang woman. Anyone who did not have clearance and was not bound—by birth or naturalization—to the ward's fealty could make a fortune with this type of information, or could bring an incumbency of shame or criminal charges against the perpetrators of this act.

It was still dark when John awoke from what could not be qualified as anything akin to sleep. It was more of a wrestling match with his consciousness than anything that smacked of rest. During the haze, he was jolted by the realization that he had only so much time and a lot of ground to cover before the race commenced, and yet, the timing of the various sequences was crucial to achieving success. Completing a task too early, too quickly, were issues he'd been told by Joe to be wary of. So he lay in that state of the in-between for what seemed like days, and conversely, like seconds.

Joe had told him that the timing of Cassandra's liberation was crucial. John agreed. Had he gone and rescued her the previous evening, his father would have had time to discover his treasonous act, and the dominoes that needed to fall after would have had to defy the laws of physics and jump the sudden gap that would be created by his grounding and/or punishment.

He got out of bed. He dressed quickly in much finer duds than was required, and he liberated a solar-powered flashlight from a charging station. He headed out into the darkness of the predawn morning and quickly trekked toward the far southwest of Impala. It was the area that had as its terminus the base of the earthen inner wall.

It was along this stretch of road that separated the buildings from the partition that he expected to find Cassandra's place of confinement.

All of the buildings were of old construction and had been left vacant to serve as a de facto barrier—a secondary element of separation between the main wall and the neighborhood. In the first days of the enclave's constitution, there was a fear that an internal rampart might be needed, but as the years passed, that initial paranoia abated. John knew that his father was the holder of the deeds for the entire measure of structures that stretched nearly the entire length of the Impala boundary.

John tracked the possible occupation by the smell of tobacco smoke that emanated from one of the windows of a building in the middle of the row. On the ground under the window, he found evidence of cigarette butts, ashes, and burned loose tobacco. An assay of the quantity and quality of the waste told him that it had been recently deposited and had been piling up for a least a couple of days.

The door that led into the structure was unlocked. He entered and climbed the two flights of stairs that took him to the landing that seemed consistent with the elevation of the window of interest.

At the outer door to the suite of offices, he knocked because there was no part of his ploy that involved just bursting in and retrieving the damsel. He waited patiently for the door to be answered. It creaked open slowly and exposed only a solitary eye in the millimeters of gap that was created.

"Hey," John said.

"What do you want?" the answerer asked.

"There's been a change in plans. My dad sent me over. We need to get her out of here."

"Who the hell are you?"

The door opened wider, and John could see into the room. The man at the door was someone he knew to be a friend of Kevin's, solidly built with a definitive hairline. There was another man loitering by the window—the smoker. He was shirtless and fit as well, though unfamiliar to John. John pegged both of them to be somewhere just north of thirty years old.

"The word has leaked out somehow that we're holding her, and my father is a little freaked out when it comes to any possible consequences, so he wants her moved out of the ward to a more neutral place," John explained.

The two men shared a look; their orders did not include anything that involved improvisation. She was to be held here until noon, then escorted back out to Woodward Avenue and released. That is all that they had been told. They did not know why she was being kept, and they did not know her affiliation.

Something struck John as a little odd. On the floor of the anteroom was just a single queen-size mattress with pillows on both sides of the bed. He found himself smiling inwardly and felt a momentary rush of fleeting respect for his father.

At least the man had the foresight to choose men to guard the woman who would not take advantage of the fact that she was an attractive female. These men were a couple, and they were chosen for this task because of that. The old man had thought of everything.

"You know who I am, don't you?"

"Yeah, you're the captain's kid," the one by the window answered.

"How else would I know that you were here if my father hadn't told me?"

They pondered that one for a beat, but they were naturally suspicious, and their uncertainty informed them that the kid's word was just not going to be enough.

"We don't have a lot of time here. I can run and go get Kevin Gatz or my dad and bring them back here so they can explain it to your face. I think you'd then be satisfied that I'm being truthful, but they would be pissed off that you didn't give me the credibility that I deserve," John said.

They shared another look, but they were still not ready to make a decision.

"There are other things that need to be dealt with here, namely how we get her to understand our motivations for detaining her and seeing if we can find a way to get her to understand that all of this is recompense for a relationship that is considered to be taboo in our society," John said pointedly.

All of this was new information to them, and it proved that the kid knew way more about the details of the situation than they did. Also, the metaphorical nature of John's explanation was not lost on the two of them. There was no implied threat hurled at them in John's statement, just the arrows of reality that they had to deal with every day. Motor City's attitude toward their orientation was one of benign neglect, but they felt the subtle discrimination most of the time and made no effort to call attention to themselves. They knew that people saw them, and others like them, as different. Whatever advances society had made in regards to acceptance had still not gone through complete osmosis within these walls. John felt that their effort to stonewall him was showing some cracks, so he asserted himself.

"I'm going to talk to her now," he said.

John moved toward one of the inner doors, and the two men did not stop him.

She was asleep. John could see that she had been bound and that a strip of linen covered her mouth. He nudged her awake and began to speak quickly in Mandarin.

"Ni shuo zhong ma?," he asked.

She nodded that she understood Chinese, and John delicately reached down and removed the gag. He evoked the name of her boyfriend and told her they were getting out of there.

"Joe song wo. Wo yao dai ni likai zheli," John said as he untied her restraints. "Wo shi John," (I am John).

"Wo zhidao ni shi shui," (I know who you are) she replied.

The two men suddenly appeared at the door.

"You guys should hang out here in case Kevin needs you," John said.

"I think you better bring him down here to authorize this. He told us that under no circumstances . . ." the smoker started to say.

"Look, I am not going to argue with you. We're going," John emphatically stated.

He grabbed Cassandra by the elbow and began walking straight at them. It was a short game of chicken, as both cleared the door and allowed John and Cassandra to pass.

"I'll tell my dad that you guys did a great job. And wait here; I'm sure there'll be something else they'll need you for later in the morning," he said as they passed through the anteroom and entered the stairwell.

They were not followed.

The cover of darkness and their hopes that most of the ward members were still sleeping off the previous night's activities emboldened them as they traveled northwest toward the boundary line of the Impala neighborhood. During their journey, John filled Cassandra in on the details of all of the related topics that Joe had determined were the most important.

Nearly every piece of information was new to her. She had not known of Joe's discovery of the Redeemer's presence; she had not known that he'd been incarcerated himself; and she had not known why—and by whom—she had been kidnapped. It was only after her freedom had been gained that she knew that it was Impala that had taken her. For the longest time, she assumed it was someone from her own ward and that the strategy had been based on a misguided attempt by that prick Titus O'Keefe to weaken Joe by threatening to hurt her if he didn't agree to perform poorly in the race.

Many questions that she had been wrestling with suddenly had answers, and her first response was to chastise herself for initially viewing them only in a negative context. Joe had not meant to be dismissive the night that he came to the museum and asked for the lawyer's name and address. He was trying to find out the whereabouts of the threat that could doom them all.

John continued to talk and did not stop until they had passed through the entire district. He delivered her to the café and told her that she should hide until he came for her later in the morning. He reminded her that though they had been successful thus far in thwarting Impala's interests in her, there were elements within her own ward that might try to use her to influence the outcome of the race.

She agreed to stay put, though the next few hours were sure to be pregnant with an anxiety unlike any she had ever experienced.

John's next task was to attempt to gather as many allies as possible to help him spread the word of the impending threat. This part was going to be the hardest of his duties, and it caused him to confront the reality that the pool that he could draw from was small. He did not really have a single person—other than Joe—that he could call a true friend. There had been Rebecca at one time, but that was over.

He chose Mr. Fedder, his former homeroom teacher, as his initial contact. Though they had been non-conversant since Mr. Fedder warned him to stay away from Rebecca, John felt that they had a connection from their previous encounters that bespoke a shared sense of duty and ethics. He also saw advantages that could be gained by the exploitation of Mr. Fedder's age and the vast amount of people that he knew. He had been teaching at the school for fifteen years, and not only the students, but also their parents, had always considered him as approachable.

It was not far from the café to Mr. Fedder's townhouse, and John ran the quarter mile just as the sun began to fire up the sky to the west.

Mr. Fedder took awhile to answer the door, and oddly, his initial response to John was one of non-recognition. John's heart sank with the realization that he had somehow created the image that this man was fond of him, remembered his travails, and was interested in where he was headed in life.

Mr. Fedder allowed him into his house but still did not seem to know who he was. He called upstairs to his wife or girlfriend—John really didn't know much about his personal life—that everything was copasetic before grabbing a pair of glasses from the counter in the kitchen.

"Jesus Christ. It's you, John. What are you doing here?" Mr. Fedder asked once he could see.

"I need your help."

"What time is it?"

"Early."

"What's up? No, don't tell me this is about Rebecca."

"No, Mr. Fedder. I heeded your advice. I haven't spoken to her since we talked," John said.

Mr. Fedder nodded. He felt venerated that the boy had taken to his counsel.

"You know me not to be anything less than truthful, right?" John asked.

"I suppose."

"There is a shit storm about to hit Motor City today. And I need your help to try to see how much we can limit the damage."

"Did you say 'shit storm'?"

"Sorry, sir, I didn't mean to be vulgar."

"It's not that, I just haven't heard that term in a while. So spill it, son."

John gave him the lowdown. As Mr. Fedder absorbed each paragraph of his speech, the elder man became more and more animated. He had a rash of questions that John could not answer. He wanted to know details that might help him know the timing, or give him a hint to the method, but these were not things that John knew—things that not even Joe knew.

"You are absolutely, positively sure about this?" Mr. Fedder asked.

"Yes, sir. I consider the source of this information impeccable. This is going to happen, sir. My friend will try and stop it, but there are so many variables, and many, many people could get hurt."

Okay, John, what do you need from me?" Mr. Fedder asked.

FIFTY-THREE

The first item on the agenda of every race day was the blessing of the driver and the vehicle at the ward's chapel. Having to attend the event was the reason that John had dressed up before he set out to retrieve Cassandra.

By the time John arrived, minders had already pushed the car into the church. He found his place alongside his family in the most forward pew. Across the aisle, he caught a glimpse of Joe surrounded by Kevin, Billy, and a small contingent from his security force. He offered a subtle signal of two fingers traversing the length of his horizontally positioned thighs to signify that Cassandra had been liberated.

Joe did not immediately acknowledge that he understood. He reached into the shelf in front of him and idly pulled out the missal.

"Where were you this morning, honey?" John's mother asked.

The question startled John, as he was focused on duplicating Joe's action and getting his hands on a similar missal that rested in the nook just in front of him.

"I was meeting some of the boys that helped decorate yesterday. We were going to try and do something special over at the stadium, but we ran out of time."

His mother smiled. Holly was looking at him with a queer eye. He silently communicated to her that she should accept whatever he said. It was a simple expression of sibling code, therefore sacrosanct. Holly went back to checking out the crowd. So few of her friends were in attendance—casualties of the previous evening's revelry, no doubt.

John finally got his hands on the missal and began to page through it. At the end of the book—between the plasticized cover and the page of acknowledgements—was a folded-up piece of paper. No one saw him palm the note before he replaced the missal in its wooden pocket.

He turned around and duplicated the actions of his sister. The turnout was as expected—full, but not SRO. One had only to scan the attendees to see that they were collectively made up of the people who had a reputation for temperance and restraint.

John's eyes found Jody Springer—his designated contestant in the pugil stick bout before his disqualification—a couple of rows back and to his right. Both of the punch-out participant's eyes were rimmed with black hematomata, and there was a recently sutured cut on the middle of his forehead. Jody was seated with four generations of the Springer clan including his grandmother, parents, wife, and his three children, all under the age of six.

That pretty much said it all to John. How could all that humanity be lost because of the stupidity of his old man and his bootlickers? It nearly motivated him to stand up and bellow the truth to the congregation.

The pastor and his young attendants entered from the back of the chapel and proceeded to the narthex. The assembled rose to their feet and bowed their heads in respectful silence. Though this was a quasi-Christian gathering, many showed their allegiance to their personal branch of religion by bowing, genuflecting, or kneeling. Much to the chagrin of the founders—men who believed that religion should only be practiced in the privacy of one's own home—the population's former adherence to the proscribed anonymity had waned. Anyone could see all variations of the accouterments of the pious among those in attendance, be it a yarmulke, cross, or hijab.

One of the altar boys approached the altar, unlocked an antique wood cabinet, and removed a silver chalice. The other took down a silver wand. Both of the youths held the implements firmly for fear that dropping the holy items might require a lifetime to live down.

The pastor waved his arms like a flightless bird, and the congregation noisily returned to their seats in a cacophony of thumps and sighs. He turned to the altar boys, relieved them of the sacred tools, and moved to a font that was tucked in the corner, opposite the pulpit.

The font was stocked with water from the fountain that once stood outside the worldwide headquarters of General Motors. One full ladle of water was dumped into the chalice before the pastor turned back and faced the crowd.

"Dear God, give us the strength to be victorious this day. Give our driver, Joe Smith, access to your unyielding greatness, and make his heart and mind true. And give this vehicle your blessing so that this machine may resemble the chariot that conveys you from earth unto the heavens, and be just as swift."

The pastor dipped the wand into the chalice and flicked a sprinkling onto the Barracuda.

"I sanctify you in the name of God and Impala."

The pastor's eyes turned to Joe, and with the nod of his head, he asked the driver to rise and approach him. Kevin and Billy were quick to remind him silently that this was also part of what he signed up for.

Joe rose and crossed to face the pastor.

"I sanctify Joe Smith, your humble servant, in the name of God and Impala."

When the arcing stream of water hit him in the face, his first reaction was to want to wipe it off. It smelled fairly funky and was likely filled with high concentrations of bacteria and mold. Joe resisted the instinct, weathered the onslaught of the fetid fluid, and allowed the pastor to spin his body around to face the crowd.

"Let us pray," the pastor said, bowing his head.

Everyone followed in his or her form of supplication.

"Dear God, be with us today. We beseech you to aid us in this time of competition. We beseech you to grant Joe Smith the power to be error free. And we beseech you to confound our enemies as you bestow upon us your blessings. Amen."

The congregation echoed him.

The pastor ceded the chalice and the wand to the boys. The youngsters carefully returned them to the wooden case and stepped to the side.

"Go in peace," the pastor said, "but do so with the knowledge that victory is attainable with God's help."

There was another moment of silence before postures began to relax and whispered voices could be heard.

"Please join us for a pancake breakfast on the patio," the pastor said in conclusion.

The invitation to dine unlocked any remnants of stuffiness, and some in the crowd began to whoop and holler just as the group broke into a communal singing of the Impala song.

Joe's responsibilities had been met, and he was ushered away by his security team, destined for Frank and Claudia's garage.

John let the note slip from his hand and into his pocket. He excused himself from his family. He wanted to see if he could pull Jody Springer aside for a moment and ask him for some help.

John found him on the patio, his eyes splitting focus on his three kids. John asked him back into the church just as the car was being pushed away by the strongest Impalans. Jody acknowledged most of them since some were also fellow members of the punch-out squad.

"What time are you heading over to the stadium?" John asked once the car was removed.

"Early. You know how it is; everyone waits until the last minute. The place isn't even full until the cars are already on the course. Besides, it is no easy feat getting this entire family to even head in a straight line let alone trying to reach a specific destination at a prearranged time," Jody said.

"What if I told you that you shouldn't take your family to the stadium today?"

"Why?"

It was more difficult to dole out this information to someone like Jody, a ward loyalist with no interest in all the machinations involved in the political maneuvering exemplified by his father and his ilk. With Mr. Fedder, there had been the basis of a previous relationship. With Jody, it was just barely more than a slight tick up from acquaintance.

"It's a long and complicated story, but I've been told that there are elements that intend to unleash an attack at some point today. I don't know if it will be at the stadium or somewhere else, but it is imminent."

"Are you saying those Mustang assholes are planning something? How do you know this?"

"It's not Mustang. The attack is against the city as a whole."

Jody's face showed signs of confusion.

"It's Redeemers," John said with finality.

Jody froze.

"What?"

"Joe Smith knows that the guy who's driving for Mustang is a Redeemer apostle, and that he's got something planned for today."

"How does he know this?"

"He's tangled with him before."

"And you believe him?"

"I do. Joe has no reason to make something like this up."

"Have you told your father?"

"My dad isn't interested in anything that is not directly related to the fortunes of Impala and the race."

"But this is related."

"Yeah. You would think he would understand that," John confirmed.

"And you are sure of this?"

"I don't know what to tell you, Jody. I believe something is going to happen. It makes sense that if you leave your family at home and nothing happens, nothing happens. You know what I mean?"

"What can I do?" Jody asked.

"Get the other punch-out team members together, and meet me at the stadium at eleven fifteen."

"I'll be there," Jody said without hesitation.

John stuck out his hand and gripped the swollen and scabbed mitt of his new friend. He turned and joined his family on the patio. There was a concentration of neighbors surrounding his father, pressing him to imbue them with confidence for the coming battle. His mother and sister had been shunted aside of this circle, and they hovered together with their plates of food.

"I'll see you at the stadium," John told his mother as he passed.

Holly tried to get his attention, but it was still too early to tell them what was going on. If he headed them off now, his father would likely shit a brick, and all of the planning that Joe and he had done would be for naught. So far, nothing had sprung up to curtail his efforts; Cassandra's guards had not informed anyone that she had been freed.

He made sure that no one was in the vicinity as he slipped the note from his pocket. It read, "Bring C 11:00 Stadium waiting room."

By the time he arrived at Frank and Claudia's, the two mechanics were availing Joe of the details of the deals that had been struck by their captain and his lieutenant.

"As I have been told, your main support is going to come from the Tigers. They're the ones that have the Impala SS," Frank said as he pointed to a phototype of the vehicle.

"Wait a minute, the Tigers? Aren't they the ones who got into trouble? I thought they were pariahs?" Joe asked.

Frank and Claudia shared a look. Kevin had briefed them before the church service of the strange alliance that had been struck, but they still wondered why the Impala officials would take such a chance. They were putting the whole ward at risk by even recognizing the Tigers' existence.

"Oh come on, you guys, this can't be a shock," John said. "This is consistent with the kind of shit that my dad does. I bet they jumped at whatever offer they received. Why wouldn't they? What are the other deals? Let me guess, the Red Wings, DeVille, and Marquis?" John asked.

Frank nodded.

"Anything specific?"

"Not really," Claudia answered.

"I wouldn't expect much from them, but if we win, you can bet they will come around with their hands out," John said.

The two other Impalans in the room concurred.

"Look," Frank said, "you don't need to think about all of this, Joe. You just concentrate on what's in front of you."

The car was scheduled to begin its trek to the stadium at around 10 A.M., and the Impala strongmen began to gather in the courtyard minutes before the top of the hour.

"Where is everybody?" Frank asked.

It was obvious that the numbers of the pushers had been thinned for some inexplicable reason. Frank's question was met with shrugs from the small group of human propellers.

John knew why some of the normal detail was absent but was not at liberty to offer an explanation. Jody Springer must have gotten to them and altered their duties for the day.

"Well, no matter. I'm sure there will be plenty of folks outside who will gladly help," Frank said.

John and Joe maintained their silence. Between the pushers and the security team, there were way too many open ears in their vicinity. John adhered to their original plan that had them consulting with each other only after they made it into the security of the stadium's green room.

As Frank predicted, a healthy crowd was waiting in the street for them when they emerged from the repair bay. Again, there were refrains of the Impala song and every other form of aural acclaim.

Joe's team of Independents gathered around him as they headed off to the main artery of Woodward Avenue. On their arrival at Motor City's primary thoroughfare, John veered northwest, bound for the café. He did not see Kevin Gatz in the crowd of the Barracuda's chaperones and therefore was not privy to Kevin's curiosity about why the captain's son was headed in a different direction from the procession.

Before the question could emerge, Kevin's attention was directed elsewhere. As they began the trip down to the stadium, there were other voices that began to compete with those of Impala. From up the street, the Impala singers started to discern some dissonance to their harmonic outpouring of patriotism. It turned out that Mustang was in the process of moving their vehicle as well, and they were only a hundred or so yards behind Impala on the road.

John tried to make himself invisible as the Mustang mob countered his movement to the northwest with their trek to the southeast. He kept his eyes peeled for a sign that Udo Lewandowski/Clarence Rigney was amongst the members of the Mustang hierarchy, but there was no one that resembled the description that he'd been given.

John found the group that contained Titus O'Keefe, and he was more than a little surprised to see that he was flanked not only by Tom Cobble but also by the lawyer Leo Rascone. Why was the lawyer aligning himself with Mustang? John picked up his pace before breaking into a sprint.

FIFTY-FOUR

J OE DID NOT hear much of the hubbub that was circulating through the group of Impalans in regards to the activities taking place both ahead and behind them.

The rear of the Impala group was preoccupied with volleying back the insults that were being lobbed at them by the southeast-bound Mustang train. Those with their nose pointed forward were making their presence felt amidst the onlookers by offering full-throated renditions of the Impala song.

With the level of random cacophony having eclipsed any semblance of comprehension, Joe narrowed his focus.

He began to exercise his finger joints. He felt that the tips that hung at the end of his hands were only the physical ends to his superstructure. There was a good five to six inches to go before one actually came to the end of his full presence. At that moment, it was best that anyone near him give him a wide berth, or they would feel the pressure on their person from the energy he was emanating beyond what they could see and touch.

He had once dispensed with a man without actually touching him. The Redeemer teetered off a ledge and fell fifty feet to his death, and the only energy that propelled him off the building had been from something beyond physical contact. Joe remembered the look in the man's eyes when he suddenly realized that he was powerless to stop the force that had pushed him over the edge. It was the only time that he'd ever felt something akin to immortal. It was the only time that he had allowed his ego to expand beyond the infinitesimally small limits sanctioned by his training.

He also remembered the penalty that was served for wallowing in that sense of pride when another Redeemer appeared from behind and slashed his leg with a hacksaw. It was his only prominent scar, and he would always remember it; a fitting result, he believed, for momentarily displaying an effervescing arrogance.

The stadium loomed up ahead. Joe surfaced to the sounds of rancor between members of his contingent and the mob of enemies that had by now become Impala's caboose. Everyone could see the officials scanning the crowd from ramps of the stadium. There would be no altercation now, as disqualification was still on the table for anyone who messed up.

The pushers needed help to get the Barracuda up the small incline before the tunnel, and every able Impalan pitched in. At the top of the knoll, Mugwumps were there to take over and deliver the car to the team of inspectors waiting on the field. Frank and Claudia split off to monitor the inspection. Joe and his minders headed for the waiting room.

At the door to the janitorial closet that had been pressed into service as the staging area for the Impala driver, Joe was able to convince his security team that he needed to be alone. There was important preparation that needed to take place. After a couple of tense moments, they acceded to his request for privacy.

He had given them no trouble to this point, and that fact went a long way toward their eventual consensus that he could be on his own for the hour or so before the race. Six of the group stood guard at the door, and the other six headed off for the bathrooms or to scare up something to eat.

Joe took a seat in the one chair that took up the bulk of the floor space and focused his attention on the task at hand. He decided that if he had the opportunity, he would take out Udo Lewandowski before they ever got into the cars. He could not make a case for letting it go to any other result.

He knew that the furor that would result from that act would place him in situation that might end up being fatal. If a Mustang mob didn't beat him to death, he was sure to be attacked by members of Impala for having the audacity to spoil their lofty expectations.

There would be no time to produce evidence of the righteousness of his deed before either group descended upon him, but many would be saved nonetheless. There were Udo's three comrades to consider, but Joe had pretty much convinced himself that they were trucklers and would not be effective without their leader.

The only perplexing problem that he had been unable to get his mind around was the possibility that the attack that Udo was likely planning might not be centered in the stadium. This thought was the basis for his biggest worry. What if the attack was to happen in another place in the city, and what if Redeemer elements from the outside were also involved?

John had said something to him about eavesdropping through the door of the Redeemer's residence and hearing them detail some of the increments of timing. They would wait until the stadium was full was the essence of John's recollections. He left out if the reasoning behind it was based on concentrating the population in one place for the purpose of exterminating them, or catching them off guard while an invasion was launched in a different location.

Joe also knew that the personage and the environs had been swept repeatedly for any devices that could cause any sort of problem. This had been part of the protocol ever since the time that a flock of Red Wings supporters tried throwing derelict flares at an opponent during the "grabbing the flag" portion of the contest. The poor unfortunate driver's suit ignited, he suffered major burns, and he nearly died. The Red Wings' suspension was lengthy, and the identified perpetrators suffered the ignominy of being banished from the enclave forever.

Joe heard a commotion at the door and heard John's voice identifying himself as the captain's son. He heard him state that he should be granted access to Impala's driver. Joe was impressed—the kid's vocal timbre expressed no hint of hesitation or tentativeness.

As the negotiation continued outside, another voice joined the discussion, Cassandra's. Joe flung open the door and was surprised to count the diminished numbers of the platoon. For a fleeting second, he thought about bolting, finding the Redeemer apostle in amongst the dank catacombs of the stadium, and killing him before they ever made their way onto the field.

With only six to stop him, he felt confident that he could disperse this group quickly and take care of his business. He had no idea where the Mustang driver was holing up, but he would find him. Cassandra could probably provide him with that information.

"Joe, we need to talk," John said gruffly.

But Joe was staring at the moisture welling up in Cassandra's eyes. He wasn't quite sure why she was on the verge of crying. Joe grabbed Cassandra by the arm, and pulled her inside before anyone could protest. John quickly followed. The door was shut, and the chair was propped up against the knob to deter any surprise entrances.

"What if I did it now?" Joe asked them.

That was not how they thought this conversation was going to begin. Both John and Cassandra needed a moment to think about what Joe was floating here.

"Yeah, actually that makes sense. It would be far better not to have to be out in public, and it might take everyone awhile to fully understand what happened. During that time, we might be able to track down the others," John said.

"Hello," Cassandra said softly.

Joe knew that there was an expectation of something here, so he reached over and brushed his lips against hers. John looked for a corner to turn to, but there was hardly enough room for the three to occupy the room as it was. He knew his face had reddened; he could feel his pulse beating just below the surface of his cheekbones.

"Okay, we can do this. Where is the waiting room for Mustang?" Joe asked Cassandra.

"It's always diametrically opposed to Impala. Six hours on the clock from here," John said.

Before Joe could open his mouth and hand out their assignments, someone from the outside began to pound on the door.

"Who is it?" Joe screamed in response.

"Frank and Claudia."

When Joe opened the door, he noticed that the full complement of guards had reassembled.

Claudia caught sight of Cassandra, and her eyes blazed with curious recognition.

"What the fuck is she doing here?" Claudia shrieked.

"No time to explain right now, Claudia," Joe said firmly.

"I'll tell you all about it as soon as we figure out what's going on," John assured her.

"Tell me now," Claudia demanded.

"No," Joe said before turning his attention to Frank.

"We passed the inspection," Frank said.

"Was there any doubt?" Joe asked.

"Not really. We made no modifications," Frank said before throwing a glance in Cassandra's direction. He was also a bit curious about her presence at this time.

"We need to head upstairs in a couple of minutes, Joe," Frank said.

And with those words, the air went out of the balloon that contained the idea that Joe could eliminate the threat before they hit the field of play.

The logistics had become too unwieldy, what with the twelve guards outside, as well as the sudden lack of cohesion among the five of them.

Again the door was opened and the five spilled out into the stadium's hallway. John headed for his other duties—to link up with Mr. Fedder and, eventually, Jody Springer. Cassandra began to separate herself also, but Joe grabbed her by the hand.

"Stay with me," he said.

She did not hesitate. She interlocked her fingers with his and floated beside him through the tunnel toward the stairwell. Frank and Claudia froze in place upon seeing this display of affection, but the contingent of Joe's guards struck them like an incoming wave and pushed them along toward the entrance to the field.

———————

It had been the lawyer's idea to send Clarence Rigney to the stadium long before the Mustang entourage would make the trip down from their neighborhood. As Leo Rascone explained to Titus O'Keefe, "Nobody really knows who the guy is anyway. Let's not present the issue until we absolutely have to. While everyone is trying to figure out what's going on, the race will have already started."

Titus agreed. He wasn't really in the mood for answering questions anyway. Clarence Rigney's job had been redefined based upon his lack of skill, and Titus, Leo, and Tom Cobble would be the only spectators aware of the change in tactics. The task now was to find a way to steer the Mustang into the Barracuda. Subtlety was important so that the act did not appear to be overt and result in any type of sanction from the committee. The plan was to have it happen at either the end of the second lap or sometime during the early part of the third.

Since Tim Rizzo had agreed to sacrifice the Tigers' entrant for their purposes, Titus had schooled Rigney to wait until the Tigers created the disruption and then use that moment to accomplish the goal.

During the instruction, Udo sat raptly, nodding his head that he would do exactly as commanded. More than once, he let the Mustang captain know that he was here to perform a job, and that whatever that task entailed, the ward was certain to get their money's worth.

There was a troupe of guards that loitered outside of the Mustang waiting room—again assigned by Leo Rascone. Leo had convinced Titus that Mr. Rigney could be a target for that zealot who was driving for those Impala fucks, and that Clarence should have an escort to stop anyone that might be a threat.

As he sat in the waiting room, Udo tried to tamp down his feelings of nervousness. He was fully aware that the prerace agenda included an inspection of all of the vehicles. If the inspectors uncovered his installation, the improvised plan that he devised would be in tatters.

If that did happen it would do nothing to preclude all of the preparations they had done to the wall at the far northwestern edge of the city, but the moment that he wanted—the moment that had caused the Redeemer Commander's hand to quiver when he read his hand-written note—would likely not occur.

To Udo, Motor City was going to be his Mercyville. He wanted to exalt his ruler with a massacre unlike any that had come before. The price for this type of status elevation was his life, but Udo was convinced that there was something more rewarding than earthly existence to ensue, and that was life everlasting with his Redeemer.

He assured himself that the other believers who resided in the afterlife would celebrate this act, and he would be welcomed with open arms. The egotist in him fantasized about a time when a beatification would take place, and Udo's martyrdom would be consecrated into sainthood. Until the end of time he would be seen as their greatest warrior ever, and he would be worshiped as the ultimate defender of the Church of the Redeemer. God had St. Michael. The Redeemer would have St. Udo.

It had been a major stroke of luck that Mustang provided him with accommodations in their mechanic's bay on the days leading up to the race. That put him in close proximity to the Mustang GT.

He figured that the pre-race inspection would encompass all of the elements associated with the drive train, and that would rule out putting the recently acquired C-4 in the engine compartment, or on the undercarriage of the chassis. He thought he might be able to remove the fuel tank and spread it across that part of the body before replacing the reservoir, but he was afraid that the concentration would be diluted and the effect he was trying to achieve would be muted.

He ruled out the trunk, behind the paltry backseat, or someplace under the dash. In these emplacements, he was concerned about the access when it came to detonation. All wiring would have to be hidden.

It took awhile, but the moment of genius eventually presented itself. He would sit on the block of high explosive and tuck the wiring into the area under the seat.

Making sure there would be no interruptions, he waited until everyone had dispersed to the all-Mustang race's-eve dinner. He had not been invited to attend.

Finally alone, he removed the driver's front bucket seat. He made a series of precision cuts in the upholstery, removed the padding, and stuffed the block of C-4 in its place. He then attached the detonation wiring and ran the leads behind the bar that held the seat adjustment levers. All he would have to do was reach down under the seat, unfurl the wires, and detonate the plastic explosive.

In the waiting room, five minutes before he was to be called out on the field, he knelt and prayed to his Redeemer that the inspectors would not detect the alteration he had made to the cockpit seat.

Joe, Cassandra, Frank, and Claudia waited at the mouth of the tunnel while Carter Pleasant announced each entrant. The security team loitered nearby, unsure of when their duties were to end.

Joe poked his head out and saw that the stadium was only a quarter full.

"When does everyone arrive?" he asked.

"It takes awhile to get everyone inside, but a lot of folks gather down on Witherell for the start. As soon as the cars take off, they begin filtering in. By the time you head up the ramp and reenter the stadium, it will be packed to the rafters," Frank said.

Joe caught Claudia's eye; she was still pouting. She still had not been given an explanation as to why Cassandra was present.

There was a roar building outside, and Joe felt a decent jolt of anticipation. Several of the wards had been announced, and it wouldn't be long until he was beckoned onto the field.

"Will you do me a favor?" Joe asked Frank.

"Sure."

"After we're loaded in, will you take your daughter out of here? Put some distance between you guys and this stadium?"

"What?"

"I know that would be hard for you, but I think something bad might go down here. In fact, I'm pretty sure that something will go down here, and I don't want either of you to get hurt," Joe said.

"What the fuck are you taking about?" Claudia asked.

She began to give Cassandra the evil eye. This must have something to do with her.

"The guy who's driving for Mustang is a Redeemer apostle. If I know their kind—and I do—he's got something planned," Joe stated.

Frank was floored by this information. Having been around for many years—including many on the outside as the shit started coming down—he knew the perils that the Redeemer ilk presented.

"What are you going to do?" Frank asked.

"If something happens, I'm going to try to stop it," Joe stated.

"Can I help?" Frank asked.

"Yeah. You can get as far away from this place as possible, so that I don't have to think about whether the two of you are safe or not."

Claudia kept her eyes on Cassandra.

"Where do you fit into this?" Claudia asked Cassandra, having already rendered a verdict of guilty on every count she had chalked onto the board in her mind.

"I don't. I didn't even know about this until this morning. And the reason that I was in the dark was that your captain had me kidnapped and held against my will so that Joe would not hesitate to do his job," she said.

"The bastard did that?" Claudia asked.

"Yeah."

"Did they hurt you?"

"No. John rescued me this morning. They don't know I've been freed."

"Well, they're going to find out," Joe said with a mischievous grin.

The next words out of Carter Pleasant's mouth were, "And in the Plymouth Barracuda, Impala!"

Above them, the small groups that were in the Impala section began to sing and holler. Joe tightened his grip on Cassandra's hand and strolled over to the car.

The security detail was caught flatfooted for a moment. Before they could close the gap and gather around their charge, Joe and Cassandra were exposed not only to the nearby Impala spectators, but also to the Mustang supporters occupying the tiers across from them.

Quickly, the tenor changed as obscenities and garbage rained down from those who took exception to the sight of this union. Those in attendance tried to understand the meaning of this. Many Impalans wondered if their driver was in cahoots with the rival ward.

Across the way, the Mustang faithful took similar exception to the spectacle. They began to scream their objections as well.

All of this chaos had the effect of flummoxing poor Carter Pleasant. He stopped the sequence of introductions and was staring at the scene, his jaw hovering just above the ground.

Joe and Cassandra made it to the car. Joe looked up into the stands and located Billy Klock and Kevin Gatz. He gave them a small wave before turning to Cassandra.

"Look, if I don't see you again, I want you to know that what we had was real to me. As real as anything I've experienced in a long, long time. It many ways, you've saved me," Joe said.

He impulsively grabbed her face with his hands, brought it close to his, and kissed her.

"Don't be here when I come back," he said sternly.

She didn't respond because she knew that this was an order she would never obey.

FIFTY-FIVE

THE NONES OF JULY

POST SEPTIMA[3]

KEVIN DID NOT hesitate upon seeing Joe and Cassandra together on the field. Seconds after watching their outrageously offensive display of affection, he grabbed one of the minions standing nearby and told him to run over to the Perry Street safe house and find out what the fuck happened.

"It's two houses up the block from Pine Street. Second floor. I need to know if anyone is still there. If you find someone, ask them this question: 'How did she get out?' Get the fucking answer and get it back to me right away." Kevin seethed.

The kid sped off.

Kevin turned to Billy Klock and indicated that he should scramble down to the field to get him some of the details regarding this perplexing predicament. Kevin needed to get some facts so he could fill in the spaces of his mind that were being polluted by his imagination. He needed to get the truth soon before Captain Brassey arrived.

The expressions of the crowd's vitriol in reference to Joe and Cassandra's union showed no signs of abating. Impalans near the rail—literally foaming at the mouth—began pelting the area where the car was parked with everything they could get their hands on. When their wayward aim resulted in a couple of dings to the body of the Barracuda, a crimson-faced Carter Pleasant rushed over to the scene.

"What hell is going on here?" Carter asked in a plaintive wail.

Frank and Claudia couldn't provide him a suitable answer, as they were also confused as to why these two would engage in such a provocative manner in this place, and at this time.

Joe didn't want Cassandra to think she was being used only for the purpose of causing a ruckus, though that was his intention. He wanted to see if this distraction could get the attention of the entire crowd and hopefully evoke the commissioner to run over to find out what all the hubbub was about.

---

3   After the noon hour. In Roman time, "septima" is the delineation for the time of day that is denoted to be between 12:00 P.M. and 12:44 P.M.

"Get your ass in the car," Carter screamed at Joe.

"I want you to make an announcement that the stadium should be cleared," Joe said.

"What?"

"You need to get everyone out of here," Joe said.

"Why?"

"I believe that there is an attack that has been planned by a Redeemer sleeper cell that has been living in your city."

Carter's eyes momentarily flashed with the recognition that something akin to that would be devastating, but he wasn't inclined—not in this super-charged moment—to take this foreigner's word for it.

"The stadium has been swept. The patrons have been searched. This is normal protocol, Mr. Smith. We've never had a problem before. Now, please take your place in the vehicle," Carter said.

"He speaks the truth, Mr. Pleasant. The Mustang replacement driver is their leader," Cassandra said.

Now Carter had to readjust. He'd known Cassandra for nearly her entire life, and he had never experienced her as anything other than forthright. If she was calling out her own clan, there must be at least some veracity in her statement.

"Do you have any kind of evidence?" Carter asked Cassandra.

A projectile—some type of balled-up food wrapper—hit Carter Pleasant smack square in the temple. As it contacted his skin, it exploded a good tablespoon of pale yellow mustard onto the side of his face.

"Ah, shit," Carter said.

He looked around for something to wipe off the goo and gratefully accepted a rag that Claudia withdrew from her back pocket.

And then there was the sound of thunder—a fifty-Hertz drone that began to drown out the crowd noise. All of the vehicles were being started at their respective stations in the stadium.

Across the field, Joe could now see Udo behind the wheel of the Mustang. He saw him shift the car into gear and head for the ramp that would take him out of the stadium to the start line.

Joe quickly took his seat in his own vehicle, adjusted the cockpit restraints, and kicked over the engine on the Barracuda. The motor roared to life, but the tone carried with it a nuanced difference. Joe immediately sensed that there must have been some work performed by his mechanics the night before because the sound he'd become inured to seemed altered—significantly more muscular. He caught Frank's eye.

"Always tuning," Frank said, leaning in through the open window.

"Go watch the race from the street. Promise me you'll get out of here," Joe said as he put his gloves on.

Joe put the car in first, slowly feathered the clutch, and crept away toward the middle of the field. He fell into line behind the Tigers' Impala SS. He couldn't see who was driving their car, and he wanted to make eye contact with him to determine whether he was going to be an ally or not.

As they congaed out of the still-filling stadium, Joe caught sight of Cassandra in the rearview mirror. She was continuing to make her (and his) case to Carter Pleasant. Frank and Claudia had disappeared back into the tunnel.

Joe did not notice that only eight cars actually left the stadium and ventured to the start. He did not see that the AMX was still parked in its spot in the middle of the field. The departing drivers did not witness the small plume of smoke rising from the crevices where the hood met the front-end body of the AMX, or the expression of oil that suddenly began pooling on the ground under the car.

The people of Ram saw it all happening in real time, and their response was to stand up, en masse, and file out of the stadium. Their day was finished before they even started, and the only logical thing to do was to get the hell out of there and get drunk. Some of their members were actually grateful that the car took a crap before it left the stadium. Had it died out on the road, they might not have known about it until the cars were returning for the finish. That would have amounted to an unforgivable waste of serious drinking time.

———

John was on the lookout for the Tigers' captain, Tim Rizzo. He knew that Tiger Tim would not be able to help him with trying to influence the other captains to his heed his call, but he had sway over his own people, and that was where John wanted to start. If John could convince Tim to remove his bloc from the stadium, there would be an inevitable curiosity that was sure to sweep through the crowd. John felt that could be exploited. Almost every attendee would have the same question pinging through his or her brain: "Why are they leaving?"

He found a visibly distraught Tim—chewing on what was left of his last fingernail—hanging out by the concession stand that served the section that accommodated his ward.

"Captain Rizzo?" John asked on approach.

Tim immediately looked for a place where he could safely lam. Why was the Impala captain's kid looking for him? He must have discovered evidence of his duplicity. Tim had told no one of his involuntary double-dealing. Who had told the kid?

"Could I have a moment of your time, sir?" John asked sincerely.

"What's up, kid?" Tim asked.

Tim's left eyelid began to flutter in a nictitating fashion. He knew it was his tell, but he was powerless to stop it. How had the kid found out?

John told him that a horrific danger was in the wind and pled with Tim to help by getting his tribe to clear the area.

As the story spilled out, Tim returned a look of perplexity. This was so opposite of his original expectations that it took him many minutes to understand what he was being asked to do.

"What are you saying? That there are Redeemers in Motor City?"

"Yes, sir."

Tim mulled the meaning, then the opportunity of this incredible news. If there was a shred of truth to what this young man was saying, he could use it as an excuse to skedaddle away from the impossible situation he had put himself in. He would not be anywhere near the stadium when the race post-mortem was conducted by either of his two secret, but opposing, "partners."

"Give me a percentage," Tim said.

"Sir?"

"What is the likelihood of this happening?"

"I want to say one hundred percent, but there will be a concerted effort made to interdict the perpetrators before they have a chance to achieve success."

Tim's face screwed up into a mask of quizzical wonder. Why did this kid talk like this? No kid talked like that.

"Okay. I'll see what I can do. I mean, we're just here for the show anyway. We ain't got a shot in hell of winning, as you know."

It was a subtle test to see if the kid had been let in on the planned ploy by his dad.

"Someday that will change," John said sympathetically.

Because John didn't address anything but their perennial snub by the rest of the city, he felt fairly secure that the secret—at least from the Impala side—was shared only amongst a very few. Maybe the kid didn't know about the deal after all.

"You'd better get started," John said.

"If this turns out be some kind of a hoax, I'm going to have a lot of explaining to do," Tim said, giving John one more opportunity to show a weakness in his position.

"It is not a hoax. I can pretty much guarantee that you will be saving lives by getting your people out."

Tim nodded and spun on his heels, briskly walking up the ramp to the tiers that held his people.

———————

Adams Avenue was packed ten deep with spectators as the eight cars tooled along on their way to the start line. From his position at the rear of the procession, Joe could not see Udo Lewandowski's Mustang up ahead, though he tried to get a view by using the ruse of veering from side to side as if his intention was to warm up the tires. With the mercury elevating in the thermometer to just above the one-hundred-degree mark, many would see this act as nothing more than inexperience or, perhaps, out-and-out hubris.

Joe could see a good amount of the fans holding up both hands in a single- (middle-) finger salute as he passed by. A brief scan of the hues of their plumage showed that they spanned all of the various wards.

Joe saw the cars making the left turn onto Witherell Street up ahead and finally caught sight of the Mustang entrant. Udo was the second competitor in the queue. He attempted to recall the preconfigured starting grid. He knew he was initially slated for the back row, but one of the officials was waving him into another place. Joe cranked the window down about halfway.

"I think I'm supposed to be in the back," he yelled to the official.

"Yeah, that's when there were nine cars in the race. We've already lost one," the official screamed back at him.

Joe intrinsically knew who it was. The lore would remain unaltered.

It was quite the blare—eight idling V8 engines, tuned and timed within a millisecond of their maximum capabilities. Joe could feel the low hum of the concussive pistons connecting to the rhythm of his heartbeat, and for a brief moment he forgot all about Udo Lewandowski. He had read many accounts in his youth of the fetishism that car aficionados attached to these machines, and for the first time, he had an inkling about why they had inspired all that lyrical poetry.

A thick nautical rope was stretched in front of the lead group of four cars. The holders had to strain to keep it parallel to the ground—somewhere just short of a tug-of-war. Joe heard the engines of the cars in the front row begin to rotate at a much higher level of RPMs. He shoved in the clutch on the Barracuda and slid the gearshift forward into first.

From his spot in the far left of the second row, he could see only a sliver of his nemesis's face through the front windshield of the Barracuda. Udo was in the forward row all the way over to Joe's right, fiddling with the rearview mirror.

The holders were relieved to let the rope give into gravity. The hemp cable hit the tarmac with a silent thud, and the entire front line of cars leapt forward.

Joe waited a millisecond before taking off. It was his strategy to take the first lap toward the rear of the field. He'd been told of all of the shenanigans taking place between historic rivals, and he wanted to steer clear until a hierarchy was established.

He kept his eyes on the Tigers' Impala SS—his supposed ally—to see if their driver made an early move to get Mustang out of the race. That outcome would turn out to be a spot of good fortune for him because if Udo's vehicle happened to become disabled, Joe could take him out wherever he came to a stop.

They made the turn onto Madison, and the pace jumped precipitously. Up ahead there was a fierce duel taking place between the Lions' GTO, Marquis' Roadrunner, and the Pistons' Chevelle. Each were angling to be the first into the violent left that would take them south to the first real straightaway down Gratiot Avenue.

Joe settled into a spot on the left side of the road that would provide him with the best angle for the turn. Directly in front of him was the Red Wings' Challenger. In front of the Challenger, there was a group of three that included the Mustang, DeVille's Gran Torino, and the Tigers' Impala SS.

The Impala SS suddenly swerved to the left and began to encroach upon the space that Udo and his Mustang were in the process of occupying. *There*, Joe thought, *I do have an ally*. They were passing by the southern end of the stadium. It was the part of the course that provided the only vantage point for the spectators in the facility to see any part of the race other than the finish line.

Joe wondered if the Tigers' feint was for show because as the cars swept through the turn, they did so in an ordered line. The Tigers' Impala SS was slightly ahead of the Mustang but was no longer driving erratically.

When they hit that first straightway, the dynamics of the contest began to change. Joe had downshifted into second to take the turn, but now that the line of the road was arrow straight, he jammed down on the accelerator and worked through the gears. He was determined to find out exactly how much power his car had compared to the others, and he was pleased to see that he easily passed both the hulking Gran Torino and the Pistons' Chevelle before they hung the quick left onto Randolph Street.

They stayed in line again for the short distance before the sharp right turn that put them on Monroe Street. In the length of the road on Monroe before the right turn that would spill them onto the longest of all the straightaways on Michigan Avenue, Joe passed the Red Wings' Challenger. As he flashed past, he could see the Red Wings' driver cursing at the top of his lungs. There was water vapor beginning to rise from inside the Challenger's hood, and the driver was looking at the temperature gauge as it zoomed upward toward the dangerous level denoted by a red bar. As the rest streaked down Michigan Avenue reaching their respective top ends, Joe could see the Challenger continuing to recede through his rearview mirror.

Joe was sitting in fifth place. He could see ahead to those who were vying for the lead: the Roadrunner, the GTO, and the Mustang. The Impala SS dangled just behind this group, directly in front of Joe.

The triad at the front adjusted for the turn onto Cass Avenue, and Joe saw that the Lions' GTO was first to come out of the turn and head up the road leading them to the gates. The Mustang had taken it easy through the curve and exited in third place. Joe was content to hang back, stay out of trouble, and keep an eye on the killer in the car two spots ahead of him.

All of the cars passed through the widest setting of the gates unscathed, but Joe could see that two of the cars had not immediately set themselves up correctly for the turn onto Adams Avenue. The GTO swept up through the curve, performed the double apex flawlessly, and barreled out of the ess to maintain his lead. Marquis' Roadrunner had been side-by-side with the GTO through the gates but had tried to pass in the small section of the straight road before the turn. It was a stupid mistake that put the Roadrunner on a course to enter the turn at too high an angle to complete the maneuver without having to significantly decrease its speed. The error allowed the Mustang to move into second place by default, and the Roadrunner nearly collided with the Impala SS as it attempted to right itself and negotiate its way through the rest of the turn.

Joe congratulated himself for having the foresight to steer clear of it all. He swept through the turn on the perfect line. He emerged directly behind the Roadrunner and the Impala SS and took the opportunity to quickly swing around both of the cars on the small part of Adams Avenue that led back toward the stadium.

For a brief moment, Joe wrestled with a frightful premonition that Udo might take this opportunity to veer off the course and return to the stadium to unleash whatever ruination his evil mind had devised. When Joe saw the Mustang follow the GTO into the sharp right that took them back to the starting line, he let out a charged breath. Lap one was complete.

FIFTY-SIX

Lon Brassey, with the rest of his family in tow, arrived at the stadium just in time to see the entire Tigers' section evacuating the area. He tried to get Tim Rizzo's attention as he led his ward down the ramps to the street level, but he was too far away, and Lon did not want to draw any interest from any of the other wards. They certainly couldn't see him deigning to talk to the captain of the ostracized ward.

Lon turned to Karen with a quizzical look on his face. She could tell that whatever innocence he was trying to portray was fighting a battle with the layer of truth that contained his dealings with Tim Rizzo as well as his other secrets about the race.

"Why are they leaving?" he asked.

"What's the point in them sticking around anyway, Dad? They can't win," Holly said, invoking the citywide absolute.

But Karen could see that her husband was truly confused. One of the elders of the ward happened past them, and Karen saw Lon physically mutate the facial bones underneath his skin to transform his look of bewilderment into a visage of assured aplomb.

"I hear we're third after the first lap," the geezer said.

"We've got the car, and the driver," Lon shot back.

The Brassey family separated themselves from the old man and headed off to their seats in the Impala VIP section.

———

Under the stands, John brought together a group that contained at least one of the lieutenants of DeVille, Marquis, and the Lions. All of these wards could be qualified as either allies or, at the very least, neutral with Impala. He hoped to convince them to talk to their respective captains about the confirmed threat and have them go the way of the Tigers by exiting the stadium. It was a steep mountain to climb, and he was on the verge of teetering off the ledge when Jody Springer and Mr. Fedder joined the discussion. The former brought the credibility of one fearless in battle, the latter a steady academic focus to complement his credentials of having lived within the walls since the enclave closed its doors to the outside world.

John thought the sage duo was helping him make some headway when two young Lions rushed up to their lieutenant.

"We're leading coming out of Adams Avenue," one of the kids screamed at his superior.

The Lion lieutenant disengaged and left the proceedings. The representatives of Marquis and DeVille got antsy for news of their own fortunes. Before John could stop them, they were gone as well. John turned to his small cadre of confederates.

"Have you had any luck with Impala?"

"Only the people that live on my street," Jody Springer said.

"Same here, though I just walked by our section and the turnout is fairly thin," Mr. Fedder added.

"Well, that's something," John said.

"You got a plan here?" Jody Springer asked.

"Just try to see whose ear I can bend," John said.

"I think we should try to get someone from Mustang to listen," Mr. Fedder said.

It was a bold suggestion, and Jody responded by initially shaking his head in the negative.

"I have someone working on that," John said.

Both of the men looked at him with an elevated level of respect before they fanned out in an attempt to inform any random individuals who crossed their path.

———

Cassandra did not mess around. She went directly to the box that housed Titus O'Keefe and his squadron of sycophants and offered the intelligence about the impending incident that she knew in her heart to be true. Amidst the scoffing by the gathered and the word "cunt" being muttered by someone at the end of the row, the lawyer, Leo Rascone, Titus's honored guest, reacted to the news personally.

"Who told you this steaming crock of shit?" Leo challenged.

"You know who," Cassandra said calmly.

Leo turned to Titus and Tom Cobble and said in a voice loud enough for nearly the whole section to hear, "Your driver isn't a Redeemer. The two of them have a history, and the Impala driver was intent on righting what he felt was a wrong. He came to me to get Clarence's location because he wanted to get revenge. When I showed my reticence, he assaulted me. Apparently Clarence kicked his ass at some point in the past, and he wants to even the score. Now he's floating the notion that Mr. Rigney is a Redeemer. The real reason—the only reason—is that he just wants to rectify a previous slight."

Cassandra was ready and willing to leave them to their stupidity, but she had friends and families of friends in attendance.

"Look, everyone, don't listen to these men. You all know me, have known me for many years. Have I ever lied to you before?"

The majority of the patrons had to weigh that question seriously. Out of the corner of her eye she found Tom Cobble and sensed that he was possibly wavering.

"Tom, what do you really know about this Clarence Rigney?" she demanded.

Tom just stared at an empty space.

"Excuse me, missy, but haven't you been having intimate relations with the Impala driver?" Titus asked in a loud, clear voice.

All eyes snapped to Cassandra in anticipation of either her obstinate denial or her contrite confession.

"Fuck you, Titus. You are going to get these people killed," Cassandra said.

"Ah, but you didn't answer the question, Cassandra. The inference from your need to deflect and change the subject can only be that you have a personal stake in all of this that goes beyond any interest you might have in our well-being," Titus said with an extra dose of congealed slime.

Cassandra just shook her head and headed up the stairs away from this group. To everyone's surprise, Tom Cobble rose, gathered his family, and joined her as she made her exit.

———

Lon, and the distaff members of his family, arrived at their seats in the VIP area of the Impala section to find that the turnout was uncommonly weak for this point in the proceedings. He slid into the row that contained Kevin Gatz and Billy.

"What's going on? Where is everybody?" Lon asked his lieutenants.

"Where do I start?" Kevin whispered.

The gofer that Kevin had sent to gather intelligence on Cassandra's release appeared at the end of the aisle. Kevin held up his finger to stall Lon, rose from his seat, and walked over to confer with the understrapper.

"Can you tell me why there are so few people here?" Lon asked Billy.

"The Mustang woman got free somehow, and our driver is out on the track trying to stop this attack that he said was sure to happen," Billy croaked through his bruised larynx.

"An attack? What are you saying?" Karen asked.

"Shush up, Karen," Lon admonished her.

"You shush up," Karen said. "What did you just say, Billy? And what is this about a Mustang woman?"

Billy fumbled. He wanted to answer the captain's wife, but he knew that would be an act of insubordination to his boss. It was best just to clam up, so he pointed at his throat as if to say that he couldn't speak.

Kevin returned from his briefing with a skin pallor resembling the albumen of a raw egg. He stopped ten feet from his seat and beckoned Lon to join him.

"It was John that freed the Mustang bitch," Kevin said when Lon had arrived.

"What?"

"John went over to the building and took her out of there. The two boys that were watching her said that he told them that you and I authorized her release."

Lon was truly confounded. Only he, Kevin, Billy, and the two nancy-boy guards knew about her abduction. How did his son find out, and what reason would he have for freeing her?

"Where is he?" Lon asked.

"I haven't seen him yet, but the Mustang bitch was on the field kissing Joe Smith before the race began," Kevin responded.

Lon's eyes darkened as he returned to his seat. Karen tugged on his arm, insisting that he pay attention to her request that he elaborate on what Billy Klock had told him before he rose to meet Kevin.

Lon ignored her, reached over, and yanked at the binocular strap hanging around Billy's large neck. Billy handed the optics to Lon, who began scanning the crowd. Lon could see the empty sections that were supposed to be occupied by the Ram and Tigers' delegations. He also noticed a smaller-than-normal presence in the DeVille and Marquis sections. He was scanning over to the Mustang area when two figures caught his eye during the pan. It was his son and Gordie Brewer, the Red Wings' captain. They were deep in conversation on the steps just above the Red Wing VIP section.

Another one of Kevin's punks appeared at the end of the aisle. He was the boy who had been designated as the in-stadium spotter, and he had run over from his perch that overlooked Madison Street.

"First lap over. The running order is Lions, Mustang, and Impala. Red Wings are out on a mechanical," the kid yelled.

Kevin sidled over to him.

"Where are the Tigers?" Kevin asked the kid.

"Fourth place."

"Did they do anything on the first lap?"

"What do you mean?"

"You know, did they try to take someone out?"

"You know, it's funny, Mr. Gatz, when they all first went past us—just after the start—the Tigers' car veered into the Mustang car, but it was kind of half-assed. Then when they just went by the second time, the Tigers' car sped up and tried to box our car in, but it was also a really weak move, you know?"

When Kevin rejoined Lon, he found his captain more unhinged than ever before. He decided not to inform him that the Tigers had failed to live up to the bargain they had agreed upon. There was no way he would bring up his growing speculation that they may have made a similar deal with Mustang.

———————

Joe was feeling pretty good about his position as they passed the start line and headed into the second tour of the circuit. He had Udo directly in front of him, and he was fairly sure that his superior driving skills would allow him to reel his enemy in whenever he desired. From this position, he could track every move of the killer.

Joe's subtle confidence was disrupted when the Tigers' Impala SS suddenly appeared outside the passenger window, not more than a couple of feet away. He had a moment to exchange glances with their driver and concluded that there was something communicated between the two that suggested that they were at common purposes. Having been briefed that Impala had entered into a compact with the Tigers, Joe assumed that this was just a tacit acknowledgement of kinship.

Joe slowed slightly to allow the Impala SS to pass him. They were passing by the stadium now, and only two hundred yards existed between them and the ridiculously tight right turn that would turn them southeast onto Gratiot Avenue. In the moment, Joe was content to have the Tigers' entrant stalk the Mustang. The Tigers' driver completed the pass of the Barracuda with only a hundred yards to go before the turn.

Joe was not prepared for what happened next. The Impala SS suddenly veered into him! Joe braked, viciously tacked to port, and smacked his left front rubber against the curb. The Barracuda's left side jumped the eight-inch ledge and rode the next fifty feet with the driver's side significantly higher than the other. Quickly, Joe veered back onto the road, righted his vessel, and downshifted as he approached the turn.

He was pissed now and confused by the Tiger driver's actions. He raced through the turn, and when they hit the straight portion of Gratiot, he accelerated up to his betrayer to see if he could find out what the fucking story was.

As he came alongside, he saw that the driver's face was blank—a veritable bust of frozen plaster. Joe knew then the incident had not been an accident. Something must have gone awry with the deal.

He was about to give the Impala SS some quid pro quo when—out of absolutely nowhere—DeVille's Gran Torino passed him on the right. Joe marveled at the demonstration of pure speed that the bulky leviathan achieved when it allowed both carburetors, and all 429 cubic inches, off the leash.

The Gran Torino zoomed by as they approached the left turn leading to the short stretch of Randolph Street. It pulled up behind the Impala SS and dove down to the left, effectively blocking the Tigers' car from creating the correct apex that the turn required at its current velocity. Then, to Joe's amazement, the Gran Torino drifted to the right, forcing the Impala SS away from any opportunity to find a way through the turn.

Because the move was so sudden, and the Impala SS reacted so slowly to the incursion, not enough speed could be scrubbed off to keep the Tigers' car from going anywhere other than directly across the curve on a straight line down the narrow spur of Gratiot Street. Joe could see the smoke rising from the tires of the Impala SS as it tried to cease its forward momentum, but it continued to travel nearly an eighth of a mile down the part of the road that wasn't part of the racecourse. He could only imagine the machinations that would be required for the Tigers' vehicle to resume racing. It involved navigating a 180-degree turn on the narrow side street before driving back to rejoin the others on the track.

Joe was in fourth now, behind the GTO, the Mustang, and DeVille's corpulent Gran Torino. They all made the quick right onto Monroe, and Joe took advantage of the nimbleness of his pony car to usurp the Gran Torino as the beast had to slow down to a crawl to make it through the turn.

As Joe flashed past, the DeVille driver gave him a rousing thumbs up. It was then that Joe remembered the protocol that had someone—anyone—running the defaulting Tigers' entrant out of the race at some point. The DeVille driver's signal was meant to signify to Joe that the deed had been accomplished.

Up ahead, the GTO had a distinct advantage on Udo and his Mustang as they hooked onto the Michigan Avenue straightaway. Joe could see the stalled Challenger at the side of the road, now surrounded by a group of pissed-off Red Wings. He knew only six cars remained in the race. He was pretty sure that the Tigers' car would not be able to rejoin.

He closed the gap between himself and the Mustang. A quick glance in the rearview told him that Marquis, DeVille, and the Pistons were more than ten car lengths behind him. Though they were only a lap and a half in, the race appeared to be between himself and the two directly in from of him.

As he approached the rear bumper of the Mustang, Joe searched the exterior of Udo's car. He rightfully assumed that the inspection team would have flagged anything that was out of order, but then he remembered that there was one thing the integrity specialists had allowed to skip past their scrutiny—the drivers themselves.

That must be it, Joe thought.

There was always the possibility that something had been planted in the stadium prior to the event, but there had been so much activity, so many people present during the run-up, that Joe had concluded that whatever device Udo intended to use to wreak havoc would have to have been brought with him or with one of his confederates.

Any scenario involving the confederates was a wild card. Only John could identify even a single cell member, and that recognition was based on the mere ten or so seconds when the guy opened the door in response to John's knocking. This whole thing was so murky. No wonder no one was willing to believe him.

They made the turn onto Cass Avenue and raced for the narrowed gates. Joe decided now was the time to challenge his enemy. He pulled out of the Mustang's draft, stomped on the accelerator, and pulled up alongside. For the first time since that early April morning back in Akron, Joe Smith looked Udo Lewandowski in the eyes.

Their exchange of glances was brief, but Joe felt that he had attained some much-needed knowledge. First off, Udo had a definite sheen of nervous perspiration coating his face, suggesting that it just wasn't the heat and humidity of the day that was affecting him. Also, Joe took note of the muscular intensity that Udo had applied to the steering wheel and likened it to a cliché—"the death grip."

This sealed the deal for Joe. He was now convinced that the instrument of death was the man and not the machine.

The gates were coming on them quickly. Joe could see the GTO pass through the threshold in the middle of the two-car-width space. There was a moment of inspiration when Joe thought that he would maintain his current position alongside his rival that would force one man to blink, but there were a great deal of spectators in and around the area—more than just about anywhere else on the course—and he thought that any sort of a debacle here might turn out to be catastrophic.

Joe relented, took his foot off the gas, and let Udo lead through the gates. He immediately set himself up for the turn at First and Adams, but Udo wasn't as precise, and the two cars took the wacky turn on completely different lines. At the center of both apexes Joe was forced to brake to avoid a collision with the Mustang. They exited as if they were one vehicle, with the Barracuda nearly locked onto the rear bumper of the Mustang.

Joe kept this connection through the entire length of Adams Avenue. If Udo decided to stay to the left and reenter the stadium, Joe would be on him before he could get out of the car.

When Udo did not deviate from the course and made the right turn onto Witherell, Joe released an actual sigh of relief. He would have another tour of the circuit to figure out what the hell he was going to do to stop this homicidal zealot.

FIFTY-SEVEN

THE IMPALA SPOTTER saw the cars pass the stadium for the final time and then sprinted around the horseshoe to inform Kevin Gatz that they were firmly holding onto third place. He was reticent to admit that the GTO had a significant lead and that unless ground was made up in the first part of the third lap, they had little chance of being victorious.

When the spotter arrived at the VIP section, he noticed that the entire Impala section was still only sparsely filled. This was a rarity. By the beginning of the third and final lap, the confines were usually at capacity. He inched down the aisle in an attempt to get close to Kevin Gatz, but his progress was blocked by a clutch of about twenty of his ward mates who had gathered around their captain.

Captain Brassey was fielding a multitude of questions being lobbed at him from every angle. All those present had heard the rumors sweeping through the stadium. Lon kept an even tone to his outward expression, though if one could strip away his skin, examine his vital organs, and take a reading of either his heart or his brain, they would see clear evidence of a raging, hegemonistic anger.

For the moment, he had it under control, but a halo of darkness was coalescing around him, and he felt whatever elasticity he retained being stretched toward its maximal tensile strength.

John had begun to make the move toward his final duty, to get his family out. The time was nigh. John hurried over to the Impala section. He was buoyed by the realization that most of the bodies that he had to dodge to forge a path back to his neighborhood's area were exiting, not arriving.

He had nearly crossed the divide—was within shouting distance of his sister and mother—when his path was blocked by two people who had just crested the stairs and were entering the ward's designated seating area. It was Rebecca LeAnn Voss and her boyfriend, Denny Regan.

John's mind began to calculate an estimation of the minutes left in his personal countdown. Did he have time to engage the couple before he tried to pry away the elements of his family that might actually listen to him?

It only took one look into the eyes of the woman who'd had such an impact on him to have the questioned answered.

"Don't sit here," John said to her without providing the minimum of context other than the desperation in his voice.

"Hey, man, back off. Haven't you figured out that she doesn't want to talk to you?" Denny said.

"Something bad is going to happen. I don't want you to be here when it does. Please, just leave," John pleaded as he reached for her and clasped her arm.

The way she recoiled in fear under his grasp shocked him, and he released her immediately. Denny grabbed him roughly by the elbow and spun him around so that the two boys were face-to-face.

"I don't want to hurt you, John. That would make me feel sad because I actually feel sorry for you, you know, but if you don't get the fuck out of here this second, I will knock you on your pitiful ass," Denny said.

John knew that he could probably surprise this lout, but now the pool of precious seconds had begun to evaporate, and he no longer had the time to avenge the slight, let alone offer any details that would get them to alter their inclinations. He held up his hands in surrender and took a step back.

"Mr. Fedder can fill you in. Find him. I really hope you get a chance to talk to him," John said.

He turned and ran the rest of the way to the Impala VIP section. John arrived just after his father had successfully quelled the clamoring of his skittish flock.

Satisfied with their captain's answers, the remaining Impalans were returning to their seats. The spotter finally was afforded an opportunity to finish debriefing Kevin Gatz on the disposition of their entry in the race. Once informed, Kevin turned to the anxious smattering and disseminated the latest information.

"We are in it. We're third, and moving on second. The last pass through the gates and First and Adams will tell the story," Kevin shouted at Lon's constituency.

The next voice to be heard was John's maturing baritone.

"Mom, Holly, let's go," John said from the end of the aisle.

All of the eyes in the row turned to the source of the request.

Lon rose and began moving toward his son.

"Sit down, Dad. You can stay if you want, but Mom and Holly are leaving with me," John said with a finger pointed directly at his old man.

"What is wrong with you?" Lon asked menacingly.

"Stay out of my way, Dad. Holly, Mom, let's go, now!"

"What's wrong, John?" Karen asked.

"I can't explain it now. Obviously, he didn't tell you. Just trust me. We have to get out of here."

Karen rose from her seat just as Lon passed in front of her. Lon reached out with his right hand, and applied pressure to her shoulder, suppressing her ascent.

"Stay put," Lon said to his wife.

Lon now picked up his pace. The other patrons who were sitting in the row were forced to hastily rise so that they could allow their captain some berth.

"What fuck is wrong with you, kid?" Lon asked as he arrived at the end of the row.

"Dad, get out of my way. I don't want to hurt you, but I'm taking them out of here. I don't care what you do, but they should not be part of this."

"Did you go and get her?" Lon asked him.

"If you mean Cassandra, yes."

"What would possess you to do that?"

"No time for a conversation on ethics, Dad."

"You can answer the question, son," Lon said.

"I took her out of there because you crossed the line."

"There is no line, son."

"There is to me."

"What the hell's this kid talking about, Cap?" the old man asked.

The geezer had not been part of the group who had surrounded Lon earlier.

"Shut up, Clem," Lon said with his back to him.

"Shut up? Did you just tell me to shut up?"

"There are Redeemers in the city, Mr. Kincaid. And they are planning something big," John said to him.

"When?"

"Now. Right now. At any moment."

"Are you shitting me?" Clem asked, aghast.

John never got to answer the question. Lon cocked his arm and swung with all of his might. The open hand swept across the gulf of air and landed hard across John's mandible bone. As John tried to maintain his bearing, he felt his body become electrified. It felt like a horse's tail, spewing sparks, swishing away a fog of gnats—its position in space determined by its reaction to the intermittent discharge of the previously sealed voltage.

The last thing he heard before the seizures began was his mother screaming something accusatory to his father.

"God bless it, Lon, you swore you would never do that again!" she cried.

———————

As the remaining cars began the final lap, Joe was pretty certain that no one was going to catch the Lions' GTO. As Frank had instructed him, he kept his vision glued forward, his supple mind focused on getting the car in the right position on the road.

He had only taken one impulsive glance into the rearview—his marking of the three cars behind him on the last lap—because Frank had told him that the action was always in front of him, never behind. Now that he assumed that the battle for supremacy in the race was pretty much decided, he felt that regulation could be eased. He tilted his gaze to get a look at all of the competitors that trailed the three who had been out front for most of the race.

Joe was surprised to learn that the distance between his third place and the two cars battling for fourth position was getting shorter. They were on the Gratiot straightaway now, and both the Marquis' Roadrunner and the Pistons' Chevelle had made up significant ground. DeVille's Gran Torino was just a small speck in the mirror's frame—well back of the other two.

The Barracuda rounded the hard left onto the small Randolph Street straightaway and then countered with the sharp right onto Monroe. Joe was hugging the Mustang's bumper again, though he could have easily blown by him at any time. Joe took a look at the gauges and checked the car's vital signs—everything was in order. He did notice that the RPMs were noticeably lower than the last time he checked, and that made him flick his eyes toward the speedometer.

On this part of the course they had earlier breeched the eighty-miles-an-hour barrier; now they were only going just over fifty. What was going on here? No wonder the GTO was getting away and those cars to his aft were closing ground, he thought. Why was Udo driving so slowly?

They passed the stalled Challenger for the last time. Joe saw the GTO—now easily a couple of hundred yards in front—near the right turn that would lead them to the long Michigan Avenue straightaway. As both he and Udo approached the same turn, he saw a larger crowd than had been on that corner during any of the previous tours of the track. From the gear they sported, they looked like the Red Wings; it was the part of the course that ran closest to their neighborhood.

Up ahead he saw a waft of smoke appear under the right side of the GTO. A second later he heard what sounded like a muffled explosion. A second after that, another puff of smoke could be seen escaping from under the left front of the GTO before a subsequent identical boom.

Joe saw the crowd of Red Wing partisans laughing and pointing up the street at the GTO when Udo suddenly swerved to avoid something, and Joe saw the reason for their joy. Someone had placed piles of nails or long tacks all along the road just past the turn.

Joe countered Udo's move, and pulled left toward the curb. He narrowly avoided a group of gleeful observers, and when he didn't hear the sounds of puncture, he believed that he passed through the obstacle without incident.

With the GTO severely hobbled, it did not take long for Udo and Joe to come alongside. The Lions' driver was pissed, spouting a string of unpunctuated expletives. The flattened front rubber meted out a synchronized rhythm on the tarmac. The damage was so complete that it did not take long for the right wheel to begin making unsheathed contact with the ground. The steel on the rim began to grind directly into the pavement, and a shower of sparks spewed up as if a lit Roman candle had been attached to the fender skirt.

The Lions' driver was not going to give up, however. If he had to drive on the rims, so be it. He was at least still moving forward.

Joe now had a dilemma to deal with, because for all practical purposes, Udo had stopped racing. Cass Avenue was next, and Joe followed Udo through the turn and looked up to see the gates looming in the distance. The two steel walls had been ratcheted closed again, and from the intersection of Michigan and Cass, the space between the two walls looked like something less than a sliver.

As they headed up Cass, Udo began to further decrease his velocity. Joe looked at the speedometer—their swiftness had retarded all the way down to thirty-five miles an hour.

This was the basis for his predicament: If he continued to stalk this killer without at least feigning that he was competing, the killer was sure to know that Joe might be onto him and his intentions.

Joe did not want that to be a possibility—the element of surprise had to be protected, so he swung around to the right, shifted into third, revved out the engine, shifted into fourth, revved out that gear, and slipped the car into fifth. By the time he had closed to within a hundred yards of the gates, he had crested 100 miles an hour.

Joe did not notice the astonished looks on the spectators who had parked their asses at this place on the course because there was usually some mayhem to witness. In their collective memory, they had never seen anyone approach this stringent barrier with anywhere close to this speed.

Joe lined himself up and continued to offer the engine more air and fuel. He slipped through the crevice as if he were a puff of air being introduced into a vacuum. He had just achieved the maximum speed that the car had reached on this day, 128 miles per hour.

As Joe downshifted, lightly pumped the brakes, and set himself up for the turn at First and Adams, he had finally formulated something akin to a plan on how he was going to deal with Udo Lewandowski.

He was in third gear when he entered the turn. Every other time he had attempted to negotiate this bizarre excuse for a curve, he had started on his line at a much lower speed, and always, always in second gear. He had once tried to adjust the reality of the physics associated with the paradoxical routing in the simulator and had failed miserably, but now he had no choice.

Because he carried so much speed into the double apex, he instinctually flattened out the normal sine wave pattern and flew around the reversely banked path in an arc, feathering the wheel with tiny turns to the right to keep the car from plunging down to the bottom.

To all of the fans viewing the action on this part of the course, it appeared that the Barracuda was out of control, flying like a rocket without tailfins, wiggling violently, and on the verge of either leaving the surface of the road or spinning out and coming to a complete stop.

To Joe, the world suddenly made sense. This was the way his training would have had him take this curve. Newtonian physics be damned: There is always an alternate method, and it would never be devised from drawing boards and simulations, but from heart and instinct.

As he neared the exit to the turn, he saw the crowd gathered across the road begin to panic and scatter. They were no doubt convinced that there was zero possibility that he would be able to successfully exit onto Adams Avenue without coming across the road and plowing straight into them. They chose to run for their lives.

Joe knew better. In anticipation of the maneuver he would have to complete, he slowed slightly and began to magnify the once-tiny oscillations. By the time the critical moment came, the car was swerving in fluctuations of three feet to the right and left.

The trick was to catch the perfect right swerve onto Adams Avenue and be in the gear where he could apply the most effective acceleration. Too short of his goal, and he would either climb the hill and slide back or vault off the edge into sure oblivion. Too long and late, and those prescient people on the other side of the road would have proved to be the smartest people in the city for fleeing a certain kill zone. Without the bodies of the spectators to slow him down he would find himself confronting a wall of a building at tremendous speed. It would take the city's pathologist more time than he probably desired to remove the steering wheel that was sure to be implanted deep into Joe's chest.

When he saw that he would be short of his intended line, Joe did the opposite of what most mortals would do. Logic would dictate that acceleration was needed to provide the extra distance required to clear the ledge.

Instead, Joe took the opposite tack. He made his correction by slamming on the brakes and whipping the wheel to the left. He then jammed the gearshift into second and watched the reading on the tachometer jump above red line as he countered the left with a sudden vicious turn to the right as soon as his front wheels crossed onto Adams Avenue. He could feel the right-side tires straining to stay on the rims and for a second he believed that the outer tread might have been ground down to the fabric superstructure that existed beneath the layers of rubber.

During the subsequent drift, he shifted immediately into third and put the pedal to the floor. Like a stone skipping across a stream, gravity finally established itself, and the car gratefully settled on the pavement. The tires dug into the road, and the trim of the vehicle was restored. He did not hear the spontaneous outburst of applause that erupted as he passed by the blur of spectators.

FIFTY-EIGHT

JOE'S SUDDEN ACCELERATION quickly put a substantial amount of distance between himself and the car in second place, Udo's Mustang GT.

As the Barracuda streaked toward the stadium, Udo had yet to successfully make his way through the gates on Cass Avenue. After Joe left him in his afterburners, Udo nearly came to a stop to make sure that he would pass through without any complications. The crowd let him know that he was the main contender for their "wussy of the year" award. The hoots, boos, and profane insults came at him like a sudden, surging tide.

If he noticed, he did not seem to care. His eyes were riveted in their sockets, his area of vision relentlessly focused forward.

In third place, the Lions' GTO was still running on its bare front wheels, gamely refusing to give up. With the gates and the turn still to come, anything could happen. His contention was that as long as he was still moving forward, he was still in the race.

The crowd's tone changed from derision to amusement as he approached. They began to laugh, and the Lions' driver could hear their hilarity over the scraping of the alloy on asphalt.

Steering the beast was an absolute bitch, but the driver had found a way to keep it on an arrow path by holding the wheel with not only his hands, but also his thighs. He was still going close to twenty miles an hour as the unrelenting gap approached.

He had not charted the progress of the cars that were following him and had nary an idea of whether anyone else was still on the course. For all he knew, the reason why none of the others had overtaken him was because they were all out of the contest for one reason or another.

His confidence soared as he approached the opening in the wall. He was stable, and on a precise line, though to keep it on that even keel he was forced to keep turning the wheel slightly to the left. He never took a second to think of why that was required.

He found out soon enough. As he began to forge his way toward the opening, the car began to list hard to the right. He had actually ground the wheel down to nothing by this point, and when the axle finally made contact with the ground, the right front of the car came to a virtual stop, and he began to spin.

The length of the car was significantly greater than the width—so much greater that to try to enter into the opening with an attitude that suggested anything but perfect perpendicularity was tantamount to suicide.

He hit the left gate first. The rear end smashed into the steel, and the rear bumper was ripped from its moorings and catapulted into the crowd. The front of the car continued to spin for another fifty degrees or so. It was enough of a rotation so that he could see the road from whence he'd come, and now he took panicked notice of the squadron of three cars bearing down on him.

It was the Pistons' Chevelle, DeVille's Roadrunner, and Marquis' Gran Torino.

The poor Lions' driver was supremely fucked. One or three of the hurtling, three-thousand-pound-plus metallic meteors was going to smash into him for sure. He looked out the rear window and saw that the ass end of his car blocked more than half the space that the third position of the gates allowed for. He had only two options: try to free the car, or get the hell out of there.

The Lions' driver threw the car into first and hit the gas, but the entrenched axle acted like the pivot point of a drafting compass, and all he did was end up completing the circle that he had drawn by traveling the next 180 degrees. The result of the maneuver left him directly in front of the corridor, at the correct trajectory for passage, now completely blocking the entrance. He immediately unhooked from his restraints and bailed out of the car.

The three heavy vehicles that were still on a collision course with the abandoned GTO slowed their pace. One of the three was going to have to eradicate the obstruction or their race was over. The drivers began to eye one another to see if there was a volunteer among them who was willing to risk self-immolation.

Ironically or not, the three were all members of wards that had no historic enmity for the other. Likewise, they were also bereft of any precedence that would have them ever working in concert.

It all came down to their fortitude. All of the colors associated with their affiliations had faded into the hues positioned on the opposite ends of the color wheel, namely black and white. Who would throw themselves on the grenade so that the others could survive?

One of the drivers had a genetic advantage in that he was not a member of one of the cushier contrade, unlike the other two. He was a Piston, and his neighborhood encompassed the region at the extreme northwestern corner of the enclave, far from the action of the center of the city.

The contrast created by friction of being inside the walls, yet somewhat ostracized, had created an ethos that labeled them as "tough guys" or "bad boys." In the end, both the Marquis driver and his DeVille counterpart knew that it would be the Piston who would take on the role of the kamikaze.

That is exactly what happened. As the Roadrunner and the Gran Torino continued to slow themselves, the Pistons' driver took the contrary path; he shifted into third and made a beeline for the occluded opening.

He wasn't stupid enough to plow into the disabled GTO at a speed that would devitalize his own efforts, so after he separated himself from the competition, he slowed down to a velocity that he felt would rid him of the clog but not destroy the core of his vehicle.

Like the others behind him believed, he was under the false assumption that the GTO had become undriveable due to some type of failure with the engine. He lined himself up and kissed the rear of the Pontiac at a speed of around ten miles an hour. Post impact, he immediately hit the gas. The GTO began to move forward, but only in a continuation of the circle the car had already scratched into the pavement. The Pistons' driver was not prepared for this, and when the GTO whipped around, its front end smashed into the right rear quarter panel of his Chevelle.

The collision came as the Chevelle was halfway through the aperture of the gates, and the force of the impact caused the left side of the car to pinball into the door of rusted steel. Unsteadily, the Chevelle continued down the road—free of the gates—with both rear fenders crushed, abrading the rubber of the rear tires. He would never make it through the turn at First and Adams, as both of the tires would blow upon his entry.

The GTO returned to its exact same position of blockage—a metallic-flecked, blue-lacquered, three-ton turnstile.

The Marquis driver and his DeVille acquaintance had witnessed the failure and were collectively stumped. They both came to a stop and tried to conjure a path of righteousness that would release them from their purgatory on the wrong side of the gates.

As their engines (and brains) idled, they did not see the elements of the crowd looking back down Cass Avenue. There was another car coming down the road, the Tigers' forgotten Impala SS. Having been left for dead by the rest of the field, the Tigers' driver had eventually got the car turned around and back onto the course.

Certain that the only status that could be achieved would be that of also-ran, the Tigers' driver took the opportunity to take a joyride around the city. He had spent the last lap wallowing three-quarters of the circuit's breadth back from the rest of the field, cruising at twenty-five miles an hour, flipping off the spectators as he languidly drove by, and laughing his pariah-burdened ass off.

When he saw the predicament in front of the gates and two of his rivals having given into the inertia of the moment, his emotions switched from whimsical resignation to full-on avengement. *Fuck the people of this city*, he thought. Hell, he had only been a toddler when the leaders of his ward had stiffed their allies; why should their misdeeds foul his life?

The fates of the affluent loiterers, DeVille and Marquis, still stagnating in front of the gates, had been circumscribed; they were done for the day. Their final act involved getting their precious relics out of harm's way. Both cars backed away from the embolus that the GTO had fabricated and parked at the curb, side by cozy side, on the western flank of the avenue.

For the spectators at the gates, the action was over. No one expected the Impala SS to try to clear the orifice as there was no point—three cars had already passed through. In race time, the three leaders were eons ahead of anyone just now passing this juncture. There was no prize for second, let alone fourth.

But the Tigers' driver was determined to finish this fucking thing. He was bent on proving to the rest of the city that—though his ward might continue existing in a state of banishment—they still retained their balls.

He slowed as the gates neared, pulled up alongside the GTO, and assessed the situation. The car had to be removed from the opening, and the methodology that was most likely to fail was attempting to push it through to the other side.

He threw the transmission into reverse, backed up to provide clearance, and turned to the right. His rear end now faced the right side of the stalled Pontiac. He then pulled forward so he could create just a little momentum, returned the car to the reverse mode, popped the clutch, and hit the gas.

The Impala SS plowed into the GTO and drove it out of the way of the opening. For good measure, he made sure that the car crossed the avenue and came to rest in front of the two quitter's vehicles—a

veritable slamming of the cell door on the now fully incarcerated DeV-
ille and Marquis.

The Tigers' driver returned the Impala SS to the correct alignment
and slipped through the gates on his way to the turn at First and Adams, his left arm out the window sustaining a one-finger-salute. He was
going be the first Tigers entrant to reenter the stadium in the era that
existed since their blacklist.

John's seizures were subsiding. He still lay on the concrete, his mother
and sister kneeling on either side of him. There was little for either of
them to do other than roll him on his side. Should he vomit, the likelihood of his aspirating his emesis into his lungs was then mitigated.

Cassandra joined the vigil, creating a circle around John. Not far
from this scene stood the impatient figure of Lon Brassey. A force field
of metaphorical electromagnetism had built up around him, and he
remained isolated from everyone in the vicinity.

His constituents had heard the incriminating words that spilled
from Karen's mouth. They were trying to process this import as they
focused their attention on the fallen boy.

Kevin had chosen to blend in with the bystanders and not stand
next to his captain. Lon's wife's implication that the kid's lifelong struggle with epilepsy may have been caused by the captain had rocked
his small and petty world. In a departure from every instinct that had
brought him to this point in his life, he began to silently pray that the
kid be returned to customary consciousness. His uncharacteristic entreaty was halted by the voice of the spotter.

"Look!" the spotter shouted, and he pointed toward the field.

A car was coming into the stadium. It would take but a millisecond for the crowd to come to the realization that it was the Barracuda.

FIFTY-NINE

THE NONES OF JULY

APPROACHING DECIMA AND BEYOND[4]

For John, the seizures had mercifully come to an end. He looked up into the faces of the three concerned women and slowly regained his visual focus. His instinct was to get to his feet and usher these people away. As he struggled to find the balance required to even raise his head, a male hand descended onto his shoulder.

"Don't get up," the male said.

"We go must now," John said.

John had no idea that he lacked any sense of his normal erudition and had jumbled the statement in a dyslexic fashion.

"I'll get them to a safe place," the male voice said.

John looked up at the face of the man. There were concentric halos emanating from above his hairline. John's intrinsic logic had not been perturbed by his seizures; he was sure of that. He knew that this person was not a spirit or an avatar, but human, and someone he had met before. He could not make out all of the facial features, and his voice was distorted, but he knew this man.

"Please hurry. Get them safely away," John said.

"I will," the man confirmed.

John heard the protestations of the women attending to him, but before he could nip their reticence in the bud, the man said, "This is what he asks of you. Please, do as he asks."

The negative outbursts ebbed when the man consented to return for John after he had removed Karen, Holly, and Cassandra.

The man gathered the group at the end of the aisle but returned to John before his departure.

"I'm going to slide you between these rows of seats. If you feel something strange start to happen—like you think the seizures are returning—let this person know."

John nodded, and the man whistled for an accomplice to aid in the redistribution. John recognized the person that the man had enlisted

---

4   The ancient Roman term "decima" refers to the time of 2:00 P.M.

to help him. It was the hulking figure of Billy Klock. That realization began to reorient his recognition abilities, and he suddenly lit upon the identity of the Samaritan. He was pretty sure the man was Kevin Gatz.

Joe came through the tunnel and entered the stadium preceding a wake of parched topsoil that followed him like an incorporeal being. The trailing apparition may or may not have been a harbinger of the future—a grimy declaration that evil was on its way. Or maybe it was just what it was, dry dirt.

The Barracuda skidded to a stop in the middle of the field, and Joe alighted from the driver's seat to the exhortations of the small but suddenly energized Impala section. They were screaming at him to go get the ward's colors, and run them up the pole. They were screaming at him to win the motherfucking race.

Joe looked up to the tiers that now contained only a smattering of his employers and felt relief that John and Cassandra had been successful in getting some people to listen to them.

Forgetting his priorities for a moment, impelled by the desire to satisfy the confidence that the people of Impala had in him (especially Frank and Claudia), he made a couple of tentative steps to complete his race duties. All the while, he had his vision centered on the stadium opening.

Joe did a quick estimation of the distance he had covered since he had left Udo's Mustang in his rearview back on Cass Avenue, made adjustments for the variance in their velocities, and tried to determine the window of time that was afforded to him before the deranged man's arrival.

At twice the follower's speed—even if Udo made it through the wicked Adams Avenue turn with no problems—he figured that he had little more than sixty seconds before the Mustang would trundle into the stadium.

Joe sprinted to the wall faced with the flags of the various wards, performed his balletic leap, snatched the Impala colors from its Velcro mooring, and turned toward the flagpole.

It had been a conditioned response and not germane to the real situation that was soon to confront him. He stopped about halfway across the field from the mast and turned to the crowd. He was suddenly intent on letting the people know that they should evacuate.

He waved the Impala pennant at the spectators. It was his way to alert them that they should leave immediately.

The Mustang fans saw it differently. Their section was still pretty full—by far the most populous of all of the other sections—and they deciphered Joe's actions as nothing more than petty taunting.

As if a choirmaster had held out his arms and beckoned them to their feet, the entire section rose and began to scream profanities and offer vulgar gesticulations at Joe's flagrant display of insolence.

More than one of the Mustang patrons gauged the distance to the ground from the railing to determine if fractures and sprains would be incurred when they jumped down to field level to beat the shit out of this cocksucker.

On the opposite side of the stadium, the small group of Impala's remaining supporters screamed at their driver to finish the job. They too migrated to the railing at the foot of their section. Though they possessed far fewer numbers, they vowed that a force of ten Impalans would meet any member of the Mustang faithful who decided to leave his confinement to exact revenge on Joe.

This was exactly the opposite effect that Joe was trying to achieve. He ceased his obviously unintelligible semaphore and dropped the green, black, and white guidon on the ground at his feet. Now, no one knew what to do. The Mustang crew was silenced as the Impala folk broke into a constant stream of scatology.

The Mustang came through the tunnel and crawled slowly onto the field. Udo took note of where the Barracuda had parked and deliberately steered his car away before coming to a stop at the base of the wall where the curve to the start of the horseshoe began.

From the first moment that the Mustang had become visible, Joe closed the gap between his position and the car. He was careful not to make any swift moves. The car was still running, and if Udo felt skittish, he could simply drive away.

The noise from the voices in the stadium drifted away as Joe's senses became attuned to stalking his prey. As he continued across the field, he noticed that Udo had not looked up and seen his advance.

Joe was ten yards away when he saw the Redeemer zealot frozen to the seat, eyes closed, mouthing unheard but definitely spoken words. His moving lips were within a millimeter of the steering wheel. Joe could see that the passenger door was unlocked. The thumb of chromed steel was in its fully pulled-out position. He could also see that his initial assumption that Udo had most likely carried the unknown device of destruction on his person was faulty. He knew the man to be big in size, but their appeared to be no added girth.

With the spell of Joe's pure intention shattered by the sudden need to improvise, the sounds of the crowd returned, and he could hear the Mustang people screaming for their driver to get out of his car and complete the required steps needed for victory.

Joe heard the noise of shoes and boots colliding with the earth, and he turned to see that many of the Mustang rail sitters had left their perches in the stands. They tumbled to the ground and briefly checked their injury status before running across the field toward their entrant.

Simultaneously, many members of the Impala hardcore leapt off of their platform. The rest traversed toward the Mustang section in an effort to get closer to the impending melee. Their target could have been the Mustang interlopers, or it could just as easily have been Joe. Maybe they intended to lodge their complaints over his non-performance by subjecting him to a collective beating.

Joe had no other choice but to hasten his advance and risk the possibility that Udo would notice his avenging intentions.

He reached the passenger door as Udo reached under the seat. Joe nearly ripped the door off the hinges to get his hands around the forearms of this demon. He got a grip on Udo's dense wrists, braced his legs against the door and the jamb, and yanked with all of his might.

It was not supernatural power that allowed Joe to extricate the much larger man through the passenger door with such relative ease; it was that Udo had submitted to his Redeemer just prior to the surprise visit from his nemesis. The moment of his death had arrived, and his mind and body had gone lax once the final commitment had been sanctified.

It took Udo a moment to recognize that the situation had changed. There was a fleeting feeling that his destruction had been completed and he was already experiencing the afterlife. Perhaps this was a last purgatorial battle before his ascendance to a life everlasting with the other devout and his hallowed savior. He truly believed that the explosive had been triggered and that he, and Joe, were preparing for combat on an amorphous plane between earth and heaven.

Udo's last thought before he found himself on the ground was the belief that he was soon to be reunited with Craig Bellows, his de facto father and mentor. The howling desire to make this a reality was the force that impelled him to release his limbs from Joe's grasp and stand to face the man. This was the final test. There would be one more earthbound human to dispense with before his Redeemer would grant his reward.

Udo did not smell the residual odor of the explosive nor the accompanying stench of burning flesh, but he still retained the surety that he had carried out his mission until he noticed that the field was aswarm with living, breathing infidels from both the Impala and Mustang wards. Both groups were advancing toward him and his foe.

Udo looked to his right. The Mustang vehicle was still intact. He did not curse his misfortune, but quickly weighed the most effective remedy to this unanticipated disappointment. He dove back into the car and reached for the wiring that dangled under the driver's seat.

Again, Joe forcibly pulled the Redeemer apostle out of the car—this time by the ankles. Unlike the last time, Udo was not caught unawares, and he fought by grabbing onto anything the interior offered. The gearshift and the console provided handholds of resistance. But a swift downward planting of Joe's boot onto Udo's testicles released Udo's grip. Joe got him out of the car and back onto the ground.

Joe caught only a glimpse of the apparatus that was meant to detonate and saw that—though the connection had been attempted—the circuit had not been completely closed. An antiquated six-volt lantern battery was dangling from the web of springs underneath the seat. Before Joe could reach in and rip it free, he was set upon by the Mustang mob.

Joe used his honed technique against the arriving horde—every block a strike, every strike a block. Within four seconds, many of the attackers were writhing on the ground in pain, each sustaining multiple sub-dermal contusions.

Udo stretched his legs and uncoiled himself from the fetal bearing he had assumed after Joe's swift kick to his crotch. As Joe grabbed him to move him away from the car, the Impala cadre arrived and chose as the subject for abuse not the driver for the enemy ward, but Joe Smith himself.

"You're fucking kidding me," Joe screamed at this new group of tormentors.

"You screwed us," one of the Impalans said upon closing in.

"Did they pay you off?" another asked.

Joe saw Udo make it to his feet. Joe sidled away from the advancing throng of ten or so and moved to block Udo's access to the vehicle and the danger dangling within.

Udo reacquired his wits rapidly and balled his fists. He took two steps toward Joe, which still left him two full arm lengths away.

"This isn't going to happen. I know who you are," Joe said calmly.

"Then you know the power of the Redeemer can will this, and there is nothing you can do about it," Udo said between gasps.

Joe lunged like a rabbit with an ignited rocket up its ass. He hit Udo with his flattened palm between the spans of ribs six through eight, just to the right of his sternum. Udo's eyes began to roll backward in their sockets as his heart was arrested in mid-contraction. When his heart tried to restart, it did so in fits and starts. The electrical components were confused as to how to reinvigorate the emptied-out chamber that Joe had completely purged with his blow. Cardiac fibrillation was invoked, and his entire body started to quiver. Eight seconds later, Udo Lewandowski was dead.

The Impalans' protestations ceased after they observed the devastation that this man had brought to one who as much larger than himself. They collectively began to back away from their original intentions.

Joe grabbed Udo's driver's suit by the collar and dragged him toward the center of the field. He wanted the gathered to know that what they had witnessed was real, and he wanted any of the Redeemer apostle's accomplices lurking nearby to understand that he was willing to do anything to quell their appetite for destruction. Joe kept an eye out in case one or all of them had designs on avenging the death of their leader.

Joe heard a sudden outburst of the crowd but did not initially see the object of their interest. He followed their pointing to find the Tigers' Impala SS was on final approach through the tunnel. He dropped Udo's body in his tracks—no more than twenty feet from where he started—and ran for the cover of his vehicle in the middle of the field.

The Impala SS slowed as the driver became distracted by his attempt to determine the identity of the race's victor. He looked at the flagpole and saw that the lanyard was devoid of any of the other ward's colors. For a second, he believed that a divine intervention had placed him in this position. He could win this race against all odds.

He laid a heavy foot on the brakes just as he crept across the surface pond of oil left behind by the derelict AMX at the outset of the contest. The Impala SS began to rotate in a counterclockwise direction. The driver tried to steer out of it and was making progress when the vehicle drifted away from his objective—the open area next to the wall containing the flags.

In a moment of panic, he embarked upon an advanced move; he engaged the transmission in a low gear and attempted a quick acceleration. He hoped that he would be able to right his vessel before it smacked into the wall on his left. By giving the car some power, he hoped to gain traction and steer clear of the looming partition.

The ploy produced the opposite result. Instead, the car fishtailed forward and smashed into the rear end of the Mustang. The Tigers' driver did not see the body of the man lying on the ground within spitting distance from the collision.

Joe was the only person in the stadium who knew what might happen next. It was the reasoning behind him dropping Udo's body and moving away from the Mustang. He completed his retreat back to his car, dove to the ground, shimmied under the center part of the frame of the Barracuda, endured the smoldering of his racing suit as the heat from the twin exhaust pipes seared his flesh, and came out on the protected side of the car. He crawled over and curled up behind the passenger-side front wheel and waited for the inevitable.

Before Joe's second attack on him, Udo had been able to manipulate the wiring so that only mere millimeters needed to be traversed before detonation. The jostling caused by the impact of the Impala SS appulsing the Mustang broke the inertia, and when the battery swung back in reaction to the jolt—like an ordinal bell—the circuit was closed.

The fireball that rose to over a hundred feet briefly preceded the concussive explosion. The report was of volcanic proportions and easily exceeded the 200-decibel threshold. Anyone within one hundred feet was likely to sustain ruptured eardrums, but this would only be confirmed during an autopsy since most, if not all of them, would be dead.

Shrapnel—both intended and unintended—dispersed onto every chartable plane of space. Layers and layers of prepackaged nails and screws joined pieces of the body of the vehicle.

Flaming remnants of both rained down on Joe. He had the foresight to plug his ears with his fingers, though after the blast they were still ringing. The force of the detonation actually moved the Barracuda nearly a foot to the south, and so Joe had to react lest he be pinned underneath the low-profile front end of his makeshift blast wall.

Joe figured that there was not likely to be a second explosion to be triggered by residual fuel since the tank would have been nearly empty by the time the car reentered the stadium. The initial deflagration would have vaporized pretty much anything anyway.

Joe popped up and peered over the hood of the displaced Barracuda. Parts of the bodies of the citizens who had earlier rushed the field were strewn about the ground. The remains only vaguely suggested that they were once of human origin. There was little but an amalgam of blood and bone sans structure and context.

The Tigers' driver was dead, and the interior of his car burned along with his body. The fabric flamed, and the plastic melted into gobs of fuming, toxic puddles with a definite Escherian perspective.

Joe could see that only Udo's torso now personified the bulk of the Redeemer's body. Every limb had been released from its respective ball and socket. The head of the evildoer had separated from its foundation as well, but not completely. It resembled the maw of a reptile with a gaping hole in the side of the neck that exposed tongue-like vertebrae ready to snatch an unsuspecting insect from the milky air to its left.

Joe's eyes panned the stands to his right. Most of the spectators within his field of vision were dead. A mass of bodies from an entire section had been blown up from their seats and smashed against the abutments separating the tiers. Joe could see that most had been dressed in some combination of blue and white. Mustangs. There was no doubt that their recalcitrance or misguided trust had hastened their departure from earth. It would take awhile to sort through them, but Joe surmised that their likes would include the corpses of their captain, Titus O'Keefe, and that weasel of a lawyer, Leo Rascone.

As the dust and smoke cleared, he saw signs of survivors, bloodied patrons staggering around the upper levels of the stadium. As Joe moved toward the Impala section, he saw more signs of life as the less critical attended to the maimed and the static. He did not see the Brassey family amongst the multitude of causalities; their section was empty.

He knew that he had banished Frank and Claudia, and he was sure that they had followed his orders. He was about to turn his attention to the wounded on the field when he saw Cassandra appear at the ramp that led to the Impala section. She darted down the aisle and ran over to a row of seats at the back of the section before collapsing to her knees. Joe immediately began to sprint toward her.

SIXTY

IT WAS FORTUNATE that John's body was positioned where it was behind a seam where two sections of the stadium were knit together.
At this juncture the engineers had reinforced the joint with an extra
four layers of imbedded-steel concrete that shielded John from being
directly exposed to the blast. The shock wave did jostle him though,
but he had regained a good portion of his wits by then and was able to
keep his head from smashing into the metal struts of the seat behind
him by rolling up into a ball. His knees had been reassigned to function as a flesh, muscle, and bone helmet.

It was the smell that he would remember—a waft of chemical
and fuel smoke immediately followed by the acrid mephitis of burning
human tissue.

John rose to a seated position and took a moment to allow for
his equilibrium to adjust. He still could not see over the backs of the
cracked plastic seats, and there was a part of him that did not want to
look at all the carnage. His imagination of the damage was far from the
reality. When he finally was able to view the aftermath, it was far worse
than any horror that his young mind could have conjured.

As he finally peered over the rim of the seat in front of him, he had
but one objective, to determine the disposition of his friend, Joe. John
had not been a witness to the proceedings for some time and was not
aware of the litany of events that had transpired.

John was sure that his sister and mother had been ferried away. He
had a gauze-like memory of a man stepping into the breech to assume
the responsibility. It made no sense to him that the face of the man
resembled Kevin Gatz, and he chalked up that incongruity to the many
images that had been scrambled by his brain during its realignment
phase. That was the only memory he had some access to, though the
quality of his remembrance was as ill defined as sludge.

He did a quick scan of those who were scattered about the field.
In the cases in which he could recognize facial features or body type, he
saw no one that shared any of the specific features of his friend.

He was just about to try to stand up when a voice called to him
from the end of the row.

"Are you hurt?"

He saw that it was Cassandra and that she appeared not to have
suffered any injury.

"I don't think so," he said as she advanced toward him with a sideways shimmy.

She helped him to his feet.

"Where's Joe?" he asked.

She responded with a look of uncertainty that appeared to him to be shadowed by doubt. She had not seen the run-up to the explosion herself, as she had been helping Kevin spirit the female members of John's family to safety. She could only assume the worst: that Joe had tried to stop the explosion but had failed and was likely a statistic now.

John looked around at the people who had been in these sections of seats and saw the first of many things that would haunt him for the rest of his life. Down at the bottom of the section—in the row that was closest to the field—was a bloodied Denny Regan, trying desperately to get his girlfriend, Rebecca LeAnn Voss, to return to consciousness.

John instinctively moved toward them. Cassandra grabbed his arm to steady him on the descent of steps.

"Denny," John called out.

When the boy turned to him, John could see that he was missing his right hand. A torrent of blood was rushing from the stump. He could also see that the body of his love no longer possessed either the aura or the essence of life.

Tears began to fog John's vision as he stripped off his shirt, ripped off a length of fabric, and applied a tourniquet to Denny's arm. Denny was in total shock, muttering something about having misplaced the sandwich he was preparing to serve his girlfriend at the time of the blast. Denny turned back to Rebecca.

"Come on Beck, we got to go now. Wake up, sweetie," Denny said.

Cassandra stepped in at that point, took Denny's arm in her hands, and raised it so that it was pointed toward the sky. Aided by the garroted bandage, the flow of blood had ebbed, and the end of the stump resembled the surface of a sliced red beet. Cassandra walked Denny away and back up the stairs as a group of first responders—Mugwumps from security and the fire division—dotted the landscape all around the stadium.

John sat down in the crimson-stained seat next to Rebecca and cradled her in his arms. She was still warm to the touch. His hand found the massive dent in the side of her head that had caused her death.

John carefully laid Rebecca's body on the ground. He wiped the moisture from his eyes and looked up toward the peristyle with faint hopes that he might attract the attention of the emergency medical personnel, though the reasoning behind his efforts was fraught with a sense of futility. After all, she was dead. He rightly assumed that their attention to triage was still what ruled the day. Body collection was something that would have to wait.

He did not want to leave her body unattended though. He sat down in a nearby seat and surveyed the scene that lay before him.

John had seen movies that had depicted similar events, but now that he was confronted with the real deal, he saw no resemblance between the fictional portrayal and what had actually occurred around him. A shift had definitely happened, and this city would never be the same. Of this he was sure.

As he scanned across the stadium, something caught his eye that compelled him to double back over a previously viewed location. Down toward the rail—two sections over in the Pistons' containment—John saw a man sitting casually, appearing to just be staring at the field in a state a catatonia. It was his father.

John was torn. He did not want Rebecca's body to be collected as part of some general clean-up operation and tossed onto the pile (and possible pyre) that was sure to be created on the field. He wanted her to be returned directly to her family and given the proper rite of burial or cremation. She had been a survivor for so long, and he had determined that her life warranted some sort of ceremonial acknowledgement of that fact. A mass grave would be convenient, if not necessary, but he did not want her to be lumped in with anyone who had been less courageous than her. The number of the deceased that would measure up to that metric would most likely sum to zero.

He reached down, took custody of her body, and lifted her over his shoulder. Even in his still-ungrounded state, she was not a burden. He traversed the two sets of aisles that would take him to the section of seats where his father sat. He had many questions for his sire, the most pressing being an elucidation of his mother's revelation that the old man had struck him before, and that that act may have triggered the onset of his disease.

As he neared the solitary figure, John became aware that his father had not shifted in his seat since he had laid eyes upon him. On his arrival, the puzzle was solved.

His father had also suffered a fatal wound. There was a chrome accoutrement protruding from his chest. Blood was still spurting forward; a prior gusher had formed a pool at his father's feet. John could see that the implement of death was a piece of the left front quarter panel of the Mustang. The rearing horse logo dangled just outside the area of penetration.

John could not process the ironic elements easily apparent in the moment. He was pissed that the man had left him before he could get some answers to the questions about why he was such a fucking prick.

He lowered Rebecca's body into the seat to his right and sat down between the two. In the ensuing minutes he spoke to both of them about a variety of subjects. He touched on topics like their mutual pasts and what the future held for him. For the first time in his life, there was no evidence of dissension from either of them.

By the time that Joe and Cassandra found him, he was mumbling to the two corpses about how one day they would feel a pride for him that they never did when they were physically part of his life.

Joe and Cassandra waited respectfully at the end of the row of seats until the Mugwumps tasked with identification and removal of the dead arrived to perform their duties.

John eventually ascended from his reverie and accepted the realization that the dead had to be taken from the area, but he pronounced his adamancy that these two should not be part of any bulk accumulation process. He would accompany these particular decedents back to their ward, back to their respective homes.

The Mugwumps had not made concessions for situations such as these. After they cataloged the names and affiliations, they left John with some materials that included propylene bags and a wide rigid board. It was up to him to figure out how he was going to accomplish the transportation of his rapidly stiffening ashen-skinned charges.

Joe and Cassandra offered their assistance. Joe assumed that they could make use of the Barracuda. Even if the leftover fuel in the car became exhausted, it would get them somewhat closer to their destination.

They respectfully draped the plastic over the victims and stacked them on top of each other on the board. It was only after they had decided on the simplest option for getting the load onto the playing field that John became cognizant that his friend Joe had survived the devastation.

"What happened?" John asked.

"I'll tell you later. You sure you're okay?" Joe asked.

"Yeah, physically I'm fine," John said.

Joe would not ask him to reveal why he narrowed his response. There would be a time to unwind all that had happened and pursue some sort of analysis, but that was not now.

Cassandra had filled Joe in on the events surrounding John's seizure, including the revelation that John's disorder could have originally been brought on when his father hit him during his infant years. Karen had admitted as much to Cassandra during their flight to safety.

Joe spied Kevin Gatz and Billy Klock down below them on the field, identifying the bodies with Impala origins for the Mugwump reapers. He called them over to the railing, and with their help they lowered the board to the ground. Joe then jumped to the field surface, and helped both John and Cassandra with the descent.

As the five pallbearers moved the ersatz casket toward the improvised hearse, Joe spied an anomaly among the bodies and random body parts that were scattered about them.

Equidistant between the smoldering hulk of the Mustang and the Barracuda was an arm. Joe found himself continuing to examine the stray limb as the funeral entourage proceeded toward the car. At one point, the cortege stopped, and Joe—still focused on the arm—nearly dropped his corner of the makeshift stretcher.

Once the board containing Lon and Rebecca's bodies was laid across the hood of the car, Joe returned to the area of the field that had drawn his interest and located the severed appendage.

At the end of the jagged humerus bone, where the arm had separated from the shoulder joint, was a flap of burnt skin that had partially obscured a jet-black tattoo. Joe smoothed some of the slack out of the epidermis by drawing his fingers across the area that sported the applied message. He saw that the tattoo was not of the crude ink-pen variety, but had been placed there by someone with a definite sense of artistry.

There was no picture or words—just a sequence of numerals and some punctuation. He knew that this limb had once been attached to the man who had committed mass murder not an hour before. He carried the arm over to the car and handed it to Kevin Gatz.

"Hold on to this," Joe said as he turned to get into the driver's seat.

Kevin first reaction was to squeamishly reject the offering, but it had already been placed in his arms. He gritted his teeth, resisted an urge to vomit, and lodged the offending article in the space between the body board and the windshield. Kevin, Billy, and John were tasked with steadying the board on the slope of the hood. Joe would keep the car's speed at a snail's pace, and Cassandra would ride shotgun.

Getting into the car was a bit of a problem. The entire driver's side had been exposed to the blast. The windows were shattered, and most of the layers of purple enamel had melted away. The scorched door handle dangled from its factory-installed moorings.

Joe slid in from the passenger side, brushed the glass to the floor, produced the car key, and inserted it into the ignition. As he began to rotate it toward the start position, there was a quaking explosion that shook the ground like an eruptive seism of the earth's core.

All of the Mugwump attendants in their vicinity looked toward the northwest before beginning to scramble about in a chaotic fashion.

"What was that?" Cassandra asked with a gasp.

Joe knew. "Round two," he said.

He got out of the car and was nearly mowed down by a cadre of Mugwumps that were frantically heading for the nearest exit. Like two wax figures of a slapstick comedy team, Kevin Gatz and Billy Klock could not adjust the expressions on their faces to portray anything other than frozen shock.

John was ready for action, and he came up to Joe's side.

"Where do you think it came from?" Joe asked.

Before John could open his mouth, he had the answer. A second, similarly violent explosion rocked them.

"Somewhere toward the northwest," John said.

Kevin's face began to thaw quickly.

"What the fuck?" he screamed.

"The apostle was a harbinger. My gut tells me that there are forces trying to get into your city," Joe said.

"We're going to have to leave the bodies here for the time being. Who's going to volunteer to stay with them?" Joe asked the detail.

John and Billy moved to help them pull the board off the hood.

"I will," Kevin said.

"Thank you," Joe said.

Joe, John, Cassandra, and Billy piled into the Barracuda. There was little if no room in the back compartment, but the four found a way to squeeze inside. Joe fired up the engine, engaged the transmission, whipped the car around one 180 degrees and sped off for the tunnel.

SIXTY-ONE

THEY MADE IT to the outskirts of the Tigers' neighborhood—just to the other side of MLK Jr. Boulevard—before the Barracuda began to sputter. Joe knew that the extra weight had seriously affected their fuel consumption, but the hunger pangs coming from the carburetor would have been felt sooner or later, he rationalized. They exited the vehicle and continued on foot up Woodward Avenue.

Joe sniffed the air.

"Oh my God," he muttered.

"What?" John asked.

"I don't believe it," Joe said.

His comment had piqued the interest of the entire party. All eyes turned to him for further elucidation.

"Greek fire," Joe said.

"What?" Cassandra asked.

"You can smell the naphtha, the sulfur, and the tar pitch."

"You can?" Billy asked.

"I think we caught a break," Joe said.

They could see many panicked individuals up ahead, all starting to stream toward them in full evacuation mode.

"Can you rally some of these folks?" Joe asked his trio of associates.

"We can try," John said.

"Tell them to gather anything that can be used as a weapon—tools, garden implements, kitchen knives, whatever. If I'm right, only a couple of these idiots will be able to breech the wall for the time being, and regardless of how many they have on the other side, we should easily be able to overwhelm these initial intruders, and then we can figure out our options for a long-term strategy."

Joe gave them a quick primer on the multi-millennial old weapon that was known as Greek fire. He explained that the recipe was secret—not a soul, other than those ancients, ever knew the correct proportions. Its manufacture required a light inflammable liquid like naphtha, sulfur, and tar pitch from the evergreen tree. The elements were intermingled somehow, and the result was a massive smoke-filled explosion. The recipient of the attack usually used conventional methods such as water to put out the ensuing wall of flames, but water only seemed to feed the inferno. Only a weak acid like vinegar, urine, or sand could snuff out the raging inferno.

"We're going to need to use their weapon against them," Joe said declaratively.

John and Billy split off to gather volunteers. Cassandra and Joe continued toward the source of the noise.

"Are there some hydrants, or is there a water source nearby?" Joe asked her.

"You said that water would only anger it," Cassandra said.

"Exactly."

A small group was gathered up ahead. Cassandra explained that the bunch appeared to be members of the small professional militia tasked with the security near the walls. A few of them sported some severe burns, but they had not completely retreated. They were all looking toward the southwest.

Joe walked up to the man that sported the most stripes on his sleeves.

"Are you in charge?" he asked.

"Who the fuck are you?"

Joe looked down the street where the smoke was billowing up toward the cloudless sky. A fifteen-foot wall of flames—easily fifty yards in width—was burning at the base of the earthen barrier.

Joe looked at the area across the street from where the explosion had occurred. There was dirt everywhere, cloaking all of the buildings directly across from the blast zone with a beige hue. He saw no evidence of any human activity and determined that whoever had used this fury to breech the wall, had not been able to traverse through the hell that they had unleashed because it was still too hot.

"Is there a firehouse around here?"

The man pointed vaguely down the street. Joe turned to Cassandra.

"Wait for Billy and John and their volunteers. This will be the staging area right here. And explain to these gentlemen my assessment of the situation," Joe told her.

"Where are you going?" she asked.

"A little recon, and maybe the execution of a temporary defense," he said.

She looked into his eyes. Something was now radically different about the soul that lurked behind them. *He's gone*, Cassandra thought. She had pried open his heart, but it had morphed back into its bolted, titanium configuration. He was no longer looking and dealing with her as if she were his beloved; she was now just another ally, nay, subordinate, in the battle.

Joe ran toward the zone of havoc, keeping his eyes peeled for anyone who might have ascended the wall's superstructure—the former I-94 bypass that was once named the Edsel Ford Freeway. He thought that some might try to cross the barrier from above, before waiting for the fire in the hole to dissipate.

He could see that there was some abatement to the intensity of the blaze, and this realization quickened his pace. If the conflagration disappeared, he was certain that an invasion would be imminent, and he would be powerless to stem the flood tide of psychotic killers who would use the hole to enter the enclave.

Joe came upon the firehouse that the militia leader had intimated was in the vicinity. The building was empty, and Joe assumed correctly that the firefighters had been dispatched to the stadium immediately after the alarm had been sounded.

He hurriedly gathered a cache of crude weapons—a fire ax and a couple of tanks of compressed air. He could use these if he had to face a few of these freaks in close combat. If there were a legion out there poised to invade, the arms would only be utile for a moment, before their forces would easily overwhelm him.

He located some lengths of hose that had been left behind, and he joined all of the strands he could find into one long cable-like skein that he loaded onto a reel. He would need to find a pressurized source to fill the hose, and all he could hope for was a nearby spigot.

He snatched a large wrench from a hook on the wall, strapped it to the rig that held the air tanks, attached the axe as well, and donned the harness. With both hands free, he began to roll the spool of hose out the gaping door of the firehouse.

He got lucky. Across the street—twenty-five yards from where the flames were shooting out from the yawning hole—there was a tap attached to the side of one of the dirt-spattered buildings. He attached the female end of the hose and rolled the spool down the street before testing the pressure of the water line. He'd experienced better in his time, but he determined the force to be adequate. The business end of the hose allowed for adjustment in flow rate, and Joe figured if the stream was too weak, he could narrow the aperture to produce an outflow that would reach the fire from a safe distance.

He recoiled the hose back behind the safety of the corner of the building and waited for the first of the maniacs to show themselves. He kept his eyes on the corner of the hole where the fire was beginning to show some signs of exhaustion.

He didn't figure on the snipers, though. Two rounds pinged off the face of the axe that made up part of the contraption strapped to his back. He scurried to cover and removed the harness. He didn't need for one of the air tanks to be penetrated; that would not be good.

The quality of the sound of the bullet on the hardened steel of the axe blade told him the caliber was of a size that wouldn't produce a lot of damage should he end up taking one or two in any place other than the head, heart, or lungs. Most likely the gun was a .22, something used to shoot small animals. It was not capable of stopping someone unless the marksman hit the subject with precision. Redeemers were not known to be that proficient with firearms.

Joe peeked around the corner of the building to get a fix on the shooter. He was hoping that the bullets had not come randomly through the wall of flame and that there was someone actually trying to hit him from a perch or other such position.

He knew one thing though. The white, green, and black racing suit had to go lest he present himself to these psychos like a phosphorescent duck in an arcade gallery. He stripped down to his underwear, found a seam in the hose where there was a dripping leak, and doused his body with water. He rolled in the dirt that had been loosed from across the street until his entire body assumed the color that made up the facade of the buildings that stood directly across from the Redeemer's forced ingress.

He camouflaged the hose with the same technique. It did not take long to cake the fabric with mud. He checked down the street to see if any volunteers had arrived with John or Billy. He wanted to warn them that there were firearms about.

He found the sniper, lying in the prone position, atop the wall at the far end of the hole. The overpass's concrete infrastructure gave him plenty of cover, and Joe knew that without a gun, he would have a hard time trying to silence that rifle.

Instead, he focused on the area of the hole nearest to him that had obviously been loaded with a weaker concentration of Greek fire because it was already waning in intensity. He could see some of the Redeemer forces marshalling themselves on the other side—clad in their customary orange jumpsuits—preparing for their first foray into town.

The fodder would be first. Even though he hated these warriors and their cockeyed catechism, he always found himself feeling sorry for some of their lot. It was always the least jaded—the ones that exhibited the strongest sense of zealotry—who would take the first steps into battle. They were almost always a unit that was comprised of the rawest of recruits, and their freshly imprinted minds beckoned them to charge into the action without fear or thoughts of consequence. Their indoctrination included the promise of a reward should they be felled during an attack on the infidels: the deliverance of their most coveted desire—life everlasting with their Redeemer. They were rarely skilled and were always given the least-functional weaponry.

It was always this group that Joe had been forced to extinguish at the outset of every clash. His realization that these weanlings had no say in the matter had never ceased to disturb him.

Shielded by fireproof blankets to protect them from the wall of flames to their right, a group of twenty attempted to make entry. Joe waited until the bulk of the squad was squarely within the zone where the explosive had been laid before activating the hose. The shower of water reinvigorated the fire like rendered fat dripping on a red-hot coal. All the intruders were either immolated or—at the very least—seriously scorched. The living ran screaming back from whence they came.

For good measure, Joe then directed the stream at the entire length of the blaze. He was able to create a great deal more vertical movement on the wall of flames, and with the water flowing to a specific area, he was able to obscure the sight of the sniper.

That didn't stop the shooter from squeezing off a few wild shots, though. Joe heard glass tinkling around him, but he had ceased to be a pure target, as the only possible thing to aim at was the source of the stream of rusty water. And that was becoming increasingly more difficult to pinpoint with the flames now licking at the guardrails of the overpass.

Joe continued to slither along the front of the buildings. Wrapped in his earthen camouflage, he was as elusive to the human eye as a yeti.

At the next structure, he found what he was seeking—a projection that he could hang the hose on for the purpose of keeping the flow pointed toward the fire without him having to direct it. The base was a concrete gothic gargoyle with an opening in the back that allowed him to feed the hose through so that it appeared to be shooting out of the creature's open mouth.

With the hose secured and directed at the center of the blaze, Joe returned to his staging area down the street, strapped on the harness with the air tanks and the axe, and ventured down the alley that abutted the back of the row of buildings.

At the terminus, now facing the western wall, he moved back toward the line of fire. From this angle, he was sure to be invisible to the sniper, and it allowed him to cross the street toward the flames. He heaved both of the tanks of compressed air into the blaze in the hopes that the heat of the fire would melt the seals.

It did not take long. Two loud explosions drove the flames ever higher, and the distraction allowed him to scale the non-burning part of the wall to his left.

Atop the overpass, he located the sniper, stealthily advanced on him, and before the shooter could react, buried the sharp end of the axe into his chest.

Carefully, he slithered across the top of the wall to the northern end of the overpass to get a view of the strength of the enemy. Spread out across the area was a number that had to total in the thousands. It was a veritable sea of orange.

"Holy shit," he said to himself in near resignation.

He retrieved the small-bore rifle and the ammunition, wiggled the axe out of the dead sniper, and was about to return to the intra-enclave side when he saw a battalion of Motor City residents marching toward the battle zone. A shirtless young man had assumed the point position. It was John Brassey.

SIXTY-TWO

In short order, John had mustered a group of volunteers that numbered well over a hundred. They were armed with everything from broom handles to rusty-toothed handsaws. Many had lost loved ones at the stadium, and they were imbued with a thirst for vengeance.

When they saw the nearly naked, mud-slathered figure of a man—cradling a rifle, cloaked in a bandolier of bullets—walking toward them with an the axe raised to the sky, they were sure that this was the enemy they were seeking. Many broke off from their ranks and raced toward the ursine creature with designs of removing this scourge from their sight.

John's scream of "Halt!" pierced the air, and surprisingly the members of his regiment suspended their charge.

"It's Joe Smith, for chrissakes!" John yelled.

To this group of volunteers, the legend of Joe Smith had already been disseminated. They had all heard of Joe's attempt to thwart the Redeemer who blew up the stadium.

When Joe arrived to stand before them, the Mugwump security apparatus that had cautiously loitered behind the attack force filled in to hear what this character had to say. As employees, their vested interests only took them so far; they could never be infused with the same fervor or patriotism as the residents.

"There are thousands out there," Joe said.

If there were gasps of surprise, they were muffled by the rattling of the weapons.

"This is no random event. This is something that has been in the works for some time, and that force of maniacs lurking out there have devised contingencies should their initial attempts at incursion be suppressed."

"Where should we position ourselves?" John asked.

"Not here."

Joe looked beyond his friend and sought out the decorated Mugwump security official that he had spoken to before.

"Do you have firearms?" he asked.

"We have a cache in the central administration building, but very few of these men are certified to handle them," the leader replied.

"You need to get them in the hands of as many of your force as you can and station them around the entire perimeter of the city," Joe said.

"We don't have enough men or guns to cover the entire perimeter."

"Well then do what you can, goddammit. Get some on top of the wall, space them accordingly, and have them shoot at anything they see. We have no idea whether they plan on trying to get in somewhere else. I don't think that this explosion was a diversion. I think the one at the stadium was, but this might not be the only entry point," Joe said.

"What can we do?" one of the residents asked.

"We need to keep that fire burning for as long as we can. We need to force them to begin considering their other options. They determined that this was the best strategy, and from my experience, they don't have the tactical expertise to really improvise effectively, so if we can stall them here we can fortify our defenses at other possible points of entry," Joe explained.

"But you said they might try to blow another hole in the wall somewhere else," someone called out.

"Yeah, they might, but it hasn't happened yet. My instincts tell me that they chose this location for its remoteness. Their limited access to the raw materials—unless they've been stockpiling them for many years—indicates to me that this was their one and only shot. This explosion was massive and definitely must have stretched their resources," Joe said.

"What about the others? The bomber's helpers," John asked.

"I would imagine they fled after the stadium explosion and probably had a hand in coordinating or triggering this thing here. We need to keep this fire going. We need to keep the gate that they've tried to open closed. The water will work for awhile, but eventually the materials that went into creating it will burn themselves out."

"The oil," John said.

Now everyone could hear the collective gasp that emanated spontaneously from the group of vigilantes.

"That'll do. Get it up here as soon as possible," Joe said.

He turned and began to head back to his position opposite the flames and the invasion force that lay behind them. As he walked away, he loaded the rifle.

John wanted to follow him, but he knew that Joe's departure had been deliberate. He was not a member of their society and would not deign to make decisions for them.

A mumbling chant, a hubbub really, began to grow amongst the avenging force. They were mulling over this request to use the oil that had been secreted away—the oil that was reserved for their yearly celebration. They all knew what this meant. If the majority of the stock were used to suppress this attack, the race and its attendant hoopla would be rendered kaput forever.

So much of their identity was wrapped up in this tradition. Their moods swung with the seasons that either moved away or approached that date that fell around or on the nones of July. Their daily existence, not to mention their external dispositions, were defined by the allegiances or enmity toward others outside their own specific neighborhoods. Without the race, how were they supposed to function?

The murmurs of dubiousness expressed by these folks went to the heart of this fear, and John took it upon himself to get them to focus on the immediate. The future was unwritten and could not be controlled, he explained to them. There was a threat outside of their walls this very second, and they must quell it or all of the other shit that they seemed to want to cling to would be gone regardless of their personal desires to retain the fucked-up status quo.

John scanned the faces of this group of enthusiastic volunteers and noticed that many of the men who had come to exact their revenge had only an hour or so before been preternaturally supposed to hate the ones who stood beside them. Maybe this was a new portal opening in their world. Maybe a significant tectonic shift had occurred, and from this day forward, they would treat each other differently.

Maybe John was wrong. The bickering began, and the predominate question being asked by everyone was how? How were they going to convince the people who lived so far away from this that they needed the barrels of crude? How were they going to be able to explain to people who hadn't seen what they've seen to help out? And even if they could get their hands on the stock, how were they going to get it up here?

Many more questions were voiced, and John let them continue for a good five minutes. When he heard shots ringing out from down the street, he called a halt to the debate.

———

Though he had not identified a specific target, Joe was not firing indiscriminately. From the reconnaissance that he performed on the top of the overpass, he knew that the Redeemer force was spread out in an arc around their objective. By adjusting for the effective range of the antiquated rifle and factoring in a little luck, Joe was hoping that some of his blind shots might reach the line of Redeemers and force them to fall back. It was just another cheap way to buy time until they got that oil up there.

Occasionally, he would have to reposition the hose when he saw certain areas of the fire begin to wane. This was still productive for now, but he feared that time was of the essence, and unless they could block the entry, the city was doomed.

He took a moment to think about the softness that had been displayed by the citizenry of Motor City and how their shunning of any sort of vigilance had led to so many deaths already. He knew now that he would never forgive himself if he allowed his consciousness to become as lax.

He had sought some quiet in this place—something that felt nurturing. He had almost found it in the food; the relationships he established with the likes of John, Frank, Claudia, and the female members of the Brassey family; and the love of a woman, his first since the death of his wife. But he was fully aware that he had been programmed for a life that differed from the norm.

He was an avenger, a killer, and the target of his rage and the sense of the responsibility he had assumed to eradicate it still existed.

His war with this evil was not over. It was not over by a long shot.

———

John stepped into the vacuum that emerged when the volunteers had talked themselves into a circle. He had felt many of the eyes of the gathered continuing to check in with him as the arguments were batted back and forth. He knew it was his place now to assume the role of the point of the spear.

"Are we done with all of this bullshit?" he finally asked.

No one answered the rhetorical question.

"Here's the deal. There is a stalled car in the middle of Woodward Avenue that is out of fuel. It is not far from here. All around the racecourse and at the stadium are other cars that did not run out of gas for one reason or another. That fucking AMX still has its full allotment, I'm sure. While some of you are breaking into the storage area to secure the barrels, others will be rounding up as much fuel as you can. We will attach the wagon that they use in the cracking ceremony to the Barracuda and bring the oil up here. Are there any Red Wings here?"

No hands reached for the sky, but that wasn't surprising. They were at the complete opposite end of the city from where their neighborhood lay.

"We're going to need their help to get to the stockpile. Does anyone know any of their officers or elders?"

"I do," someone responded.

The voice was female, and John recognized the timbre. It was Cassandra, and she stood in front of another entire group of volunteers. To their left, he could see Billy Klock coming up the street with a mob of his own making.

"I can talk to their captain," Cassandra said.

"Okay, we'll find a bike or something, and get you down there. In the meantime, let's put our hands on the gas, refuel that car, and start working to bring the barrels up. Who here has experience behind the wheel?"

"That would be me," the voice of Billy Klock rang out.

Of course, John thought. Billy had once been the back-up driver not that long ago.

"Here's how it's going to go: All of the folks with Cassandra will head on down to the river. All the people with Billy will head out in search of fuel. And all of those with me will stay here and figure out what we can do to stop an invasion. Along the way, tell everyone you can about the situation. See if they can get word to those who live near the walls so that they can be prepared to defend our city should they try to get in somewhere else," John said authoritatively.

There was little dissent in the defenders' responses. Someone had stepped up with a plan, and for now, they were willing to go with it. The distinct groups began to disperse, though Cassandra wasn't happy that she was going to be separated from Joe again. She asked John if someone else could cover that part of the task, but John did not have a moment to listen to her; he was focused on the Mugwump security people still loitering on the fringes. He strode up to the man who Joe had earlier singled out as their leader.

"Why are you still here?" John barked.

"We're trying to figure out the chain of command. We're trying to make an assessment of where the authority is supposed to be coming from. We aren't going to take the word of that guy down the street. He isn't even a resident of the city," the leader said.

"That guy down the street will save this city and your fucking job. But I will do everything in my power to explain to the populous that when the shit came down, you stood here with your thumb up your ass trying to figure out how to protect your own self-interests," John said.

The Mugwump leader felt the force of the threat but instead affected an air of nonchalance toward this sixteen-year-old son of a captain. Who the fuck was he to be ordering him around?

John pushed him aside and grabbed the man who stood closest to the leader. John's assumption was that—though there seemed to be little in the way of insignias to identify a hierarchy—the one standing nearest to the leader probably retained some sway over the others.

"Go get the guns, and bring them up here!" John said.

"Yes sir," the Mugwump said.

"Take five men, and do it now!"

"Yes, sir," the Mugwump said.

"And tell your superiors what my friend told you about stationing some of your men on the walls all around the city."

There were more rounds fired from down the street, and John reacted to the sound of the reports as one does to a clarion call. He turned to his group of volunteers—their minds and weapons at the ready—and waved his arms toward the action.

He then pivoted and ran in a direct line toward the center of the tempest.

EPILOGUE

THE CITIZENRY OF Motor City endured the siege of the Redeemers for a grand total of 128 days.

On November 12, after four consecutive days of white-out blizzard conditions, scouts affiliated with the Motor City Defense Unit found irrefutable evidence that the hold-out Redeemers who remained amidst the slaughtered of their numbers had abandoned all of their previously held positions.

More penetrating recon missions into the environs of Hamtramck confirmed that the Redeemer force had fallen into retreat or evacuation. The entire area was bereft of life.

The threat of being overrun had been expunged, and as the year came to an end, life in Motor City began to return to an altered definition of normal.

In all, nearly 85 percent of the stock of oil that the city had reserved for their festival and the race was used to keep the initial inferno alive and to repel the Redeemer contingent on the other side.

There were incursions, but the city's founders had designed their enclave well, and though they never thought they would ever have a reason to do so, they were able to transform the purposes of their dream from protected cantonment to offensive citadel.

Motor City began the struggle against the Redeemers somewhat behind the curve, and during the initial days, there was serious concern among the residents whether the enclave would survive.

One of the reasons why the circumstances became so dire stemmed from an insurrection that the Mugwump population staged during the first week of defense. The basis for their protest was centered on the newly devised conscription regulations that were imposed on them in the wake of the attack. A new duty—"defense technician"—was added to their job description, and anyone who failed to participate was threatened with expulsion.

The short-lived "strike" was settled when the panicked administration consented to change the regulation from compulsory to volunteer, with all enrollees being granted full citizenship after the completion of their mission.

The following year, an entire new Independent workforce was summoned, and the newly consecrated residents from the volunteer fighting force moved into domiciles within the areas that had been vacated by those who had perished on the nones of July.

These initial hiccups aside, the tide of the conflict turned in the favor of the enclave when intelligence gathered in the aftermath of a bloody firefight included many coded messages from the Redeemer command structure to their plebes on the ground. The format of these messages matched many found during a forensic examination of the apartment that had once housed the Redeemer cell.

John Brassey, with help from some of his more erudite classmates, was able to decipher the missives using a copy of *The New Testament for Now* that had been liberated from the Redeemer's lair. The cryptographers were lucky in that there were many notations in the margins of the confiscated book that led them to break the code fairly quickly.

On a brisk October day, the body of man named Kip Timmons was found during a battle assessment one kilometer from the front gates. On his person was the original coded note that he had carried to the Redeemer commander. It was the personal message that informed the Redeemer hierarchy that its writer—Apostle Udo Lewandowski—needed materials to blow up the stadium at the conclusion of the race.

Eventually the bodies of all of the cell members who had aided Udo Lewandowski were discovered.

The final death toll from the blast at the stadium was significant: 4,345 men, women, and children. Certain wards—like Mustang—saw their numbers decrease by more than 50% of the total of their previous population as result of the initial attack.

———————

Joe Smith became the most trusted advisor to the city elders who had been tasked with coordinating the efforts to protect the population. His intimate knowledge of the tendencies of the raiders in regards to strategy was invaluable at not only the planning level, but at the operational phases as well.

Joe personally trained cadres of Motor City's most vital residents in the art of close combat. The men and women who served their city performed admirably. In the end, they sustained less than 4 percent of the overall causalities attributed to the combat phase of the conflict.

The entire ward structure was abolished. No longer would the previous segregations be tolerated. The race was never run again.

The remaining oil from the city's stock was used to light a lamp at the nones of July memorial that was constructed near the outskirts of the stadium. A new yearly festival was conceived that marked the date—a week of feasts and remembrance.

In January, Joe Smith left Motor City with two companions, John Brassey and Cassandra Montgomery.

One of the items in young Brassey's knapsack was a small container of formaldehyde. Suspended in the liquid for preservation was the tattooed skin from the upper right arm of the Apostle Udo Lewandowski. Only part of the coded numerical message had been deciphered. It was the same sentence that the killer had been able to decode, "The Redeemer Lives." The delineation of the rest of the message—the bottom line of numbers—remained a mystery.

ACKNOWLEDGMENTS

First off, thanks again for reading. I am indebted to so many people for their selfless assistance by providing me with the valuable information I required to construct this narrative. I readily admit to being a pain in the ass to most of them, but I hope they are at least minimally aware of the depth of gratitude I retain for them and for their massive contribution.

My Uncle Harry Brassey and his business partner, Steven Copp, were instrumental in providing me with all of the doings that took place before, during, and after the incident at the armory in Rubber City.

The man who was given the mantle of the "tracker" in this story is really the late Ricky Medina, and it was with his help that I was able to reconstruct the details of Joe Smith's journey back to his home state. He also provided much-needed information about the early life of Udo Lewandowski via an interview he conducted with Anna Cremins (nee Lewandowski) when, for my sake, he took a detour through central Ohio while on another job. Unfortunately, Ricky passed away a few years after the time of these events when he was killed during a situation involving a case of mistaken identity.

I would like to thank Joe and Eileen Smith of Big D for their information about Joe Smith's youth. I apologize to them for the rudeness I displayed by demanding that they comment on the effects associated with their estrangement from him during his early years as an adult, the death of his children, and the end of his marriage.

Thanks to Dr. Mitchell Stephens, PhD, for answering my never-ending list of questions on the subject of Motor City's history. The titles of the last three chapters are so named in homage to you and your academic endeavors. I hope that Elysium has accepted you with open arms.

Finally, I would like to thank, once again from the deepest depths of my heart, the extraordinary Katherine Harris for all she has done to help this story to be realized. Without her, neither this nor the first book could have ever been written.

— John Brassey

Heartfelt thanks demand to be extended to the following:

My dear wife, Saxon Trainor. There is nothing concrete to be gleaned from the definition of the word luck. It will forever be amorphous and personal. For me, the murkiness that surrounds that word has been quantified because I have seen and felt it having united with you.

My mother, Ursula Kantor. The human personification of viral marketing. In every conversation with every community that has been given the gift of her presence, she has—without a trace of guile—pushed my work into the hands of friends, colleagues and strangers.

My esteemed brother-in-law, Tad Kelly, who exposed me to the real life events that inspired this entire saga. His generosity is boundless.

Rick Price, Lane Witz, Tom Ramirez, Matt Craven, and my sister, Susan Anderson, all readers of this piece in manuscript. Observations, criticisms, comradeship, and support logged and appreciated.

The Helen's Circle Book Club of Lafayette, California for their warm invitation, insightful conversation, and delicious meal.

Katie Pyne for her continuing cover design and the map drawings—another ball in the air for her. I will be shocked when one reaches the ground.

Barrett Briske for consenting to add developmental editor duties to her stellar and precise copyediting work. Fairness and efficiency must be stamped upon her paperwork.

Karen Richardson for her style in mounting the text. Impediments for her are something to be brushed away like lint or stray dog fur.

As always, Daniel Pyne, my mentor and icon.

Finally, Robert G. (Max) Flynn, who opened my eyes to the worth of a Stanford University degree in English. Max and the nearly undecipherable scribble of his red pen had as much to do with shrinking the initial bloat and shaping the final narrative as anything or anyone else.

— Erich Anderson

About the Author

Erich Anderson is a professional actor who has appeared in over three hundred episodes of television, fifty theater productions, and twenty feature films. As a writer he has written multiple episodes of television and has a filing cabinet full of unproduced screenplays. He was born in Sagamahara, Japan. He is a graduate of Hilltop High School, Chula Vista, California. He holds a B.A. in Biochemistry and Molecular Biology from the University of California, Santa Barbara. He is married to Saxon Trainor and they reside in Los Angeles, California with their dog, Becky. *Thy Kingdom Come* is his second novel, and the second installment of the Pater Noster series.

Printed in Great Britain
by Amazon